COMPLIANCE

THE BELLATOR CHRONICLES: BOOK ONE

CLARE LITTLEMORE

BRIT ALERT!

If you are reading this book and not from the UK, a brief warning that I am a British author and use British spellings throughout. In Bellator, the pavements have 'kerbs' rather than 'curbs', the students of the Danforth Academy may be disciplined for their bad behaviour (not behavior) and one or two of the characters might, on occasion, have to apologise (rather than apologize).

Happy reading!

CONTENTS

CHAPTER ONE: NOAH

" **M** ove!"

Noah looked up into the eyes of Harden Porter. The older boy loomed over him from the other side of the table, eyebrows raised, a cocky smirk on his pale face. Behind him stood several of his friends, most of them leering like Harden.

"I'm not finished." Noah gestured to his plate, which still held a few good mouthfuls of food.

"And?" Harden slammed his plate down opposite Noah and slid into a seat on the bench, his knees colliding painfully with Noah's. "We need the table now."

Noah stared back at him, wondering whether it was worth standing his ground. Harden was an idiot, but his ma was on the council with Noah's, so taking him on was never a good idea. As a newly elected Eremus raider, Harden was even more full of himself than usual, and Noah was an easy target.

Usually, Noah resisted his taunts, but something about today was different. Staying where he was, he stabbed his fork into a potato and brought it to his mouth.

Opposite him, Harden stiffened. His buddies, who had surrounded the table and were preparing to take a seat, froze, awaiting further instructions. As Noah continued to chew, Harden leaned closer. "Hey, Madden. I said move."

As calmly as his shaking hands could manage, Noah scooped up some gravy from his plate and shovelled it into his mouth. Holding the gaze of the boy who sat opposite, he swallowed and speared the last couple of vegetables on his fork. It wasn't a powerful protest, but in keeping his seat for even a few minutes, Noah knew he was making a stand.

Harden's eyes flared and he pushed to his feet once more. "You little—" He snapped his mouth shut and sank back into his seat; his eyes fixed on something behind Noah.

"Everything alright?" Noah's heart sank at the familiar voice.

A heavy hand landed on his shoulder and he turned to face his older brother. Making a stand wasn't quite so effective when it looked like he was relying on Paulo for backup.

"Evening, Noah," Paulo nodded to the rest of the table, as though they were a group of friends sitting down to eat dinner together. "Harden. Boys."

A full nine years older than Noah, Paulo was everything he wasn't. And, if he was honest, he wasn't his real brother, though they shared the same living quarters. An expert raider with many years' experience, everyone respected him, and Harden knew it. There was no way he was going to mess with Noah when Paulo was around.

As for later . . . well, that was another matter.

Noah shoved back the bench and picked up his plate. Shrugging Paulo's hand off his shoulder, he moved away from the crowd of boys who took their seats and began cramming food into their mouths as though the incident had never happened. Passing his plate to Cora, the older woman who was on kitchen duty, Noah walked away, trying to ignore his brother.

"What was that all about?"

"Nothing."

"Didn't look like nothing."

Noah shrugged. He looked around the cave, filled with many people coming and going, eating dinner, discussing the day's chores, greeting friends and family before they readied themselves for their night's rest. Too many people in too small a space. It was suffocating.

Noah knew where he wanted to go, but he'd have to get rid of Paulo first. "Harden was being his usual charming self. That's all."

Noah braced himself for another lecture. Years of enduring the taunts of Harden and his friends had made him mostly immune. And he certainly didn't provoke them. He didn't need Paulo to tell him he had to stay away from the idiots of their community. Yet his family seemed to believe he somehow went looking for confrontation. It was maddening.

Eremus was a small community. Their home was a series of caves and tunnels hidden in the depths of the forest. It kept them safe, but made it difficult to escape people, be it bullies like Harden or overbearing brothers. As for seeing the sky, that was almost an impossibility. Whilst not banned from venturing outdoors, the council discouraged people from such activities, undertaking such trips with great caution. They only went outdoors in small numbers when their job required them to do so.

Right now, Noah wanted escape. He didn't want to talk to Paulo. He didn't want to face the taunts of Harden and his stupid friends, made worse now because Paulo had stepped in to rescue him. He wanted to be alone.

But Paulo wasn't going to let it go. He placed a hand on Noah's arm, turning him to face him.

"Is he still giving you trouble?"

"Not really."

"Want me to speak to him?"

"No."

Paulo's face darkened. "Look, you need to stay away from him. Do you hear me? Confronting him will lead to trouble you won't be able to deal with."

Noah glared at his brother.

"I mean it. I can't always be—"

"Saving me?" Wrenching his arm from Paulo's grasp, Noah took a step back. "Is that what you were going to say?"

Paulo drew himself up to his full height. "Well, you don't exactly have the best record for saving yourself, do you?"

"I never asked you to protect me." Feeling a familiar rage burning inside him, Noah forced himself to draw in a deep breath. "I never do."

"Suit yourself." Sighing, Paulo took a step back. "Be careful, little brother. One day, you'll look around for rescue and I won't be there."

Paulo turned and stalked away. As Paulo collected his dinner, Noah watched the way people responded to him. He was Eremus, born and bred. And a raider, to boot. He had proved himself over the ten years he had been on the team which made regular visits to Bellator to bring back supplies. They respected him. He belonged in a way Noah had never felt he did.

Turning away from the rest of the diners seated in the large rock cavern, Noah checked that he wasn't being followed before wandering down a series of tunnels which led deep underground. His destination: a tiny crack in the rock at waist height which allowed a single body to fit through, as long as that body was laid flat and slithered. Noah had no fear of small spaces and had discovered this hideout as a child of eight. Running away from the taunts of another of his supposed playmates, he had rushed crying into the maze of tunnels and gotten lost.

When he had spotted the crack in the rock and peered into it, he'd spied a faint light beyond. Curious, he had slid his skinny, eight-year-old body through the gap, making like a snake for around three metres, until the space beyond opened before him. The small cavern hidden behind the crack was only large enough to stand in the centre, but wide enough for one or two bodies to lie flat and gaze upwards.

In the cavern's rocky ceiling was a fissure that ran all the way up to ground level. The space above was clear of trees. During the daytime, Noah could lie down and see a small piece of the sky. Best of all, at night, the stars above gazed down at him like old friends. Nicknamed the den, it had become his place of refuge over the years.

He used to worry that one day he'd be too large to wriggle through the gap and gain entrance to his little haven. But as he had grown older, his body had remained stubbornly skinny. Even though he had just turned sixteen, his shoulders broader and his chest wider, he was still able to slip through to the other side. It was the only real advantage of his lean frame.

Reaching the entrance, he checked there was no one else around and bent down to slide into the space, making his way through with the ease that came from years of practice. On the other side, he found he wasn't alone.

"Hey, loner."

"Hey, yourself."

Ruth Murphy sat cross-legged at one end of the cavern, scribbling on a pad of paper. His best friend, she was the only person Noah had ever shared his hiding place with. At ten, they'd been able to fit into the den with plenty of room to spare. At thirteen, they could still co-exist comfortably. At sixteen, it was a bit of a squeeze, but they were old friends, very relaxed with one another, and the closeness required for the pair to inhabit the cavern together now did not bother either of them.

She took one look at his face and wrinkled her nose. "Harden giving you a rough time again?"

He shrugged.

"Gah. I swear, since he got raider status, he's become impossible."

Extracting his legs from the rock, Noah folded himself into the space beside her and leaned back against the wall of the cavern. Ruth went back to her drawing. For a few moments, they were quiet. Busying herself with her sketch book and pencils as usual, Ruth didn't look up, and Noah was happy to close his eyes and breathe. The irony of the smallest space in the Eremus caverns being the only place he felt free was not lost on him.

A little while later, he opened his eyes and found Ruth staring at him, her brown eyes earnest. Calmer now, he smiled.

"Let's have a look then?"

Ruth handed him the sketch pad. She had filled the page with intricate pencil strokes, crisscrossing and overlapping, an image of a machine emerging amongst the brushstrokes.

"It's brilliant." He grinned at his friend. "What is it?"

She threw her pencil at him. "Don't know. It's not done yet."

He shifted so he could glance up at the sky. Above him, the light was seeping away. It would soon be dark and the stars would creep out of their hiding places, fanning out across the heavens in the intricate patterns and shapes which had always fascinated him. He wondered how long he could get away with sitting here before his ma started looking for him. There were chores to do before they went to bed tonight, and he knew from bitter experience he wouldn't escape them.

"So, want to tell me what happened?"

"You were right." He shrugged. "Harden was being his usual idiot self."

"What'd he do?"

"Not much. Tried to muscle me out of my seat when I was eating."

"Did you let him?" Ruth's tone was darker. "I told you not to —"

"I know. I know." Noah held up his hands in a gesture of self-defence. "I didn't, as a matter of fact. I held my ground." He remembered Paulo's hand landing on his shoulder. "Well, I tried to, at least."

"How'd he react?"

"Well, he didn't have much of a chance to react, to be honest."

Ruth frowned. "Paulo?"

"Paulo." Noah rolled his eyes. "All he had to do was stand behind me, and . . ."

"Let me guess, they backed right off." Ruth shook her head.

"They did."

"I'm sorry."

"S'alright. At least I didn't get a kicking."

Ruth grimaced. "You know that's not what they'd do. Flynn and Paulo'd never let them. Nor would your ma."

"True. But they'd have found another way to make me miserable, I'm sure."

"You going to tell her?"

"Ma?" Noah shifted, easing the familiar numbness which had crept into his legs. "No. She'd worry. And she frets about me enough."

"I know, but—"

Noah reached out his hand and squeezed Ruth's shoulder. "Look, I know you mean well, but it's not a big deal. It doesn't even bother me all that much these days."

"Maybe not. But I still think there's something you could do to get him off your back." Ruth shook off his hand with uncharacteristic irritation. "Look. I'm a raider now. Harden's a raider. You could be one too."

"We've talked about this. She'll never let me." Noah turned away. "There's no point having the same conversation with her again."

Ruth slapped a hand against his arm so hard it stung.

"Ow!" Noah frowned at her. "What was that for?"

"For giving up. Yeah, you've asked before. And she said no. But you're sixteen now. She can't stop you forever." Ruth packed up her supplies, sliding them into the cloth bag she carried everywhere and smoothing it flat. "Ask her again. And don't get all angry with her. You don't know what she'll say this time."

"Maybe." Noah rubbed his arm, frowning. "Okay. I'll ask. But I'll have to pick my moment."

"Well, don't wait too long." Ruth gestured to the opening. "I have to go. Dawn'll be expecting me. She likes me to get a good rest before the raid, and I've chores to do first. You staying?"

Noah shook his head. "I'll walk you back, give you a hand." He began angling his body so he could ease his way back through the gap in the rock.

"Are you avoiding talking to your ma?" Ruth crouched behind him. "Chicken."

"Hey!" He chuckled. "I'll talk to her. Later. Or in the morning. I promise. But Dawn's right. You need some rest. If I help with the chores, you'll get to bed faster."

Ruth had only been a raider for a few months and was still in training. The large raids on Bellator took place at night, under cover of darkness. Making their way into the city via tunnels allowed the Eremus citizens to access various buildings and stores within Bellator where they could obtain vital resources. Their council paired new raiders with more experienced ones, allowing them to learn the positions of key targets in the city, the various tunnels and their exits, plus the rules they had to follow to ensure the Bellator authorities never discovered them. This kept the community safe and enabled the raiders to bring back much needed supplies.

In the past, the community had travelled above ground, using trucks to assist them with the raids, but it had become quite challenging to obtain the fuel needed to keep the trucks running. As Bellator's transport system became more sophisticated, the fuel used by their older vehicles had become almost impossible to get hold of. And, since Eremus had started to use the tunnel system, the vehicles had become pretty much obsolete.

As ever, the community had adapted, recruiting larger numbers of raiders who went into the city on foot, carrying the supplies back by hand. It was hard work, but the raiders were proud of their role as providers, Ruth especially.

Ruth's mother had died when she was a baby, and she had shared a home with Dawn, who'd been a close friend of her mother's, for as long as she could remember. Dawn had a daughter of her own, Ella, who was six years older than Ruth. The three of them shared a small cave on the lower level and were fiercely independent. But Ruth would get little enough sleep with the raid tonight, and tomorrow she would need to rest. If Noah helped with her chores, things would be much easier for her. Dawn never seemed to mind Noah's presence in their small, cosy cave the way she did other people.

Not bothering to wait for a response, Noah shuffled through the gap in the rock, knowing Ruth would follow him. As he reached the far side, he paused as he always did, listening to ensure no one was passing by. The tunnel was not a major thoroughfare and was usually empty, but he always checked. One time, some older Eremus residents returning from a foraging trip had almost caught him coming out of the den. Since then, he'd been cautious.

Hearing nothing, he eased his body out of the crevice and turned to offer a hand to his friend. She batted it aside, rolling her eyes at him as she slipped through the rocks and righted herself.

"Are you sure?" Her face was hopeful. "Your ma won't miss you?"

Truthfully, he was needed home to help with his own family's chores, but he wasn't in any hurry to have the same argument with his mother, and he knew Dawn would appreciate his help. Ruth had been his friend as far back as he could remember, playing with him when none of the other Eremus kids would. He'd always felt at home with her, and the same went for her family.

"I'm sure." Elbowing his old friend, he grinned. "Let's go."

CHAPTER TWO: FAITH

The needle loomed closer, seeming larger than usual. As the technician bent over her, the heavy floral scent she wore assaulted Faith's senses. What had the woman said her name was? Margaret? Maisie? Faith had forgotten already. She bit the inside of her cheek, trying not to gag. Staring upwards at the ceiling, she willed herself not to flinch. She had done this before. So many times, she'd forgotten. But it never got any easier.

The blood tests were a part of life. Vital for the girls who attended Danforth Academy. It was a privilege to be a student at the school, and came with *many* benefits, but the flip side was the regular testing.

Still, it was worth it. A Danforth girl was special.

Since it had first opened, the academy had been responsible for testing some of the most cutting-edge technology that Bellator had to offer. Its students had been the first to experience comcars, the next-generation self-driving vehicles which had cut the commute times of the wealthy Bellator citizens in half. Fabric which was able to harness body heat and use it to charge small devices, an application for wristclips which enabled a wearer to discover the exact nutritional content of anything they ate, and even a gadget which could thoroughly clean teeth in fewer than ten seconds: all had begun their journey to city-wide release at Danforth Academy.

It was the reason so many Bellator youngsters were desperate to be selected for a place. And the reason the students, once selected, had such great healthcare. Still, it didn't mean Faith enjoyed the needles.

She glanced back at the technician, waiting for the procedure to begin. For a moment, nothing happened. Anxious, she glanced back at the syringe. It was still empty and had yet to even make contact with the delicate skin on the inside of her arm. The technician leaned closer, wiping the swab of cotton across the pale skin. Faith shivered.

With an expertise borne of many years of extracting blood, the woman flicked the used cotton ball into the bin and grasped Faith's elbow firmly, brandishing the silver needle like a weapon. "Ready?"

Focusing determinedly on the sterile white walls, their shelves stacked with boxes no doubt full of similar glass tubes and syringes, Faith nodded.

"Here we go."

A sharp pinch in the crook of her elbow. A deeper, penetrating sensation, and then the familiar lurch of her stomach as the blood started to flow out of Faith's body and into the empty vial. Would she ever be used to this? She closed her eyes, waiting for it to be over. The procedure never took long, and soon she would be out of the medical centre and walking back to school in the early morning air.

There was a clicking sound as the technician removed one vial and replaced it with a second one. Faith's eyes flew open and she watched as the first vial was placed on the counter beside them. The woman returned her focus to Faith's arm again.

"Two?"

"I'm sorry?" The technician looked puzzled.

"Two vials of blood today?"

The woman tapped the clipboard beside her. "Just following instructions."

Faith sighed and forced herself to stare at the shelves which took up the entire wall of the exam room. They provided a focal point which allowed her to ignore the unpleasantness of the procedure. Row upon row of different coloured boxes, all labelled with complex medical terms, filled the shelves. She ran her gaze along them now: amitriptyline, benzonatate, ciprofloxacin, clindamycin, femgazipane . . .

Faith had long ago memorized the names on these shelves as a distraction from the blood test. Femgazipane was definitely unfamiliar. Come to think of it, there was an awful lot of it. Usually, the shelves were stocked with roughly equal amounts of each drug, but there was an entire shelf dedicated to this new one. Faith turned the word over in her head, enunciating every syllable. She loved the way the alien words sounded.

Faith winced as the technician removed the needle from her arm without warning. Glancing across at the second vial, Faith could see it was filled with deep scarlet liquid, and the technician had placed it next to its partner on the counter. Snapping off the needle, she flicked it into the bin and busied herself placing the tiny green caps on the tubes of blood. Removing the ready-printed labels from the tiny machine on the desk, she smoothed them onto the vials with a perfectly-shaped nail painted the exact colour of the liquid inside them. Faith wondered if the tech had chosen the crimson shade on purpose and had to disguise a smile at the thought.

"What's funny?" The sharp tone brought Faith back from her daydream.

"Nothing." She straightened her face. "Can I go now?!"

Shooting her a disapproving look, the technician grabbed her clipboard from the desk and thrust it at Faith.

"Sign here."

Hastily, Faith sat up and scrawled a signature so untidy she was certain it would have horrified her teachers. Ignoring the dizziness, she yanked down the sleeve of her uniform, covering the arm before the technician could tape the obligatory cotton ball over it.

"Don't you want—?"

But Faith was out the door and halfway down the corridor. She followed it until she reached the central lobby of the medical centre. Danforth girls came in for their monthly appointments before the facility opened to the general public. This ensured they received the undistracted attention of the medical staff. The preferential treatment was just another privilege of attending the school.

Despite the early hour, the reception area buzzed with activity. On the desk, a secretary tapped her fingers on the datadev in front of her, accessing patient records and organising data. There were a few drudges scurrying about, transporting supplies from one place to another, cleaning and tidying the various treatment rooms. Bellator's serving class, they had their faces covered in the traditional manner, only their eyes visible as they moved around in the background, preparing the medical centre for another busy day.

Originally called *doulos* after the Greek for slave, their name had been changed several years earlier. The newly elected chancellor, Abigail Danforth, had reclassified them, considering their earlier name too elegant. In her words, *drudge* was a true reflection of the nameless labourers they were and prevented them getting ideas above their station.

A technician in a shocking pink tunic stood at the doorway to one treatment room, consulting a list of names, and another dressed in royal blue wheeled an overloaded trolley past Faith, tutting when she didn't dive out of the way fast enough. There were even one or two doctors strolling through, their slow pace indicative of their importance. They were deep in conversation and didn't even glance at the gaggle of girls sprawled across the central waiting area.

The pink technician called out a name, and another of Faith's fellow students was ushered into a treatment room. The blood test was not relished by any of the girls, but it was thankfully brief. Knowing they would soon be back at school devouring pancakes topped with a variety of sugary delicacies, certainly made up for the minor discomfort. Faith was savouring the prospect of fresh strawberries and whipped cream.

Her eyes scanned the crowded seating area. For a moment she couldn't see who she was looking for, but then she spotted the familiar pale-blonde hair blending in with a larger group of their other classmates. Sophia had far more friends than Faith, simply because she was so nice. It was easy to be friends with a girl who went out of her way to make your day better. But that was Sophia. Faith often found it difficult to believe this girl was her best friend.

She made her way over, picking her way through the other still-sleepy students. Reaching Sophia's group, she flashed a smile at her friend. As she settled into a chair a few feet away, she found herself yawning widely. Being selected to attend Danforth was an honour. But, sometimes, it was a drag. The monthly appointment which required a five a.m. wakeup call always exhausted Faith, and she still had a day of school ahead.

"Avery Lassiter."

The pink technician had returned to the door. She glanced around, her face twisting in irritation at the need for repetition.

"*Avery Lassiter?*"

The group, which had hushed slightly to listen, glanced around at one another. Hissed whispers grew in volume as the girls speculated about Avery's whereabouts, and there were a few raised eyebrows as the technician's face turned the same shade as her uniform.

"*Avery. Lass—*"

"Here!" A figure swept in through the outer doors of the medical centre, her face a mask of innocence.

The technician blinked. "You're— you're not supposed to . . ."

Avery had reached her side and smiled warmly. "My apologies." She tapped a manicured nail against her temple. "Had a bit of a headache, so I stepped outside to get a little . . . fresh air. It's done me a world of good." Dropping her hand to the pendant all the Danforth girls wore, she twirled the delicate gold chain around her finger idly. "Are you ready for me now?"

She sashayed past the technician, gliding through the door to the treatment room, leaving a waiting room full of stunned faces behind her. Students were not permitted to leave the building until all the treatments were done. But Avery paid little attention to rules, and Faith had no idea why people were surprised by her behaviour.

What should have shocked them, Faith thought, was the ease at which she got away with it. Avery was nineteen, a whole three years older than Faith, but for as long as she could remember, the girl had been adored by the school's entire staff. Her angelic face, sweet smile, and silver tongue allowed her to escape blame from even the harshest of teachers, and Faith, whose face was an open book that betrayed her every thought, cursed Avery's ability to fool everyone so thoroughly.

A movement startled her out of her reverie, and Faith looked up to see Sophia standing over her.

"No prizes for guessing your thoughts." She held out a hand and hauled Faith out of the seat. "C'mon. Let's follow Madam's example."

Though they didn't actually leave the premises, the two of them stood close to the door of the medical centre while the last few students were ferried in and out of the treatment rooms. Every now and again, a welcome rush of fresh air cut through the stifling heat of the lobby as a doctor or technician passed through the doors.

Twenty minutes later, they were all ready to leave.

"Finally!" Faith hissed at Sophia as they waited for the rest of their peers to get in line.

Sophia smiled, her eyes gently rebuking Faith's trademark impatience. Once every other girl from Danforth school had hurried past them, pairing up to giggle their way back along the quiet morning streets, they slipped through the doors and brought up the rear. They always held back so they could return to school last, and put as much distance between themselves and the teacher who led the line, as possible. It meant they could wander more slowly, chatting or simply enjoying each other's company.

They crossed the street outside the medical centre and began their walk along the pavement on the opposite side. It was too early for the shops to be open, but the scent of freshly baked bread hung in the air as they passed Meriton's bakery on Bronte Street. A few citizens, those whose jobs required an early start, were up and about, and the odd delivery truck or comcar swished past, but otherwise they were undisturbed.

A pale sunlight filtered between the buildings which lined the street. Breathing deeply, Faith slowed her pace, watching the figures ahead of them retreat even further into the distance.

"Best not to walk too slow." Sophia was more cautious, as usual. "They'll notice if we arrive *much* later than the others."

"Ah, live a little, Soph," Faith protested, turning to face her friend. "Breakfast can wait a few minutes."

"Alright." Sophia smiled, slowing her own pace to match her friend's.

"How was your test?"

Sophia wrinkled her nose. "Really? There's nothing else you'd rather discuss?"

"No." Faith kept her eyes on the street ahead as she waited for an answer which didn't come. "So, how was it?"

"It was fine."

Faith frowned. "They took two vials from me this morning."

"Me too. So?"

"So, usually it's only one."

Sophia thought for a moment. "I'm sure there's a good reason. They must *need* additional blood this time. Maybe they want to see the benefit of that new vitamin supplement they've been giving us before they roll it out to the other citizens."

"I suppose."

They fell into a companionable silence, watching as a small group of girls lined up to collect the newspapers from the depot further up the street. Most people accessed their information on their datadevs these days, but there was a growing trend among the richer citizens for getting news the old-fashioned way. These newsgirls would deliver the broadsheets to the wealthier Bellator households, before hurrying off to school themselves.

Education was considered important in the city, as was training for the various roles a Bellator woman might take on as she grew into an adult. The younger citizens were given the opportunity to test out their aptitude for a wide range of jobs before they specialised at the age of sixteen. Danforth girls remained in the academy for an additional four years after this, ensuring their education was among the very best in Bellator.

"Do you ever wish you were them?" Faith pointed to the line of girls. "I mean . . . to have a job . . . responsibility, to earn your own money . . .?"

"We have responsibility." Sophia took her hand. "It's just different, that's all."

"But we don't actually . . . *do* anything . . . make stuff or fix machinery or sell things or . . ." Faith paused, struggling to make her point. "Aren't you anxious to get out there into the world? Get on with life? Twenty still seems like a long way away."

Sophia squeezed her hand. "You're so impatient. Our education doesn't lead to instant success, you know that. It's not like selling a paper, getting a few credits, using them to buy something. It's more long-term than that. But the jobs the academy opens up for us will be far more rewarding in the end. You'll see."

"I know." Faith watched as the door to the depot swung open and, one-by-one, the girls took a stack of papers, stashed them in identical packs, and strode off in different directions. "But sometimes I think it would be nice to just . . . have something simpler . . . to know what our . . . oh, it sounds so stupid, but . . . our *purpose*, instead of . . ."

She trailed off as something in the distance caught her attention. Ahead of them, a few paces past the newspaper depot, was a large food store which should have been closed, considering the early hour. The light had been reflecting off its windows, but as the clouds drifted over the sun, she caught a glimpse of rapid movement inside the building.

"What?" Sophia was staring at her.

Faith sped up, hurrying ahead to get a closer look inside the store. As she passed the newspaper depot, several things happened at once. The line of Danforth students turned the corner ahead of them, disappearing into the street beyond. The final newspaper seller, a girl with short, flame-red hair, stepped into the street, a stack of papers clutched in her arms. The door of the depot slammed sharply, the sound echoing around the almost empty street.

And then the door to the food store was wrenched open and a figure darted onto the pavement.

Something about her was strange. As Faith stared, she noticed the woman was shabbily dressed, the shirt she wore patched and worn, as well as very old fashioned. She carried a large pack on her back which looked like it weighed her down and Faith felt bad that she didn't have a comcar waiting at the kerb to help her transport the goods home.

And then, from behind her came a second figure. This one too, wore clothes which were old and shabby, but as Faith stared, she registered something else. This person had a much broader build than the first. Like her, this figure was laden down with a pack, but she had a hat pulled low over her forehead and a dark scarf wound loosely around her neck. Beside Faith, Sophia gasped and grabbed hold of her arm. The figure carried a gun.

And then, as Faith looked more closely at the face of the second figure, she understood. It wasn't a woman at all. It was a man.

Her eyes fixed on this figure of intrigue. For the moment, he had his back turned to them as his gaze swept the street from the north end. Faith sucked in a breath, trying to decide what to do. A few paces ahead, the redhaired girl lost hold of her newspapers, sending the entire pile fluttering into a heap at her feet.

Faith cursed, her eyes glued to the strange figures ahead. Edging forward, she searched for a place to hide.

The man's gaze rotated through its circuit, coming to rest on the three girls huddled at the far end of the street. His jaw dropped as he spotted them. Hastily, he pulled up the scarf to cover his face, then raised his gun. Sophia cried out. The man's accomplice spun round, her eyes catching the three of them. She laid a hand on the man's arm and turned to mutter something in his ear.

For a second, time was suspended, as each of the five figures in the street gauged the response of the others. And then, little Red dropped to her knees, scrambling to gather the papers.

Faith shot forward, grabbing the girl by the arm and pulling her into a standing position.

"Oww!" she complained, rubbing her arm where Faith had hold of her.

"What're you *doing*!" Faith hissed into the girl's ear.

Her eyes fixed on the man brandishing the weapon, Faith clamped a hand over Red's mouth and hauled her into the empty doorway of the newspaper depot. Sophia followed, cramming her body as far back as she could into the space, which wasn't deep enough to safely house the three of them. For the second time in as many minutes, Faith grasped her friend's hand, keeping her other arm firmly fixed around the younger girl.

Hearts pounding, they waited.

There was a brief silence in the street, and then they heard the sound of footsteps pounding towards them. In her arms, the child shuddered violently, the danger of the situation finally dawning on her. Sophia had closed her eyes and was muttering indistinguishable words under her breath. Faith, however, kept her eyes on the street.

The sound of the footsteps grew in volume, thundering, until the pair who had invaded the quiet Bellator streets was almost on top of them. Tensing, the three girls huddled together and bowed their heads. Faith held her breath, bracing for the blow.

But it never came. The interlopers sped right past the doorway and down the street.

When the noise died away, the girls emerged from their refuge. Creeping out of the doorway, they peered in the direction the strangers had run. A few scattered newspapers blew across the pavement, their headline reading *Danforth Guards Triumph Again.*

Otherwise, the street was empty.

CHAPTER THREE: NOAH

The following morning, Noah entered the canteen for breakfast feeling as if he hadn't slept the previous night. He nodded at his Ma and Dawn, who were eating with Harden's ma, a fearsome woman who never seemed to smile. She was leaning forward, gesturing wildly with her spoon as she told a story, no doubt a boast about her son's success in the previous night's raid.

Noah crossed the cave and slid onto the bench next to Ruth, elbowing her when she was slow to notice his arrival. "What's the matter? You tired or something?"

She stuck her tongue out at him and continued eating. With a successful raid, there was always a treat, and this time was no different. The usual breakfast of oatmeal was transformed into something special. The previous night's raid had provided the community with fresh fruit, and there was even a little sugar to sprinkle on it.

Noah dived in, filling his spoon to overflowing. Pausing to enjoy the mouthful, he regarded his friend closely. Her eyes were bloodshot and her face paler than usual, but the raiders always made it a priority to eat and share their story before heading off to get some rest. Noah had nothing more than a day of log-splitting to look forward to and was determined to see how his friend was before she disappeared until dinnertime tonight.

"Went well, then?" He grinned, wiping a hand across his mouth, savouring the rare sweetness. The berries were delicious, picked fresh from the Bellator fields, and the crunch of the sugar one of the raiders had taken from one of the shops in the city made the porridge into something special.

"Well enough." Ruth's face flushed. "I guess."

"Well enough?" Stopping with the spoon poised halfway to his mouth, Noah peered more closely at her. "Not very convincing. Tell me more."

Ruth glanced sideways to check there was no one in earshot. Noah didn't really understand why. It wasn't like they had tons of friends queueing up to be their dining companions. But he let it slide, intrigued by Ruth's cloak-and-dagger attitude. Leaning forward slightly, she kept her gaze on the table as she began to speak.

"We were almost caught." A flush of red worked its way up her neck. "I can't tell, though . . . I promised . . ."

Noah's head was spinning. Ruth was currently partnered with Paulo. Which meant, logically speaking, that . . .

"My darling brother messed up, then?"

"Wasn't really his fault. We were delayed exiting the tunnels, something to do with the guards being out patrolling late, I think. That's what Evelyn said, anyway."

"Evelyn?" Noah frowned.

"She's one of the Bellator citizens who helps us out." Ruth explained. "It made us late, anyway . . . by the time we reached the supermarket we'd been assigned to it was light. Still early morning though . . . no one about. Street was empty. Or so we thought." Ruth stuffed another spoonful of the porridge into her mouth, swallowing the food before she continued. "When we got outside though . . ."

"No." Noah sucked in a breath. "Guards?"

His friend shook her head. "Nope. Just a kid, really . . . starting work, I think? And a couple of older girls. Around our age, I guess. Dressed in some kind of uniform." Fascinated, Noah waited for more. "Smart, like. Pale trousers, buttoned-up shirt, a tie-like thing round their necks. And a fancy hat. Really odd-looking. And not very practical, if you ask me. They weren't heading off for a day working the fields, if you know what I mean."

Noah tried to picture the scene, intrigued. "I wonder where they were going."

"Who cares?" Ruth shrugged. "I was just glad they weren't six feet tall with guns strapped to their shoulders." She hesitated for a moment, then leaned closer as she continued. "Thing is . . . Paulo didn't have his face covered."

"What?"

"Male raiders are supposed to have their faces covered at all times, because—"

"I *know*." Noah cut her off. "But . . . Paulo? Not masking his face? Was he *seen*?"

"Oh yeah. Clear as day. We were no distance from these girls."

"Would they recognise him again?"

"I don't know . . . maybe." Ruth looked uncomfortable. "With his bright blue eyes? Probably."

"Woah. He'll really be for it if Jacob or Flynn find out."

"Well let's not tell them, hey?" Ruth jabbed him with her elbow. "Look, I know you and he aren't always close, but . . ."

"Don't worry. I'm no rat. I might not always like him, but . . ."

"Okay, good." Ruth relaxed. "He wouldn't thank you for it. Anyway," she changed the subject, "Bellator's amazing. You should see it!"

At the far end of the cavern, Noah spotted Harden entering. Spotting his friends, he began making his way towards them, but before he could reach their table, Harden was accosted by his ma. Sarah Porter strode over to him, her face even more thunderous than usual. The boy's face fell as he saw her, but he slowed his pace, allowing her to catch up to him.

Noah watched with interest. The conversation was very much one-sided, with Sarah doing most of the talking. She barely let Harden get a word in, and even when she did pause for him to speak, presumably to respond to a question, his answers did not seem to satisfy her. Eventually, she grasped hold of his arm and hurried him off in the opposite direction, steering him towards the table where Jacob, the head of the Eremus council, was sitting with Flynn and Paulo. Thrusting him down onto a bench, she plonked herself beside him and sat expectantly, as though Jacob might need her at any moment.

Noah watched as Harden gazed around the room, eyeing the table where his friends sat laughing. For a moment, Noah almost felt sorry for him, but then his enemy's eyes met his. They narrowed for a second, but then Harden raised an eyebrow and jerked his head at Jacob, his usual arrogant expression back in place. Noah ducked his head and hurried to finish his meal as Ruth continued to talk. Whilst Harden usually didn't try anything when there were adults around, Noah didn't want to risk antagonising him.

"I mean . . . you know I've been on three raids now. But I've always been sent to the fields . . . the outskirts. This was, you know, my first chance to see more of the city itself." She paused, cocking her head to one side. "It's kind of beautiful, you know. The buildings are so tall in places, and the streets are clean, and . . . well, I guess you'd have to see it for yourself."

Noah scowled. "Not much chance of that, is there?"

"You never know." Ruth narrowed her eyes. "What duties are you assigned this week?"

"Log splitting." He rolled his eyes. "And when I've done my quota of that, I join the tunnelling crews. *So* dull."

"But the physical work strengthens you. That'd go in your favour, I mean if you wanted to raid."

"You know I want to raid. I'm just not allowed."

"Did you ask her?" Ruth gestured to the other side of the cavern, where Anna and Dawn were just getting up from their seats. She returned their smiles as they exited the cave before turning back to Noah. "Last night, I mean."

Noah didn't want to admit the trouble he had gotten into the previous night. Returning after helping Ruth with her chores had left him little time to do his own, and his ma had not been pleased. The timing had to be right when he brought up the subject of raiding again and talking to her last night would have been a disaster. There had been no hope of escaping his chores either. Not when his mother was in charge. She was all about responsibility.

"You choose to come home late, that's fine," she had told him, "but the chores still have to be done."

So, he had spent two hours repeating many of the tasks he'd already done for Dawn and Ruth. Knowing his ma would check, he made sure each task was done properly, working long after she, Flynn, and Paulo had gone to bed.

His mother was a stickler for every job being done to the best of your ability. She refused to allow him any slack, ever, and was harder on him as her son than on anyone else he knew. It was one of the main reasons he spent as much time as possible with Ruth's family. Between his ma and Paulo, life at home wasn't the easiest. But staying at Dawn's for so long the previous night had been counter-productive, as the time he'd spent basking in their gratitude had been far outweighed by his mother's fury when he returned home.

In the end, he had flopped down on his own mattress exhausted, which hadn't helped his energy levels this morning. The knowing look Anna had shot him when he'd stumbled out of bed this morning had screamed 'I told you so.' He had been glad to head off to breakfast, despite his exhaustion.

He realised Ruth was still waiting for a response. He didn't like to lie to her, but he also knew how she'd react to the fact he'd yet to bring up the touchy subject with his ma. He opened his mouth to speak, but was saved by Jacob's appearance on the small platform at the side of the cave. All around, voices petered out as he held up a hand for silence.

At fifty-two, Jacob was one of the oldest men in the camp and had held the position of council head for as long as anyone could remember. He was responsible for the development and growth of the Eremus camp from fewer than a hundred people, to the thriving community of citizens who inhabited the caverns today. Through bringing their community underground, and hiding it from Bellator's sight, he had ensured their safety and survival, and his people were intensely grateful for this. When he talked, they listened.

Once the cave was silent, he gave them his trademark grin, and ran a hand across his closely-shaved head.

"Morning, all. Look, this isn't an official meeting, but I thought I'd say a few words of thanks for those raiders who went into Bellator last night. Their visit was a successful one," he paused, his smile widening, "as I'm sure our breakfast has demonstrated." A smattering of applause echoed around the cave, and many of the raiders received congratulatory slaps on the back.

Jacob held up a hand for quiet, his face more serious now. "As we're all aware, Bellator currently believes it has all but eradicated the Eremus community. This is, in large part, down to us keeping a low profile and making sure our raids are stealthy and subtle." Noah thought about Paulo's lack of face covering and exchanged a glance with a guilty-looking Ruth as Jacob continued. "In the days to come, it may not be possible for us to stay so well-hidden, as we strive to further expand, ensure we have enough supplies to sustain our growing community and, eventually, work towards regaining our rights and our freedom."

Jacob's face darkened at the words. His hatred of the Bellator system was well-known, and he often referenced the progress Eremus was making towards what he called a *better future*. But something in his expression today was different. More serious. Noah thought back to stories he'd heard over the years from his ma and Flynn. Tales of Jacob's bravery, his devotion to making Eremus a safe place, to prevent the many losses they had suffered at the hands of the Bellator guards.

Paulo had lost his father, Tomas, at a young age. He had died fighting to save other members of the Eremus community from a particularly vicious attack. And Flynn spoke often of a friend of his, Robert, who'd been gunned down during a raid by a guard who hadn't stopped to ask questions.

Everyone in Eremus had suffered at the hands of Bellator. Until Jacob had devised the plan for them to live out of sight. A fact for which they were all thankful.

But Noah had heard his ma and Flynn many times in recent years, discussing Jacob's obsession with regaining equality for men in Bellator. Whilst his parents were mostly content to live as they did, putting the survival of the community first, Jacob seemed bent on invading Bellator and forcing them to reinstate men's rights. It was the reason he had worked so hard to expand Eremus in recent years, swelling the numbers of citizens so they were stronger, more able to take on an enemy.

But as Noah refocused on Jacob's words, he couldn't ever imagine them having the might to conquer Bellator.

". . . owe a debt of thanks to the large numbers of you on excavation duty, who have continued to dig out the tunnels in the North and West, despite the tough work. Everyone here," Jacob thrust out his arm in an all-encompassing gesture, "*everyone*, is a part of making this community what it is now and what it will be in the months to come." His voice grew in volume as he continued. "Chancellor Danforth has no idea . . . *no idea* that almost a thousand Eremus citizens, both male and female, inhabit the woods so close to their precious, single-gender city. This is a fact which should be celebrated, but also something which requires us to proceed with even more caution as we work towards our ultimate goal."

He paused, nodding confidently. "But one day, *one day*, she will know. There are plans in place. Big, bold plans. The day will come when we no longer have to hide but can live in the open: proud Eremus people, for all to see."

He punctuated the end of his speech with a hand thrust skyward and a broad smile for his adoring crowd. Leaving the podium, he was greeted by several of his most ardent fans, eager for a moment of their fearless leader's time. Noah glanced sideways to find Ruth rolling her eyes as she continued with her meal. As the conversations around them began to buzz again, he leaned closer.

"What is it? You don't believe him?"

She shrugged. "Ma says he's fooling himself. His *great plans*, and all."

"What do you mean?"

"She doesn't think it's realistic." Ruth paused to jab her spoon at the cavern above. "I mean . . . she thinks he's achieved a lot, of course. We all survive down here, the number of patrols has reduced over the years, no one's died in a while. But we've done this by *hiding*." She sighed. "I don't know. She just remembers the days when Eremus citizens lived every day in fear for their lives. She doesn't want to go back to that. And she definitely doesn't see a time when Eremus can just come out and be all 'Hello, Chancellor Danforth!' Not when Bellator's so big and powerful and all."

Before she could continue, Ella, Ruth's sister, approached their table. Without asking, she placed her bowl of oatmeal on the table next to him and sat down, flicking her long blonde hair backwards so it almost whipped against his face.

"What's up, sis?" Ruth stiffened, though her tone remained even. "You need something?"

"Ma asked me to check on you." Ella rolled her eyes as she took a small spoonful of porridge and brought it to her lips. "I know, you don't need me to, and all that." She fixed her sibling with a hard stare. "But she said I had to make sure you didn't stay in here too long chatting about last night."

Ruth bristled. "I'm only–"

Ella waved her spoon at Ruth, cutting her off. "Don't shoot the messenger, okay? She only wants to make sure you get a decent rest before your next shift." There was a lengthy pause, where Ruth was clearly expected to reply but did not. Eventually, Ella continued, "How was the raid, then?"

There was a minimal pause before Ruth muttered her reply. "Fine."

"What?"

"I said, it was fine." Ruth seemed to force the words out, and Noah knew she was almost choking on the lie. "It was fine."

"You were with Paulo again, right?" She shot Noah a wide grin, acknowledging his link to the golden raider. Ruth nodded, keeping her gaze fixed on the bowl in front of her. "Then I'm sure it went well."

Ruth's head jerked up. "He's not quite as perfect as everyone seems to think, you know."

"Really?" Ella leaned forward, her gaze darting between her sister and Noah. "Did something go wrong?"

It was Noah's turn to look at the table. The siblings' relationship had always made him slightly nervous, and he tried to stay out of things between them. Ella cared about Ruth, but his best friend often saw the interest Ella took in her life as stifling. The fact that Ella was Dawn's biological daughter didn't help, and he knew their relationship was strained because Ruth felt guilty for disrupting Ella's life when she had become a part of their family so suddenly.

"No." Ruth's reply was sharp. Noah shot her a warning look and she calmed her tone. "Nothing went wrong."

A shadow crossed Ella's pretty features, but she rallied quickly. "Alright. As long as you're okay." She glanced away, her eyes wandering the room as though searching for someone. Noah followed her gaze, but it didn't seem to settle anywhere. Eventually, she picked up her half-finished bowl of food and stood up. "Promised I'd talk to Harriet before I started my shift," she muttered. "See you later?"

Ruth didn't look up. "I'm sure you will."

Ella looked for a moment like she was going to lean over and grasp Ruth's arm, forcing her sister to meet her gaze. She looked over at Noah and seemed to change her mind. "Don't forget to get some rest, then."

After a brief pause, she turned and hurried away.

Noah waited until she was out of earshot before speaking again. "Weren't you a little . . . hard on her?"

A look of guilt crept over Ruth's face, but she quashed it quickly. "I wish she'd just keep out of my business, that's all. They treat me like I'm a child sometimes." She sighed. "So overprotective. You feel that way too. With Paulo and Flynn. Don't deny it."

Noah took a breath before answering. "Yeah. I sometimes wish they'd give me a bit more space." He softened his tone. "But they mean well. And I think the protectiveness just . . . kind of comes with the territory." Bracing himself for an angry response, he pushed on. "I mean . . . you lost your ma . . . Dawn took responsibility for you. I guess Ella feels it too."

"Feels what?"

"Like they have to care for you . . ." he hesitated before finishing his sentence, "because *your* ma can't."

Ruth's face crumpled, and he knew his words had hit their mark. For a moment, she was quiet, busying herself with her food. Noah followed suit. Eventually, she looked up.

"I guess that only proves my ma's right. The damage done when people here lose someone to Bellator is . . ." she glanced over at the table where Ella had settled with her back to them, "well, it's long lasting." She swept the remains of the oatmeal from her bowl in one final spoonful. "I think she's right. Jacob's not going to find it easy to free Eremus from Danforth's stronghold."

"He's convincing, though." Noah jerked a hand at the number of citizens who still swarmed around the council head. "I mean, you got to give him that."

Ruth shrugged. "Guess so." She stood and picked up her tray, glancing around at the still-busy cavern. "Your ma went straight to work?"

Stiffening, Noah shrugged. "Must've."

"Well," Ruth leaned closer, so only Noah could hear her, "you'd better make sure and speak to her later on today then . . . before the next raids are announced."

"But I—" Noah spluttered.

Ruth patted his shoulder. "I know you too well. There's no *way* you asked her last night." She leaned closer, her face growing serious. "But you heard Jacob. There's going to be another raid soon. You could be a part of it." Picking up her bowl from the table, she stood up. "All you have to do is persuade your folks."

"Yeah." Noah made a face. "Piece of cake."

"You'll just have to turn on the charm." Ruth winked. "Now I'm off to bed. Make sure you have some good news for me when I wake up, okay?"

Noah glared at her retreating back as he finished his oatmeal, dreading the day ahead.

Chapter Four: Faith

The encounter on the way home from the med centre had made Faith and Sophia into temporary celebrities. All through breakfast, they were quizzed by the other senior girls at their table who were desperate to hear about the events which had taken place outside the offices of the *Bellator Blade*. Girls from the lower years stopped by their table with tentative smiles and curious expressions. Sophia fielded questions in her usual good-natured way, but Faith tired of the attention quickly and took to dipping her head and ignoring everyone.

"I'll be glad when it's time for lessons," she muttered to no one in particular, "and that's saying something."

But it seemed they were destined for even more attention. Just as Faith was finishing the last of her pancakes and Sophia was shooting anxious glances at the large clock which loomed over the breakfast room, Avery sauntered over. The other girls clustered around the table fell silent, glancing uncertainly at the queen bee.

Once she knew she had everyone's attention, Avery smiled, a picture of innocence. "I hear you two had a little *adventure* on the way back from the med centre this morning."

"Yeah. That's right."

Faith stared at the older student, trying to work out her angle. The senior section of the school spanned girls between the ages of sixteen and twenty, and Avery, at nineteen, was one of the oldest. She regarded herself as a cut above and didn't usually go out of her way to speak to anyone younger. As one of the newest to join the senior class, she considered Faith distinctly beneath her.

Avery nodded at Fiona, a mousy senior who was seated to Faith's left. She gave out a small squeal and vacated the chair immediately, scurrying away, her face flushing. Avery took her time, gliding into the empty seat and settling herself. Finally, she turned to Sophia and Faith.

"So, you think you saw . . . what? A *man*?" She was practically sneering.

"We don't *think* we saw anything." Faith drew in a breath and fought to keep an even tone. "We *definitely* saw a man."

Avery looked away. "I hardly think that's likely." Faith felt a cool hand on her arm as she bit back a sharp response. She looked across at Sophia, who had flushed pink. She shook her head at Faith as Avery continued. "I mean," Avery looked at the others sitting around the table, "you were at the back, right? Everyone else from school had turned the corner onto Morrison Street? So . . . there were no other, um, *witnesses* to your little drama?"

Faith could feel the change in the atmosphere around the table. Where before the other girls had been enthralled, intrigued, even horrified by Sophia's story, now their expressions were doubtful, filled with disdain and pity. One word from Avery and they were willing to change their minds completely. It made her sick.

"Think what you like, Lassiter." Faith took her time picking up her tiny purple vitamin pill. Swallowing it with a large gulp of water, she eyeballed the older girl. "We know what we saw."

Avery threw her head back and treated them all to her delicate, tinkling laughter. "I'm sure you do, um . . . Faith, is it?" She threw a knowing glance at another of the younger girls who stood next to the table, winking in a conspiratorial manner. "I'm *sure* you do."

Desperate to leave before she slapped Avery, Faith shoved her chair under the table in a very unladylike manner and waited for Sophia to follow suit. She was unable to avoid hearing Avery's next words, which followed them out of the room. "The lengths some people will go to for attention." The girls at the table around her erupted into giggles as Avery had known they would, just as Avery had meant for Sophia and Faith to hear her final comment.

Sophia clutched her hand tightly as they walked away, though Faith wasn't sure whether her friend simply shared her embarrassment or whether she was trying to stop Faith from doing something she would later regret. As they were just about to exit into the corridor, Avery's voice trilled across the room one last time.

"Ladies? Um . . . Faith? Sophie?" Faith felt her friend's nails digging into her palms and knew she too was fighting for control.

As one, they turned. Sophia spoke through gritted teeth. "Yes?"

"Message from Professor Kemp. She wants to see you in her office." Avery's eyes flashed with delight. "*Now.*"

Without bothering to reply, Faith spun around and exited the room, Sophia hot on her heels.

"That girl!" Faith muttered as they reached the hallway which led to the rear of the academy where their teacher's office was located. "She's such a—"

"There are no words that do her justice." Sophia cut her off as they passed another of their professors descending the staircase.

"Morning, girls." Professor Lannion nodded slightly as she passed. "Don't be late for class now, will you?" She frowned as she passed them but didn't wait for an answer.

By the time they had reached the corridor containing Professor Kemp's office, Faith and Sophia had regained some composure.

"What do you think she wants?" Sophia speculated, chewing on a fingernail. "I mean, we haven't done anything wrong, have we? I mean, *I* haven't." She peered more closely at Faith. "Have *you*?"

Faith rolled her eyes. "No more than normal. And anyway, if it were something I'd done, why would she want to see you?"

Accepting this, Sophia smoothed her already perfectly straight tie and glanced over at Faith as she raised a hand to knock on the office door. She managed a smile which told Faith she looked as well presented as she was ever going to and rapped her knuckles smartly on the polished wood.

"Enter."

Sophia twisted the handle and pushed on the door. It glided open, revealing a light, airy office beyond. Seated behind the desk was an elegant woman in her early forties, with light brown hair scooped into a neat bun on the back of her head. She sat regally, as though there was an invisible thread attached to the top of her head which kept her upright. The desk contained a datadev—one of the very newest versions—a miniature bonsai tree, and a single, delicate cup and saucer which, Faith knew from experience, contained green tea. Otherwise, the space was bare.

At the girls' entrance, she lifted her finger from the datadev and touched it to her lips with the ghost of a frown. "Yes, I understand."

"No one. Do you hear me?" The disembodied voice drifted upwards from the datadev.

"I do." The woman motioned the two girls into the seats in front of her desk, waving a hand to imply her conversation was almost over. "They're here now. Don't worry, the matter will be dealt with swiftly."

"I trust it will." A sharp clicking sound indicated the call was over.

Tapping a finger lightly on the screen, Professor Kemp checked the call had properly disconnected, before swiping a finger across to access a different information source. Only then, did she turn to the girls.

"Sit, then." Again, she waved her hand at the seats in front of her desk, which both girls had ignored. "Sit!" Awkwardly, they slid into the seats as their teacher continued. "I presume Avery passed on my message. Thank you for seeing me."

"That's alright, Professor Kemp," Sophia breathed. Faith could tell she was nervous. "What can we do for you?"

There was a long silence where Professor Kemp regarded them both over the rim of her elegant spectacles. Faith resisted the urge to glance at Sophia and see what she was making of the situation. When an interminable amount of time had passed, Professor Kemp opened her mouth to speak.

"Now girls, you know it's up to me as your personal tutor here at Danforth to keep you, *ahem*, on track, so to speak." The teacher seemed to hold her body more stiffly than usual, and her hands clenched on the desk in front of her so hard that her fingers were white. "I've just been speaking to Principal Anderson. She has become aware of some . . . um . . . gossip which is circulating around the school. She believes the source of the gossip is . . . well, you two."

Kemp sat back in her chair, her eyebrows raised, clearly awaiting an answer. Faith went to open her mouth, then changed her mind and closed it again. The only thing she and Sophia had been talking about was the incident in the street that morning, and she didn't feel that constituted gossip. But perhaps through another person's eyes, it did. Glancing at Sophia, she saw the uncertainty in her friend's eyes and took a deep breath.

"The only, um . . . information . . . we have been discussing is what we saw on the way back from the medical centre this morning."

Faith was sure her teacher's face paled. "And that was?"

Faith realised her hands were shaking. "A man."

"Really?" The smile which Professor Kemp gave them seemed strained. "A man."

"Yes." Faith nodded vehemently, furious at being questioned once again. "Why does everyone keep asking us about that?"

"And where did you see this . . . man?"

"Coming out of Rochester's store."

"At that time of the morning?" Professor Kemp looked down her nose at the two of them. "You must be mistaken. Rochester's isn't even open then."

"I *know* it's not!" Noticing Sophia's warning glance, Faith moderated her tone. "It *wasn't* open. But there were people in there anyway."

"People?" Kemp's eyebrows went up. "What, you're saying there were *two* men now?"

"No. There was a man. And a woman."

"So, a Bellator citizen and, what . . . her drudge?"

"No!" Faith almost exploded. "We'd know what—"

Sophia's fingers were suddenly digging into her arm. Puzzled, she peered at her friend, wondering what she was doing.

"Of course, you're right." Sophia spoke quickly, as though to cut off whatever Faith might have come out with next. "That must have been it. One of the wealthier Bellator citizens, with her drudge."

"But—" Faith stopped abruptly as Sophia dug her nails into the skin of her arm.

"We made a mistake, didn't we Faith? *Didn't* we?"

Turning her gaze back to her teacher, Faith paused until she knew her voice would sound steadier. "That must have been it. Silly us." Sophia relaxed her hold on her arm, but even as she let go, Faith could still feel the pressure, her skin pulsing from the fierce touch.

Professor Kemp relaxed somewhat, her face breaking into a small smile for the first time since their entry. "A mistake, then. Easily made."

"It was early, I suppose . . ." Faith continued, the frustration still surging through her veins. ". . . and they took more blood from us than usual. We must have felt . . . lightheaded and . . . imagined it."

"Yes, well . . ." Professor Kemp looked down at her desk, "if that's all cleared up, you are free to go now." She picked up her datadev and began tapping at the icons impatiently.

Sensing they had been dismissed, Sophia tugged on Faith's sleeve. "Let's go."

Faith was at the door before she turned back. "Why did they double up on the blood tests this morning, Professor?"

Her teacher stiffened, then took her time raising her head to return Faith's gaze. "I'm sure we don't need to worry our heads about that, do we? Changes to the tests can only mean good things. More progress, new discoveries, and so on. Hurry along now, or you'll be late for class."

As Faith and Sophia closed the door behind them and moved towards their first lesson of the day, they exchanged glances.

Sophia waiting until they were out of earshot before commenting. "That was a little . . . odd."

"More than a little." Faith's hands curled into fists at the thought of the lies they had just been forced to agree to. "As if we can't tell a drudge from a real-life man!"

Sophie stifled a giggle. "Drudges *are* real life men."

"I suppose." Faith considered the drudges, the only remaining male of the species left in Bellator. A servant class, they were specially bred and treated so that they did not have the cruel, violent urges so characteristic of other men. Bellator made use of them all over the city. Wearing a specific uniform which included a face mask that covered everything but their eyes, they were entirely subservient. Most of the Bellator citizens barely noticed them. "They don't act like men," Faith mused. "And the person we saw this morning didn't *act* like a drudge."

"I agree," Sophia whispered, as they slipped into a group of girls heading for their first class. "You know what's strange?"

Faith turned the corner, heading for their first class of the day. "What?"

"The man . . . and the woman. They were together, right?"

"Yeah. So?"

"Well, everything we've been told about men tells us they treat women horribly. Abuse them, are cruel to them."

Faith saw where Sophia was going with it. "You mean the pair this morning didn't seem like that?"

"Exactly." Sophia dropped the volume of her voice as they entered their classroom. "They seemed . . . almost friendly." She headed for her seat towards the back of the room, leaning closer to Faith to make one last comment. "Anyway, Kemp doesn't want us to talk about it. And she *definitely* doesn't want us telling other people about it."

"Well Avery made sure no one would believe us anyway." Faith was still fuming. "I think we'd be laughed out of any room we tried to tell the story in now."

"Maybe that's for the best." Sophia's face twisted into a worried frown.

"Maybe." But as she slid into her seat at the back of the Biology Lab and opened her textbook, Faith wondered.

CHAPTER FIVE: NOAH

" Absolutely not."

Noah stared down at the rough woollen blanket on his bed. He had known what his mother's response would be in advance, so he didn't know why he was so angered by it. But as a wave of helplessness washed over him, he clenched his hands into fists and refused to look at her.

He had worked hard all morning and finished his shift early. After speaking to Ruth at breakfast he was feeling energised about the conversation with his ma, so he hurried straight to his family's cave, knowing she was likely to be there, alone. She had worked a morning shift in the gardens, and often chose to eat a cold lunch and read, enjoying what she called "blissful peace and quiet."

She had been alone when he arrived and everything had gone well. Her anger from the previous night seemed to have left her, and his immediate efforts to tackle the stack of dishes that needed washing had gone a long way towards making her happy. After ten minutes, when he judged her to be in the optimum mood and knew he'd have to speak up before her afternoon shift, he had come straight out with it, knowing his mother hated anyone who "beat around the bush," as she put it.

But her response had been just as it had been so many times before. A big, fat *no*.

Sick of the silence which had followed her refusal, he forced himself to look over at her. She was sitting, a hunk of bread in one hand, the other propping open a book, her eyes squinting in the dim light of the candle to read the words on the page. It was a type of medical tome, with ancient, yellowing pages, one which Noah knew she'd read many times before. The words were faded and hard enough to decipher in the brightest of lights, but still she continued to read.

"Can you tell me why, at least?" He could hear the whine in his voice and hated it but knew he couldn't just let it drop.

She shook her head almost absent-mindedly. "You know my reasons. They haven't changed."

"But I don't think you understand how—" He was stopped as she held up a hand, letting him know she wanted to finish the page before discussing the matter further.

His first memory of his mother was of books. Eremus was a simple society, and the formal education of its children was not paramount. Jacob Williams insisted all the children born in the community were given a grounding in the basics. They learned to read using the minimal supply of books the society had access to, mostly those taken from places visited on the raids. Jacob made sure they all gained a thorough understanding of the mathematical concepts they might use during the course of their work in Eremus. Other than that, school was not prioritised and only took place a few mornings a week. The rest of the children's time was spent learning more practical things.

Not Noah though. For some reason, his mother was a stickler for learning. She had read to him regularly since early childhood, often the same books over and over. Whenever Flynn went on a raid, she would beg him to bring back a new book or two, which she always shared with her son before passing it on to others in the community. And when he was older and had finished school for the morning, she would insist he return to their cave after his on-the-job training and dinner for more reading and lessons, which she delivered herself.

It was another reason he had issues with boys like Harden. Whilst they competed to see how fast they could finish their training, exercised to build muscles they could show off to the others, and found ways to sneak out of the caves so they could brag about it later, Anna insisted Noah be home to further his learning every evening.

In a community where what you were capable of providing was prized far above anything else, additional education did little for him. Of course, understanding which plants were safe to eat was important. And knowing how to make available ingredients stretch to feed the largest number possible and which herbs were useful in creating salves for wounds were attributes the community prized. Anything beyond that was unnecessary.

Noah just didn't fit in.

Ruth had become his only friend, encouraged by Dawn to attend the evening lessons with Noah which she, surprisingly, seemed to enjoy. And Noah had to admit, having her there made the sessions a little more bearable. If he was totally honest, he should admit he enjoyed the reading, and had an excellent memory for the facts his ma insisted he retain. When Flynn, and more recently Paulo, came home with a new book for them to devour, he was just as excited as his mother, but that was beside the point. He appreciated the love of reading and education his mother had instilled in him, but in a place like Eremus there seemed little opportunity to use what he had learned, and he wondered all the time why she invested so much effort in teaching him these things.

Finally, his ma tore her eyes away from the page and looked at him. With a sigh, she closed the book and put it to one side, coming over to sit alongside him on the bed. He had to force himself to remain still and not shift away from her and knew she could see how angry he was.

"Look," she laid a hand on his knee, "I understand, you know."

"No. I don't think you do." She looked hurt. "I don't understand why you won't let me be a raider. Paulo's done it for years. Now Ruth raids too. Why not me?"

She removed her hand. "I don't want you going into Bellator. It's too dangerous."

"But you're okay with Paulo doing it? And Flynn?"

She looked away. "I don't want you getting hurt."

"Who says I'd get hurt?" He stood up, afraid if he stayed where he was, he might punch something or, worse, burst into tears he was far too old for. He had to stay calm, appear mature, or he had no chance of convincing her. He changed the subject. "Jacob spoke at dinner today."

"I heard."

"Said there'd be another raid soon. Said the raids are vital. Said—"

His ma held a hand up for silence again. "Jacob says a lot. But Jacob has a different motivation than most citizens."

"What kind of motivation?"

Noah's ma shook her head. "Never mind. Some of Jacob's words are dangerous, that's all."

"But he understands how the raids keep our community going. He *respects* the raiders."

She turned to him, her eyes narrowed. "Are you suggesting I don't?"

He shook his head. "No. But . . . but Jacob prizes the raiders above everyone. You know that. And he's the one who's kept Eremus going over the years."

"Oh, he's the *only* one who's done that?"

"You know what I mean." Noah struggled to find the right words. "If I don't become a raider, how can I ever hope for him to notice me . . . to become something . . . better?"

"Like I said, Jacob has his own reasons for wanting the raids to continue. For wanting to increase the size of our raiding team." His ma sighed. "Some of them I agree with. Some . . . well, I'm not so sure about."

"What do you mean?"

"Forget it. You don't need to concern yourself with it." She paused for a second, and he knew she was trying to change the subject as she always did. "What did Jacob say about the raid, then?"

"It went well. But apparently there were a few things they didn't manage to get hold of."

"Ah yes, the analgesics." Anna was one of the unofficial Eremus medics and, along with a man around Flynn's age named Sam, did her best to treat the illnesses and injuries of the community. She was regularly frustrated by their lack of provisions, which made it difficult for her to treat some of the more serious ailments. "Whoever they sent to the medical centre this time didn't manage to get in. Or brought back the wrong meds . . . I don't know."

"You see!" He jumped on the idea. "They don't know what they're looking for. But if *I* were a raider—"

"But you're not going to be a raider. I can give better instructions to the others next time. Or they'll have to look elsewhere." Anna shrugged. "I don't want you going, and that's final."

She turned her back on him as Flynn pushed aside the cloth which covered the entrance to their home and strode inside. At six feet tall, he dominated the space. He wiped a hand across his face, which was streaked with sweat, and reached up to pull his shirt over his head.

"Phew. It's warm down in those lower tunnels today." He tossed the shirt into the empty basket at the side of the bed. "We're making progress though. I just wanted to grab a wash before I meet with Jacob this afternoon." Stopping to pour himself a large cup of water from the pitcher which stood on the table at one side of the room, he looked around. "Everything alright?"

"Everything's fine." Noah muttered. Flynn was a gruff man who Noah got along well with, but he knew how hard the man who had always been a father to him could be on those who failed to follow orders.

Anna shot a look at Flynn as he gulped down the water. "Same old argument, I'm afraid."

Flynn placed the cup back down on the table, refilling it for a second time. "Jacob's been filling their heads with tales of Eremus' future triumph over Bellator. You can't blame him for being curious."

"I don't *blame* him." Anna sniffed and stood up, brushing crumbs from her lap. "But we don't all have to give in to our curiosities, do we? You know how I feel about it, and why. And you know my concerns about Jacob's motivations."

Flynn shot Noah a glance behind his mother's back. It conveyed sympathy, but also a lack of power. Whilst Flynn was a formidable man within the Eremus community, and one of Jacob Williams' closest advisors, when it came to Anna, he was a total pushover. Rumour had it he had been a loner until Anna had stolen his heart, but since then, as Jacob sometimes put it, he was a goner.

Noah was Anna's child, and not Flynn's, in the same way Paulo, though Flynn was his uncle and not his father, was his relation. And though the four of them cohabited as though they were a family with blood-ties, Anna took care of Noah's discipline while Flynn dealt with Paulo. It was, they argued, what kept them happy. In any case, Noah knew Flynn had no real control over his mother's decisions. He would no more be able to change her mind, once made up, than Noah could.

Flynn strode across the floor to Anna. He circled his arms round her, pulling her close. "Alright. I know better than to try and change your mind."

She relaxed into him for a moment before pushing him gently away. "Did you get some lunch?"

"Not yet. I'll grab something on the way to Jacob's." He relinquished his hold on her reluctantly. "Oh, and I think we might have to deal with a swollen head from Paulo this evening."

Anna shot him an amused glance. "Why's that?"

Flynn chuckled. "When I left the tunnels, he was busy recounting his heroic antics on the latest raid to several of our female citizens. They were hanging on his every word." Noah's mind strayed to Ruth's version of events and wondered how much of the truth his brother was telling those who were in such awe of his raiding prowess. "But I'm sure we'll manage to bring him back to earth. I mean, the last raid was pretty textbook. Very quiet. No issues whatsoever. I don't really see how he can spin it as all that exciting."

Knowing it was no use bringing up the subject of him raiding again, Noah pushed himself off the bed. Seizing the almost-empty pitcher from the table, he waved it at them and turned to head out the door. "I'll refill this before my shift this afternoon."

He didn't wait for a response. Exiting their cave, which stood at the junction between two of the main thoroughfares in Eremus, he ducked into the second one and headed for the canteen, nodding to the few Eremus citizens he passed. When he got there, it was empty. Most people ate their lunch on the job or in their own dwellings.

He made a beeline for the three large barrels of water which were filled every morning from the river which ran through the cave system. After refilling the pitcher, he was about to set off back down the tunnel when he heard footsteps. Emerging from the same tunnel he was headed for was Dawn. Her hair was swept back under a bandana and she looked like she had been working hard.

"Hey Noah." She smiled tiredly. "How's it going?"

"Alright." He gestured to her dusty overalls. "You on tunnel-clearing this morning?"

"How'd you guess?" She winked at him, the gesture reminding him very much of Ruth. Helping herself to a cup of water, she drained it in one long gulp. "Gave Flynn a run for his money down there. He's such a—" Stopping abruptly, she stepped closer to Noah, peering into his face. "What's the matter?"

"What?" He shrugged. "Oh . . . nothing."

Noah had known Dawn all his life. She wasn't an easy woman to get to know, but once earned, her respect and loyalty were steadfast. She and his mother had been friends since before he was born, and the warmth she felt for Anna extended to Noah by association. Unlike other members of the Eremus community, who were pleasant to him only because of his relationship with Flynn and Anna, Dawn seemed to genuinely like him for himself. Sometimes, he felt more welcome in her home than his own.

"Don't give me that." She stepped towards him. "I know when something's wrong. Is it Harden? Don't think I don't see how he treats you. If his ma would only get off his back, I think he'd—" She stopped, narrowing her eyes. "Or is it something closer to home?"

Another reason Ruth was such a good companion was her own family setup, which was similar to his own. Not actually related to Dawn by blood, she had been taken in by her when her own mother, Mara, had been killed in a Bellator guard attack. Dawn had been Mara's best friend, the two of them looking out for one another from the moment both their partners had been killed in the same attack on Bellator a few years earlier.

When Mara suffered the same fate, Dawn had taken Ruth in and brought her up alongside her biological daughter Ella. Not that she treated Ruth any differently. But the fractured household gave them something in common. As did the fact that Dawn usually understood the difficulties which could occur with such a setup.

He shrugged again. "It's Ma. I asked her if I could raid . . . again . . . same old argument, you know."

Dawn nodded wisely. "Same response, too?"

He nodded miserably. "I just, I just don't get why she's so against me being a raider. I mean . . . it's not like I have a lot going for me here. If I could, I mean . . . if they gave me the chance to raid, at least I could show people round here I'm worth something . . . gain a little respect . . ." He trailed off, suddenly embarrassed.

"Stop being so down on yourself, Noah." Dawn slapped him on the arm, then bent to refill her cup with water. "All the important people know you're worth something."

"But if I could just—"

Dawn held up a hand to stop him. "Noah, I'd love to tell you your ma'll come round one of these days. But I'd be lying to you if I did . . . I think," she sighed, "I think you have to find a different way of gaining the respect of others."

Noah didn't feel any better. "But I don't understand *why*. When Flynn, and Paulo . . . and *Ruth*, even . . . Does ma think I can't do it?"

"It's not that." Dawn soothed. "I promise you. Look, she has her reasons. You just have to accept them."

Betrayed, Noah glared at his mother's oldest friend. Of course, she would take his ma's side. She frowned, and he knew she could see his disappointment, but she didn't waver.

"I'm sorry, love. I really am." Dawn shook her head sadly. "But you need to let this one go."

"Maybe." Swallowing hard, Noah turned away. "I need to get this back. See you later."

Dawn's eyes followed him as he left. He waited for her to call him back, to offer more comfort, but she didn't.

CHAPTER SIX: FAITH

That afternoon, Faith was exhausted. The early morning wake-up call and the shock of their encounter on the way back had been trying enough. But the curious nature with which she and Sophia had been silenced and the tedium of the three lessons which followed had wiped her out. The weather was hot, too. Any time spent outdoors today had been unbearable and sent her racing back to the comfort of the airconditioned academy.

As she and Sophia headed through the door of the Herstory classroom for their lesson, they were both dragging their feet.

"Ugh. First this, and then Bellator Lit last period." Sophia lifted her arm and tapped on her wristclip, navigating between different screens with dizzying speed. "I hope I didn't . . ." Faith cast a questioning glance at her friend and nodded at Professor Kemp, who was waiting impatiently for the class to arrive. "Phew!"

"Phew, what?"

Sophia lowered her voice. "Thought I'd forgotten to save that report for Principal Anderson. The one due today." She frowned at her friend's confused expression. "You know . . . the analysis of Sylvia Plath's *The Bell Jar* from a post-abolition perspective?" Faith's heart sank. "You did do it, didn't you?"

"I did it." Faith slid into her seat in the third row of the room, hissing the final comments over her shoulder. "But I don't have it on me."

She cursed herself, having forgotten to transfer it to the portable clip on her wrist. Unlike other teachers who encouraged girls to submit their work remotely, and ahead of time, Anderson liked the girls to hand in their work during the lesson. She claimed it encouraged a sense of pride and less dependence on technology. But it was a nightmare for the less organised students, like Faith.

Sophia only had a second to shoot her a look of concern before Kemp cleared her throat loudly. The last few students hurried in as she waited in front of the huge screen which dominated the front of the room, her expression cold. Sliding into their usual seats, the students tapped the screens of the datadevs integrated into their desks, ready to begin.

Faith remembered Professor Kemp once telling them that, in days gone by, teachers had to call out the names of every student to check their attendance. There was no need for that now. A simple tap on the datadev established their presence, and the fingerprint identification system knew who was sitting in the chair. It made teachers' lives much easier. Skipping lessons was a difficult, almost impossible process. You had to be a tech genius, and even then, it was easy to get caught.

When they were all checked in, Professor Kemp nodded. "Welcome. Today we will be watching a video, followed by a brief discussion of the following debate topic: could the abolition of man have happened faster than it did? After that, you'll be assigned a paper on the subject, to be submitted next lesson."

Faith straightened in her chair. The day was looking up. Herstory was a subject she enjoyed and debating the great female revolt would definitely be interesting. Plus, the video would take up at least the first portion of the class, and not demand too much of them.

"Activate your earcoms, girls, and read the introductory task. Complete the questions on the recall quiz from last lesson." Professor Kemp shot a look at some girls at the back of the room who had been whispering to one another. They fell silent. "We'll begin in a moment."

Faith took the earcoms from their tiny drawer, paired them with the datadev, and slid the buds into her ears. Scrolling her eyes over the screen, she scanned the quiz. The questions were fairly standard, only requiring students to remember key facts from previous lessons.

Sophia's head was already bent low, her finger rapidly selecting responses. On the screen at the front of the room, the counter next to her name scrolled upwards faster than anyone else in the room. Every answer was highlighted in green. Gaining full marks in record time was pretty standard for Sophia.

It took Faith far longer to complete tasks, especially if she wanted to do well. Casting her eyes down the datadev, she read the first question.

1. List three common symptoms of the 2051 Vardicus virus.

An easy one to begin with. Seventy years earlier, a new virus scientists named Vardicus had swept the world, affecting every country. Millions of people had died over the next few years, despite many countries closing their borders in a desperate attempt to stop the spread. By the time any kind of immunity had developed, the global population had been dramatically reduced. A nasty illness, the symptoms were extremely debilitating. *Swollen glands, vomiting,* Faith typed, *a purple-coloured rash.*

2. List two long-term consequences of the virus.

Faith had no trouble remembering the first. *A gender imbalance in the population.* Where a large percentage of women recovered well from Vardicus, men were more seriously affected and far more likely to die. As a consequence, the work force in male-dominated industries had been decimated. Farming, engineering, construction and, most notably, the military had all suffered. The solution had been found in the surviving women, many of whom had stepped in to be trained and fill the gap in these vital areas.

Chewing her lip, Faith racked her brains for another major consequence. She eventually typed *Disintegration of international exports.* It was true. Once the borders between countries were closed, most governments were too frightened to open them again. The virus had left behind a severely-reduced population in every country, and most leaders, wanting to protect their remaining citizens, preferred to stay isolated and manage their own affairs. It was one of the reasons the island had become so isolated.

3. In what year was the Women's Independent Party formed?

This one wasn't difficult. It was even part of the Bellator shield, emblazoned on their uniform. Quickly, she tapped the response: *2085.*

4. Why was the WIP formed?

This one was multiple-choice, and the correct answer was easy to locate: *Once the threat of the virus was reduced, the women of the island rose up to condemn the violent actions of the remaining men who sought to retain their original control, even with their reduced numbers.* Again, Faith selected her response with confidence.

5. Name the two drugs successfully employed by the WIP in the abolition of man?

This time, Faith deliberated for a moment. In the early years of the WIP, a number of revolutionary meds had been used to reduce incidences of aggressive behaviour in males. Members of the party had used them in secrecy, adding them to various food and drink products commonly consumed by men, and increasing the levels as time had gone on. This had been key in allowing the female gender to weaken men who had survived the Vardicus virus.

Later, the WIP had employed more severe measures, including regular public executions of men who continued to commit violent acts against women. Many men chose to flee the city, forming small rebel communities in rural areas of the island. In subsequent years, the WIP, now in total control of Bellator's government, sought to destroy them all.

The drugs had been the start of it all, though. Their complex names were tricky to remember. Eventually, Faith typed *haloperidol* and *risperidone*, and waited anxiously to see if she was right. When she heard a satisfactory 'ping' through her earcoms, she grinned.

Moving on, she scanned the next question.

4. What method was employed to enable procreation in the early days of Bellator?

This time, Faith didn't hesitate, but as she gave her answer, she shuddered. When Bellator had first turned single-gender, it had retained a number of men so their seed could be used for the purposes of reproduction. These males had been kept in captivity, to ensure they couldn't pose any threat to the women of Bellator, but the idea of several violent men living within Bellator walls was enough to make any citizen fearful.

A few years later, several of them had escaped and gone on a violent rampage across the city— a horrific event which was etched into the memories of all the older Bellator citizens. The city had gone into lockdown as the guards tracked down and eliminated the fugitives one by one. After that, leading bioengineer Abigail Danforth, now Bellator's Chancellor, had implemented a procedure by which scientists took huge quantities of seed from the remaining males in captivity and froze them in a vault for future use. A public execution of the few remaining males had reassured the city they were no longer a threat. Everyone agreed the seed bank provided a much safer solution to the procreation issue. And now, the only males in Bellator were the drudges.

There were several more questions, but as Herstory was a subject Faith enjoyed, she didn't find them too much of a challenge. Satisfied she had answered all the questions correctly, Faith sat back and waited for the rest of the group to finish.

Avery was sitting a few seats over, her chin resting on her hand as she stared out the window. Clearly, like Faith and Sophia, she had finished earlier than the others. Unlike other Bellator schools, where students were loosely grouped with those pupils whose day of birth fell in the same year, students at Danforth found themselves in classes with girls up to five years older than them. Despite her age, Avery shared all their classes with them.

Faith exchanged glances with Sophia, who looked increasingly frustrated at the length of time it was taking some of the girls to finish. Faith jerked her head towards Avery and made a face, turning her eyes in towards her nose and sticking out her tongue. Sophia burst out laughing, stifling the giggle with a hand over her mouth, but she wasn't quick enough. She was rewarded with a scathing look from Avery and a sharp rap on the desk from Professor Kemp, who seemed as eager to start the video as the girls were to watch it.

"Alright now. Are we *ready* yet, girls?" Kemp's tone was exasperated. Faith spotted a few girls blushing and hurrying to finish. When the tally chart on the large board at the front displayed a full cohort of student responses, she glanced at her own datadev. "Hmmm. Mostly correct, though a few of you need to put a *little* more effort into your revision." Another series of taps followed her disgruntled announcement.

Moments later, the lights were dimmed and the blinds on the windows descended. The screen flickered to life and the film began with the usual images which accompanied the subject. The Abolition of Man was not a topic for the faint hearted. Close up shots of female faces emblazoned with angry purple bruises, arms and torsos covered with blood, horrific images of the millions of women who had suffered and died at the hands of men flashed across the screen one after another.

When she had first seen this kind of film, Faith had found the images stark and upsetting. The faces of the women, battered and bruised, were distressing enough, but for Faith, it was their eyes that were the most disturbing. Some women had hollow stares which told the viewers they were broken. Others had eyes filled with fire and fury. These were the women who had risen up to form the WIP. Faith had left the first few lessons like this in tears and had even gone as far as to petition Principal Anderson to stop showing them.

"Of course, they're upsetting, girl." The principal was not one to be argued with. "They're *meant* to be." Faith had opened her mouth to argue, but the older woman had jabbed a finger at her. "If we don't study the past, learn from our mistakes, see men for the *treacherous* creatures they truly are, then we are doomed to repeat our mistakes."

And so, the discussion was closed. Since then, Faith had become almost immune to the images, as most of the girls were.

Next, a calm female voice echoed across the classroom. "We are all aware that, in the not-too-distant past, our beloved land was dominated by the male species. Men, those base, violent creatures, ruled over us with their fists and their weapons of steel. The Vardicus virus, though devastating, gave women the chance to redress the imbalance. To stand up and say, 'No. There *has* to be a better way.'"

A large red X appeared on the screen, slashing through the devastating images as the voiceover continued.

"The rise of the Women's Independent Party and the successful Abolition of Man is a vital part of our herstory. But should these changes have happened *earlier* than they did?"

The film continued, now displaying shots of the men who had caused the horrific damage: always action sequences, the limbs blurring as they attacked their female victims with venom, the faces further away than those of the women and usually out-of-focus. Faith often wondered what emotions lurked in the eyes of these men, whether their expressions were filled with the hatred that fuelled their attacks on the vulnerable women.

The video lasted ten minutes, and when it was over, Professor Kemp switched off the film, opened the blinds, and turned on the lights. Faith blinked as her eyes adjusted.

"So, that's the crux of it." Kemp waved a hand at the now-empty screen. "We all know our great land has been free of men for twenty-six years now. With males in charge, the land we love was unfairly and unjustly managed, and women were treated as little more than slaves. The question for today's paper is on your screens now."

Faith glanced down at the assignment, which had just popped up. *Two decades on: could the abolition of man have been brought about more rapidly?*

"Now," Kemp continued, "what questions might we explore as part of this topic?" Sophia's hand shot up. "Yes, Sophia?"

"Why did the abolition happen when it did?" Sophia ticked off the ideas on her fingers. "*How* could it have been brought about earlier? What were the key things which made it a success?" She paused for a second, thinking. "Oh, and—"

But Kemp held up a hand for her to stop. "Yes, yes, Sophia. I think you have most of it covered there. Don't forget, you could also explore the potential *effects* of an earlier abolition. What might some of those have been?" Ignoring Sophia's hand, her hawk-like eyes settled on a quiet girl sitting towards the back. "Serene?"

Under her freckles, Serene flushed. She was another one of the older girls but had none of Avery's confidence. "Um . . . a larger number of lives saved?"

"That's right." Professor Kemp nodded her approval. "Any other suggestions?"

One of Serene's friends, a girl named Diane whose seat was directly behind Sophia's, raised her hand. "Could we look at it from a different perspective?"

Professor Kemp looked confused. "Whatever do you mean, Diane?"

"I mean," Diane was quite controversial, and Faith always enjoyed her debates with their teachers, "where would our society be if the abolition had never taken place at all?"

There was a silence in which every girl in the room waited for Kemp's reaction. Her face went through a number of different shades as she struggled to find words. First she paled, then turned almost green, and finally her cheeks blazed scarlet as though she had been branded.

"*No*. I'd rather you *didn't* cover that side of the issue, Diane." Kemp struggled to draw breath, then managed to continue. "The fact is, the abolition *did* occur, and we are, *of course*, better for it." She looked back at her datadev, as though trying to discourage further questions, but behind Sophia, Diane had raised her hand again. With a sigh, she nodded stiffly at her. "*Yes*, Diane?"

"Would it be advisable to mention Eremus in our papers?" An almost audible gasp filled the room as Diane mentioned one of the forbidden communities of men who had fled Bellator in the early days. Eremus was the most famous, fabled to still exist in the woods not far from Bellator's outer limits. Vivid descriptions of it often featured in horror stories told by the older Danforth students. "I mean, Bellator used to send regular patrols out to the woods looking for any men who had escaped its notice, didn't it?"

"It did, yes." Kemp appeared to be speaking through gritted teeth "You're right of course Diane, but that community was eradicated *years* ago, of course, along with all the others. Any patrols sent out there recently have found no sign of them. A brief mention of Eremus *might* be worthwhile, but no more than that." The professor sagged with relief as another student raised her hand. "Yes, Emily?"

"Don't be so sure." Diane's comment was muttered under her breath, but Faith heard it. She exchanged glances with Sophia, marvelling at the other girl's daring.

After Kemp had dealt with the next question, she instructed the class to use their individual datadevs to research the topic further. Faith felt they could have had more of an in-depth discussion and was disappointed she hadn't gotten the chance to contribute, but Kemp seemed in no mood to listen to them anymore. Giving up, Faith bent her head over her datadev and dove into the past.

The rest of the lesson flew by. At the end of it, Faith was the first one to exit. The girls had only five minutes to move to their next lesson, giving them enough time to visit the bathroom and walk across the campus, but not much more than that. With her homework stored on the datadev in her dorm, Faith would be in trouble, but she was cutting it close to make it up there and back, before the datadev alerted Anderson of her absence.

Dashing in the opposite direction of everyone else, Faith had to fight her way through the crowd of students, like a salmon swimming upstream. Once she reached the stairway at the end of the corridor, the crowding eased and she was able to sprint up to the floor above with no more delay. Skidding to a stop in front of her dorm room, she thrust her weight against the door and burst in.

It wasn't empty.

Standing at the opposite end was one of the Danforth Academy's drudges sweeping the floor. Faith shuddered to a halt, her stunned expression mirroring his.

The fact she could *see* his expression doubled her shock. Drudges always, *always*, had their faces covered. It was law. These men were only allowed to exist within Bellator because they weren't classed as men. They served its women, and their entire role depended on them completing their tasks unnoticed. The drudge's naked face was an act of sedition, punishable by death. Yet his shock suggested it wasn't an intentional act of rebellion.

It wasn't an unpleasant face. In truth, the male face was not unlike her own. Narrow cheekbones framed intelligent-looking eyes, and the mouth was pleasantly curved. As she continued to stare, the drudge's face coloured, with embarrassment or, more likely, fear. Slowly, he reached down to his belt, where he had tucked his mask.

Within seconds, he had donned it, hiding the lower part of his face. Faith could now only see his eyes. She found herself staring into their depths, unable to move. And then the drudge ducked his head and continued to sweep the floor as though she wasn't there.

Remembering the time, Faith moved past him to her desk, tapping on the datadev to activate it. The vital homework was still on the screen. Pressing her wristclip to the Transfer symbol at the top of the screen, she waited until it beeped, indicating the file had been copied to her portable device. Satisfied she'd be okay now, as long as she moved fast, she turned to leave.

As she reached the door, she turned one last time to find the drudge was staring at her again. Faith offered him a small smile before stepping into the hallway and closing the door. As she hurried down the hall, she realised she was shaking.

Chapter Seven: Noah

N oah stared into the forest. Today, he'd been assigned to tunnel duty, tasked with removing the excess rubble for a team who were digging a new branch to the south of Eremus. There were several exits to their cave settlement, and they were used to bring out the excavated soil and rocks. The exits were rotated to avoid alerting the outside world to what was going on beneath the surface.

Some of the citizens were used to bring the rubble to the surface in wheelbarrows; others were in charge of distributing it throughout the woods, carrying small amounts of it in packs and scattering it as widely as possible. Noah preferred the second of the two jobs, as it allowed him to be outdoors, but today he had not been lucky in his assignment. Removing the rubble was a hot and tiring job, and he was damp with sweat. But the trip to this particular exit came with its advantages.

People called it the sky cave. It had two exits, one at ground level, which was narrow and concealed, as usual, by dense foliage which kept it from being discovered. The other was set high in the rock, tipping upwards so steeply that you had to climb hand-over-hand to reach it. It was often used as a lookout point, as the view from the opening was wide-ranging and magnificent. Towering trees fringed the edges, their emerald leaves swaying in the breeze or whipping back and forth, depending on the weather conditions. The sky could be glimpsed through the fronds of green, glowing an intense turquoise, a pale blue, or a lead grey. And if you looked down and stayed still long enough, the forest floor beneath was alive with creatures.

A noise behind Noah startled him, and he spun round. Standing at the cave entrance was Paulo, a wheelbarrow in his hands. Noah watched as Paulo tipped out the contents, adding to the heap which was waiting to be transferred outside. When he was finished, he glanced upwards, frowning.

"Wondered where you'd got to." Paulo abandoned his wheelbarrow and climbed up to join his brother. As he approached the top, he stretched out a hand. Surprised, Noah reached down to pull him up. Together, they stared out at the view. "I'm aware most people believe you to be our resident weakling, Noah, but I know how fast you can move."

Noah regarded his brother warily. "I don't know what you mean."

Paulo laughed. "I've been keeping an eye on you. Timing your movements. Figured you were either crawling here and back again, or . . . *stopping* for some reason." He noted Noah's sharp intake of breath and continued, a sudden wicked grin on his face. "Don't worry, little brother. I'm the only one who's noticed."

Noah felt a slight sense of relief. The journey between the rock face and the rubble heap was a long one, but over time, he had made it into a game. He raced between the rockface and the outer cave as fast as he could, using the glimpse of freedom at the end as his reward. If he returned for his next barrowload of rubble and got yelled at for dawdling, he was disappointed in himself.

And he knew he was getting faster. The barrows were heavy, and the work hard, but he had managed to shave several minutes off the trip, and as a result, increased the time he spent at the cave mouth. When he'd first started, he'd hoped the strenuous exercise would strengthen his body and increase his muscle mass. But over time, the racing had only made him leaner. He had none of the obvious muscles some of the others had. It was beyond frustrating.

"Be careful, though." Paulo turned to look at Noah, his expression serious. "If you show them, even once, the speed with which you can *actually* get between here and the workers, well . . ."

"I know, I know." Noah shook his head. "They'd roast me."

"I was going to say they'd recruit you to be a raider." Noah shot a glance at his brother. "You'd be good at it, you know. It's not all about muscle."

"Pity Ma won't let me then, isn't it?" Noah scowled.

"You know you're sixteen now, right?" Paulo stretched his tired arms above his head, displaying the thick cords of muscle which roped around his biceps. Noah looked away. "You goin' to follow her rules forever?"

Noah stared at the distant trees, picturing the city he'd heard so much about. "You think I should defy her? What? Just go on a raid without telling her?" He snorted. "How'd that work? Flynn'd have told her before I'd even left Eremus."

Paulo's face darkened. "Who cares what she thinks? Isn't the golden boy *ever* going to disobey his beloved ma?"

Once again, Noah found himself flushing. "One day, maybe. But it's not like I have a ton of allies, is it? I don't want to fall out with her."

"What can Anna do?" Paulo shrugged, turning to clamber back down the rocks. "Sure, she'll be mad for a while. But she'd forgive you in the end."

"You think so?" Noah set off after his brother, scrambling to keep up with him. "You've seen how she is whenever I bring it up."

Paulo had reached his barrow. Skillfully, he maneuvered it to face the opposite direction. Pausing briefly, he faced his brother. "You chicken?"

"No!" Noah snapped. "What would you know, anyway? It's not like you—"

"Yeah." Paulo cut him off, his eyes flashing with a hurt which he quickly masked. "Not like I've got a ma of my own, is it?"

Paulo's ma had died giving birth to him. Eremus medical resources were limited, and the occurrence was not uncommon. As his father had been killed in a Bellator attack a few years later, Flynn was the only real parent he'd ever known. Noah knew his accusation had been unfair and inwardly cursed himself.

"Sorry," Noah muttered. "I didn't mean . . ."

But his brother had already headed up the tunnel, his empty barrow rattling along in front of him. He was several metres ahead before he turned and called back over his shoulder. "So, *little* brother, think you're fast enough to make it back to the rockface before *me*? Maybe, if you can, I won't tell them how much time you waste when you're down here."

Noah grasped the handles of his barrow and scuttled after the retreating figure. But he was fighting a losing battle. Those few precious moments staring into the canopy of green where he had felt, for once, that perhaps his brother was on the same side as him, were gone. And in their place, the sense that sharing a secret with Paulo wasn't such a good idea.

It had been the same for as long as he could remember. Paulo: older, taller, stronger, ready for anything. Yet his brother always seemed dissatisfied, as though he wanted something *more*. Paulo had always blown hot and cold with him, one moment seeming to rejoice in the company of a brother, the next finding him nothing but an annoyance. There was the age difference, of course, and the fact he wasn't related to Noah by blood, but

Noah had always felt there was something more to it. He just didn't know what.

He didn't stand a chance of beating Paulo, but he kept up a fast pace anyway. When he reached the rockface, he thought his heart would stop. Paulo was talking to Flynn and Jacob on the other side of the tunnel. Their heads were bent close together, as if they were discussing something of great importance. Noah had visions of their intimidating leader turning to stare at him, disappointment carved into his craggy features.

Glancing down at his barrow, he considered loading it up again as fast as possible and scurrying back the way he had come. But the word *chicken* rang in his head. Instead, he set the barrow down and approached the three men, steeling himself to deal with the consequences of Paulo's revelation.

Flynn spotted him first, nodding to the others, who turned to face him. The conversation stopped. Noah frowned at Paulo, who held a subtle finger to his lips. Jacob was the last to turn.

"Hey, Noah."

"Hi, Jacob."

"We were just discussing the next raid." Noah's thundering heart slowed at the words. Of course, Jacob had better things to do than bother himself with Noah's little game. He shot a brief smile at Paulo, thankful his brother had not betrayed him.

"Will there be another one soon?" he managed.

"Soon as we can arrange it," Jacob continued. "There are a few things we still need."

It crossed Noah's mind he could ask Jacob directly about becoming a raider, but before he could pluck up the courage, the older man spoke again.

"We were also considering the possibility of Eremus being able to do a lot *more* than sneak in and grab supplies."

Flynn frowned. "I told you. It's too soon."

Jacob held up a hand to stop him. "You're wrong."

"But—"

"No. We're almost ready."

As he spoke, Sarah Porter appeared from another of the central tunnels, a line of citizens following her. She stood aside, gesturing with her hand for them to continue. Aside from Sarah, they all carried large, sealed boxes. Their focused expressions suggested the contents were heavy, and possibly fragile.

"Almost done with moving these, Jacob." Sarah stepped closer to their leader, her expression serious as usual. "This is the last load."

"Thank you for supervising, Sarah." Jacob grinned. "You've done a good job."

Much to Noah's surprise, Sarah attempted to return the smile, the expression looking alien on her permanently-sour face. "Thank you. It was my pleasure."

She turned to usher the last of the citizens through. Bringing up the rear of the line was Harden, who stumbled slightly as he passed them.

"Careful, son!" Flynn warned.

Harden righted himself, shooting a quick glance at his ma's face. Noah followed his gaze, noting the fury which had replaced Sarah's unfamiliar smile. Without speaking to her son or offering to help, she turned and hurried after the other citizens. Harden lowered his head, his face blazing scarlet.

"Need a hand, Harden?" Paulo mocked.

Noah almost felt sorry for his enemy but couldn't help but enjoy Harden's embarrassment just a little. Glancing up for a brief second, Harden caught Noah's expression and shot him a look of venom. As he disappeared down the tunnel after his ma, Noah wondered how Harden might make him pay for his amusement later.

"You see?" Jacob gestured at the retreating figures. "This is what we've been working towards all these years. What we have here will make *all* the difference."

Noah's curiosity outweighed his lack of confidence in front of Jacob. "What's in the boxes?"

Jacob took him by the shoulder. "The future, Noah."

Confused, Noah opened his mouth to ask again, but a dark look from Flynn stopped him.

"You don't need to know. Not right now, anyway." He turned back to Jacob. "Look, you know I support this idea, but if we go in too early, things could go badly."

Jacob shook his head. "I've explained the plan. I've spoken to Madeleine. She's talked to her contacts in the resistance and they're certain Danforth won't see it coming. It's perfect." His face darkened. "And it's about time we fought back." Flynn looked like he wanted to argue, but Jacob's attention was elsewhere now. "In the meantime, how are things going with the tunnel extension?"

Flynn's expression transformed. The extension project was his responsibility, and as he began to speak, his pride was clear. "We're making real progress." He grinned at Noah, all previous frustration gone.

"Good, good." Noah glanced at Jacob, wondering whether he had distracted Flynn on purpose. Their leader took a step towards the citizens who were working on the tunnel. Sweat glistened on their skin as they plunged the picks into hard rock, grunting with the effort. Wrestling their weapons back out, they raised them to attack once again. "That sounds very promising."

Encouraged, Flynn continued, "As you can see, the teams are managing to excavate a large amount of rock each day, and we're almost ready to begin carving out individual caves for people to move into."

The Eremus population had grown over the past few years, which meant there were now too many people for the number of homes within the cave system. Many citizens were currently sharing cramped accommodations, and the extension would create much-needed extra space for the community.

Jacob tapped his knuckles on the tunnel wall. "And how much further do we have to go?"

"Not too far at all now. And we have great plans for the development of this area—"

Sensing his part in the conversation was over, Noah returned to his abandoned barrow. As he moved it towards the citizens who were chipping away at the tunnel wall, a few of them shot him a sharp look, jerking their heads at the pile of rubble which had only grown while he'd been talking to Jacob. He picked up the shovel and began filling his barrow.

When he left the cave moments later, the three men were still talking. Intrigued by the contents of the mysterious boxes and cheered by Jacob's confident talk of progress, Noah made it to the sky cave in record time. He flung the rubble out of his barrow, sending clouds of dust spiralling upwards.

And then, clambering up into the shaft of sunlight which slanted into the cave from the opening above, he stood on the edge once more and allowed himself to dream.

CHAPTER EIGHT: FAITH

When Faith woke up on Saturday morning, she lay in bed for several minutes, relieved she didn't have to get up right away. She looked around the dorm room, letting her eyes adjust. Bright sunlight streamed through the window, reflecting off the polished mahogany of Sophia's desk, which was far less cluttered than Faith's. Danforth Academy senior rooms were spacious, with queen-sized beds, en-suite bathrooms, carpets your feet could sink into, and plenty of closet space. Faith and Sophia had been assigned to the same dorm at the age of ten and had been friends ever since. Pairing up to share one of the more select rooms, which were the privilege of the senior girls, had been a no-brainer.

Glancing at the other bed, Faith noticed her friend was already up. Sophia rarely slept late and could often be found in the library on a Saturday morning before the rest of the Academy was even awake. Faith stretched widely. Grabbing her robe from the floor where she had left it pooled the previous night, she slung it on and shuffled to the window.

It had been an interesting week, and she had been exhausted at the end of it. On Monday, after making it into her Bellator Lit class with seconds to spare, she had submitted her work to Principal Anderson and barely listened for the rest of the lesson.

Her lack of focus had almost led to detention when she failed to answer three of the questions Anderson had fired at her. Sophia had hissed the response to their teacher's final question under her breath, allowing Faith to narrowly escape the sanction.

Afterwards, Faith had told her about the incident with the drudge. Her friend had been fascinated, quizzing her about it for hours and staring intently at every one of the servants they passed. She had even started to research information about them in her spare time. Faith had not seen the drudge since, though she had also kept a keen eye out for him, knowing she would recognise his eyes anywhere. Though she didn't admit it to Sophia, she was dying to see him again.

Outside on the lawn, some of the older girls were doing a morning yoga class, stretching and bending their limbs into impossible-looking positions. Faith grinned as Serene, never the most graceful of girls, wobbled in the midst of a complex pose. Next to her, Diane grabbed her arm in an attempt to prevent her from falling, but the two of them collapsed sideways, landing hard on the grass. There was a second of shocked pause before they burst out laughing.

Avery, who was leading the group, stepped forward, making a remark which Faith couldn't hear. She could imagine what was said, though. Avery's face screamed disdain, and when she stopped speaking, many of her followers turned and sneered at the pair on the ground. Serene scrambled to her feet, her face flaming. But when Diane stood up, she glowered at the girl who led them. Faith was glad she wasn't on the receiving end of such a stare, but Avery merely shrugged and continued with the next pose, which looked even more complex. Faith was convinced she'd chosen an even trickier one on purpose, aimed at further humiliating Serene.

Across the courtyard, Professor Kemp was standing at the rear of the school reception area, perhaps waiting for a comcar. Over the weekend, the teachers were permitted to travel off-campus.

They visited friends from outside the school, frequented the high-end mall in the centre of Bellator, or spent the day at one of the local beauty spots. Students were not allowed the same freedom.

Envying her teacher's escape, Faith pushed open her window and breathed in the scent of newly-mown grass, which must have been trimmed overnight by the diligent drudges. It never failed to amaze her how the Bellator servants completed their jobs so invisibly, and under such difficult circumstances. If she hadn't witnessed it for herself over the years, Faith would not believe it was possible to mow the lawns under the cover of darkness and do it so competently. Usually, the drudges kept themselves apart from the Danforth students, only interacting with them when it was unavoidable. It was the very reason her encounter with the drudge the previous day had been so surprising.

It was a beautiful day, but Faith's mood did not match it. After toying with the idea of skipping breakfast in favour of getting back into bed and sleeping for another hour, she forced herself to get washed and dressed. When she was ready to go, she tapped a quick message into her wristclip, telling Sophia she would meet her in the dining hall. Suspecting her friend's early morning research might be focused on the drudges, Faith was eager to hear what she had discovered.

Since her encounter earlier in the week, Faith had noticed a few things about the servants who inhabited almost every area of life in Bellator. Firstly, they were not all the same. Though their uniform created an illusion of similarity, in reality there were actually stark differences between them. Some were taller than others, and though they were all fairly slight, their body shapes varied in the same way the girls' figures did. Another thing she had learned from her drudge-watching was no one else paid them any attention. As long as they were doing their jobs, keeping their heads down and their faces covered, they escaped notice altogether.

Faith wished she knew more about the drudges. Bellator didn't generally permit the birth of male babies. Faith was aware the drudges were different: specially bred, genetically-created as male, but without the rough and violent nature which was typical of that half of the species. The process was complex, but Faith's Biology lessons had taught her the seed used to create the drudges was specifically chosen for its genetic makeup, which was highly submissive. Once born, the drudge babies were given frequent doses of a special hormone which ensured their passive natures endured.

Thus, the drudges performed the tasks asked of them without question, unseen and indistinguishable from one another, at least to those who didn't look too closely. Faith didn't even know if they could speak. And though she and Sophia had discussed the subject until well into the night, they still couldn't explain why a single drudge would remove his mask in a place where he could be so easily caught. Faith sighed. No amount of consideration had brought her any closer to a conclusion, but she found herself longing to see the drudge again so she could get answers to her questions.

Maybe Sophia would have something for her. Pulling her hooded sweater over her head, Faith thrust her hands deep into the pockets and headed for the door. As she pulled it open, there was a figure about to enter. Expecting Sophia, she smiled, but the greeting died on her face as she came face to face with the very drudge she had spent so much time thinking about. She stepped back in shock.

Under normal circumstances, a drudge would back away from a Bellator citizen respectfully, allowing them to pass. But the figure standing in front of her didn't move. Standing in the way of a woman in Bellator was unheard of, but even as Faith gasped in a breath, the drudge held up a hand in appeal, gesturing for Faith to return to her room, where they couldn't be seen.

Nodding her understanding, she went back inside, taking a seat on the bed. After a moment, the drudge followed her, glancing around to make certain they were alone, before shutting the door behind them. They stared at one another in silence for what seemed like eternity.

"Um . . . hi." Faith tried eventually.

The drudge looked at her. She felt like he might be smiling, and echoed his expression, not feeling at all threatened. "Look, about the other day, I want you to know I haven't told anyone . . . I'm not going to tell anyone." She peered into the large green eyes, but the drudge merely stared back at her. "So, you don't need to be afraid . . . or worried . . . or . . ."

She trailed off, unsure of what else to say. For a moment, the drudge didn't move, but then, almost imperceptibly, he bowed his head.

Taking this as a positive sign, but not expecting any more, Faith stood up from the bed. "Well, um . . . I'll be getting to breakfast then. Leave you to . . ." Faith gestured at the room, knowing as she did it was too early for it to be cleaned. The drudge had not come here to do his chores.

She took a single step towards the door, not wanting to startle him. As the drudge shifted to one side to let her pass, he raised his head, angling his gaze to meet Faith's. She stopped, waiting, her heart pounding.

"Thank you."

It was a whisper, and as she left the room, she thought perhaps she'd imagined it. But as she turned, she saw the expression in the jade eyes above the mask and was certain she hadn't.

"You're welcome." She nodded her head and closed the door.

As she made her way to the stairs, Faith heard someone calling her name, and turned, half expecting the drudge to be calling her back. Instead, Diane was beckoning to her from the doorway of her own room further up the corridor. Intrigued, Faith did an about-face and headed back the way she had come, pausing for a second at the older girl's door. Diane had disappeared inside, and Faith wasn't sure whether or not to follow, but a tentative knock brought a sharp "Come in!" so she stepped inside.

The room was on the opposite side of the hallway from her own, but its layout was much the same. Serene stood in front of the mirror, a towel tightly wrapped around her body as she smoothed cream onto a face still pink from her shower. Diane was still dressed in her yoga clothes, her hair tangled and sweaty from the workout. She stared at Faith as she entered.

"Um . . . morning?" Faith fiddled with her wristclip.

Diane only nodded in response.

"Did you need something?" Faith racked her brains. "Notes for a class you missed?"

"No. I wanted to ask you about last Monday morning after the med centre visit. Sit down." Diane gestured to the chair which stood next to her desk. Nervously, Faith took a seat. "Can you tell me what happened? On the street?"

With shaking legs, Faith remembered Professor Kemp's warning and attempted a neutral expression. "Last Monday?"

Diane glared. "It was testing day, remember?"

"Oh, yes. That's right."

Again, Diane waited for Faith to continue. When she didn't, Diane grew openly hostile. "You and your pal . . . what's her name? Sophie?"

"Sophia," Faith corrected.

"Soph*ia*, then." Diane rolled her eyes. "You and she were last in line. You got left behind, somehow . . . is that it?" Diane stepped closer, so close Faith could see the sweat beading on her forehead. "And you saw something unusual."

Squirming under Diane's gaze, Faith tried not to show she was trembling. From the other side of the room, Serene frowned.

"Leave the girl alone, Di. She's not under interrogation."

Diane shot her a look, but when she looked back at Faith, her expression had softened somewhat. "Look, there's no one here except us. And you can *trust* us. That's the reason I wanted to speak to you outside of the more . . . *communal* settings." She stressed the word as though spending time around others was distasteful. "I'd just like to know what happened that day. I know you were telling your story to some of the girls at breakfast on Monday. But then you . . . stopped."

Faith thought of Kemp's warning. Leaning as far back in the chair as she could manage, she tried to resist blurting it all out. But her curiosity was getting the better of her. Why was Diane so interested? Closing her eyes briefly, she began to speak, hoping against hope she wasn't plunging herself into a heap of trouble. "Okay then. Sophia and I thought we saw . . . no, we definitely saw, a man in Bellator. And it wasn't a drudge."

Diane glanced over at Serene with a triumphant glint in her eye. "Told you." She backed away from Faith and settled herself on the bed to listen. "Go on."

"There were two of them. Not two men. Two people. Came out of Rochester's before it was even open." Faith hesitated, but Diane's face had lost some of its frustration and glowed with intrigue. Encouraged, she continued. "The first one was a woman, but she seemed . . . different."

"Different how?"

"I don't know . . . she looked . . . poor. I mean, *really* poor. Like, her clothes were very odd-looking. Old-fashioned, I suppose. When she saw us the girl seemed . . . scared. Then, behind her, there was another person. At first I thought it was another strange-looking woman." Faith stared Diane straight in the eye. "But then I saw it was . . . a man. Honestly."

Diane grinned. "You're worried I won't believe you?" Faith stared at her in confusion. "Don't worry, I believe you. In fact," she leaned closer, "I think this kind of thing has happened before."

"Before?"

"Sure! Sightings of men who are supposed to be long dead, right here in the city." Diane seemed almost excited by the news. "Authorities don't want us to know they still exist. And you said," Diane crept closer, clasping Faith's arm so tightly it hurt, "they tried to convince you it was just a drudge?"

"Yeah." Faith stared at her, incredulous. "That's exactly what they did. I mean . . . the drudges are . . . different . . . this man was tall, muscular . . . I don't know. And he didn't have his face covered, for a moment, at least. He *wasn't* a drudge."

"You don't have to tell me!" Diane leapt up from the bed. "It's just *another* thing they hide from us."

"Sshhh!" Serene left the mirror and came to her friend's side. "We talked about this. You have to keep quiet. If they get suspicious, you'll be expelled."

Diane rolled her eyes, but she listened to her friend, coming back to sit on the bed, muttering to herself. "Too many things don't add up. Too many suspicious sightings."

Faith jerked her head at Serene. "Is she okay?"

"She is." Serene made a face. "Well, as okay as she ever is." She came over to crouch next to Faith. "She believes, no . . ." she corrected herself after a dark look from her friend ". . . *we* believe, Eremus still exists."

Faith's eyes widened. They had been taught all about the various male settlements scattered about the island in Herstory. Eremus was infamous. In the early days, it was rumoured to have been one of the largest, filled with angry male fugitives plotting revenge on the city. One of the earliest missions of the Bellator guards had been to eradicate these communities, which they had done to great acclaim. Now Eremus was simply a part of the past. Long gone. Something Bellator used to fear but no longer needed to. Or so they'd been taught.

"We think there are still some men out there. Hiding, in the woods, but still alive, still around." Serene's calm stood in stark contrast to Diane's fervour, but was somehow more convincing. "And the fact that you saw a *woman* with one of them, well . . ."

"It means maybe the Eremus community isn't all male." Diane was off again, a jab of her finger punctuating each word, though she kept her voice below a whisper. "Did the woman seem to be under the man's control?"

Faith thought for a moment. "No. At least, I don't think so. She came out of the store first, and she looked to him, perhaps for help or guidance, but they left together, side-by-side."

"Interesting."

"Well, interesting or not, don't you think we'd better get ourselves to breakfast? Before there's nothing left for us to eat?" Serene rubbed her stomach and groaned. "Nothing like a humiliating yoga session to help you work up an appetite."

"Don't listen to Avery." Diane stood up and slung an arm around her friend. "She's an arrogant—"

"I know." Serene grimaced. "Doesn't make her taunts any easier to bear though. She turned to Faith. "You coming?"

Surprised but flattered the older girls wanted to be seen walking to breakfast with her, Faith stood up. Her own stomach rumbled as she hurried to join her new friends, hoping to discover something more about the secrets Bellator kept from its citizens.

B y the time Noah's shift was finished that evening, he was exhausted. Dodging into the cave to fetch a towel, soap, and clean set of clothes, he headed to wash up before dinner.

Keeping clean underground had always been a challenge. Several years earlier, some Eremus citizens had almost been caught by a Bellator guard whilst washing in the river in the woods. After that, Flynn had been tasked with finding a way for the people to bathe without having to leave the caves.

Flynn was very inventive. He'd been assigned a small team, and worked with them for several months, carving out trenches and damming up sections of the underground river so they were diverted into several different pools. There were three: one for laundry, one for male bathing, and one for females. Flynn had even created an ingenious system where temporary gates, fitted at one end of each trench, could be removed to allow fresh water to flow into them.

The only issues the system had were the chilly water temperature and the lack of privacy. Noah liked to get down there as soon as he could after a shift, knowing the hazards of being there at the same time as Harden and his buddies. Today he was early, but when he entered the cave mouth he cursed: so was Harden. He was alone, which was good; he was never as nasty without an audience. But it also meant there was nowhere for Noah to hide.

Stripping off with his back turned, Noah made his way to the edge of the pool as far away from his enemy as possible. He slid into the water hurriedly, barely even shivering at its coolness. As soon as he was fully submerged, he began scrubbing, dragging the rough soap over his body as fast as he could. The combined grime of sweat and rock-dust was never easy to remove.

Harden seemed content to simply linger at one edge of the pool in a leisurely fashion, barely even attempting to wash. He was waiting for his buddies, no doubt. Noah worked faster, turning his attention to his scalp now, knowing his hair would be three shades lighter by the time it was free of the dirt. Finishing up, he ducked his head under the water, running his hands through his hair. He knew from bitter experience any leftover soap would make his head itch.

When he came up for air, wiping water from his eyes, he found himself face to face with a sneering Harden. Fighting the urge to swim away, Noah raised his eyebrows in a question. "Want something?

"Good day at the rockface, *No*-ah?" Harden over-emphasised the first syllable of the name, stressing its negative sound.

"Yeah, thanks." Noah sluiced the water over his head once more, pretending they were just passing the time of day. "You?"

"I had a *very* good day." Harden's face split into an unpleasant grin. "Mostly training, you know, improving my skills for the next raid, and then I was specially chosen to help Jacob with a couple of specialised tasks."

"I know. I saw." Noah couldn't resist reminding Harden of his earlier humiliation. "You enjoy your trip? Not sure you were handling those *special tasks* all that well." He smiled as Harden tensed. "And what exactly was it you were you doing? Carrying boxes? Hmmm. A real *tough* job."

Harden looked like he was about to explode. His nostrils flared as he searched for his next words. "Shut it, Madden. It was what was *inside* the boxes that made the job important."

"Oh, really?" Noah was curious, despite himself. He hadn't even thought *Paulo* knew what was inside the boxes, so he doubted Harden, a brand-new raider, would have any knowledge. "What was it, then?"

"Top secret." Harden glanced away as he said it, and Noah was certain he didn't know. "Nothing they'd tell little *weaklings* like you."

Noah took a deep breath. He knew Harden was trying to goad him. Silently counting down from twenty in his head, Noah ignored him as he shook the excess water from his hair.

"I mean, guys like me were born to be raiders." Harden's voice continued to taunt, as Noah began moving towards the side of the pool. "And runts like you, well, *weren't.*"

"Look." Noah stopped. "I'm sixteen now. Who says I *won't* become a raider?"

Harden threw back his head in an exaggerated laugh. "As if your ma would ever let you. She has a stick so far up her—"

"Don't talk about her like that." This time, Noah couldn't ignore the fire that surged through him at Harden's words.

A nasty smile spread across Harden's face. Stepping so close to Noah that he could smell the sourness of his breath, he sneered. "Like what?"

Noah knew he couldn't beat Harden. Not even when he was alone. Up close and without clothing, the fact Harden was twice as broad as Noah was patently obvious. He ached to slam a fist right between the bully's eyes. But he knew such a punch would be a waste of time, and seconds later he would be the one nursing a sore jaw, as well as a sore fist. Hauling in a deep breath, Noah took a step back.

Disappointed at the lack of reaction, Harden mirrored his movement in reverse, grasping hold of Noah's shoulder. Clearly, a peaceful retreat wasn't going to be permitted, even without Harden's avid supporters cheering him on. Instead, Noah fell back on his wits, knowing his only chance was to outmanoeuvre the bully with a clever retort.

He leaned even closer to Harden, so their faces were a mere inch apart. "Hey Harden," he kept his voice at whisper-level, "you seem awfully close for someone who claims he doesn't like me." Harden narrowed his eyes, trying to work out Noah's meaning. "I mean, unless you do? *Like* me, I mean?"

This time, Harden understood. Instantly releasing his grip on Noah, he stepped back a fraction, glancing around the cavern and flushing. "That's not what I meant. Makes no difference to me if a boy likes another boy, but I don't like you. *At all*." Harden took one more glance around the cavern. "Someone needs to teach you a lesson."

"Really?" Noah eyed the side of the pool, where his towel and clothing lay. "And you think that someone should be you?"

"Maybe."

"Okay. Well, I'll be ready to learn. You just name the time and place." Noah grinned at Harden, who stood with his fists clenched by his sides. "Now listen, I'd love to stay and chat, but I have places I need to be."

Thrusting his body backwards, Noah took off across the pool. Harden looked stunned at the sudden movement and attempted to follow, but his size made him fairly ungainly, and in the water his thick muscle did him no favours. Noah swam well, propelling his body rapidly through the water and reaching the side well before his enemy. Wasting no time, he hurried out and pulled on his trousers rapidly, ignoring the uncomfortable way they clung to his legs.

By the time Harden had exited the pool and found a towel to cover himself, Noah had a t-shirt and shoes on and was ready to go. Throwing a little wave over his shoulder at the bully, he turned and rapidly made his way out of the cavern, passing other men and boys heading to bathe. There was no way Harden would follow him now, but he feared the retribution that would follow in the weeks to come. He'd survived Harden's bullying for this long because he had managed to ignore him and rise above it, but now that he'd made a stand, who knew how Harden would react?

As he charged up the tunnel, passing the growing number of Eremus citizens returning from their daily shifts, he cursed his lack of control. By the time he reached the tunnel leading to his own cave, he was out of breath. He knew his mother had been on shift in what counted as the Eremus medical centre that afternoon. It didn't render her filthy like the more physically demanding jobs, so there was a good chance, if she hadn't had many patients to see, she would already be home. He slowed his pace to a steady walk and took the time to calm himself. As he approached, he was grateful to see the door curtain still covering the entrance.

Perhaps his mother wasn't home yet. His heart leapt, relishing the opportunity of a few minutes to himself in the peace of an empty cave. He was just about to pull back the cloth and duck inside when he heard Flynn's voice within. Pausing, he stood and listened as fragments of speech drifted out from the cave.

". . . speaking to Jacob . . . tried to get him to listen but—" Flynn's voice was soft and deep.

"Well, what did you expect?" Noah cringed at his mother's more strident tone. He had no problem hearing Anna through the thin curtain. "You know how he is."

". . . seems serious about it though, and I . . . well, it's worrying."

There was a pause for a few seconds, and Noah was about to go inside, when Flynn spoke again. ". . . asked Jacob, when Noah was gone . . ." Freezing at the sound of his name, Noah shifted closer to the curtain. "He'd be happy to . . ."

Again, his mother cut across Flynn. "You asked him without telling me? You know how I feel—"

". . . thought if I . . . time to adjust . . ." Flynn's voice grew in volume. "Look, I know you're dead set against it, but we need every raider we can get, and I thought . . . I thought maybe it would help Noah to—"

"No." The flat refusal was familiar. "He can't."

"He isn't as fragile as you seem to think." Flynn sounded like he had moved closer to the cave entrance, as Noah could hear him quite clearly now. "Paulo told me he moved at least fifty barrows of rubble today in a single shift. He's a hard worker. He's fast and strong."

"I *know* that, but—"

Flynn cut off Anna's protest, and Noah found himself cheering inwardly. "And he's clever. Being a raider isn't just about strength and speed. It's about instinct, keeping your wits about you. He's brighter and better educated than most of the kids in Eremus. What have you spent the last sixteen years teaching him for, if not to *use* that knowledge?"

A lengthy silence followed Flynn's speech, and Noah strained his ears, leaning closer to the doorway so as not to miss his mother's response. Eventually he heard a sound, not a voice, more like a gasp, followed by something else unidentifiable. Was his ma *crying*?

He stood for another moment and had just decided to leave the two of them alone when his ma spoke again. Her voice, usually so strident, quavered.

"I know all that. But I worry . . . no, I *fear* . . . him having access to Bellator will make him ask questions. Questions I don't want to have to answer."

Flynn made soothing noises, and Noah could picture him sliding an arm around his partner. "I know you don't want to, but maybe the time has come? To tell him the truth, I mean."

"The truth?" Noah could hear the horror creeping into his mother's voice.

"Yes, the truth." Again, there were sounds of movement from inside the cave, and Flynn's voice came from closer to the entrance. Noah prepared to step back and act as though he was just returning from the baths. "Look, Anna, you know I've always respected your wishes, kept the secret, as has everyone else who knows. But one day, he'll find out. Don't you think he should hear it from you?"

Now it was his mother's voice he could barely hear. "But what if . . . what if he—?"

Outside, Noah heard voices approaching from the opposite end of the tunnel. Other citizens were beginning to return from their shifts and would notice him standing outside the door. Still, he couldn't move. Leaning as close as he could to the door, he held his breath and strained to hear Flynn's next words.

"He *won't*. He loves you, and he'll understand. Maybe not at first . . . I mean, finding out you originally came from Bellator has to come as a shock, but . . ."

Noah didn't hear any more. His head spinning, he found himself having to hold on to the wall to stay upright as figures further up the tunnel came closer.

"Hey, Noah!" Through a haze, he heard Dan Clark, a neighbour of theirs, calling out. "You alright there?"

And then, from inside the cave, a silence, followed by the sound of someone scrambling to get up out of a chair. The curtain across the doorway was thrust open and Flynn's face peered out, etched with concern. Behind him, Anna stood frozen, her face pale and her eyes haunted. She knew Noah had heard. She knew he understood.

And then, Noah was running.

It was late when Ruth found him. Noah had been crouched in the cave for what felt like hours, his thoughts racing, his body numb. When his friend's face appeared, it was flooded with relief. She didn't speak, but crawled in and curled up next to him, taking his hand in hers.

Eventually, he found his voice. "Did you know?"

Beside him, Ruth went rigid. "Did I *know*?"

"Yeah." Noah sat up, jolting her away from him. "I need to know if you're one of the people who've been keeping a secret from me my entire life."

"No." She eyeballed him from the other side of the space, her eyes flashing. "I didn't. I haven't." There was raw hurt in her tone, and he knew she was telling the truth.

"Alright then." He allowed his body to sag against the cave wall.

There was another silence, where he could almost *feel* Ruth searching for the right words. Eventually, she shifted her body alongside his again. Somehow, it was easier to speak when they weren't making eye contact.

"Your ma sent me looking for you. I made her promise she wouldn't follow me." She paused, picking at a loose thread on her shirt sleeve. "She's pretty upset."

Noah stiffened. "*She's* upset?"

"Sorry. That came out wrong." Ruth nudged him with her shoulder. "She's upset with herself . . . that she hurt you. She feels bad for the way you found out . . ." He felt Ruth let out a long breath. "I think she knew . . . you'd be like this . . ."

He laughed without humour. "What'd she expect?"

Ruth fell silent for a moment. Above them, the sounds of the night creatures in the woods floated down through the gap in the cave ceiling. An owl, screeching in the darkness. The plaintive howl of a fox hunting its prey.

"Want to talk about it?" Ruth tried again. "I mean . . . you're from Bellator, originally, I mean. That's so . . ."

"Pretty shocking, right?" Noah ran a frustrated hand through his hair. "I mean . . . I guess now I know why people treat me the way they do."

"No." Ruth's reply was abrupt. "I don't think many people know. I mean . . . how've you got to sixteen without finding out?"

Noah turned to look at her. "You *really* think people don't know?"

"Some people do, obviously." She thought for a moment. "But we're talking sixteen years ago. Eremus has grown a *lot* since then . . . the younger citizens outnumber the old by, like, a *lot*. I really don't think people our age know. *I* definitely didn't, though my ma did." She shrugged. "Apparently, Anna's arrival here was kept fairly low key, and I think the people who knew about you kept the secret."

"Maybe."

"Look, I know you're mad, but think about it." Ruth's tone grew earnest. "Anna came here from Bellator, pregnant with you, desperate to save your life. If she'd have stayed in the city, you'd've never been born." Her voice dropped to a whisper. "I think that's pretty brave."

Noah closed his eyes. "But she never *told* me. Don't you get it? She goes on and on about trust and honesty and—" He slammed a fist into the cave floor. "She's such a hypocrite."

"She tried to protect you." Ruth shuffled forward, twisting her body so she was looking at him. "Ma said Anna had to work, like, *really* hard to get people here to accept her. Think about it . . . her life in Bellator was great, she had pretty much . . . well, everything . . . and she gave it all up to save you."

Noah met her gaze steadily. "Guess I know whose side you're on." Her eyes flashed with pain and he looked away, ashamed.

"Look." Ruth wasn't giving up. "I'm on your side. You know that." She paused, grasping hold of his hand. "But I think, when you calm down, you'll understand."

"Maybe." Noah shrugged off her touch, turning away. "But if she thinks I'm going to do as she says now, she's in for a shock."

"Look," Ruth lowered her voice, "you're my best friend. Always have been. I don't want to fall out with you. So, I'll tell you this. That next raid? It's happening soon. Jacob wants to recruit more raiders. Why don't you put yourself forward? Might help get this Bellator thing out of your system."

Noah stared at her. "Jacob won't take me without a recommendation."

Ruth paused for a second, thinking. "I know who might recommend you." Ruth mused. "Someone I might be able to persuade . . ."

"Who?"

"Look, it's a longshot. But let me see if I can . . ." She was already moving towards the gap in the rock. "Meet you in the sky cave?"

He nodded, but she was already disappearing through the gap in the rock.

Twenty minutes later, Noah sat staring out of the cave's elevated exit. The forest was so different at night, the velvet blackness hiding the canopy of dark green leaves from view. He could still hear the leaves whispering in the dark. As the unmistakable sound of footsteps echoed up to him, he turned to see Ruth enter from the tunnel, the thin beam of a flashlight illuminating her path.

Behind her trudged a bemused-looking Paulo. "Why you couldn't just bring him—"

"He needs to see you," Ruth interrupted.

"Anna won't sleep til she knows he's safe." Paulo came to a halt at the base of the climb to the cave's lofty exit and glared up at Noah. "Come down, little brother."

"You *knew*."

"Yes, I knew." Paulo met his gaze steadily. "Come down, if you want to talk to me."

Noah took his time. When they were standing face to face, he found he was shaking.

"They made me promise not to tell you." Paulo's voice was so calm, it was infuriating.

"You didn't think I deserved to know?"

Paulo shrugged. "Flynn's the only parent I got, as I believe you pointed out earlier today." Noah flushed. "I did what he told me to, cos if I hadn't, he'd have roasted me."

Noah stared at him. What Paulo said made sense, but it didn't make things any easier. His brother took a step towards him.

"Look, Anna's frantic. She's had Flynn and I looking everywhere for you . . . Dawn's been with her all night, and even *she* can't calm your ma down." Noah opened his mouth to argue, but Paulo continued. "No. All this fuss is . . . Don't you see?" Noah shrugged. "She kept it a secret cos she was trying to protect you."

"Don't you think Noah deserves to see Bellator?" At Ruth's words, the brothers turned. Noah had almost forgotten she was there. "More than anyone?"

Paulo eyed her warily. "I suppose."

"You'll recommend him to Jacob, then?"

Paulo glared at her.

"You know he wants more raiders. Noah'd be good. *You* told me that." Paulo flushed, and Noah felt a stab of pride at his brother's faith in him. "You're experienced. Jacob would listen to you."

"Do you know the trouble it would cause for me at home?"

Ruth shrugged. "I thought you'd understand. See how much it means to Noah."

"Didn't you just call me coward today for not being prepared to go against Ma?" Noah narrowed his eyes.

Paulo switched his gaze to his brother. "Guess I did."

Sensing his brother was wavering, Noah pressed their advantage. "Listen, *technically* you promised not to tell me the truth about my origins. You *never* promised not to take me to Bellator . . ."

Paulo turned away, gazing up at the dark sliver of sky just visible at the top of the cave. "You know, there *might* be a way you can come along on the raid without your ma or Flynn finding out."

Noah turned back. "I'm listening."

"The next trip to Bellator is just a small one. We're lower on meds than we'd like to be. Jacob's trying not to broadcast it to the entire community." Paulo paused, glancing over at Ruth. "He's asked me to lead the raid. Keep it on the downlow. So people don't worry."

"He and Flynn aren't coming?" Ruth's mouth dropped open.

Paulo shook his head. "If they stay here, people are less likely to notice."

Ruth's eyes glowed. "So . . . if Noah were to come, no one would need to know?"

"That's right."

"And you'd let me?" Noah felt an unfamiliar rush of warmth for his brother.

"I guess so." Paulo's expression turned stern. "You'd have to partner me, so I could keep an eye on you. And you'd have to do the basic training, or you'd put everyone at risk."

"I'll do it."

Paulo's eyes bored into him. "The *only* way this works is if you show up at the last minute and it's too late for anyone to blab. Got it?"

Noah found his voice. "Got it. I won't tell a soul."

"Alright then." Paulo sighed. "But I hope you're ready to deal with the fallout when we get back and Anna finds out where you've been."

"I'm ready." Noah grinned. "You know, if this works out right, maybe when Ma hears how well I handled myself on the raid, she'll come round to the idea of me doing it full time."

"Dream on, brother." Paulo rolled his eyes. "Talk to me about training tomorrow, then?"

"I will. And Paulo?" Noah stepped towards his brother. "Thanks."

"S'fine." Paulo shrugged off the sentiment as he turned to go. "Now will you come home? We all need some sleep, and no one's likely to get any until you're safely in bed."

He crossed the cave in a few strides and disappeared into the tunnel, flicking on his flashlight to light the way. Noah exchanged an excited smile with Ruth before following, sensing everything was about to change.

Chapter Ten: Faith

As Faith filed into the assembly hall on Monday morning, she was still thinking about the conversation with Diane and Serene. If, as they suggested, the Eremus community still existed, living undercover in the woods surrounding Bellator, then the authorities had to know about it. There was no way, with all their hi-tech surveillance equipment and well-trained guards, the government could be unaware of a sizeable community living in the vicinity.

There was no other explanation. They didn't want the rest of Bellator to know.

As she settled into a hard-backed chair towards the rear of the hall, Faith glanced up at the stage. On it sat a row of young girls, dressed in crisp new Danforth uniforms and wearing identical smiles of pride. Faith groaned loudly and received an elbow in the ribs from Sophia.

"Hush, they'll hear you."

Faith rolled her eyes, but straightened up as Principal Anderson appeared on the podium. Tapping a finger on the datadev next to her, she smiled widely as a holoscreen appeared above her head.

"Good morning, ladies," she trilled. "We are here today, not for our usual assembly, but for our bi-annual welcoming ceremony. The young ladies behind me have been specially selected to attend the Danforth Academy. They are all extremely excited to be here, and to join you in this *honoured* position. As always, please be sure to make them feel welcome in the days to come."

She used a finely-manicured nail to tap another button on her keypad. Above her, the holoscreen filled with images and triumphant music boomed from the speakers all around them: the Danforth Academy Song.

The voiceover began. "Established in 2102, the Danforth Academy has always been a symbolic beacon of Bellator's progress. Twice a year, an elite group of ten-year-old girls is selected to . . ."

The video droned on, explaining the academy's purpose, its traditions, its goals. Faith remembered her own Welcome Ceremony. Had it really been six years ago? She'd been excited to start at the academy, but had also felt very homesick for her old community.

From birth to the age of 10 she'd lived in the Garner Borough, an area on the outskirts of Bellator. It was surrounded by rolling fields rather than city blocks, and many of its citizens were employed in the nearby farms and orchards. Faith had loved the scent of the countryside. Many of her early memories centred around playing games with the other girls as the older women who supervised them worked in the fields and barns around them.

Bellator's attitude to child rearing was a communal one. Once a baby was born, she was taken back to the area her mother was from, but from that point onwards, became the responsibility of the entire community. A child's early days could be spent being looked after by any number of women, and close bonds between a baby and her biological parent were discouraged.

Faith couldn't remember much about her own mother, other than her name, which was Grace. She was an engineer who worked in one of the manufacturing plants on the other side of the city. Her role was an important one, and took her away from the borough for long periods of time each week. But there were so many other women closer to home who had cared about Faith and made sure her needs were met that she had never resented her birth mother's absence.

When Faith had been selected for the academy, she'd had mixed feelings. Her other friends would continue their schooling close to home, beginning to supplement their studies with short placements in the different fields of work they might eventually go into. Academy students received a higher level of education and did not complete vocational training until they were much older. The academy enabled girls to secure better jobs in the future, but a little part of Faith envied the maturity she knew the other girls would gain as they began working to support the adult community.

Sophia, meanwhile, had been brought up in the Parker Borough. More central, she had found it far easier to adjust to city life when she and Faith had first arrived at the academy. But where Faith missed the friends she had left behind, Sophia had been more than glad for the fresh start at Danforth. Her upbringing had been far less idyllic, she had confided to Faith, because her own mother, Thea, had rejected the communal style of upbringing supported by Bellator.

Instead, she had tried to care for Sophia in a far more independent way, insisting on feeding and caring for her daughter as exclusively as possible. After several months of issues within the community, things had come to a head. Thea attempted to take a lengthy period off work to look after Sophia during a period of illness, despite there being plenty of other women around to care for her. Her employer had reported her to the authorities, who had felt it best to resolve the issue by removing Thea from the Parker Borough altogether.

Sophia assumed her birth mother had been transferred elsewhere in the city. And whilst having no real memory of Thea meant she didn't miss her, living with the notoriety of having a parent who had gone against the *Bellator way* had been hard. Sophia had always been treated differently by the other women in her community, who had always looked upon her like she might turn out the same way as her biological mother.

As a consequence, Sophia had never felt accepted, and her eventual selection for the academy had been a huge relief. She found the Welcome Ceremony far more interesting than Faith, and was always friendly and respectful towards the new students, understanding how much of a difference the academy could make to their lives.

Feeling guilty for her own lack of focus, Faith turned back to the row of awestruck young girls on the stage. Would they be as thrilled to be here six years down the line? She was struck by an unexpected pang of sympathy, knowing what the girls were giving up.

Surprised by the feeling, Faith forced herself to sit up straight and pay attention to the video, which was just finishing. It ended with a shot of a smiling Principal Anderson shaking hands with Chancellor Danforth, Bellator's leader.

Abruptly, the holoscreen dissolved, and from the rear of the stage, the real-life Anderson came forward. "And now to properly welcome our newest students. First, Maisie Rogers." Anderson cast a hand behind her at the first candidate, a dark-haired girl who quivered, but stood up and shuffled forward. "Welcome, Maisie."

Anderson reached down to the table at one side of her. When she brought her hand back up, a brand-new Danforth Academy pendant hung from it.

Anderson bowed her head. "May you feel at home inside the walls of the Danforth Academy. May you soar under the protection of its staff. May you thrive in the friendships you make here. And may your presence be a sign to all Bellator that women will always prevail. To good health. To strength. And to sisterhood."

Along with every other girl in the room, Faith reached up to touch the necklace which hung around her own neck. "To sisterhood," she intoned, in unison.

Anderson fastened the shining necklace around Maisie's neck and began the first of many rounds of polite applause. The ceremony continued, girl after girl being introduced, welcomed, and awarded their very own pendant, then joining the group of girls facing the stage, symbolically taking their place in the Danforth Academy Community.

When it was over, Anderson held up a hand for silence. Waiting until she was satisfied all students were listening, she nodded solemnly.

"Ladies, I have an announcement to make." She clapped her hands excitedly. "As you are well aware, Bellator's scientists have been making huge strides recently. In fact, your recent blood test results show the benefits of the new vitamins you have all been receiving, and these will be rolled out across the entire city very soon."

There was a smattering of applause as Sophia elbowed Faith. "What did I tell you?"

Faith hid a grin behind her hand as Anderson continued. "The medics say a small number of you have responded *so* well to the vitamins that you may find yourselves selected to trial some even more cutting-edge health supplements over the coming days. Ones which will improve your focus, your mental capacity, your fitness levels . . . Imagine that!" Anderson beamed.

"It might mean, for the time being, that some of you are required to make more regular visits to the medical centre for monitoring purposes," Faith jabbed Sophia in the ribs, "but in the long run, we will *all* benefit." Anderson put her hands together in front of her heart and made a small bow. "As always, Bellator will be extremely grateful to you.

"In the meantime, enjoy the feast which follows this ceremony, and welcome our new friends."

Anderson nodded to Professor Kemp, who stood and began dismissing the girls, row by row, into the annex on the side of the hall. Its tables would, as always, be groaning with platters of steaming hot food and pitchers of fresh lemonade. Faith tapped her foot impatiently as she waited. When their line was allowed to enter the annex, she made a beeline for the plates filled with tiny cream-cheese pastries.

"Wow," Sophia caught up with her a minute later. "Wait for me next time, won't you?"

"These are my favourite." Faith grinned mid-chew, her mouth crammed with two of the delicacies. "Phsh-orry."

Ducking a shower of crumbs, Sophia grimaced. "Classy, Faith." She selected a single pastry and nibbled the corner delicately.

"Get away with yourself," Faith swallowed, grabbing her friend's arm and swiping a platter of cakes as she moved past the dessert table. Ducking through the heavy curtains which fringed the edges of the room, she took a seat on the carpeted floor behind and pulled Sophia down after her. Satisfied they hadn't been spotted, she placed the overloaded plate in between them, before selecting an éclair bursting with cream and taking an enormous bite.

Sophia chuckled. "Will you ever change?"

"Nope." Faith stifled a yawn. "They can try to make a lady out of me, but . . ."

On the other side of the curtain, they heard the sounds of polite chatter, plates clattering, glasses being clinked. The feast was definitely the best part of the welcome service, for everyone except the nervous newbies. Faith recalled her own ceremony when she had felt uncomfortably on display. At the banquet afterwards, she had slipped behind the curtain to hide from prying eyes and discovered she wasn't the only one with the idea. That was the first time she had met Sophia.

The curtain-hiding had been a tradition ever since, though their escape there had gotten bolder as the years went on. These days, they tried to up the ante with their daring, attempting one year to get away with staying there for a whole hour, stealing the largest platter of food possible from the banqueting table without being noticed, or snatching one of the wines meant solely for the adult teaching staff and taking it to their hideout to drink without being caught.

This year, they had promised to attempt to remain behind the curtain until the entire event was over, but their plan was doomed to failure. After only a few moments, they heard the microphone-projected voice of Professor Kemp ringing out across the room.

"Could new admissions and senior girls in Group A proceed to the entrance hall for tours immediately, please?"

"That's us." Sophia jabbed her in the ribs with an elbow. "Time to go."

"No!" Faith widened her eyes in exaggerated horror. "The challenge!"

But Sophia was already on the move. "Can't deny our senior responsibilities, can we?"

"Nooooooo!" Faith took Sophia's arm and held on for dear life. "You *promised*. Imagine how it'd feel to get away with missing the entire feast and all its *required* activities." Exaggerated air quotes punctuated the last words.

"Don't be silly." Sophia was unmoved. "How could they *not* notice we're missing? They'll have planned the groups and accounted for everyone." She pressed on, ignoring Faith's pout. "Actually, I'm kind of looking forward to it. Aren't you? Even a *little* bit?"

From behind the curtain, Kemp's voice boomed again. "Group A seniors. We need you *now*, please."

It was one of the senior girls' tasks to take the new students on a tour of the school buildings. Once they turned sixteen, they were afforded certain privileges, like a twin room rather than the shared dorms of up to eight students, but they were also expected to do their bit in terms of helping the staff. Sophia was excited about the prospect, but Faith had little time for the younger girls and suspected she would find this part of the senior role dull.

Still, Sophia was right. They wouldn't get away with missing the tour, which all seniors had been assigned to. Reluctantly, she slid into the room behind Sophia. With all eyes on the students leaving, no one noticed them emerging from the curtain, and they were able to head for the door without being questioned. When they reached the entrance hall, several of the groups had already left, and Professor Kemp's glare told them they had taken too long to arrive.

At her side stood four of the new girls, all identical in their brand-new uniform, the silver D of their school pendant shining proudly. Most of the older, more experienced girls in the school preferred to keep their pendants hidden, inside buttoned-up shirts or under the scarf which was an optional extra. Displaying them so boldly marked a girl as brand new.

"Faith. Sophia." She motioned to one of the pairs of new students standing beside her. "This is Jenna and Beth."

"Hello." Sophia beamed. "How are you both?"

The two girls returned the smile nervously.

"Sophia and Faith are the seniors assigned to take you around the school. They'll give you the full tour, make sure you know where your dorm is and then bring you back here to enjoy the rest of the buffet." Professor Kemp nodded briskly at Sophia before directing a glare at Faith. "*Do* take good care of them, won't you?"

She didn't wait for a response but turned to growl at the next seniors emerging from the doorway behind her. Faith stifled a giggle as Diane and Serene entered the hallway.

"Girls, you're late. Your tour should have begun by now and you do these new girls a great disrespect by not arriving on time. You should have . . ."

Kemp's scolding faded into the background as Faith trailed behind Sophia, who had begun the tour by climbing the impressive staircase rising out of the entrance hall. As they ascended, Sophia offered an enthusiastic lecture about the history of the school which, of course, she knew by heart. She sounded like one of the guides who took tourists from the outer provinces of the Bellator region around the city.

To begin with, Jenna and Beth trailed silently behind Sophia, drinking in her every word and paying Faith no attention whatsoever. They passed through the hallway with all the junior dorms, where Sophia pointed out what would be the girls' own room and the corresponding bathrooms, then headed upstairs to the senior apartments, which the girls were warned not to enter without an express invitation. They headed back down to view the library, the gymnasium, and various other leisure facilities: tennis courts, a 50-metre swimming pool, and full-sized athletics track among them, and then headed to the area at the rear of the building which housed the classrooms.

As they wandered, Sophia kept up a steady stream of chatter. The two girls relaxed enough to begin asking questions and pointing things out for themselves, and Faith marvelled at her friend's ability to set people at ease. They passed the science labs and were heading for the hallway which housed the staff offices when one of the girls, Faith thought it was the one Kemp had introduced as Beth, fell into step next to her.

"So-oh, aren't you going to participate in the tour?" Startled, Faith stared at the girl. "I mean . . . you're both assigned to take us around, and it's supposed to be about getting to know us, so . . ."

"So what?"

"So, what can *you* tell us about the school?"

Faith laughed. "You don't need to know what *I* can tell you. Believe me, Sophia knows more than I do and recounts the anecdotes with a lot more charm."

Beth frowned, but fell silent. They were approaching the very end of the bottom corridor, which led to Anderson's office. The official tour required the girls took in the entire building, every storage closet and administrative office, but *finally*, they were on the home strait. Vaguely annoyed at the implied criticism, Faith strode ahead, stopping abruptly outside their principal's office where she motioned a dramatic hand at the door.

"This hallowed ground," she declared in an overly loud voice, "is our esteemed principal's office," she dropped her voice to a dramatic stage whisper, "otherwise known as her *lair*."

Sophia shot her a warning look as the two new girls gaped, their eyes wide.

"Be careful to follow *all* the school rules to the letter . . . especially those concerning not being up and about after lights out." She leaned closer to Jenna, the more mousey of the two girls, and widened her eyes. "Some of the teachers like to . . . umm . . . go *roaming about* after midnight, if you catch my drift, and you do not want to be found by them when they're in their . . . *altered* state."

Both girls were leaning close now, and even the bolder Beth seemed alarmed. Behind them, Sophia stifled a fit of laughter and stepped forward, placing a hand on the girls' shoulders.

"Now then, don't listen to Faith. She's only—"

But a noise from behind Faith stopped her, a look of horror marring her amused expression. Faith turned around, praying she was wrong about where the noise had come from.

Standing in the doorway of the office behind her was Principal Anderson, her face impassive.

"I hope you're enjoying your tour, ladies." She nodded at Sophia. "Could you complete the rest of the route *without* Ms. Hanlon now, Sophia?" With a humourless smile, she beckoned to Faith with a finger. "I'd like a word."

Her heart sinking, Faith followed the principal into her office.

"Close the door, Ms. Hanlon." Faith turned to obey, noting Sophia's sympathetic glance as she made her way up the hall with the new girls. She turned back to Anderson, who jerked a hand at the chair facing her huge mahogany desk. "Sit."

Faith did as she was told. But before the principal could begin to scream at her, her wristclip emitted a series of beeps, indicating she had an incoming call. Jabbing a finger at Faith to stay put, Anderson disappeared into her inner office, smiling broadly at the holo which appeared in the air in front of her.

"Chancellor Danforth, what a pleasant surprise! I was wondering when . . ."

As the door closed behind her, Faith sighed, wondering when she might get back to Sophia and, more importantly, the food at the buffet. Gazing around the room, her eyes landed on the built-in datadev on Anderson's desk. A glint of light on the screen suggested Anderson had not locked the display when she had come out of the office to reprimand Faith, and Danforth's call had interrupted them the moment she had returned.

Intrigued, Faith leaned forward, but saw there was only a report on the screen. Disappointed the datadev had not revealed some gossip about the staff she and Sophia might have laughed about, Faith sighed. She was about to give up when her eye was drawn to two small images at the top of the document: the Bellator Government emblem and the logo of a company named BellaLab Corp.

Leaning closer again, she looked at the document more closely. It appeared to relate to a new drug. Amongst the complicated medical terminology, Faith spotted a familiar word, *femgazipane*. She remembered seeing it on the boxes at the medical centre. Scanning the rest of the information, she managed to read a few more words before the screen flickered and went blank.

Faith sat back in the chair, her mind spinning. *"Dramatic results . . . extremely hopeful . . . significant side effects . . ."* femgazipane was a drug, then, and the report Anderson had been reading suggested it related to the girls at the academy. And although the word *hopeful* suggested femgazipane might have positive results, the *significant side effects* didn't sound so promising.

When Anderson ended her call and returned to the room, Faith barely listened to the lecture. Desperate to get back to Sophia, she had nodded in all the right places and apologised, knowing it was the only way the principal would let her go. But when she returned to the annex it was filled with people, and Faith had been forced to make polite small talk with the new students until the meal was over.

The rest of the day was filled with a whole-school tennis tournament to celebrate the new arrivals, a music recital, and *yet another* assembly where the student council gave speeches about the different extracurricular activities available to the Danforth first-years. Time dragged, but eventually they were dismissed. On the way out of the hall, Faith hurried to catch up with her friend.

"Hey." Faith poked her friend with a finger. "Can we talk?"

"Sure." She turned to Faith, a worried expression on her face. "Is it about Anderson?"

Faith frowned at the girls who swarmed around them as they waited to exit the hall. "Let's wait til we're upstairs."

Sophia shot her a curious look but didn't say more until they were safely back in their shared room. Hurrying inside, Faith closed the door and turned to her friend.

"What's up?" Sophia loosened her scarf, unwinding it from around her neck and folding it carefully. "Anderson come down heavy on you earlier?"

Faith shook her head. "Not really. That's not what I wanted to talk about." She walked to the window and stared out. "Remember the last time we were at the med centre? You notice anything different?"

"Nope. Don't think so." Sophia sank down on her bed. "Wait, you're talking about the double blood test again?"

"No." Faith shook her head. "The meds on the shelves in the exam rooms."

"But there are *hundreds*. I barely notice them." Sophia laughed. "What? You mean, you do?" She stopped. "Wait, you *actually* do?"

"I kind of . . . count them." Faith flushed. "It distracts me."

"Oh. Sorry." Sophia straightened her face. "What did you notice, then?"

Faith walked over and perched on the edge of her friend's bed. Keeping her voice low, she filled Sophia in on the new drug, the number of boxes on the shelves in the exam room, and the report on Anderson's datadev. When she had finished, she looked at Sophia expectantly. "Don't you think it's a little . . . suspect?"

"Um . . . I guess a little." Sophia fingered the pendant around her neck absentmindedly. "I mean, the centre stocks all kinds of drugs though . . . couldn't femgazipane be linked to these health supplements Anderson was talking about?"

"Maybe." Faith shifted away and folded her arms. Sophia was so rational she always made things seem possible. "But it said the side effects were . . . *significant*."

"All meds have side effects, Faith." Sophia said gently. "It's a case of them balancing the level of the side effects with the effectiveness of the treatment. I'm sure they wouldn't give us a drug unless they knew it was harmless."

"You trust them? I mean, totally trust them?" Faith leaned closer to her friend. "Even after their cover up the other day?"

"You mean the male on the street?" Sophia nudged Faith with her shoulder. "I'm sure they just wanted it dealt with quietly. They didn't want to cause a panic, especially with the new students coming this week."

Frustrated by her friend's lack of concern, Faith stood and moved to the window again, pulling the curtains closed on the darkening sky outside. The courtyard below was empty, and many of the windows were already dark. It had been a long day, and with mandatory gym classes starting at 6:30 a.m., most students would want to get a good night's sleep. She knew she should do the same.

But as she lay down on her bed, Faith couldn't shake the feeling of unease. She wondered whether Diane might take her words more seriously. The older girl had certainly been interested in what Faith had to say about the interlopers in the city on their previous med centre visit.

When Sophia went into the bathroom to shower, Faith grabbed her datadev. Opening her messages, she hit *New*, and scrolled through the school's list of students until she found Diane. Hitting the unfamiliar contact ID before she could change her mind, Faith tapped out a message.

HEY. YOU KNOW ANYTHING ABOUT THESE NEW HEALTH SUPPLEMENTS?

She would keep it simple. Hitting send, Faith watched the tiny speech bubble in the corner of the screen. It turned orange, indicating Diane was reading the message, then began flashing green. A reply.

ONLY WHAT ANDERSON TOLD US TODAY.

Faith stared at the screen, wondering whether Diane would think she was crazy, like Sophia. Before she could lose her nerve, she typed a second message.

WHAT ABOUT NEW MEDS? ONE CALLED FEMGAZIPANE.

The speech bubble repeated its pattern.

NEVER HEARD OF IT.

Disappointed, Faith hesitated. Diane's message seemed dismissive. She might not welcome a reply. Eventually, she typed.

SAW A **LOT** OF IT ON LAST VISIT TO MED CENTRE.

For several moments, the screen remained blank. And then, just as Faith was about to give up, the bubble flashed green again. The message seemed to take longer to come through this time, as though Diane was typing more. But when it came through, the reply was disappointingly brief.

TALK ABOUT IT TMR?

Faith let out a breath. At least the older girl seemed interested in hearing what Faith had to say. Before she got cold feet, she tapped a brief reply.

SURE. WHEN/WHERE?

This time, the response came quickly.

I'LL FIND YOU.

Faith replied with a thumbs up and stashed her datadev in her bedside drawer just as Sophia came out of the bathroom.

"I'm beat." Sophia stretched widely, and slid into her bed, pulling the covers right up to her chin and curling into a ball as she always did. "Not still fretting about femgazipane, are you?"

Faith stood up and made for the bathroom, shaking her head. "No."

"And you're not worried about Anderson? She's had a go at you before. I'm sure she'll get over it."

"I'm fine, honestly." Faith managed a smile, knowing Sophia wouldn't settle if she thought her friend was worried. "Go to sleep."

"Good. I'm sure there's nothing to fret about." Sophia gave a tired smile. "Sleep well, okay?"

"Sure. You too."

Faith showered and then climbed into bed, pretending to read while she waited for her roommate to fall asleep. It didn't take long. When Sophia's breathing evened out, Faith knew she wouldn't wake. Slipping out of bed, Faith pulled on a pair of dark full-length pants and a t-shirt which didn't have the school emblem on it. Grabbing a sweatshirt and deactivating the location function on her wristclip, she crossed the room to the window and eased it open.

Faith had thought about the conversation she would have with Diane the next day. She didn't want Diane to think she was making a fuss without good reason. Something was wrong, Faith could feel it. But if she were to convince anyone else, she needed more information. And the only place she was going to get that was the medical centre itself.

She had sneaked out this way before when Marcy Robinson had dared her to. There was a helpful beech tree in the courtyard outside. It was within reach of the window and had a large number of branches sturdy enough to support a fair-sized human being. Glancing back at her sleeping roommate, Faith slipped through the window and closed it quietly behind her.

Descending the branches with ease, she paused at the bottom and listened. When she heard nothing, she let go of the last one and dropped noiselessly to the ground. Then it was a simple matter of scurrying quickly around the edges of the courtyard to the side entrance, where the fence met the corner of the building. Using the window ledge as a first step up and the thin strip which ran along the centre of the panel as her second, she was up and over it in a matter of seconds.

On the other side, she glanced up and down the darkened street. Taking a cap out of her pocket, she tucked her hair inside it and pulled it low over her face. Then, head down, she scuttled off into the night.

Chapter Eleven: Noah

Noah was tired by the time they reached the city. Paulo had explained the hike was a long one, but not that some of the tunnels were better formed than others. In places, the low ceiling had required him to duck his head or even walk bent double for several minutes. The raiders came to a halt where the main tunnel split into several smaller ones. They waited while Paulo slid his hand into a small hole in the tunnel wall. For a moment, he groped around, a concerned expression shadowing his face. Then, he relaxed and drew his hand out again.

Glancing down at his open palm, he grinned. "All good. Let's go."

The other raiders headed off in different directions immediately. Within minutes, the brothers were alone. Puzzled, Noah approached Paulo, staring down at his brother's hand. In it lay a smooth, grey pebble.

"Madeleine's system. A grey stone means all is well, we can proceed. White would be a warning. Take care. A black one means danger. Stay away." Paulo replaced the pebble in the hole. "Come on. We need to hurry."

Jerking his head at Noah, Paulo strode off along the only unoccupied tunnel. Noah followed, determined not to hold his brother up. It wasn't long before the tunnel roof sloped lower, and they had to bend to continue onward. In places, the rough stony roof scraped against their backs. Eventually Paulo stopped, and Noah found his heart was racing.

There were several exits from the tunnel system, situated in different locations. Some came out inside buildings; others were hidden on side streets, where Bellator citizens rarely strayed after dark. Noah was aware Eremus had some sympathisers in the city. People who were aware of their existence yet protected them. Who disliked the way Chancellor Danforth ran things. Many of these citizens lived or worked in the buildings where the tunnels came out and allowed the raiders access to the city whenever they could.

Several uncomfortable minutes went by. Finally, there was a noise up ahead. Noah could see nothing beyond his brother's feet, until a light flooded the space, blinding him for a second. Paulo began to move again, and Noah struggled along behind him, blinking furiously.

He crawled out into a different world. As his feet touched the ground, he found the floor beneath him was perfectly flat and even, and covered with a layer of highly polished wood. Taking a step into the room, he approached an object which looked a little like a chair, but was much longer, and lower. It was covered in a soft-looking material with a complex pattern woven into it. Next to this was an ornately carved table, on which lay a shiny object that looked a little like the old wristwatch Jacob owned, and a delicate cup filled with a steaming yellow liquid. Beautiful melodic sounds drifted from somewhere close by, and the opposite wall was home to an enormous screen filled with moving pictures.

Noah tore his eyes away, forcing himself to focus on his brother and the mission. Paulo stood in the centre of the room, next to the strangest woman Noah had ever seen. She was old, older than any of the citizens he knew in Eremus. Her hair was a silvery shade, and instead of being cut short or tied back, it cascaded around her shoulders in waves. She wore something he recognised as a dress from pictures his ma had shown him. It was bright blue, and drawn in at the waist, with a long, floating skirt that finished just above her ankles.

Noah stared at her as she secured a picture on the wall, covering the tunnel entrance. Despite her age, she moved with grace and dexterity.

"Hello, Noah. I'm Madeleine." The woman took a step towards him. "It's nice to meet you."

Noah found his voice had deserted him. He felt Paulo's glare as he managed a slight nod in response to the woman's greeting.

"Paulo here tells me you're heading for the med centre on Bronte Street."

"Uh-huh."

"First time nerves?" She turned back to Paulo with a wink. "Centre's closed this evening. You shouldn't run into any trouble."

"Anything we need to know?" Paulo sounded different, more commanding.

"I did hear some whispers." She frowned. "Not sure your last raid went totally unnoticed."

Paulo's eyes widened, though he disguised the look quickly. "Really? What happened?"

"There was talk of some schoolgirls spotting something unusual. They hushed it up though."

"But they're getting suspicious?"

"Maybe. They don't like the ordinary citizens to know about . . . well, anything really." The woman walked over to the table, bending to open a small drawer beneath it. "When you're noticed, it causes them . . . a problem." She straightened up, a notepad and pencil in her hand. "Look, once Eremus went underground, Danforth and her government believed they'd gotten rid of most of you. They're arrogant. Thought any few stray loners they'd missed wouldn't pose a threat.

"And there are enough resistance sympathisers in the city to cover up the stock disappearances after each raid." Madeleine sat down, leaning over to write something on the paper. "But you *have* to be careful. Danforth was furious when she heard the girls had spotted the raiders last week. She's been on the warpath ever since."

Noah wondered if Madeleine knew Paulo was the raider who'd been spotted. His brother certainly looked uncomfortable, and Noah understood why. This woman was someone they depended upon. Citizens who allowed the raiders into the city risked their own necks for the Eremus people. There had to be trust. If the tunnel locations were ever discovered, the entire Eremus settlement would be in danger.

But Madeleine didn't seem to notice Paulo's discomfort. Tearing the slip of paper from the pad, she stood up and held it out. "You'll be needing this."

Paulo took the note and pocketed it. "Thank you."

"And you'll let Jacob know? Warn him about Danforth's mood?" She peered at Paulo closely. "The need for caution?"

"Of course."

Noah wondered if Madeleine's warning would have any effect on Jacob's plans, which he seemed pretty determined to carry out. He didn't have much time to consider the idea though, as the older woman ushered them to the door at the opposite end of the room. On the other side, a set of steps rose steeply upwards. They followed her up and into a small hallway, where she led them to an outer door. Tapping her hand on a device which was fixed to the wall, she peered at a small screen, which showed her a grainy image of what Noah thought was the street outside.

"All clear," she muttered, as she tapped in a series of codes. Noah heard several locking mechanisms move within the door. Finally, she pulled it open. "I'll listen for your call." Paulo nodded as he passed her. Noah went to follow but found Madeleine's cool hand on his own. Surprised, he stopped.

"Enjoy your first glimpse of the city, Noah." She squeezed his hand, and he could feel the hard edges of the rings which decorated her fingers. "But be careful." She let go, and he took a step forward, turning to reply. But the door behind him had closed and he was standing in darkness.

Paulo was already way ahead, creeping along in the shadows. Straining his eyes upwards, Noah could only just see the darkened sky above the towering buildings, a sliver of it revealed between the structures which jutted upwards on either side. They reminded him of the high cave, except this glimpse of sky was more regulated, a long rectangular shape rather than the jagged edges created by the rocks back home.

Sensing Paulo's impatience, Noah focused. The street they were moving along was not a well-travelled one, Paulo had explained, which lowered the risk of them coming across anyone. Noah had memorised the route as part of the thorough training Paulo had put him through over the past few nights. He'd made it clear Noah was only coming along to observe and to stand watch when necessary.

At the end of the street, Paulo stopped to check the one ahead. This one was a major road, which would probably be empty this late at night, but Noah hurried to catch up as he knew their next move was a risky one. Checking that his brother was close behind, he jerked his head and they darted across the street together. Noah's eyes glimpsed a couple of stores, their windows filled with various products, before they dove into the darkness again. He had to admit, he felt less exposed in the shadows of the narrower streets, but part of him longed to linger in the wider thoroughfares and see the city properly.

The concept of using currency you had earned in exchange for goods fascinated him. He knew all about how Bellator worked from his mother's lessons, but seeing it in reality was far more thrilling. Over the past few days, he'd thought a lot about his mother's obsession with education, and her extensive knowledge of Bellator. It made much more sense now. Having been brought up there herself, she prized education in a way that most Eremus citizens did not. And her knowledge of the way the city was run was born of firsthand experience.

Things between them had been distinctly cool since his discovery. On his return to their cave after the conversation with Paulo, he had found her sitting with Dawn, her face pale and her friend's arm around her shoulder. Once Dawn had left, Anna had begged Noah to talk to her. He'd told her he didn't want to, ignoring the hurt expression on her face.

After he'd gone to bed, he'd overheard Flynn smoothing the waters. "Leave him be. He needs time."

His mother's reply had been hushed, but the next day she hadn't brought it up again. She seemed to be leaving it up to Noah to let her know when he was ready to talk. And that suited him fine.

Noah was still struggling with the number of people who'd kept the truth from him. It felt like a betrayal. He'd decided he wanted to see the city himself, make his own judgement. Perhaps when he returned, he'd be ready to ask his mother questions, begin to understand the choices she had made. He was grateful to Paulo for making it possible.

He followed his brother across two more intersections, noticing another store, fancier than the last one; two restaurants, the screens in their windows flashing menus displaying a dizzying array of food options; and a theatre, where he knew from his mother's description you could pay to sit and watch people performing stories on a raised platform. At the corner of the fourth alleyway, Paulo took longer glancing out at the street ahead. Then he turned to face Noah.

"See that glass-fronted building over there?" He jerked his head at a larger property which had a sign outside with a green star emblem on it. "That's our target. Shouldn't be anyone in there at night." He pointed. "The delivery entrance is round that side, okay?"

He waited for Noah to nod before darting across the street, Noah close on his heels. The side street they dodged into was cleaner than some of the others they had walked along, the bins here filled with medical waste, rather than the food leftovers he had spotted outside the restaurants and food stores. Paulo stopped outside a door which was grey and nondescript. The sign above read Deliveries. Noah found himself hoping the centre didn't receive any at night.

Paulo retrieved something from his pocket and peered closely at the number pad to one side of the door. Noah recognised the slip of paper Madeleine had given to him, as his brother tapped in a code. After a second's pause, the door gave a tiny click.

With a sharp tug on the dull metal handle, Paulo opened it, and Noah followed him into a warehouse of some kind. It was filled with shelves, many of which were stacked with neatly labelled boxes. Noah started to make his way towards them but felt a hand on his arm.

"No." Paulo shook his head. "We were in here on the last raid. The meds we need are more likely to be inside the main building. He nodded at the other side of the warehouse. "Over there."

Thankfully, the door was unlocked, and they moved into the hallway beyond. It was gleaming white and had a number of identical red doors leading off it. Noah wondered how many people attended appointments at the centre each day.

An elbow in his side brought him back down to earth. "We'll try the treatment rooms on this floor first." Paulo muttered. "The closer we stay to our exit, the better. I'm going to find somewhere for you to keep watch, so you can warn me of trouble. Stay close."

Together they crept down the hallway until they reached a more open area. It had a number of chairs laid out in small clusters and facing in different directions. At the front was a desk which contained a smaller version of the screen he had seen at Madeleine's house. At the moment, it was blank. He caught a glimpse of the double entrance doors he had seen from across the street, only this time he was on the other side. He shivered at the tall, dark figures reflected in the glass.

"Stay low." He glanced back at Paulo, who was indicating the space behind the desk. "Watch the street. You see anything heading this way and not just passing by, you come and get me."

"What do I do if there's someone already *inside* the building?"

"There isn't."

"But what if—"

Paulo held up a hand to silence Noah, nodding at the knife fixed to his belt. "Then, you'll have to do something about it."

Swallowing hard, Noah nodded. He slid into the space behind the desk, positioning himself so he could see the doors but remain hidden. Shifting until he was comfortable, he made sure he had a hand on the weapon at his belt. When he glanced into the waiting room once more, Paulo had vanished.

CHAPTER TWELVE: FAITH

T he closer Faith got to the medical centre, the less confident she felt. The adventure had seemed like a good idea back in the safety of her room, but the night was dark and the streets eerily quiet. She couldn't stop thinking about the man they'd seen outside Rochester's store last week. Still, she had come this far, she couldn't back out now.

As she turned the corner onto Bronte Street, she shivered. In the darkness, the streets seemed unfamiliar and eerie. The Danforth students occasionally slipped out of their rooms after dark, but only to meet friends in the school's gardens, or to play harmless pranks. Faith had heard rumours of older girls sneaking out to attend concerts on the other side of the city, but that broke so many rules she had always doubted the stories.

Reaching Rochester's, Faith hurried past, but couldn't resist a brief glance through the window. The store looked no different than usual. It was hard to tell they'd had a break-in a matter of days ago. Not a broken window in sight, and every shelf neatly stocked as usual. Faith wondered if the store owners even knew there'd been a breach. But how could they not notice the goods which had gone missing?

Reaching the medical centre, she stared at the large glass doors of the main entrance. Of course, they were locked at night, and she had no way of accessing the building without a key code of some kind. Instead, she wandered along the front of the building, peering in the windows and trying to spot a way in.

It all looked normal: the rows of chairs, the tables with magazines for those who were kept waiting, the coffee machine the academy girls were never permitted to use. Her eyes moved to the reception desk. For a moment, she froze, certain she had spotted movement. But when she peered closer, all was still. *Get it together, Faith.*

She moved on, working her way around the side of the building, trying a number of doors with no luck. At the back of the centre, she discovered what looked like a small kitchen. Low down in the wall which faced into the alleyway, there was a square metal cover. Faith pulled on it, surprised when it lifted off with little effort. Behind it, was a narrow chute which led upwards.

The bags and boxes stacked at its base were sealed and fairly clean, or Faith might not have considered the waste disposal chute as a potential point of entry. Figuring it was her best chance of entry without breaking in, Faith thrust herself into the chute, pressing her feet against the smooth metal sides. She shimmied her way up, appreciating the academy's mandatory yoga classes for once, as her legs burned with the effort.

When she reached the top, she was panting. She placed her hands on the chute cover and pushed hard, praying it would open as easily as the other end had. Thankfully, it did. Thrusting it up and over, she heard it hit the wall behind it with a loud clang and stopped, cursing silently. When there was no sound of running footsteps, she clambered out into the kitchen, brushing herself off and hoping the building was as empty as it appeared to be.

Easing the cover closed, she crept through the kitchen and out into the hallway beyond. It took her a few minutes to work out where she was in the dark, but eventually she made her way through the centre in the direction of the treatment rooms. If she could find a box of femgazipane, she could take a copy of the dosage instructions and safety warnings. That was the kind of information she needed for Diane to take her seriously.

As she reached the central reception area she slowed, taking her time to work out which treatment room she had been in on her last visit. The girls were assigned a random room each time, and she had been in most of them over the years. Though it might be true *every* room on this floor had the femgazipane, she wanted to spend as little time here as possible. If she could find the same room on the first try, she could be back in her bed listening to Sophia's snores all the more quickly.

She had passed by the reception desk and was moving into the hallway when she heard a noise behind her. Before she could turn round, a pair of arms had grabbed hold of her, and she found herself thrust against the wall so sharply she hit her head. A second later, a hand was wrapped around her mouth and she felt the sharp edge of a knife at her throat.

Closing her eyes, she tried to thrash out backwards with her arms, but the figure behind pushed against her even harder. She heard ragged breaths in her ear. Opening her mouth, she was about to bite down hard, when she heard a voice.

"Stop struggling, would you?"

Faith went still. The voice was strange. Deeper than she was used to.

Somewhere, she'd read if you relaxed, an attacker would be fooled into thinking you'd given up, so you could surprise them by striking when they weren't expecting it. She forced her muscles to relax, melting against the body which was pressed against hers. The person was tall, she figured, but not hugely broad.

"Okay." The hold on her was relaxed slightly. "I'm going to let you turn around. Don't fight me. And *don't* scream."

The hand left her mouth, and the knife was removed, for now at least. Strange hands took hold of her arms and Faith found herself being turned to face her attacker. Suddenly, the strange voice made sense.

It was a man.

Well, not a man. More like a boy her own age. Faith had seen numerous images of men in her Herstory lessons over the years. The violent ones. Those who sought to rape and kill and maim. Huge beasts, with rippling muscles, ready to rain down blows on any female who dared to question them. Terrifying creatures.

The figure in front of her looked nothing like those men.

She'd been right, he was tall. He had at least four inches on her. But he wasn't broad. He wasn't so muscular he could crush her. The rest of his face was masked by a bandana of some sort, which reminded her of the facial coverings the drudges wore. But she could see his eyes. And the look in them mirrored hers. He was wary. Nervous. Frightened, even.

Faith's plan had been to start struggling the second she faced her attacker. To take them by surprise, slip out of their hold, and race back the way she had come. What choice did she have? She couldn't hope to defeat them. But she was fast. Her only hope was to outrun them.

But even as she started to wriggle, tried to drop into a crouch to try and loosen the boy's hold on her, she knew she was unlikely to beat him. He was strong, despite his slight figure. His hold on her arms was tight, so tight she imagined she'd have bruises later. Her attempt to duck out of his arms didn't work. His face twisted in surprise, but he refused to relinquish his hold on her, so as her body slid down the wall, his followed.

He pitched forward, banging *his* head and wincing. She felt a sense of satisfaction at avenging the blow to her own head. But he didn't let go. They ended up on the floor of the lobby, his body pressing down on hers, his face inches from her own. Scowling, Faith tried to shift away from him, but found she couldn't move. He recovered quickly, pushing himself up from the floor with one hand while the other found the knife again and thrust it at her.

"Get back." He pointed, and Faith shifted her body until she felt the wall at her back. A large cabinet to her left hid them from view now. Glancing back and forth, the boy seemed satisfied they couldn't be seen. His eyes bored into her as he spoke again. "Do. Not. Move."

She held up her hands in surrender. With the knife at such close quarters, she didn't dare try anything else. Not that she had any other ideas.

He knelt in front of her, his eyes narrowed. "Who are you?"

"Does it matter?"

He frowned. "What do you mean?"

"Does it matter who I am?" She found herself whispering, unsure whether it was driven by fear or a desire to make herself seem vulnerable. "I mean, it's not like you care. Aren't you just going to kill me?"

He blanched. "Kill you?"

"That's what you *do*, isn't it?" Faith shifted slightly, trying to ease the tension in her legs which were cramped beneath her.

"What we . . . *do*?" He looked even more perplexed.

"*The human male is a machine programmed to hurt and maim and kill. It's built into his genes. He can't help himself.*" Faith recited the opening chapters of her Herstory study book, watching his face closely.

He stared at her, his eyes widening with every word. "*That's* what they teach you?"

Faith glanced at the knife sharply. "Well, I'm not seeing too much evidence to the contrary right now."

He flushed, relaxing his grip on the knife slightly. Faith sucked in a breath, feeling slightly calmer. He hadn't attacked her yet. Perhaps she could talk her way out of this. She tried to shift her body into a more comfortable position, but the boy's face darkened again. He moved the knife closer again, until it was millimetres from her skin.

"Don't think I'll be falling for that trick."

"It wasn't a trick. My legs hurt." Faith glared at him. "Well? Are you planning to use that thing?" She gestured to the knife at her throat. "I mean, you haven't so far."

"I don't . . . I'm not . . ." he trailed off. "Look, you don't know anything about me."

"I know you're from Eremus." Faith hazarded a guess.

The shock which flashed across his face told her she was correct, but it had been the wrong thing to say. Naming the place he called home only made him more determined to protect it.

"What do you know about Eremus?"

She stared at the ground, refusing to answer. Closing the gap between his knife and her throat, he pressed it against her skin so she could feel its tip. She gasped, her eyes flying to meet his. Was she imagining things, or had he thrown a glance down the hallway over his shoulder? Faith's memory of the previous week's encounter came back to her. If this man *was* from Eremus, it seemed they travelled in pairs. The look told her he was searching for a partner.

"You're not alone?" He shook his head and her heart sank. "Why don't you just call your partner, then? Maybe he can get it done, if you're not able to."

"Get *what* done?" The boy frowned. "What . . . you still think I'm going to kill you?"

"Well aren't you . . ." she paused, ". . . isn't that what you—?"

Looking once more at the knife he held to her throat, he lowered it. Shifting further away from her, he sighed deeply. "No."

There was a long silence. Faith raised a hand to her throat, tracing it across the place where the point of the knife had been. She drew it back, staring at the droplet of blood which stained the end of her finger. The boy watched her, a look of horror in his eyes. He certainly didn't *look* like he wanted to kill her.

"Why not?"

His eyes widened. "Why aren't I going to kill you? That's a crazy question."

"I don't understand." Faith didn't know why she hadn't tried to run again. The knife was still in his hand, but he had backed away and he wasn't holding it in a threatening manner. She'd stand a good chance if she left now. Instead, she stayed.

"What don't you understand?" He tucked the knife back into his belt. "I'm not going to kill you."

"But *why* not?" Faith glanced up the hallway in the same direction he had. "I– I mean, isn't that what they'd expect?"

"Who? My people? Or the *good* citizens of Bellator?"

"Your people. It's what you *do*, isn't it?"

He shrugged. "Guess so. I mean . . . you're a danger."

She bit back a laugh. "*I'm* a danger?"

"To Eremus." His eyes hardened. "Any Bellator citizen who knows of our existence is a threat. I'll be blamed." He dropped his gaze. "I'm not even supposed to be here."

"*None* of you are supposed to be here." Faith countered. "*You're not even supposed to exist.*"

His head snapped up, startling green eyes boring into her own. "*That's* what you're told? That Eremus is a myth?"

She frowned. "Not a myth, no. But a place Bellator has eliminated."

He seemed to think about this. "I see."

"They sure don't want us knowing about you." Faith sat up straighter. "I mean . . . they try to hush up anyone who—" Stopping abruptly, she closed her mouth.

"Anyone who what?"

She shook her head firmly. "I don't know why I'm telling you this."

For a moment, they stared at one another. Neither of them moved. Eventually, the boy cocked his head to one side, eyeing her with curiosity. "How old are you?"

"Sixteen."

"Me too."

In the hallway beyond, a noise made them both stiffen. A door, opening. And a voice.

"Noah?" Even in a whisper, the voice was far rougher than the boy who sat in front of her. "You alright?"

Noah tensed. "Sure, I'm fine."

"No disturbances at your end?"

Noah hesitated for a second, then blinked rapidly. "No. Nothing here."

"I've one last room to check, then we'll head back."

"Fine."

Another door closed. Faith breathed again. The cabinet had screened them from view. For now. She glanced at Noah again, finding she was no longer scared of him.

"He's your partner?"

"My brother."

"Your *brother*." Faith's eyes widened. "Why didn't you give me away?"

Noah shrugged and said nothing.

"Will he . . . be as . . . lenient as you?"

Noah shook his head. "You'd better hide." He gestured to the reception desk "He won't be long now."

Faith glanced back the way she had come. If she made a run for it, she might make it to the end of the hallway and out of sight before Noah's brother emerged from the room. On the other hand, if she was only halfway there when he spotted her, and if he had a gun . . .

Noah moved across the lobby, gesturing behind the desk. "Plenty of room to hide behind here."

"How do I know you won't . . .?" Faith trailed off. She didn't know why she was even asking. It wasn't like she had a choice.

Noah looked frustrated. "If I were going to tell him, I'd have already done it, wouldn't I? I'll make sure he doesn't notice you. Now get down and stay quiet."

She nodded, slipping past him, and ducking her body behind the desk. Once she was hidden, he began to back away, then stopped.

"What's your name?" She hesitated, wondering how wise it was to tell her enemy more than she already had. He looked almost hurt, as he gestured in the direction his brother's voice had come from. "You already know mine."

"Faith." She managed a small smile. "My name is Faith."

"Faith." His tone was gentle. "Nice."

He rounded the desk and leaned on the front of it, as a door clicked open further up the hallway. Praying she could trust him, Faith squeezed her body as far under the desk as possible, praying Noah's brother wouldn't come back there. The air felt electric as she waited, the footsteps on the tiled floor growing louder as they approached. When Noah's brother reached the desk, he stopped. Faith held her breath.

"Not having a whole lot of luck. I got a few boxes, but not as many as we were hoping for." He sounded defeated. "All clear out here?"

"All clear." She tensed for a moment as she heard Noah's reply. "Shall we go?"

"Sure. Let's get out of here. Don't want to be . . ." The voices faded as the two males moved away from the lobby area.

Faith waited a long time before she crawled out from under the desk. Abandoning her original mission, she retraced her steps to the waste chute. She crept back through it, sliding all the way. When she landed with a harsh bump in the alley at the other end, she got up and sprinted back to the academy, praying her absence hadn't been noted.

Chapter Thirteen: Noah

As Noah crawled out of the narrow tunnel which led from Madeleine's apartment, his head was spinning. He had expected to look around the city he had heard so much about. He had not expected he'd actually *meet* one of its citizens. A girl who was the same age as him and, in many senses, his equal.

Faith's ma would have been pregnant around the same time as his. She might even have attended appointments at the same med centre, in the same area of the city. Until, that is, Anna had run away from Bellator. Since then, things had been very different for them.

He'd expected to hate any Bellator citizen on sight. But after meeting Madeleine, one of several Bellator citizens who sympathised with Eremus folks, he'd had to rapidly adjust his view. As for Faith, well, she had not been what he'd expected at all. She wasn't a sympathiser; she had clearly been taught males were the enemy, yet she hadn't seemed scared of him.

At first, perhaps. But then, he'd held a knife to her throat, what did he expect? Later, when he had backed off, she'd seemed interested in finding things out about him, rather than afraid. And clearly, what she'd discovered went against everything she'd been taught. Obviously, Bellator lied to its people.

He and Paulo appeared to be the first ones back. His brother had rested the mostly-empty pack against the wall and they had taken a seat on the tunnel floor as they waited. Paulo's lack of success at the med centre had put him in a foul mood, and he was tense and silent. It meant he hadn't asked Noah too many questions about his Bellator experience so far. Unsure what he would say, Noah was grateful.

All the way back, he'd felt like he'd been holding his breath. Until Paulo had passed by the reception desk where Faith was hiding, he'd felt an almost physical pain. He wasn't sure what his brother would have done if he'd caught a Bellator citizen, but he knew he didn't want to find out.

Yet he doubted himself for allowing her to go free. The questions had been running through his head ever since. What if she told someone? What if she'd screamed as soon as they were out of earshot? What if the Bellator authorities came looking for him the very next day?

But she had told him her name. Seemed interested in finding out where he came from. Trusted him enough to hide her, when she could just as easily have tried to run. On the walk back through the quiet Bellator streets, he had managed to get his thoughts in some semblance of order. Now, as they crouched in the tunnel waiting for the others to return, he wondered if he could lie to his brother.

A noise behind them made him jump. Paulo gave a humourless laugh, as Denton, one of the other raiders, emerged from a different tunnel. Harden, who'd been partnered with him, followed. They nodded at Paulo.

"Don't mind Noah, he's a little tense." Paulo shrugged. "First-time nerves, you know."

Harden laughed. Noah shot his brother a dark look and turned away, feeling foolish.

Paulo ignored him, all-business. "It go well tonight, Denton?"

"We weren't seen, if that's what you mean."

Paulo frowned. "But . . .?"

"Sorry, boss." Denton sighed. "We didn't even get inside. Some medical emergency. Hospital was all lit up . . . people everywhere. We couldn't get near without compromising ourselves."

"I see." Noah knew Paulo was fighting to keep the disappointment from his voice. "Well, better to be safe, I guess."

Harden's laughter had also died on his lips as his partner reported their lack of success. Noah found it difficult to muster any sympathy for the boy who had been making fun of him only a moment ago. As the last few raiders returned, they also shook their heads at Paulo. Clearly, the haul of drugs they would be taking back was not as large as they'd hoped it might be. Paulo's mood grew darker.

When Ruth hurried into the tunnel with her new raiding partner Beth, she shot him a look, her eyebrows raised. He nodded, and she gave him a subtle thumbs up, glancing away before anyone else noticed. He fully expected to be grilled about his experience later. When Paulo had made sure everyone was there, they began making their way back to Eremus. The walk was a lengthy one, but there wasn't much in the way of chatter. The raiders were exhausted and their mood sombre.

As they approached the camp, Paulo directed them down a tunnel Noah was unfamiliar with. The raiders' section was deep in the caverns, but Noah had rarely been down there. The area was quiet, and far from any of the residential areas of the community. There were many large, empty caves down here, reserved for training and storage of various supplies. As they walked, Noah noticed several caves filled with items from the recent raid, and one cave which was packed full of the mysterious boxes he'd seen being moved recently.

Paulo made a sharp left turn, leading them into a cave covered by a distinctive red curtain. Inside, Noah could see the space was already partially stacked with boxes. Paulo pointed to a section at one end, and the raiders began unloading their supplies. Seeming determined to ensure his raiders felt appreciated, Paulo thanked each one in turn as they stacked their packs on the shelves and headed for bed.

Tired of waiting for his brother, Noah turned to Ruth. "Walk you back?" He knew he was only putting off the moment when he had to return to his own cave. He was fervently hoping he could make it inside without waking his mother and Flynn. The less they knew about tonight's events, the better.

"Sure." Ruth looped an arm through his, yawning widely as they wandered through the tunnels. "It went okay then?"

"Yeah." He nodded. "Tell you everything tomorrow?"

He wasn't sure whether or not he was going to tell her the whole story. As his best friend, he had never kept anything from her, but after her reaction to Paulo's indiscretion with the face covering on the previous raid, he wasn't sure how she would react to him coming face-to-face with a Bellator citizen. For now, he decided to keep it to himself, at least until he'd had time to consider what had happened.

"Sure." Ruth's eyes glowed with curiosity, but she didn't press him. "I'll wait to hear about it. Think you'll cope with your shift tomorrow?"

The raiders were all allowed a day off usual duties the day after a trip into Bellator, but since Noah was not officially a raider, he still had a day of normal duties to complete.

"Guess so." He shrugged. "Don't have much choice really, do I?"

"You don't." She laughed. "I'll think of you when I wake up nice and rested."

In the tunnel ahead, the entrance to Ruth's cave came into view. There was a faint light shining out of it.

"Strange." She quickened her pace. "Ma doesn't usually leave the light on."

Noah hurried after her with a growing sense of dread. As they approached the doorway, they could see the curtain was tied back. Inside, Dawn sat on one of the chairs, a cup of something steaming by her side and her eyes closed. Ruth was at her side in seconds.

"Ma." She shook her mother gently. "Ma, wake up. Is everything alright?"

Dawn's eyes flickered open. She smiled at Ruth fondly, then her gaze moved across the room to Noah. They widened, then relaxed into something which looked like relief.

"You're back. Did you—?" She hesitated. "Did you go? On the raid, I mean?"

Noah nodded slowly.

"And you knew?" Dawn turned her gaze back on her daughter.

Ruth chewed her lip and said nothing. Dawn's face fell.

"Look, I get why you felt you had to, but . . ." She pulled herself out of the chair. "Your ma knows you went. I spent most of the evening trying to calm her down. She's had half the camp out looking for you, in case you *weren't* on the raid, but . . ." She shook her head sadly. "Noah love, you'd better go on home."

"But he only—"

"I know." Dawn held up a hand at Ruth's interruption. "I understand why he went. But Anna won't. Not right now, anyway."

Ruth fell silent, casting her eyes towards Noah. "Sorry."

"It's fine." He shrugged. "I chose to go, didn't I?" He smiled at Dawn weakly. "Thanks for the word of warning. Guess I should go and hear what she has to say."

"Tell me tomorrow?" Ruth reached out and squeezed his hand as he turned to go. "Whatever happens?"

Noah managed to nod as he moved back into the tunnel and headed for home. The walk to his own cave wasn't a long one, but he dragged his feet all the way, delaying the confrontation ahead. He'd hoped he might get away with the mission, with Paulo's support, but he should have known his mother wouldn't be so easily fooled.

When he reached his own cave, he could already hear raised voices. Paulo had made it back before him and, from the sounds of it, was taking the brunt of the adults' fury. Feeling protective of his brother, he picked up speed, steeling himself for the onslaught.

". . . don't understand how you could—" Flynn sounded angrier than Noah had ever heard him.

"Did you think we wouldn't find out?" Anna's strident voice cut across her partner. "How could you take him with you?"

Paulo was silent.

Noah reached the doorway as his mother was about to launch into another tirade. She stopped when she saw him, her face contorted in fury. Her body sagged, and she made her way across the room to his side, flinging her arms around him. Over her shoulder, Noah saw Paulo's face. It flashed with something he couldn't identify, before turning white with fury.

His mother thrust him away from her as fast as she had pulled him close. Standing back from him, she straightened. "What did you *think* you were doing?"

Noah met her gaze, trying to stop his legs from shaking beneath him. He had never deliberately gone against her this way. Her reaction was terrifying.

"I said, how . . . could . . . you?" A fleck of spit flew out of her mouth as she spoke. "I mean . . . I know you've had a shock recently, but to just . . . go . . . and not even ask me about it?"

"Would you have said yes?"

The words were out before Noah could stop them. He stared at his ma, her breathing ragged and her eyes wild. For a moment, she didn't respond. And then she pulled her hand back and slapped him. His hand flew to his face, instinctively shielding the cheek which stung from her attack. She reared back, as though to strike him a second time, but Flynn flew to her side, catching her hand before she could.

"Maybe we should sit down. Talk." He guided Anna into a chair and nodded at Paulo. "Set a kettle on to boil, would you. I think we need a cup of tea."

Paulo stared at Noah for a moment, a strange, half-smile on his face. Then, as Flynn cleared his throat pointedly, he moved to the small range and lit the stove. Pouring water from the pitcher into the kettle, he set it on the burner. Noah stood in the doorway, unmoving. His mother refused to look at him, staring instead at the ground as though she were hoping it would open up and swallow her.

Flynn approached Noah with caution. Pulling on his arm gently, he moved Noah inside the cave and pushed him into another chair before returning to tug the curtain down and cover the cave entrance.

"Look, it's been a long night, and I think we all need rest. Your mother told you not to go to Bellator. You even knew *why* she didn't want you to go, but you went anyway."

"I'm sixteen. I'm old enough to raid now. I don't see why—"

Flynn held up a hand to stop Noah. "You deliberately disobeyed your ma's wishes." He turned to Paulo. "And as for you, well, we thought you knew better. To discover that, not only has Noah decided to go on a raid without permission, that *you*, his *brother*, were the one that made it possible for him to go . . . well, that's more disappointing than him going in the first place."

Paulo stiffened. "He begged me. And I understand why he wants to go. I've never really got why she had such an issue with him going."

"You *knew* our feelings on the subject."

"No. I knew *her* feelings on the subject." Paulo jabbed a finger at Anna. "I also know *you* don't necessarily agree with her." Flynn's face coloured at the accusation. "But you go along with her, cos you'll do anything for your precious Anna."

"Paulo, be careful what you say." Flynn avoided Anna's eyes. "You don't—"

"I don't what?" Paulo's voice grew to a shout. "I don't *get it*, is what. You've been fine with me being a raider for the past six years, yet when it comes to your darling Noah, he needs *special protection*. What's with that? You're willing to risk *my* life, but not his?"

Noah's gaze volleyed between the two men, horrified at the turn the fight had taken. Beside them, the water in the kettle had begun to bubble, steam rising into the already-warm air of the cave.

Flynn moved towards his nephew, his hands outstretched. "It's complicated, you know that. Your brother—"

"He's *not* my brother."

For the first time, Anna's head jerked up from the ground she'd been fixating on. "Don't say that, Paulo."

"We're a family, you know that." Flynn took a step towards his nephew. "We look after—"

"Yeah," Paulo spat back, so viciously that Flynn stopped in his tracks. "I know. We look after each other. Except some of us get better looked after than others, don't we?" He gestured a hand at Noah. "Sorry I took him on the raid. I guess now I can see the way things are around here. Clearly, some of us are more dispensable than others."

Wanting to stop the argument from worsening, Noah willed himself to interrupt. But when he opened his mouth to speak, nothing came out. The kettle had begun to whistle softly, and he wondered whether he should remove it from the heat.

Flynn jerked forward again, his face pained. "That's just not —"

"—true? I'm afraid the evidence points elsewhere, *Uncle* Flynn." Paulo sneered around the room looking at each of them in turn. "Look at you? The perfect little family. Guess you don't need me around to ruin the picture."

Before anyone could stop him, he spun round and made for the door, almost tearing the curtain as he thrust it aside. The three of them sat listening to his footsteps as he moved off down the tunnel.

Anna turned to Flynn, her eyes worried. "Where will he go?"

Flynn shrugged, troubled. "Someone will take him in. He'll be alright . . . when he's had a chance to calm down." But he didn't seem convinced.

On the stove, the kettle was now boiling furiously. Flynn lifted it, blowing out the flame underneath. He poured water into three of the four cups which Paulo had laid out, making the tea in silence.

"I was worried sick about you." Anna's voice interrupted Noah's thoughts.

"I know."

"You *knew* I didn't want you going."

"I'm sorry." Noah turned and met her gaze. "But I'm sixteen now. You *have* to stop trying to . . . protect me or whatever. It doesn't . . . it doesn't *help*."

She took a deep breath as she accepted a cup of tea from Flynn, her hands shaking. "It's hard for me though . . . you don't understand."

"No." Noah wrapped his hands around his own cup. "I really don't."

Anna turned to Flynn, gesturing at the doorway which Paulo had disappeared through. "And now *this* . . ."

Flynn sat down beside her, wrapping his free hand around hers. "Let's drink these and get to bed. Things'll look better in the morning."

They fell into an uncomfortable silence as they drank their tea. Noah hoped Flynn was right. But in front of them on the table, the single cup stood empty, suggesting otherwise.

CHAPTER FOURTEEN: FAITH

When Faith walked into the dining hall for breakfast the following morning, her head was pounding. Whether it was lack of sleep or the fact she had suffered what felt like several minor heart attacks the previous night, she had no idea. But after she had helped herself to a large bowl of fresh yogurt and a selection of luscious-looking berries, she looked up to find Sophia observing her curiously.

"What's up?" her friend asked, as they sat down to eat.

"Can't talk now." Faith shook her head. "Tell you later."

She still hadn't decided how much she should tell Sophia. When she'd crept back into the academy the previous night, her roommate had been fast asleep. She hadn't even stirred when Faith had pulled the window closed with a bang. It meant Faith hadn't needed to explain her absence, but Sophia wasn't stupid, and she knew something was going on. Faith would have to tell her something.

For now though, her friend simply nodded and continued with her breakfast, reading over some lesson notes for a quiz they had later in the week. The room was quiet, as it often was at breakfast. Many of the students wandered around like ghosts until they'd had a hot coffee or a sugar-sprinkled pastry to wake them up.

Faith found her mind straying back to the events of the previous night. The darkness of the medical centre, the unexpected male visitors, the fact Noah had seemed the polar opposite of her previous beliefs about men. She massaged her temples, trying to ease the ache. Things were more confusing than ever. All she knew for certain was what Bellator was telling its citizens wasn't adding up. That, and the fact she hadn't been able to stop thinking about Noah.

There was a disturbance at the front of the dining room. Faith looked up, spoon suspended halfway to her mouth, to see Professor Kemp stepping up to the small podium. It was unusual for their meals to be interrupted by announcements of any kind, and the room quickly fell silent. The teacher's eyes roamed the room, checking she had everyone's attention before she began to speak.

"Good morning, girls. As the principal mentioned during the Welcome Assembly, the doctors have been extremely impressed by the results of your recent blood tests following the new health supplements you've all been taking." The professor paused for a moment, glancing around the room.

When she continued, her smile seemed forced. "As a result, they have selected a number of you to be the very first to receive their most recent compound, which promises to have cutting-edge effects, and will ultimately be developed for city-wide use." Her gaze travelled to the senior tables, and Faith knew what was coming. "To this end, the following seniors should meet outside in the quad immediately after breakfast. Marion Court, Faith Hanlon, Eve Jakeman, Serene Joseph, Diane King, Avery Lassiter, Farrah Stewart, and Sophia Thompson. You'll be escorted to the med centre at 9 a.m. sharp and are, of course, excused from lessons this morning."

With that, she snapped off the microphone and stepped down from the podium, her heels clicking on the polished floor of the dining room as she left. Her exit was greeted by silence, followed by a sudden surge in conversation. The announcement had woken up everyone, and every girl in the room seemed anxious to discuss the news.

Faith and Sophia stared at one another. Others at their table seemed excited by the prospect of being the first to experience the new supplement. With the previous night's experience fresh in her mind, Faith was far less eager.

"Their most recent compound?" Faith wasn't relishing the idea of returning to the med centre. "What do you suppose that means?"

"Not sure." Sophia had abandoned her notes. "She was pretty vague."

"You think it means more needles?" Faith shuddered. "I'm sick of needles. Bad enough we have to endure them once a month. This sounds like it might be more regular than that."

"Guess we'll know soon enough." Sophia nodded at the time on the wall display. "We only have a few minutes."

They gulped the rest of their breakfast and exited the dining room, joining the rest of the girls waiting in the quad. The group was quiet, the selected students muttering to one another, fidgeting, glancing around as though they were hoping someone else might know more about what was happening. Even Avery seemed a little nervous, though she strutted out of the dining hall with her usual swagger, her good friend Farrah by her side. Circling the group, she eyed the rest of them as though she couldn't see what she could possibly have in common with them, before positioning herself a short distance away and shooting occasional worried glances at the clock on the wall.

At exactly nine o'clock, Professor Kemp appeared, with two drudges in tow. With a start, Faith recognised the eyes of the one she had encountered in her room. Both servants kept their gaze at ground level, never meeting the eyes of the girls. Faith noticed how no one else paid them any attention. As the girls arranged themselves into pairs to begin the walk to the med centre, the drudges fell into place guarding the rear of the line, while Professor Kemp led from the front. Faith wondered if they were intended as additional protection after the events of their previous journey.

She lined up next to Sophia and was readying herself to leave when she felt an elbow jab into her side. Turning slightly, she saw Diane, who was gesturing for her to hang back. Realising what she wanted, Faith tugged on Sophia's arm, forcing her to wait, so Diane could slip into the line directly in front of them, a pale-looking Serene in tow.

As they began walking out of the quad, Diane shot her a pointed look over her shoulder. "Told you I'd find you."

Beside her, Faith felt Sophia stiffen, clearly curious about the older girl's sudden interest in them. Faith placed a hand on her friend's arm in reassurance. Waiting until they were further up the street, the gaps in the line widening so no one could overhear, Diane began to speak.

"This new drug. What do you know about it?"

Faith blushed, wishing she'd managed to find out something more concrete the previous night. Between her suspicions about the new drug, her encounter with Noah, and the unexpected med centre visit today, she was certain Danforth was keeping things from her citizens. She wanted Diane to take her seriously. But, as yet, she had no more than a few suspicions that things in Bellator were not as they seemed.

She took a deep breath. "Not much, I'm afraid. And I'm not sure if it's relevant. I just have a hunch. Last time we were in the med centre I saw large amounts of a drug called femgazipane in the treatment room. It's definitely new. I've never noticed it before, and I kind of . . ." she shrugged, embarrassed, "well, I notice these things."

"Alright. But what made you *suspicious* about it?"

Faith dropped her voice so the girls behind were unable to hear. "I saw a document about it in Anderson's office the other day. Didn't get a chance to read it properly. But it mentioned serious side effects. And I wondered . . ."

Diane and Serene exchanged glances. "Was it specific?"

Faith shook her head. "No. Or if it was, I didn't see that part. But it worried me. And you seemed . . . I mean, the other day you knew things . . . well, that I didn't. So, I figured you might —"

"You're right. I have . . . shall we say . . . suspicions, about certain things. But I don't have any real . . . proof." Diana punched a fist into her palm. "It's so frustrating."

"Sshh." Serene interrupted, casting a glance at the students who walked ahead of them. "Someone'll hear you."

"Alright, paranoid." Diane chided her friend, but she lowered her voice. "I'll keep it down." She shot her friend a concerned look. "You alright? You don't look good."

"I just wish they hadn't picked today to do this." Serene fanned her face with her free hand. "Haven't been feeling well all morning."

"Lean on me if you need to." Diane took Serene's arm, tucking it under her own. "I'll make sure you get there in one piece."

"Thanks." Serene took a deep breath. "I'm a little dizzy, that's all. Probably just a cold."

"Hopefully whatever this is won't take long." Diane reassured. "And we get the morning off, remember? When we get back, you can rest."

Serene raised her head and smiled at her friend. The two fell silent for a while, as the line of girls continued down the street. It was a beautiful day, warm and sunny, and the fact they were missing lessons should have made her happy, but Faith was still concerned about what awaited them at the medical centre.

Beside her, Sophia leaned close. "Since when do you talk to Diane?"

"Since she hauled me into her room the other day asking about the man we saw." Faith peered ahead as they rounded the corner onto Bronte Street, remembering how different it had looked in the darkness. "Wanted to know more about what we saw."

"You heard what Kemp said." Sophia glanced sideways at Faith. "She didn't want us talking about it."

"I know. But Diane *asked*. I didn't just offer the information. She seemed to know about the man already . . . I mean, the men . . ." Faith checked no one was close enough to hear her before continuing. "She thinks Eremus still exists. And so do I."

Sophia's eyes widened in alarm, but they were approaching the med centre now. Lining up outside, they waited as the doors swished open and they could file inside two by two. A technician in green scrubs sat behind the reception desk. Faith's heart beat faster as she imagined herself crouching under it the previous night, praying she wasn't caught. She waited her turn, approaching the technician and pressing her finger on the datadev to confirm her identification.

Usually their appointments were early morning, before the general public used the centre. Later in the day it was filled with the rest of Bellator's citizens, attending routine appointments and receiving various treatments. But not today. For some reason, the entire building was empty of anyone except the Danforth girls. They sat down in the waiting room, Diane and Serene seating themselves across from Faith and Sophia. Professor Kemp chose a seat close by, so any further conversation was impossible for now. Faith could see her own frustration mirrored in Diane's face.

Once they were settled, the technician came out from behind the desk, a datadev clutched in her hand. She was joined by a doctor, an older woman dressed in dark blue scrubs to indicate her position. She beamed as she waited for their attention.

"Good morning, girls. Today's procedure is simple but will require you staying in the treatment rooms for a little longer than usual. You will each be given a small dose of the new compound, and we need you to stay . . . just so we can monitor its effect. We believe this supplement is going to change the face of Bellator medical care forever, and you can be proud of the role you are playing in its development." She gestured to the tech on her right. "I'll leave you in these capable hands now, but don't worry, I'll be closely observing your results."

The tech stepped forward, all business. "As the doctor said, each individual appointment will take a little while. Please bear with us while we deal with each of you in turn." She consulted the datadev in her hand. "Could I have Serene Joseph?"

With a pained look, Serene got to her feet. She still looked pale and shaky, but as she passed by Professor Kemp, she managed a weak smile. All eyes followed her as she joined the technician and was led up the hallway.

"Hey, Serene!" The call came from Avery, who was holding court on the other side of the waiting room. Serene turned around. "Best of luck." Serene looked confused but nodded and continued to follow the technician. "You'd think they'd've picked a better specimen to be the first to experience something so, *cutting-edge*, wouldn't you?" Avery stage-whispered. "Still, perhaps they're doing it in reverse order, starting with the weeds. They'll be saving the best til last."

Despite her usual audience being absent, her cruel comment still provoked a chorus of giggles from Marion and Eve. Almost, but not quite out of earshot, Faith saw Serene stiffen as the technician ushered her through the door of the exam room, and it was clear she had heard.

Her fists clenched at her sides, Diane glared at Avery. Beside them, Professor Kemp sighed, and Faith glanced over to catch her also shooting a frustrated look at the popular girl. Faith was surprised. Diane's protective attitude she understood, but teachers were not supposed to have favourites, or openly dislike students. She caught Kemp's eye, and the teacher masked her expression quickly, covering it with a brief, strained smile.

"Did any of you bring your lesson notes with you?" she said. Sophia reached inside her bag and took hers out, waving them in Kemp's direction. "Ah Sophia, a girl after my own heart." Kemp's smile was warmer now. "You could always revise while you're waiting."

With a nod, she stood up abruptly and moved across to speak to the technician at the reception desk.

Faith scowled. "What's the point of a morning off school if we still have to study?"

"What else are we going to do?" Sophia pointed out. "It might mean less revision this evening." She rustled the papers in Faith's face. "Test me?"

"What's the point? You already know it all anyway."

"Okay, then I'll test you."

Across from them, Diane rolled her eyes. "She's just like Serene." Sophia's face fell. "No. I mean . . . no offence." Her tone softened. "Serene's my best friend. She keeps me on the straight and narrow. She's always so . . . *good*. Most of the time I wonder how she puts up with me. And I hate it when cretins like *that*," she darted a look at Avery, who was still basking in the glory of her earlier taunt, "are mean."

Faith smiled at Sophia. "She's right you know. We all need a friend like Serene." She nudged her friend playfully, trying to lighten the mood. "But you also need friends like *us*!"

Sophia wrinkled her nose. "Why's that?"

Snatching her notes out of her hand and passing them to Diane, Faith turned to her friend. "The type that tells you when to stop working and shows you how to have some fun."

Sophia giggled. "Alright, rebels, how much fun do you think we can we have right now, with Kemp watching us like a hawk?"

Diane was already glancing around. "How about we play a trick on Avery?"

"Sounds like a *plan*." Faith leaned closer. "What can we do?"

"Anything which cracks her perfect exterior." Diane stared at the golden girl. "She's all about not losing her cool. What could we do that might make that happen?"

The three of them fell silent. Faith racked her brain to come up with a prank that might leave Avery feeling foolish, yet not reveal their part in it.

"We need some dirt on her," she began, "something she wouldn't want anyone else to know."

Sophia was sceptical. "How're we going to find that out?"

"Dunno." Faith racked her brain. "Could we figure out her password? That way we could access her datadev, see if she keeps a diary."

"You think that airhead keeps a *diary*?" Diane frowned. "How about we accidentally spill something on her? Mess up one of her perfect outfits. She'd *hate* that." The older girl's eyes were already searching for a likely substance. "Or maybe we could—"

She didn't get any further. A shrill alarm pierced the air around them, and a red light began flashing. Technicians and doctors came running from all directions, heading for the room where Serene had been taken. Professor Kemp paced by the empty reception desk, trying and failing to mask her worried expression. The Danforth girls froze, their eyes glued to the door of the treatment room. Above it, the red light was still blinking madly. All around them, the whine of the alarm continued.

Finally, a medic emerged from the treatment room and made her way towards the waiting room. Noticing Kemp, she approached her, leaning close and hissing something into her ear. Her expression darkened, but she nodded as the medic continued up the hallway.

"Ladies," she had to shout to be heard over the shrieking alarm, "we need to make our way back to the academy. No one else will be receiving the compound today." Her face was unusually pale.

"Why not?" Diane was on her feet, her hands on her hips.

"Don't question me," Kemp snapped. "Just get in line!" She gestured to the girls, her arm sweeping across the waiting room. "All of you."

For a moment, the group was still, but eventually the girls began to stand, shuffling back into their original places. Diane headed in Kemp's direction. Without knowing why, Faith followed her. As she approached their teacher, Diane's usually fierce expression was replaced by something far more vulnerable.

"We're waiting for Serene," Diane's voice wavered, "right?"

Professor Kemp shot a nervous glance at the door of Serene's treatment room. It was still closed, though the light above it had stopped flashing. She turned back to Diane, her face sympathetic.

"We need to leave her here for now. But the medics will take good care of her." As she finished her sentence, the alarm stopped abruptly. Professor Kemp's final words cut into the silence that followed. "I'm afraid she's not well."

She swept past them, heading for the door. With no alternative, the girls joined her, lining up in their original pairs. As they left the med centre, Faith was very aware of Diane walking alone behind her, an empty space where her best friend had been.

CHAPTER FIFTEEN: NOAH

Noah was grateful his shift that morning required him to work outside, and he took his time with his assigned tasks. He always enjoyed being outdoors, but the respite was doubly welcome because it allowed him an escape from the suffocating tension inside the caves.

It had been more than a week since the raid, and Paulo still had not come home and slept in their cave. Flynn and Anna had argued about it, several times, and although Noah had tried to speak to his brother himself, so far, he'd had no luck. He always seemed to be assigned to shifts on the other side of the community, though Noah suspected he'd been switching some of his duties with others so he could avoid them all. When Noah *had* managed to track his brother down, he'd always been with a large group of people and it had been difficult to talk.

Harden had also heard about the argument, and had been extra nasty, mocking Noah for being a Mama's boy as publicly as possible. All in all, Noah was glad to get out, even for a short while. He was on shift with Dawn, who knew when to talk and when to leave well enough alone, and for the first time in days, he felt a sense of peace.

This morning they were foraging. The woods around the camp contained many edible plants, and Dawn was an expert at knowing where to find them. Over the years, when raids had not been as fruitful as the community had hoped, foraging had sustained their community and saved lives. Noah and Dawn had worked side-by-side all morning, collecting nettles, wild garlic, chickweed, and even some beech nuts. By mid-morning they had brought several packs brimming with food back to the south cave and were satisfied enough with their progress to take a break.

Dawn bent to grab her canteen and took a long swig of water before passing it to Noah. Settling herself on a conveniently comfortable tree stump, she pulled out one of the flatbreads they had brought for lunch and began to eat. Noah lowered himself onto the ground next to her and ate one of his own. They sat for a few moments in companionable silence.

"Things still bad between you and Anna?" Dawn kept her tone casual, but he wasn't fooled.

"I guess." Noah shrugged. "It's more about Paulo. I mean . . . I knew she'd be mad with *me* for going on the raid. Just didn't think it would . . ." He glanced at his shift partner, who took another bite of bread and let him continue. "I mean . . . Paulo and me . . . we don't always get along . . . but I kind of miss him now he's not there."

"That's normal. Just like it's normal for siblings to fight. You'd think Ella and Ruth hated each other sometimes, the way they carry on. They're so different." Dawn chuckled. "But they'd defend each other if the need came."

"Wonder if Paulo'd defend me."

"Course he would!" Dawn scoffed. "He took you into Bellator with him, didn't he? Risked his position with Jacob, his relationship with Flynn and Anna?"

"I never looked at it like that. Like he was the one taking a risk." Noah cringed, thinking back to the confrontation. "He was *so* angry with them, Dawn. And I understood why. It was like . . . like they blamed *him* . . . like I was his responsibility . . ." He found his hands had curled into fists and released them slowly. "And then he said all this stuff . . ."

"What stuff?"

"Like how they'd allowed him to raid without an issue, but they wouldn't let me . . . he said . . ." Noah dropped his voice, ashamed, ". . . he made out like they cared more about me than him."

There was a silence, as though Dawn was considering how to respond. Embarrassed, Noah continued to eat, just to give himself something to do. After a moment, Dawn placed a hand on his arm.

"Maybe he's been feeling like that for a while, Noah." Her voice was kindly. "And if that's the case . . . well you shouldn't blame yourself. That's between him and Flynn. And Anna."

"But I—"

"It's unfortunate it all came out now, as a result of him helping you." Dawn held up a finger to stop him interrupting again. "I know it's hard. But they need to work it out between themselves. It's not on you."

"I guess not." Noah stood up and stretched, needing to keep himself active. "We don't even know where he's sleeping."

"I'm pretty certain the first night he bunked with some friends." Dawn began packing away the remnants of the food. "But he's staying with Jacob right now."

"Jacob?" Noah knew their leader lived alone. "Really?"

"Sure." Dawn stood up and shouldered her pack. "And you can't get safer than living alongside our fearless leader now, can you?"

"I guess not."

"He'll be fine." But Dawn broke eye contact with him as she spoke. "Shall we get on?"

They got back to work, moving to an area of the woods which bordered Swallow Lake, a water source which had been used as a bathing pool before the community had moved inside the caves. Dawn knew of a large hawthorn thicket close to the water, where they could gather leaves and possibly even berries for making into jams and jellies. Noah usually loved being by the water. As children they'd been brought there regularly, once the Bellator raids had become less of a threat. He remembered Flynn teaching him to swim and splashing about in the shallow waters at the lake's edge with Paulo.

Today though, the setting didn't seem able to work its usual magic. He couldn't help but think Dawn's words about Jacob had been less than convincing. He trusted Dawn. If she had her doubts about Jacob, they had to be genuine. His mind drifted back to the raid, which seemed like a dream now. Alongside his worries about the family argument, and now Jacob, he'd been struggling to drag his mind away from the mysterious girl he'd met in the darkness.

He still didn't quite understand why he'd trusted Faith. He knew if *Paulo* had discovered a Bellator citizen, an enemy, lurking in the med centre, he'd have dealt with her in a very different way. Noah hoped he would have felt able to defend himself against a trained guard or a Bellator police officer. But attacking a sixteen-year-old girl? No. It would have been like attacking Ruth.

He had yet to tell his friend about the encounter in Bellator. The conflict with Paulo had left his ma in a terrible mood. She had loaded Paulo's chores on to Noah, ensuring he had enough time to go to work and to eat, but little else. The rest of the time he was pretty much confined to home, until she decided to forgive him. If she ever did. As a result, he'd had no time to spend with his best friend.

But he wasn't sure what he would say when he finally spoke to Ruth. He suspected she might have a problem with his actions. When he thought about it, he wasn't even sure *he* approved of what he'd done. On the way into Bellator, he had been tense, ready to despise everything about the place which would have eliminated him before birth. He'd fully expected to hate any Bellator citizens he might come across. After all, they were a part of the system which had tried to eradicate the male of the species.

Yet it seemed like the Bellator girls were brought up to believe a pack of lies about men. Faith had been convinced, at first, he was going to kill her. But she'd listened to him. Been brave, intelligent, even shown some empathy. If he was completely honest with himself, he had been fascinated by her. She was nothing like the girls he knew in Eremus. But she believed men were violent monsters.

Over and over, he found himself hoping his treatment of her had shown her they weren't. He wondered why he cared. It wasn't as though he was likely to ever see her again. But the thought made him sad.

A sudden noise in the bushes startled him. He stiffened, peering in the direction of the disturbance. Dawn continued to work on the other side of the large hawthorn thicket, unaware of any issue. He was about to whistle to her when a figure emerged from the greenery.

"There you are!" It was Harden, a trademark smirk on his face. He laughed. "Scare ya, did I?"

Noah felt a surge of relief, closely followed by the sinking feeling which so often accompanied his dealings with the bully. The expression on the older boy's face was one of smug satisfaction at startling Noah. He took his time approaching, a broad grin on his face.

"Hey, Harden." Noah kept his tone even, willing himself to remain calm. "Anything wrong?"

"Wrong?" Harden's tone dripped innocence. "No. Apart from it taking so long to track you two down. You're a ways from camp."

"Well, why are you—"

But he didn't get the chance to finish. Wrapping a beefy arm around Noah's shoulder, Harden pulled him into what was almost a stranglehold. If Dawn saw them from a distance, of course, it would look like he was giving Noah a friendly squeeze. He struggled, but Harden's hold only tightened.

"Can't a man come and pay a friend a visit while he works?" Noah seethed at Harden's mocking words. "I mean . . . it's a while since we've talked, and we haven't had much of a chance to catch up since your first raid . . ."

"Everything alright there, Harden?" Dawn appeared around the side of the bushes. "I'm presuming you didn't abandon your own shift *just* to come and say hello to Noah."

At last, Harden released him, but not before he jabbed a sly punch into Noah's stomach. Noah straightened, fighting the urge to wince. He would *not* give Harden the satisfaction.

"Jacob sent me." Harden was beaming. "Wants to see Noah."

Noah's heart almost stopped. Since Paulo was staying with Jacob, he *had* to know Noah had been on the raid without permission. He wondered what trouble he might be in. A lot, if Harden's face was anything to go by.

"You'd better get going, then." Dawn appeared at his shoulder, taking the secateurs from his hand. "I can finish here."

"Jacob told me to stay. Help you finish." Harden said, picking up the pack from Noah's feet. "S'hardly a haul to be proud of, Madden." He sneered. "Think you can start slackin' now you're a big-time raider?"

"Enough, Harden. Noah's been working hard all day." Harden shot Noah his usual look of disdain as Dawn continued. "If you're here to stay, you'd better take these. You can take over the section where I was working." She thrust the secateurs into his hand and stared pointedly at the other side of the thicket.

Frowning, Harden leaned close enough so only Noah could hear. "Other people fightin' your battles again?"

Before Noah could reply, he turned and walked away, heading in the direction Dawn had pointed. As he reached the other side of the bushes, he shot Noah a poisonous smile, clearly anticipating the roasting he was going to get from their leader.

"Ignore him." Dawn passed Noah a rag to clean his hands. "It's probably nothing."

But as Noah made his way back into the tunnel, he doubted it. It didn't take long for him to find Jacob, who was waiting for him in the canteen. It was empty, aside from the few citizens assigned to prepare the food. They were busy at the far end, peeling and chopping vegetables and ignoring their leader's presence.

Jacob sat alone, a half empty cup of coffee beside him. Noah found himself wanting to offer to refill it in an attempt to delay the conversation, but as he stopped at the table, he lost his nerve. Jacob glanced up from the documents he was pouring over, waving a hand at a chair on the opposite side of the table. Noah sat down.

For a few minutes, they sat in silence. Jacob didn't pay him anymore attention, focusing his attention instead on the maps he had in front of him. Noah began to think Jacob had forgotten about him, when Paulo entered the cave from the opposite side.

Spotting Noah's brother, Jacob gathered his papers together into a pile and sat back as Paulo joined them. Noah's heart sank. A telling off from the Eremus leader was one thing. But it taking place in front of his brother? Humiliating.

When Paulo had settled into his seat, Jacob turned to Noah with a wolf-like smile. "So, Noah, your brother tells me you went along on the raid the other day."

Noah shot a brief glance at Paulo, who refused to look up from the scratched surface of the table. No help there, then. He sat up tall. "I'm sorry, Jacob. I know I shouldn't have done it . . . but I did the training . . . I was prepared . . . and I didn't . . ." an image of Faith flashed into his head and he swallowed hard, "I didn't do anything to put Eremus in danger . . . or . . ."

Jacob raised a hand to stop him. "I haven't called you here to chastise you, Noah. Quite the opposite. Paulo says you did well. Followed orders, didn't get scared, moved quickly and quietly through the tunnels *and* the city." He exchanged a knowing glance with Paulo. "You'd be surprised how many don't manage that their first time out."

Noah stared at his brother. Had Paulo praised him? It was the last thing he'd expected after the argument.

"I've been in charge of Eremus a long time," Jacob continued, oblivious to Noah's confusion. "The supply raids are *vital* to our survival. And, as you know, I have bigger, bolder plans for *Bellator*." He spat the word out, a bitterness in his eyes. "Anyway, I'm *always* on the lookout for more raiders. Ones who know what they're doing. Ones who won't panic if things go wrong."

Paulo leaned forward, meeting his brother's gaze for the first time. "Jacob's saying he'd like you to join the raiding team."

Jacob nodded, his eyes serious. "We could really use someone like you. If Paulo says you did well, I believe him. Now, what shift do you have tomorrow? I'd like to see you—"

But he never finished the sentence. One of the younger boys came skidding into the canteen, dread clouding his features.

"Guards! Bellator guards!"

Jacob stood up. "Where?"

"In the woods . . . east of Eremus."

Noah's heart gave a jolt. He and Dawn had been foraging to the east of the camp.

To his credit, Jacob did not panic. Snatching up the walkie talkie from his belt, he jammed his finger against the button. "Guards on the outer perimeter stay hidden, but alert. All other citizens back inside the caves. Immediate disguise mode. I repeat. Immediate disguise mode."

Noah and Paulo were also on their feet. At the command, they both raced from the table. Bellator raids were few and far between these days, but they had once been the biggest single threat to the community. The fearsome female guards had never found their way *inside* the cave system, mainly due to a rigorous system which every Eremus citizen knew by heart. The community protected itself from such an invasion by disguising the entrances to their caves and hiding.

A constant lookout was maintained on all sides of the camp. Whenever Bellator guards were sighted, an alert was given, and the citizens retreated. While the guards were close, all work stopped, and the citizens played dead. A glance into any of the exterior caves revealed nothing more than random piles of rock. It had worked pretty well in the past.

But as Noah followed his brother into the lower caverns to hide, he wondered whether it would work this time. And whether, by putting his trust in a girl from Bellator, he had made the biggest mistake of his life.

Chapter Sixteen: Faith

F aith trudged back across the fields from the morning training session. The workout had been particularly gruelling, and her body ached. Without explanation, Professor Leyland had doubled the length of their physical education lessons this week. She seemed set on pushing the girls harder every day, working their muscles until they screamed for mercy, as though she were on a personal mission to totally exhaust them.

The Danforth professors had all been acting strangely this week, and there had been several alterations to the usual timetable. In addition to the longer physical fitness sessions, extra yoga and meditation had been added, and, strangest of all, Professor Kemp had cancelled homework for the time being. Not that any of them were complaining about it.

No one was sure why. In the seven days since they had returned so suddenly from the med centre visit, they'd been given little information. Serene was still absent from the academy, and every time anyone had asked about her, they had received the same response: Serene had gotten sick before the technicians had given her the supplement. She was being treated by the doctors and wasn't up to receiving visitors. After getting herself into trouble several times, even Diane had given up asking questions.

There had been plenty of gossip about their fellow student and the details about what had happened at the med centre. Faith had heard Serene was throwing up, had a fever, and was suffering from an ugly rash which covered her whole body, or needed her tonsils removed. Every time Faith heard a story repeated, there were several changes to it, the details exaggerated or altered to ensure the most dramatic reaction. But no single explanation rang true.

Having been tasked with collecting the equipment at the end of the session, Faith was one of the last ones to reach the school. When she entered the building, the lower hallway was empty, most girls having raced back to their rooms to shower. Faith hauled the box of tennis balls and rackets to the Physical Training Equipment storeroom. Reaching it, she pulled on the handle and was surprised to find the light inside already on.

At the rear of the cupboard, tidying and cleaning the shelves, stood a drudge. *The* drudge. He turned at her entrance, his eyes flaring with recognition. They stared at one another for a moment.

Eventually, Faith gestured to the box. "Leyland asked me to bring it back . . . put it away."

The drudge inclined his head. All Faith had to do now was turn and go, leaving the box where it was. The drudge would put it away: it was part of his job. But something stopped her. Instead, she pulled the door closed.

"I know you can talk . . ." she hesitated at the tension in the drudge's eyes. "That's all I want to do. Will you talk to me?"

The drudge paused, his body tensed. He glanced at the door behind her, then nodded slowly.

"Thank you." Faith smiled. "Are you– I mean . . . do you have . . . a name?"

The drudge raised his eyebrows, as if this were the last question he'd expected.

"I'm Faith. My name is . . . Faith. And you?" She gestured towards the drudge. "You are?"

"Drudges don't have names." The voice was husky, as though he wasn't used to speaking much.

"That's awful." *How must it feel to have no identity.* "I'm so sorry." The drudge stared at her. Growing braver, she continued. "I mean, everyone should have a name. If we're going to be friends, then . . . I have to call you something."

"Friends?" The whisper was incredulous.

"Yes." Faith found his shock at her offer saddening. "If you'd like?"

The drudge bowed his head. When he raised it again, his eyes were large and wide. "You could call me . . . Arden." He blinked rapidly as he continued. "I . . . others have . . . called me that in the past."

Arden. "Alright then." Faith wondered who these *others* were. Did the drudges talk amongst themselves, perhaps? "It's . . . um, nice to know you, Arden."

The reply was hesitant. "You . . . you too."

"Can you—?" Faith took a tentative step forward. "Can you take off your mask?"

Arden flushed, obviously remembering their first encounter. He shot a nervous glance at the door. Faith reached behind her, demonstrating it was completely closed. After a moment's hesitation, Arden slid a hand up and pulled the covering down, revealing a hesitant expression.

"Do you—?" Faith found herself at a loss. "Do you want to ask *me* anything?"

Arden's face reflected his shock. He took his time, seeming to choose his words carefully. "Are you . . . sad?"

Faith cocked her head to one side. "Am I . . . *sad*?"

The drudge's expression changed, as though he was unsure how she had taken his question, but he tried again. "You don't look . . . happy. Like you're . . . worried?"

Faith considered his query. He was certainly observant. "My friend . . . I mean, one of the other girls I know here . . . she's older . . ." She was babbling, but in the privacy of the cupboard she found she was desperate to unburden herself. "She's sick. Been in the med centre for a week. Teachers won't tell us anything."

Arden frowned. "This girl. She is called . . . Serene, yes?"

"*Yes!*"

"Then she is not . . ." he faltered but seemed to steel himself to continue. "She is not in the med centre . . . was transferred to Bellator Hospital."

"Transferred? But how do you—?"

"They don't think we listen." Arden tapped a finger to his ear. "But drudges hear things."

"To Bellator Hospital? You're sure?"

"I'm sure."

"Do you know when? And why?"

"I heard Kemp talking." Arden thought for a moment. "Her sickness got worse . . . I think. Kemp said she was moved the night after she reacted badly to her treatment."

"Hold on. She was given some *treatment*?" Faith was surprised. "But we were told . . ."

On the stairs above the cupboard, there was the sound of footsteps. There was an assembly this morning, and the girls were beginning to make their way to the main hall. A glance at Faith's wristclip told her she had fewer than ten minutes to get showered and be there before Anderson started talking.

"I have to go." Arden nodded, covering his features with the mask again and retreating to the rear of the cupboard. Faith smiled. "Thanks for telling me . . . what you know. Can we talk again sometime?"

Arden didn't speak, but his eager nod indicated he was looking forward to the prospect as much as Faith was. As she took the stairs to her room two at a time, she considered how lonely the drudges must be. Other than the fact they did most of the menial jobs around Bellator and would be severely punished for conversing with a Bellator female, Faith knew very little about them. Yet she was sure the conversation had made him happy. Resolving to find a way to speak to him whenever she could, she hurried off to take a quick shower.

When she sat down next to Sophia in the assembly hall, her hair was still damp. Her friend glanced over at her, frowning. "Where were you? You were gone ages. I waited, but . . ."

"I'm fine. Tell you later." Faith slid lower in her seat as Anderson took to the stage, her face even more serious than usual. She tapped a button on the datadev at her side to activate the microphone and cleared her throat.

"Good morning, girls," she began, "our assembly today will be fairly short. I don't have much to say, other than I appreciate you embracing the alterations to your timetables this week. You have all responded well to the additional lessons, and we're certain the extra time devoted to exercising the body and stimulating the mind will have done you good.

"Until now, we haven't really given you an explanation for the changes, but rest assured we made them with good reason, and as a direct result of a recent event. It is that event which I want to speak to you about this morning."

Beside Faith, Sophia shifted, darting a glance at Faith. Most of the senior girls were exchanging similar looks, anticipating an announcement which would explain Serene's extended absence. As Anderson continued, the entire hall hung on her every word.

"Last week, as most of you know, some of the senior girls were selected to receive a revolutionary new health supplement. When they arrived at the med centre, however, Serene Joseph was taken ill. Seriously ill. Of course, the medics sent the rest of the group back to school so they could focus on treating Serene. It is always," she paused and looked around the room as though daring the girls to object, "*always*, our priority to ensure the Danforth girls are properly looked after. We wanted to ensure Serene was well again, before administering the new compound to any more of our students."

Professor Anderson looked down at her hands for a moment, an odd expression on her face. "So it is, with a heavy heart, I now have to inform you that last night, despite receiving the best treatment Bellator had to offer, Serene Joseph left this world."

A shockwave reverberated around the hall. Faith turned to look over her shoulder at Diane, whose face was white. Next to her, Sophia took her hand.

Anderson ploughed on stiffly, the words sounding scripted. "Serene was a valued member of the academy. Her death will be thoroughly investigated. The recent timetable changes have been made as a direct result of what happened to your fellow student. We hope they will ensure you are all as fit and healthy as possible, and guard against anything like this happening again."

Faith couldn't drag her mind away from the conversation she'd had with Arden fewer than twenty minutes ago. Her grip on Sophia's hand tightened as Anderson continued, her voice so low they had to strain to hear her.

"Please know, girls, you're all very precious to us. We mourn the loss of any student deeply and must find a way to help each other through this. A service will be held in a few days' time, to give us all a chance to celebrate the life of a young woman who was taken from us far too soon. And now," Anderson raised her voice suddenly, startling some of the girls sitting in front of her, "we ask you to bow your heads and take a moment's silence to remember our friend, Serene."

Faith closed her eyes and dipped her head, hoping the students sitting around her would think her body was shaking with tears, rather than the fury which threatened to consume her. She thought back to Arden's words again. Serene had been given the treatment, he'd said. And Serene had died.

He'd had no reason to lie. Anderson was the one who was lying to them. And not for the first time.

CHAPTER SEVENTEEN: NOAH

Noah felt like he had been sitting in the same cramped position for hours. His retreat location was a small cave deep in the settlement, and he shared it with thirty others. Since the last citizen had arrived and they'd hauled rocks over the entrance, the room had been close to silent. Now, a faint scent of sweat drifted through the stagnant air and the odd hushed whisper broke the quiet stillness.

The Eremus strategy had proved successful in the past. Ever since the community had retreated inside the caves, the number of citizens killed by the Bellator guards had drastically reduced. And they'd *never* made it inside. Bellator had almost stopped looking for them altogether. So much so, this lockdown had come as quite a shock. As they'd waited, Noah's thoughts had ricocheted between worrying about Dawn and wondering if Faith had anything to do with the sudden appearance of the guards.

Beside him, his ma was tense. When she had reached the cave, she'd headed straight for him, pulling him into a rough embrace. They hadn't spoken, but he knew her anger over the raid had been replaced by her concern for his safety. He hoped she would remain in a forgiving mood once the danger was over.

After letting go of him, she had attempted to repeat the process with Paulo, whose body had stiffened at her touch. His ma had turned away quickly to speak to Cora and Beth, but Noah had seen the flash of disappointment on her face. Flynn had arrived moments later, having finished concealing one of the outer entrances before making his own retreat. He had thrown a worried smile at them all, before doing a head count and pulling the heavy cover across the doorway.

When the all-clear was finally given, the group in the cave let out a collective breath. Flynn and Paulo pulled the rocks away from the door, peering into the darkness beyond before venturing out. The scouts never gave the signal until they were certain the guards were gone, but it was still sensible to be cautious. Aside from one or two citizens completing essential outdoor jobs, the community would stay in the caves for several days after a raid, just to be certain.

When the cave started to empty, Noah hurried into the tunnel beyond. The cramped space had begun to feel like a tomb, and he was desperate to reach a cave closer to the surface, where he could breathe more easily. As he approached the tunnel end, he almost crashed into Ruth, who was approaching from the opposite direction, her face pale.

"Everything alright?"

She shook her head. "Have you seen Ma? We had to shut the retreat cave before she reached us." His friend clutched at his arm, her face hopeful. "I mean . . . you were on shift with her this morning, right?" Noah went cold. "If you made it back inside . . . then she must have . . ." She trailed off, the expression fading.

"I'm s-sorry." Noah stuttered. "Jacob called me back in early —needed to see me. I wasn't out there when the alarm sounded."

Ruth's eyes blazed. "You mean you left her alone out there?"

"No!" Some of the citizens hurrying past shot Noah a warning look, and he lowered his voice to a whisper. "Jacob sent a replacement . . . Harden . . . stayed out there with her when I–when I—"

Noah turned as his ma appeared, her face creased with concern. "What's the matter, Ruth?"

"Dawn is . . ." Noah took a deep breath. "She was outside, foraging in the woods to the east. Ruth can't find her."

His ma reacted instantly, turning to Flynn, who was hurrying up the tunnel behind her. "Got your walkie talkie?"

He slipped it from his belt and waved it. "Why?"

"Dawn's missing. Did everyone make it back inside?"

Flynn shrugged, raising the walkie to his mouth. "Come in, Jacob. We have reports of missing citizens down here. Dawn Murphy was . . ." he shot a questioning look at his partner.

"In the woods to the east, close to Sparrow Lake."

Noah elbowed his mother. "Harden was there too."

Flynn continued, ". . . east. Near Sparrow Lake. Also, Harden Porter."

They waited while the walkie talkie went silent, then crackled sharply to life. "A patrol has gone to look."

"Thanks." Flynn lowered the walkie talkie. "They've sent people to check." He shot a comforting look at Ruth. "They'll find her. There's nothing you can do right now."

They walked the rest of the way to the large cave where the community met to eat. Several of the kitchen staff for the day were handing out rations: cereal bars—stolen from the very city who threatened them—and hot coffees. Citizens spread out across the cave and spoke in hushed voices as they waited for the rest of their community to gather.

Flynn went to speak to Jacob while Noah guided Ruth to a table where Ella was already sitting. The older girl clutched a steaming cup in her shaking hands. Her hopeful expression was dashed as she exchanged glances with Ruth and read the despair on her face. As Ruth sat down and wrapped an arm around her sister's shoulder, Ella leaned heavily into her.

"Here we are." Noah was grateful to see his ma approach with a mug of coffee for Ruth. She handed it over and Ruth nodded her thanks. "No problem. Drink it all up." She leaned closer to Noah, so only he could hear her. "I'm going to fetch my first aid supplies, just in case."

Noah nodded. As Anna stood, there was a disturbance at the far end of the room. Voices, raised in panic. From the entrance closest to the surface, a number of figures stumbled into the room. They were moving awkwardly, looking like they were somehow attached to one another. Noah leapt to his feet, peering at them, trying to understand. And as they came closer, he understood. There were three citizens, holding another in their arms. And behind them, another two, also staggering under a similar burden.

The entrance led to the east side of Eremus. The direction from which he had exited this morning, then entered again to speak to Jacob. Taking a few paces forward, he heard Ruth and Ella's twin cries as they all realised what they were seeing.

Dawn and Harden were being *carried* into the cave.

It seemed like the entire community surged forward. And then, from the front of the room there was a shrill whistle and all movement stopped. Jacob stood on the podium, waiting for their attention. "Would all citizens please return to their caves and stay there until told otherwise. We need time and space to deal with this crisis. Only medics and family of the . . ." his voice faltered very slightly, ". . . injured should stay behind."

As the room began to empty, Noah felt a hand grasp his arm. "Go and fetch my meds bag." His ma hissed in his ear. He stared at her for a second, uncomprehending, until she jabbed a finger in the direction of the cave which served as their medical base. "*Now!*"

She hurried off towards Harden and Dawn, with Ruth and Ella following closely behind. Finally understanding the urgency, Noah sped out of the cavern, choosing the least populated exit and pushing past anyone in his way, calling a quick 'Sorry, emergency' as he did. Most people moved quickly out of his way.

Once away from the more crowded tunnels, he increased his pace until he reached the medics base, where he grabbed Anna's bag and retraced his steps just as quickly. As he re-entered the cave, he stopped to survey the scene. Dawn and Harden had been laid on tables side-by-side, his ma attending to Dawn while her fellow medic Sam looked at Harden, whose face was twisted in pain. The older man held a torn-off piece of material to an injury on Harden's arm. Already the blood was beginning to show through it as Sam applied pressure and held the limb aloft.

Harden's mother stood a few feet away, her lips drawn back into a fine line as though she were bursting to ask questions but had been ordered not to. The only obvious sign of distress was her hands, which were clasped in front of her, their knuckles white. As Harden let out a groan, she released them and took a step forward. Ignoring Sam's glare, she clasped the hand of his good arm in hers.

By contrast, Dawn lay completely still and silent on the other table. Recognising the more serious situation, Noah moved to his mother's side. He placed her bag on the ground and flipped its lid open, waiting for his mother's command. Eremus had limited medical knowledge, but his ma had been working with the sick and injured as long as he could remember. Her choice of profession made far more sense in the light of his recent discovery. Anna had received an intensive biology education in Bellator, which made her far more qualified for the role than anyone in Eremus.

Right now, she was facing the challenge of a lifetime.

Avoiding looking at Dawn, Noah turned instead to her children. Ella had her head buried in Ruth's shoulder and her shoulders were shaking with sobs. Ruth's eyes were fixed on her adopted mother, but they did not shed tears. The intensity of her gaze seemed to be willing Dawn to live.

Noah forced his attention back to his ma. She was holding something, a shirt, perhaps, over a wound in the centre of Dawn's torso. She pressed down hard with both hands, almost unaware of Noah's presence.

"Bullet wound to the stomach," she muttered, half under her breath. "Apply pressure to stop the bleeding."

"Ma." Noah touched her arm lightly. "Ma. What do you need?"

Startled, his ma looked up. Her eyes travelled to the medical case, to Ruth and Ella, and back to Dawn. He saw something change in her expression.

"Take over, Noah. Apply pressure to the wound. A *lot* of pressure."

Gulping and trying not to balk at the task, Noah stepped closer to his best friend's mother and covered Anna's hands with his own. She slid hers out from under his and he felt the warmth of the blood-soaked shirt ooze between his fingers.

"More than that." Anna covered his hands with her own and pushed down on Dawn's body harder. A long, low moan, more animal than human, escaped her lips.

Noah winced and attempted to loosen his hold. "We're *hurting* her."

Anna gripped his hands, not allowing him to withdraw them. "We *have* to stop the bleeding."

When she was certain he was following her instructions, she leaned away and looked in her bag. Her hands were stained scarlet and he could see them shaking. He raised his eyes to meet Ruth's and tried to look encouraging, but as the blood continued to pump from the wound beneath his fingers, he knew he wouldn't convince her. Instead, he looked away, staring at the ground and feeling like a coward.

Behind them, a figure entered the cave. Flynn. Anna looked up, her face flashing with relief at the sight of her partner. She beckoned him over, lifting a knife from the medical kit.

"We have to see if the bullet's still inside. I can't sew her up if it is."

Without question, Flynn moved to the opposite side of the table. Anna joined him, taking hold of her friend's shoulder.

"Noah, we're going to lift her. You *have* to keep the pressure on the wound." Anna's voice seemed to come from far away. He managed to nod. Satisfied, she turned to her partner. "Together?"

"Got it." Flynn secured his hands under Dawn's hip. "One. Two. Three."

As he finished counting, they levered Dawn's body upwards, rolling her towards Noah. He held his breath, trying to keep the pressure stable on the wound, though it was incredibly difficult. There was a silence as Anna examined the body, then they lowered it back to the table.

"It's still inside." Anna's voice rang with despair. "I'll have to try and . . . remove it. But it could be . . . it could be anywhere. I might do more damage if I . . ."

Flynn leaned over Dawn, putting his ear close to her chest, then moving to her lips. Withdrawing, he leant close to Anna, gesturing at Dawn's body. "Are you sure she's . . .?"

Ella's sobs grew in volume and she clung to her sister, but Ruth's eyes remained fixed on Dawn and she did not cry. Noah looked down at the woman who was like a second mother to him. Her face was chalk white, and she hadn't opened her eyes since he had entered the room. And she was so *still*.

"She had a pulse when they brought her in." Anna sounded strangled. "She was breathing."

Noah glanced at Dawn's chest. When he had taken over from his ma, it had been rising and falling. Not evenly, not with much power, but there had been movement. And he'd felt the blood seeping from the wound, soaking through the shirt. He relaxed his hold very slightly as Flynn leaned close to Dawn again, placing his fingers on her neck and feeling for a pulse.

"I'm so sorry." Noah watched the colour drain from his ma's face at Flynn's words. "She's gone."

CHAPTER EIGHTEEN: FAITH

L essons were suspended for two days while Serene's memorial service went ahead. The academy felt very quiet, a sense of shock pervading the entire campus. Faith could only recall one previous death at Danforth Academy, a few years before. A young girl had sneaked off alone during a field trip to the city's museum and been hit by a Delivery Transporter. Her death was often used by the Danforth professors as a moral tale which proved the rules were there for the girls' protection, but Faith thought the story was sad. She had often wondered what had caused the girl to run away.

Serene's death was different. Bellator was pretty advanced, medically, and for a healthy young woman to die of what appeared to be a minor illness was devastating. Aside from some mild cold symptoms, Serene had seemed fine on the day of their appointment. If what Arden said was true, the supplement Anderson claimed to have been delayed had never existed. Instead, the selected girls had been on their way to the med centre for some kind of treatment, one which had actually been administered to Serene. Faith couldn't see any reason for Arden to lie, and when she had confided in Sophia, her friend had agreed with her. But no one else knew the truth.

Since the announcement of her friend's death, Diane had been locked away in her room, and Faith did not feel able to knock on her door uninvited. She had seen the other girl at the service, looking pale and drawn at the back of the hall. When Professor Kemp had stepped forward to deliver her speech about Serene, Diane had bowed her head, clearly moved by their teacher's kind words. But at the end of the ceremony, she had disappeared again.

Faith longed to speak to her. Diane didn't yet know Serene had been given the treatment, and Faith knew she'd be furious when she found out. Cursing herself for not managing to gain access to the meds at the centre on the night she met Noah, Faith was desperate to find out more. But she was also wary of Anderson now, and in no hurry to be hauled into the principal's office again, over what would be far more serious charges.

When classes resumed the day after the memorial, Diane didn't appear. Faith searched for her in every lesson, with no luck. She was even absent from the dining hall at mealtimes. Not daring to ask after her, Faith had begun to wonder whether something sinister had happened when, in the midst of a Physical Education lesson the next day, Diane was marched across the field by Professor Kemp. Pale and silent, she refused to make eye contact with anyone.

"Professor Leyland, Diane seems to think she is excused from lessons this week. Please ensure she works *very* hard this lesson."

A wicked smile brightened their teacher's face. "No problem, Professor Kemp."

Faith pitied Diane. Leyland was a tough cookie at the best of times but given a direct order to be tough on a student was an invitation for her to excel at what she did best: physically demanding workouts that left students begging for mercy. Faith groaned internally as she considered what this meant for the rest of them: any physical exertion she doled out to Diane would have to be reflected in the entire class' workout. The resentful expressions on the other students' faces told her they had come to the same conclusion.

Leyland turned to face them all. "Today, I thought we'd start with a long-distance run. Around the field twenty times, I think." She bared her teeth in what was presumably supposed to be a smile. "Ready, ladies?"

She blew her whistle and the keenest of the group shot off. Faith started slowly, planning to align herself with Diane if she could, and talk to her as they ran. They were all kept pretty fit at the academy, so running and chatting at the same time wasn't much of an issue, as long as they stayed close to the rear of the group so no one could hear them. But Diane took off before Faith could get near her and set a pretty punishing pace.

For a few laps, Faith attempted to keep up, but had to admit defeat and abandon the effort. Perhaps this wasn't the time to talk to Diane. She ran like something terrifying was chasing her, pushing harder with every lap. Despite not being first to leave the starting blocks, she worked her way through the group until she was almost leading the pack, aside from the students who always excelled in their workouts. Faith had to smile at the panic of the usual champions, forced to accelerate rapidly to retain pole position.

When it was over, Leyland made them do half an hour of various strength exercises followed by a 'fun' game of basketball, a sport which Faith despised. Even here, Diane pushed herself, racing up and down the court, attacking other players with a razor-sharp focus and retaining control of the ball with terrifying aggression. When the session was over, she was drenched with sweat and panting.

Even Leyland looked impressed as she dismissed them, slapping Diane on the back. "Great job today."

Diane shrugged her off, attempting to sprint from the field, but Faith made sure she was standing in the way.

"Can we talk?" Scowling, Diane tried to push past her. "Please? I've something I need to tell you."

"Not now." The older girl circumnavigated Faith to find herself faced with Sophia, her gentle face sympathetic.

"How are you, Diane?"

"I'm fine." Diane's reply was cutting, her face poisonous. "Not that it's any of your business."

Sophia stepped back, a little stung by the comment. For the third time, Diane tried to leave, but Faith stepped in front of her, taking hold of her arm.

"Stop. I mean it. We just want to talk to you." Faith waited, until Diane's arm relaxed slightly. "I heard something which might be linked to . . . to Serene . . . to her . . ."

"Her death?" Diane glared at them. "You can say it, you know."

"Okay. Her . . . death, then. I think you should hear it."

Diane glanced to the left, where Professor Leyland had locked up the courts and was heading their way.

"Alright. Not here though." Diane ducked, as though she were tying up a shoelace. "Come to my room later. This evening."

"Don't loiter, ladies." Leyland's voice was sharp. "Get inside and get showered or you'll be late for your next lesson." Faith glanced down at Diane, who was still fiddling with her shoelace. Leyland followed her gaze. "Miss King, could you wait behind? I need to speak with you."

Faith and Sophia set off across the field together, leaving Diane to speak to their professor.

"Think she's telling her off? Or asking her to join the team?" Faith wondered aloud. "She was acting like she was possessed today."

"She's grieving for her friend." Sophia's tone was gentler and more understanding. "I wish the teachers would cut her some slack."

"Will you come with me to speak to her later?" Faith glanced over her shoulder at the fierce expression on Diane's face. She had to admit she was concerned about how Diane might react to the information.

"Sure. I'll come." Sophia chewed her lip. "Maybe knowing the truth will make her feel better."

The rest of the day dragged. Diane managed to avoid lessons and didn't appear until dinner time, when she sat by herself, her face sullen. Professor Kemp loitered nearby, watching the older girl as she ate. It looked like she had to force the food down, but she managed most of her meal and threw a defiant glance at Kemp as she stood to clear her plate.

After dinner, they headed for Diane's room, thankful the hallway was empty as they knocked on the door.

"C'm in." Faith opened the door and peered around it. Diane was standing at the window, gazing out into the courtyard below. Sensing their reluctance to enter, she turned and waved a tired hand in their direction. When Sophia had closed the door behind them, Diane walked to her bed and sat down. "Sorry about earlier. I just can't . . . can't seem to find the words." She shrugged helplessly. "I was never great at talking to people, but I got along okay because . . ."

She stopped, her gaze roaming to Serene's bed, which was still made up with a set of pretty flowered sheets. A small stuffed bear sat on the pillow.

"It's understandable you're . . ." Sophie shifted from one foot to the other, ". . . feeling strange without her."

Diane's gaze shifted to the floor. "She was . . ." She tailed off, then straightened, clearing her throat. "Anyway. You were coming to tell me something important. Do you . . . want to sit?"

Faith and Sophia looked around. It didn't feel right sitting on Serene's bed, but there were limited options. Eventually, Sophia sat in the chair at one of the study desks, and Faith lowered herself to the floor, making herself comfortable on the plush rug. She leaned back against the desk drawers and took a deep breath.

"I wanted to tell you I spoke to one of the drudges a few days ago, and—" Faith began.

"Wait a minute." Diane sat bolt upright. "You *spoke* to a drudge?"

"I did." Faith shifted awkwardly. "I've never talked to any of them before, but I've seen this one several times, and the other day, I actually had a conversation with him."

"What about?"

"Well, we didn't talk for long. But what he did tell me, and I don't know what he'd have to gain by lying about this . . . was Serene was only transferred to the Bellator Hospital after she received treatment at the med centre."

"So?" Diane looked puzzled. "She was sick. And if she was *very* sick, she'd need the hospital. That'll be why they transferred her."

"No. You see, he said before they transferred her they'd actually given her some kind of treatment. In fact, I think all eight of us were supposed to have it."

There was silence as Diane digested Faith's words. "So, Anderson lied to us."

Faith shrugged. "The drudge seemed to think so."

"But that means . . . means she might have gotten sick . . . *because* of this treatment." Diane sounded choked. "Whatever they did to her . . . killed her."

"Well, I don't know for certain." Faith leaned closer to Diane. "But it's possible, isn't it?"

"That's right. You *don't* know anything for certain," Sophia interrupted. "You need to be careful, making these kinds of accusations . . . I mean . . . you're already on Anderson's radar."

"Think about it though, Soph." Faith turned to face her friend. "They give Serene a dose of something new and she reacts badly to it. Then they hustle the rest of us back to the academy *without* giving it to us. Don't you see? What they gave her must've caused a pretty bad reaction."

"You're probably right." Diane's voice was hard. "We'd have to find out more, though. There's no evidence of anything other than a tragic death at the moment."

Faith thought again of the mysterious drug, wishing she had managed to get information about it on her midnight visit to the med centre. "Diane, do you think this could be linked to femgazipane?"

"That drug you mentioned?" Diane nodded. "Maybe."

"It would make sense, though. Especially if there were worrying side effects."

"You think they gave Serene a dose of a *drug* they weren't sure was safe?" Sophia looked horrified. "No! The academy would never risk our lives."

"Maybe not intentionally." Diane stood up from the bed abruptly, making Faith jump. "But if they believed it would have one effect, and instead it did something else, then . . ."

Sophia blanched. "If the papers got hold of this, the academy'd be in a real mess."

"Too right." Diane began pacing. "I mean . . . people wouldn't stand for it. Questions would be asked."

Faith stared up at Diane. "So, what do we do?"

"What do we *do*?" Sophia leaned forward in her chair. "I don't think we should—"

Diane cut across her. "We need to get into the hospital. Find Serene's records. They'll have more information about the cause of death." She punched a hand into her fist. "I can't go, though. You've seen Kemp. She's watching me like a hawk at the minute."

"Really?" Faith sat up straighter. "Why?"

She sighed. "I haven't exactly got a stainless record. And since Serene's death, well, they're afraid I'll act out. You saw the way I was hauled over to practice this morning."

Faith's mind was racing. She had managed to get into the med centre. But the hospital was a whole new level of breaking and entering.

"I don't think it would be that difficult," Diane continued, as though she'd read Faith's mind. "The hospital's not far, and it's *open* at night. No break-in necessary."

Faith tried to picture the building. She didn't know it well. She'd only ever been there for her annual checkup, which involved a full body scan the med centre didn't have the equipment for. It was much larger than the med centre, but maybe its size and the number of citizens who used it would make it easier for her to go unnoticed.

She pushed herself into a standing position. "I suppose *I* could go."

Sophia's face creased with concern, but Faith ignored her.

Diane turned to look at her. "Would you?"

"Guess so." Faith shrugged, attempting nonchalance. "How hard can it be?"

"Hopefully not very." But Diane seemed to see through her bravado. "I'll sketch you a map of the layout. I probably know it better than you."

"Thanks." Faith nodded. "And you'll cover for me here?"

"Of course."

Sophia nodded too, but still looked troubled. As Faith considered the undertaking, thinking back to her previous nighttime excursion and her brush with the Eremus people, she felt her own heart race a little faster.

A s he made his way into what served as a medical area of the Eremus caves that evening, Noah felt nothing but dread. Since the incident the previous week, his mother had been insistent he help her out with Harden's treatment, in addition to his daily duties, and he was exhausted. But it was the scent of sickness that hung over the cave, rather than his tiredness, which brought on the sense of despair.

The days since Dawn's death had been among the worst of his life. Both her daughters were struggling in their own way: Ella seemed unable to stop crying and Ruth had been walking around like a zombie. His ma said Ruth was burying her feelings, and it wouldn't do her any good in the end. He'd tried to talk to his friend, encourage her to spend some quiet time with him, to grieve, even visited the den every night since the Bellator attack, but so far she hadn't appeared.

His ma was just as bad. She was obviously devastated at the loss of her friend, a woman who had been there for her from her earliest days in Eremus, when she was a refugee fleeing from Bellator. But Anna's response to the situation was to throw herself into healing Harden with every fibre of her being, as though saving him could make up for her loss. She was with him every waking second of the day, and when she couldn't be, she had Noah or Flynn watching him. Harden's past treatment of Noah made it difficult to handle him with sympathy. But he did it for his ma.

As he turned into the narrow tunnel which led to the medcave, someone coming from the opposite direction barrelled into him, sending him flying backwards.

"Watch it!"

As Noah recovered, he looked up into the cold eyes of Sarah Porter.

"How's Harden today?" He took a step towards her.

"No different." Harden's ma sidestepped him, heading for the more central community area.

"Oh, I'm . . . I'm sorry."

"Why?" She turned back, her face unreadable. "He's *hardly* a close friend of yours."

"You must be worried, though."

"Oh, he's strong. He'll be fine in a few days. Your *hero* of a ma will see to it . . ." Sarah turned and swept away down the tunnel. "She'd better, anyway."

He watched her go, grateful for once his own ma was less formidable. Sarah was the most unforgiving woman he'd ever come across. Aware of how she envied Flynn's close relationship with Jacob, Noah hoped her threatening tone wouldn't lead to trouble for his family.

He moved towards the cave where his ma was caring for Harden. Inhaling deeply, he swept the curtain out of the way and entered, going straight to the bowl of water to scrub his hands clean. His ma, who had been slumped in a chair next to Harden's bed with her head in her hands, jolted upright. He sloshed the water around noisily, pretending he hadn't noticed she'd been sleeping

"How's he doing?" he offered, in the way of a greeting.

Sighing, his ma rubbed her eyes. "He's alright, I guess. The wound isn't healing as well as I'd like." She jerked her head at the tunnel he had entered from. "Presume you bumped into his ma?"

Noah rolled his eyes. "Literally."

"She's not happy." She glanced down at her sleeping patient. "I wish we had more in the way of antibiotics right now."

Guilt knifed Noah's gut as he thought back to their unsuccessful raid. "Is he in danger?"

She shrugged. "Wound could get infected. If it does, I'm all out of solutions. I've given him everything I can."

She reached for her medical book. Well-thumbed and falling apart at the seams, it was her best source of knowledge when helping the sick and injured. He knew it frustrated her she didn't know more, she wasn't able to help people as much as she could have done if she was in Bellator with unlimited medical resources.

"I'm sorry." He laid a hand on her shoulder, not knowing how to comfort her.

"It's okay." She managed a tired smile as she stood up, stretching. "Look, Noah . . . I should probably tell you . . . tell you about my background sometime." She seemed hesitant, choosing her words carefully. "Back in Bellator, I was studying to be a medic, before I . . . before we ended up here. I . . . I never finished my training."

Noah blinked, but when he thought about his mother's revelation, it made total sense. Her choice to become the unofficial Eremus doctor alongside Sam, who was well-meaning but lacking in the medical expertise the Bellator training had given his ma; her obsessive pouring over the medical tome; her anger when she lost a patient. A mysterious sickness had swept through the community two years ago, killing thirty people. Despite staying awake for days on end caring for the sick, his ma had been furious with herself for not being able to save more of them. Dawn's bullet wound had also caused her great anguish.

Noah had heard her crying late at night more than once in the past week.

He turned to her, trying to keep his expression neutral. "Figures, I guess."

"Anyway . . ." she flushed, "now's not the time." She moved towards the door.

"I'd like to hear about it." She stopped and turned back to him, a small smile on her lips. There was a moment of awkwardness, where Noah busied himself refilling Harden's water before taking his mother's seat. "You go and get some rest."

"Alright." She nodded at the patient. "He's only just dropped off, so it should be a while before he needs anything. Come get me if anything changes?"

Noah nodded, knowing better than to protest. His mother needed sleep badly, but if Harden's condition worsened and he didn't call for her, there'd be trouble.

With one final smile, his ma pulled the curtain aside and disappeared up the tunnel, her slow trudging step betraying her exhaustion. Noah was glad they were talking again, at least. Settling back in the seat, he said a small prayer Harden wouldn't wake up at all while he was there. The injury he'd sustained wasn't major, and Harden was quite capable of delivering his usual abuse when Anna was out of earshot. It was only his slight fever that kept him here for observation.

Harden had also been well enough to tell them about the Bellator attack. Even as far out as Swallow Lake, he and Dawn had been alerted to the emergency via the call system which involved the scouts whistling birdcalls repeatedly through the woods. They'd been on their way back to the caves when they'd heard the sound of heavy boots approaching. Shots had been fired through the trees before they could react. One had caught Harden in the arm. The next thing he knew, Dawn was pushing him over.

He'd struggled at first, but eventually given in. Dawn had forced him to the ground and rolled him beneath the cover of some bushes. He'd pressed his hand against his wounded arm and waited, expecting her to follow. Seconds later, he'd heard the guards express surprise as they discovered Dawn. They had attempted to capture her, presumably with the intention of taking her back to the city.

But they hadn't bargained on her attachment to Eremus. Determined not to be separated from her daughters, she had struggled and attempted to run away from them. Eventually, Harden had heard the guards muttering something about a *lost cause*. There were additional shots, and Dawn's body had collapsed not far from his own.

Unable to reach her without giving his position away, Harden had stayed hidden until the guards moved on. The entire thing sounded horrific. Noah shuddered every time he considered that it should have been him out there.

Flynn felt Dawn's actions had not only saved Harden, but also ensured the Bellator authorities would be less likely to return to search the forest. Finding an unarmed woman in the woods was one thing. Finding a strong, able man was entirely another. By hiding Harden from the guards, Dawn had probably saved the entire community from weeks of anxiety whilst additional patrols stalked the woods looking for signs of life.

"Back *again*, Madden?" Beside him, Harden had stirred. "You just can't keep away, can you?"

Opening his eyes, Noah forced himself to smile. Being injured had definitely not altered Harden's attitude.

"Can I get you anything?" Noah gestured to the cup beside his patient. "Water? Are you hungry?"

Harden shook his head, scowling. "I'm okay. Bit hot."

Noah stood and made his way over to the other side of the room, where there was a bowl of water. Dipping a clean rag into it, he wrung it out so it was just damp, and made his way back to the bed, placing it on Harden's forehead.

"See if that helps any." Harden grunted and closed his eyes again. "Is it painful?"

The boy lying in front of Noah didn't open his eyes. "Course it is."

Noah paused, feeling the familiar guilt spear through him. "Wanted to say I was sorry."

Harden's eyes flew open. "*Rea*-lly?" He drew out the word, as though he was enjoying the moment immensely. "What for, exactly?"

"Well . . ." Noah hesitated, "if it hadn't been for Jacob's message, it would have been me out there."

Harden grimaced. "Wish it had been."

Noah ignored the slight. "Can you tell me about the guards again?"

"I've told you. Several times. I was hit. Then I lay low and hid." Harden's face flushed. "I didn't really see the guards. Dawn was the one who . . ." He sighed. "Guess I was lucky."

Noah agreed, surprised at Harden's appreciation of the fact.

"Got any more meds?" Harden shifted, wincing as he moved the injured arm.

Noah crossed to the table at the side of the room again. "We don't have all that many left you know, after that last raid . . ."

"Just give me *something.* Hurts like a bastard." He stared at Noah. "Or am I not worth wasting the drugs on?"

Noah didn't answer, tipping a small white pill out of the bottle on the counter. Bringing it to Harden, he pressed it into his palm and offered him the glass of water. Harden struggled to come up onto the elbow of his good arm and manage the meds. In the end, Noah had to support him from behind and hold the glass of water to his lips. Noah could see how much Harden hated needing him. But when he collapsed back on the pillows, his heavy breathing told Noah how much effort taking the pill had cost.

They sat in silence for a few minutes, while Harden steadied his breathing. Noah was about to go and refill the cup of water when Harden spoke again, his voice almost a whisper. "When she fell, I knew."

Noah stared at the boy in the bed. His eyes were closed and his tone totally different.

"Knew what?"

Harden didn't answer for a long time, and when it came, his response was barely audible. "Knew she'd been hit bad. That's when I decided not to try and get to her." He paused, opening his eyes and shooting a dark look at Noah. "There was no point us both ending up dead."

"S'pose not." Noah didn't know if he'd have done any different in the situation.

"My arm was bleeding, and it hurt bad. I just . . . held my breath while they examined her. Prayed they didn't see me."

"Didn't they realise she was still—?"

"I dunno." Harden hung his head. "Seemed like they thought she was dead. Or on the way."

"Ma said her pulse was only faint when they brought her in."

"I heard them talkin'." Harden had closed his eyes again.

"What did they say?"

"Well . . . they were surprised to find a woman so deep in the woods."

"Surprised?"

"Yeah. Like . . . I don't know . . . first they thought she might have wandered away from the city . . . like she might've been a Bellator citizen . . ."

Noah frowned. "Didn't they notice her clothing?"

Harden nodded. "In the end they did . . . it confused them . . .and when she started fighting them off, like she wanted to be out here . . ." His voice faded in and out now. "They couldn't believe a woman might actually have chosen to live out here . . . in Eremus, with us *men*."

Noah touched the cloth on Harden's forehead, wincing at the heat which radiated from it. "They really hate us, don't they?"

"Not as much as I hate them . . ." Harden's words were slow, and Noah wondered if he was falling asleep. "Wait til I'm in Bellator next . . . they'll be . . . be sorry when . . ."

"Try and rest."

There was a silence for a moment, then Harden spoke once more. "Got another one a' them cloths, Madden?" Noah got up and changed the damp cloth, replacing it with a fresh one. Harden lapsed into stillness, the relief clear on his face. ". . . was brave though . . . really, really brave . . . saved my life . . ."

A few moments later he was sleeping again. Noah closed his own eyes. He had read enough of the medical book and been around his mother long enough to know a high fever was bad. If Harden got worse, he probably had an infection, and if his body couldn't fight off the infection, he would need antibiotics. Antibiotics they didn't have.

His thoughts turned back to Dawn, and the actions she'd taken to save Harden. His nemesis had been right about one thing—she'd been extremely brave. And loyal. But that was Dawn all over. He wondered where Ruth was right now. He wanted to go to her, ease her pain, but he didn't know how to. He shifted in the chair, unable to get comfortable. Eventually, he drifted off, dreaming of the kindness on Dawn's face as she'd sent him back inside the caves to Jacob, reassuring him about the reason for the meeting.

Minutes later, they'd been under attack.

When he woke, his body was stiff and cramped. He glanced at Harden, immediately knowing something was wrong. He still appeared to be asleep, but was tossing and turning, and moaning under his breath. That must have been what had woken Noah.

When he placed a tentative hand on Harden's torso, it was burning up.

Noah changed the cloth again but knew it wouldn't solve the problem. He had no choice but to go and fetch his mother. Stripping the bedclothes back from Harden's body, he made him as comfortable as he could.

"Harden?" Noah shook his arm. "Harden, can you hear me?"

Harden stirred and mumbled something, but the words were incoherent.

"Look, I'm going to get Ma. I won't leave you for long, but you're sick, and she'll know best what to do."

Hoping the words had gotten through, he went to the door and fastened the curtain back so it would remain open. Hopefully, the faint breeze from the tunnel outside would help to cool the room a little. With that done, he hurried to his own cave.

When he approached, he could hear raised voices. Flynn's. And Jacob's. He slowed up slightly, trying to work out whether his interruption would be welcome.

". . . *have* to do something . . . can't let them get away with this . . ." Jacob's tone was angry.

"But Bellator haven't been here for months . . . this is the first death we've had in a long time . . . Yes, it's tragic, but they didn't get inside, and our cover wasn't blown. It could have been a lot worse."

"That's not the point! We *have* to take action . . . I'm not going back to the old days, where they just show up out of nowhere and . . ." Jacob's voice was lost for a moment.

". . . what can we do?" Flynn was the voice of reason. "How can we . . . their forces are . . . not enough resources . . . just not strong enough."

"Maybe not yet." Jacob's tone had changed. It was harder, more determined. "But we're almost there. You know I have plans. We just need to bring them forward, that's all."

"Are we ready for that? The council needs to know . . . everyone has to be on board . . ."

"One more raid. For weapons, this time. Explosives. And reconnaissance." There was a loud scraping sound, as though Jacob had stood up, shoving his chair back. "*Then* we can plan our next move."

". . . not sure whether . . ."

The discussion sounded like it might go on all night. Noah backed up a little and deliberately stamped his feet on the tunnel floor, knowing it would alert the men who might not want to have their conversation overheard. As he hoped, they had stopped talking when he approached the cave entrance for the second time and were looking at him in surprise.

"Noah. Is something wrong?"

"I have to wake Ma."

Flynn's face creased with worry. "Is it Harden?"

Noah nodded. "He's burning up. I mean, really burning. And raving . . . talking like he's not making sense. It's not right."

From the rear section of the cave, his mother's head appeared. "Harden's worse?" She was already pulling an old sweater on and preparing to leave.

"He's got a really bad fever. I'm sorry to wake you . . . but . . ."

"'S fine." She looked at Flynn and Jacob. "You two *still* talking?"

There was an air of disapproval in her tone, which made Noah think she wasn't happy to have their leader in her cave so late at night. But there was no time to question her. He waited for her to pull on a pair of shoes and, shooting a final glance over her shoulder, they left the two men and their discussion behind and hurried to the cave where Harden lay.

When they reached him he was in the same condition. Anna persuaded him to take an additional pill, crushing it up into powder and mixing it with water to form a liquid he could swallow. Her worried gaze told Noah she wasn't certain it would work. As she took his dressing off, a look of horror swept over her features. The wound was an angry red colour and oozing something yellow which didn't smell good.

Noah watched as his mother began to clean it up. "An infection?"

She poured a saltwater solution over the wound. Harden didn't even wince. Running a swab over the area, she seemed satisfied it was clean. "He needs antibiotics. And we don't have any."

"Could his body fight it without them?"

"It's possible." She nodded. "His immune system could kick in. He's young . . . strong . . ." But as she fastened the cloth over the wound, her face paled, and she did not seem convinced.

CHAPTER TWENTY: FAITH

As Faith approached the hospital, she didn't feel particularly confident. It had taken her longer than she'd anticipated to find her way here, since she'd had to deactivate the location function on her wristclip. A bit of a tech-whiz, Diane had shown her how to do it, accessing a hidden menu with a password she had discovered by hacking into one of the professor's personal vaults. Faith found herself in awe of the older girl's rebellious actions.

Diane had also sketched a map, as promised, but the building was a lot larger than the medical centre, and she didn't know it well. Parts of it were open twenty-four hours, which meant the doors would be unlocked, but also that there would be medical staff on duty who could easily spot her.

They had waited several days to carry out their plan. Sophia had insisted on making sure they chose a night where they knew a large number of teachers were off duty. Somehow, she had managed to access the teacher's schedules so they could check the staff rotation. It meant Faith's absence was far more likely to go unnoticed and was the first time she'd ever known her friend to break the rules. Still, she'd felt on edge all day.

She headed for the Emergency Medicine department, as Diane had directed. There, at least, she could pass herself off as a patient if she had to. As the glow of the entrance lights appeared, Faith cursed. Diane had labelled a side door but warned her the best time to enter would probably be whilst the main entrance was busy and the technicians were tied up with patients. Right now, it was deserted.

Faith skirted around the side of the building, locating the door without a problem. Peering inside, Diane was right. The hallway it led into was fairly busy, even this late into the night, and she would have to time her entrance so she wasn't seen. Heading back the way she'd come, she crouched on the ground behind a wall, where she had a good view of both the main entrance and the side door, and waited.

She had two objectives. Firstly, finding a datadev where she could access Serene's records. To do this without being noticed, she needed to find an empty office, away from the areas of the hospital which were busier at night. Her second aim was to locate a stock of femgazipane so she could read more about its effects. For this, she would need access to a medical storage room or treatment room. Before she could do anything, she had to get her hands on a staff ID card which would allow her to move around the building. Since staff kept these on their person at all times, this would probably be the most challenging of all.

Faith was beginning to wonder how long she'd have to stay hidden, when a medi-pod screamed into the bay outside the emergency entrance. Inside the building, a loud speaker announced the emergency, and several technicians flooded towards the medi-pod. Wasting no time, Faith hurried to the side entrance and slipped inside, closing the door behind her as quietly as she could.

On the other side she found herself in a hallway which ran the length of the Emergency Ward. Faith hurried along it, glancing into a couple of the bays on the left as she moved. Most of them were curtained, but she spied an old woman in one of the beds, an oxygen mask covering most of her face, and a girl of around six sleeping in another.

Moving swiftly, Faith made it to the doors at the end of the hallway without meeting anyone. She had dressed carefully, borrowing a hat from Diane to help conceal her face. Keeping her head low to avoid the security cameras, she eased the doors open and crossed into the hallway beyond. It appeared to run along the back of the hospital, away from the emergency ward, and was thankfully deserted.

She took a moment to glance at the map, detouring at the next lobby to avoid a bank of elevators. Instead, she followed signs for the stairs. In an elevator, you were trapped, no matter who appeared when the doors slid open. At least with the stairs she stood a chance of darting onto a different floor if she heard someone coming. Locating the stairwell which led up the west side of the building, she stopped for a moment to glance at the detailed plan of the hospital layout mounted on the wall.

The list was mind-blowing. There were operating theatres, consultation rooms, general wards, wards for patients with heart problems, wards for children, rooms where scans and blood tests were carried out, plus several research laboratories and storage facilities. The hospital was one of the largest in Bellator, and also home to the fertility unit, where those selected to bear children came to be inseminated.

After a moment of confusion, Faith worked out how Diane's map fit with the plan on the wall. The older girl had done a decent job of sketching the layout. Faith's heartrate settled slightly as she noted the number of the floor which housed the general recovery wards. She set off up the stairs towards them.

Diane had suggested they might be a good place to get hold of a keycard. She had spent some time in the hospital herself a few years ago after a routine operation and knew recovery ward patients were not so sick that they required round-the-clock observation. This meant the staff had less to occupy them and were often less-than-alert at night. As she exited the stairwell and headed for the first of the wards, Faith hoped she was right.

The door of Ward R1 was closed. At first, Faith feared it was locked, but it gave way when she leaned against it. She peered through, holding her breath. Inside, the space was dimly lit, and there was no one in sight. Sliding the door closed, Faith crept into the space. The first bay of beds she came to was silent. Faith glanced around, spotting the office at the far end. Her heart leaped. There looked to be only a single tech in there.

As Faith crept closer, she could see the woman was asleep. The button at the top of her shirt collar was undone and she was wrapped in a warm cardigan which was definitely not part of the uniform. The datadev on the wall scrolled quietly through a twenty-four-hour news channel and on the desk at her side lay her keycard, next to a cup of coffee and a half-eaten snack bar. Diane had been right. This was a tech expecting a quiet night shift.

Faith contemplated sneaking in and taking the keycard while the woman slept but found the prospect terrifying. If the tech woke up and discovered her, she'd have nowhere to go. As she racked her brain for a different plan, a buzzer sounded and a small orange light started blinking on the datadev screen.

Anticipating trouble, Faith ducked behind a stack of chairs which stood outside the office and peered out at the technician. Moments later she jerked awake, rubbed her eyes blearily, and stared at the winking light. Then, heaving a sigh, she pushed herself to her feet and lumbered off towards the bay at the far end of the ward.

Wasting no time, Faith darted into the office and snatched the keycard. She was back in her hiding place in seconds, waiting for the tech to return. From the bay at the other end of the ward, she heard the murmur of low voices. The tech was taking care of a patient. Hoping against hope the tech would be gone for a few minutes, Faith took a chance. Slipping the keycard into her pocket, she retraced her steps and, a few seconds later, was standing in the stairwell again.

Now she could access some of the more restricted areas of the hospital. All she had to do was find an office which was abandoned for the night and activate the datadev without being seen. Feeling for the first time like the plan might actually work, she moved further up the stairs to the top floor where the map had indicated the private offices were located. Most of the upper floors required permission to gain entry. Her hands shaking, Faith held the stolen keycard up to the entry panel and heaved a sigh of relief as there was a click and the light turned green.

The hallway Faith found herself in had many doors leading off it. That made sense, she reasoned, since offices took up less space than wards. Thankful the plush carpet muffled her footsteps, she began walking along it, wondering which of the offices she should try. She tapped the wristclip on her wrist to illuminate the flashlight and shone it around her. The office to her left had a nameplate which said Doctor F. Constance. It was as good as any, Faith figured.

Taking a deep breath, she touched the keycard to the entry pad. There was no green light, no clicking sound to indicate the lock had released, nothing. Her heart pounding, Faith tried the next office along, and the other after that, with no success. Panic began to engulf her as she hurried onwards, desperate to find a door which her keycard permitted her to enter. Every minute she stood in the hallway, she risked someone finding her.

Beginning to wish she had never set foot in the hospital at all, Faith approached the two doors at the very end of the hall. They were spaced further apart than any of the previous offices, and Faith suspected the rooms behind them were larger and perhaps had a different purpose. When she reached the first one, she shone the flashlight on the sign, which said Records Room. Stepping across the hall, she repeated the process. That one read Medical Storage.

Holding her breath, Faith tried the Medical Storage room first, almost weeping with relief when she heard a magical click. Opening the door as quietly as possible, she hurried in and closed the door behind her, collapsing against it. It took her several moments to regain control of her breathing. Once her heart had stopped pounding, she tapped a finger on her wristclip to activate the flashlight function.

She appeared to be in a large storage room which contained numerous closely-packed shelves. Each one was stacked high with boxes of medicines, in a wide range of sizes and colours. Faith cursed under her breath. There were far too many to make her search a quick one.

Just inside the door, a datadev was mounted on the wall. It looked like the ones she used at the academy. Touching the screen, an icon appeared which prompted her to use her keycard to access the database. Scanning the chip on the back of the card, she held her breath.

The name Tech Jackson appeared on the screen. It had worked. Faith wondered for a moment how much trouble Tech Jackson might get into for accessing this particular datadev but reasoned the med room was probably visited regularly by most of the staff. Hopefully, this single access would go unnoticed. Scanning the options available to her, she tapped on the Meds tab, and then the search box. With a shaking hand, she typed in femgazipane, and held her breath while the datadev considered her request.

Seconds later, a page popped up, the name of the medication in bold at the top. Underneath was a list of ingredients. Faith skimmed over it. None of them meant anything to her really; the chemistry she'd been taught at school didn't really cut it when it came to cutting-edge scientific discoveries. Scanning the other options on the page, she selected the Research tab, and waited once again. When the information popped up, it was disappointingly brief.

There was a date of creation and a date of testing. Both of these were very recent, which confirmed Faith's suspicions the drug was new. The third column, Date of Approval, was blank. When Faith pressed on the tab for more information, she was greeted with a large warning which blinked in the centre of the datadev screen: Access Prohibited.

Tech Jackson was clearly not superior enough to gain anything other than basic information about the new drug.

Faith cursed. All she had established so far was femgazipane was new and access to it was severely restricted. She supposed that was suspicious, but she *had* to have more information to take back to Diane than this. Activating the camera on her wristclip, Faith captured an image of the femgazipane information, then tapped on the home screen again. This time, she tried a different tack. Selecting Patient Access, she typed in *Serene Joseph* and waited for the database to find her. Seconds later, Serene's file flashed up on the screen.

Clicking on the file, she found herself on a page of general information. At the top, next to the name, was a photograph. Serene was wearing her academy uniform and smiling. Blinking away tears, Faith cast her eyes down the rest of the page, trying to remain focused. At the bottom, there was a section with dates of medical centre and hospital visits. Next to each entry, the reason for visit was listed.

Most were simply a record of Serene's annual checkups, but as Faith's eye darted to the bottom of the list, she spotted a more recent date, which confirmed Serene had been admitted to the hospital in the last fortnight. Next to the date was a ward number, FEX1, and the code Res. *Restricted, perhaps?* The final column said 'Adverse/Allergic reaction to drug.' Faith snapped another screengrab before tapping on the Further Information button next to the entry.

As she had feared, this was the point at which Tech Jackson's access expired. Faith was taken to another page where a warning stated she'd have to request permission to see any more detailed information about this patient's treatment. But just as Faith was about to exit the page, she noticed the URL in the address bar at the top of the screen. It consisted, as they always did, of a series of seemingly-random letters and numbers, but Faith knew from her Tech lessons that programmers often used tags within the sequences.

She read it closely, running her eyes over the numbers until the patterns began to make sense. Part of the URL contained FEX1, the ward where Serene had been treated. And then, towards the end of the sequence, Faith noticed the letters FGPN. Her heart raced faster. Was this proof Serene had been given the mysterious new drug?

Returning to the home page, Faith typed in Diane's name. The results from her new search were similar, except there was no recent entry, and no issue with accessing any of Diane's information. As she closed the screen, Faith's mind was spinning. Serene had been treated here, in a ward which was probably restricted. She had probably been given femgazipane, a drug which was not actually listed as approved. And her recent medical records were extremely well-protected.

This was enough to go back to Diane with. Now all Faith had to do was retrace her steps.

She ran the sleeve of her shirt over the datadev to clear it of prints and turned to the door, the keycard clutched in her hand. Easing it open, she peered into the hallway beyond. For a moment, she was certain it was empty. She opened the door wider, ready to dodge out into the space beyond. And then, at the far end of the hallway, she heard a noise.

Someone was coming.

Chapter Twenty-One: Noah

The raid had been hastily planned. With Harden sick, the usual raiding party was already one person down, and Jacob had decided a grieving Ruth should also stay behind. Too much of a risk to have someone so vulnerable on a dangerous mission. Noah had volunteered to go in her place. His ma hadn't been happy, but when he'd suggested he might be in a position to find meds for Harden while he was there, she'd reluctantly agreed.

Most of the raiders had been sent to the city's military base to see if they might gain access to additional weapons. Eremus did not have a direct contact in Bellator's military yet, so the mission was a risky one, but they knew from previous visits the facility had external storage facilities. The hope was that, with help from one of Madeleine's contacts, they might gain access without being seen. Jacob had advised caution but insisted on the weapons' stores as key targets. Whatever he had planned, it was big.

Noah and Paulo, however, had been tasked with targeting the central hospital in Bellator. Their assignment was to return with an up-to-date sketch of its layout, specifically, the access points of the labs and storage areas at the rear of the building. Paulo had kept quiet about the reason why, but Noah had accepted the partnership with his brother, hoping it might help repair the rift in his family.

Paulo had been friendly enough so far, and Noah knew his brother didn't blame him for the argument, but he hadn't dared to bring up the subject of his mother. He was planning to tackle that on the return journey. What Noah had done was asked Paulo if he might access some of the drug storage areas in the hospital. After lecturing him about being careful, Paulo had agreed, and led him to the upper floors of the hospital where he knew there were some storage rooms.

Noah crept up a deserted stairwell behind Paulo, his palms damp with sweat. The hospital had been far more difficult to get into than the medical centre. His brother had been forced to break a window at the rear of the building, as the front entrances were too busy. Knowing they were not alone in the hospital was terrifying.

At the top of the stairs, Noah found Paulo staring at a plan of the hospital, which was mounted on the wall. They were on the fourth floor. Paulo pointed to the door which led into the hallway beyond. "This area is mostly offices and medical storage. You know what you're looking for, right?" Noah pulled Anna's crumpled list from his pocket. "Okay. Get in quickly. Try to locate the drugs, but remember to—"

"I know," Noah parroted his training instructions, "take small numbers of each box to reduce the chances of them noticing."

"Look, the raid proved they're really nervous about Eremus at the moment," Paulo warned. "If they notice large amounts of drugs going missing, it'll only get worse." Paulo pressed a keycard into his hand, on loan from Madeleine. "You'll need this."

"Thanks." Noah took the card. "Where does she get these?"

Paulo shrugged. "Mostly, we don't ask. She has a lot of contacts across the city, but she's very cagey about revealing her sources."

Noah gestured to the map. "Where are you headed?"

Paulo swept his hand across the plan, indicating the large building at the rear of the hospital site. The label on the map read Fertility Unit.

"Here." He reached into his pocket, pulling out a pencil and the plan of the city he always carried on raids. Turning it over, he began copying down the locations of the main hospital departments from the map on the wall. "It's where Bellator impregnates the women they select to have babies. And stores what they call the *seed*." He gave an exaggerated shudder. "You know, cos they can't do it the old-fashioned way . . ." he grinned, as Noah blushed, "what with there being no men here and all."

Noah looked away. "Yeah."

Seeming to recognise his discomfort, Paulo changed the subject pausing his sketch to flip the map and jab his finger at a specific point. "When we're done, I'll meet you here. There's a doorway around the side of this department store . . . corner of Atwood Street and Jackson Ave. Can you remember that?" Noah nodded. "It's pretty deep . . . whoever gets there first should be able to hide until the other one gets there. Thirty minutes, and no more, right?"

"Right."

Paulo turned the map over again and continued drawing. "Do me a favour, huh?" He didn't look up, but his tone had changed. "Be careful."

"I will."

"Go on, then." Paulo gave a pointed look at the stairwell's exit. "Off you go."

Swallowing hard, Noah opened the door in front of him and found himself alone in a darkened hallway with multiple doors. He made his way along it, straining his ears for any sign of other people. Most of the doors appeared to lead into offices, and he bypassed them. At the very end, he was about to give up when he noticed one marked Medical Storage. Glancing both ways and seeing no one, he held the keycard close to the entry panel. To his immense relief, it gave a quiet *click* and he heard the catch release. He listened, but could hear nothing, so he pushed the door open and slipped into the space beyond.

Inside he was greeted by many identical rows of shelving filled with boxes. Setting his pack down on the floor, he pulled out the list and a flashlight, and began to read. His ma had requested several different drugs, listing alternatives in case the ones she wanted weren't available. He stepped towards the first set of shelving, the flashlight still illuminating the list. As he swept its beam from the paper in his hand to the shelf, something caught his eye.

A figure, standing in the space between the shelving. Instinctively, Noah snapped the flashlight off, plunging the space into total darkness. In the silence that followed, he became aware of the other person's breathing. It was rapid, uneven, as though they were as frightened as he was. He thought about it. Someone who had been in here before he entered, without the light on. Someone who, when he had entered, had not announced their presence, as they surely would have done if they worked in the hospital.

Whoever it was didn't have permission to be here either.

Taking a chance, he snapped the flashlight back on, but kept the beam low. Knowing he should back out of the room and make a run for it, he found himself curious to know who else might be in here illegally. Slowly, he ran the beam of light over the figure, starting at the feet and working his way up. Whoever it was did not appear to be wearing a hospital uniform, but a dark pair of jeans and a hooded sweatshirt. Unlikely to be a patient either. Surely, someone here for treatment wouldn't be dressed for the outdoors in the middle of the night.

As the beam of light reached the figure's head, he heard a gasp, as though the stranger had been holding off making any noise until they were certain they'd been caught. Something told

Noah the female in front of him was young, though her hands covered her face.

He stayed where he was, not wanting to alarm her further. "I don't want to hurt you."

He was still trying to decide what to do when the figure removed her hands from her face and took a step towards him. "You?"

The voice was familiar, as his had clearly been to her. He moved around the side of the shelf, shining the flashlight closer.

A hand was thrown up in protest. "Watch it, would you?"

Something clicked in Noah's head, and he felt his brain scrambling to make sense of the situation. He had never been one to believe in fate, but, incredibly, inside the storage room with him was the same girl he'd met in the med centre. She sounded angry rather than terrified, but perhaps his earlier treatment of her had allayed any fears she had about men, or him in particular.

"Faith?"

"Noah?" Her tone mocked him.

"W-what are you doing here?"

There was a brief pause, and he almost felt her drawing herself up to her full height. "I was just leaving actually." She pulled down her hood, taking a step closer to him. "If you'd just let me pass."

For a moment, he didn't react. She stood a foot away from him, her eyes blazing. But as he glanced down at her hands, he could see they were shaking slightly.

"I mean, since the last time we ran into each other you behaved like a decent human being and let me go, I presumed . . ." she trailed off for a second, a brief flicker of panic in her eyes. "Or have you adopted the usual male traits since then? Did you get found out, the last time? Going *soft* on a woman?"

Noah didn't move. He hated the accusation, though he knew it was just what she'd been taught. Again, he found himself wanting to convince her men weren't all beasts.

And then he remembered the attack. His guilt over allowing Faith to escape, and his questions ever since. He stepped towards her, making her jump. She stumbled backwards until she hit the wall and gave a small cry before dropping her eyes to the floor.

Noah took another step. "Who did you tell?"

"What?"

"I said," Noah moved closer still, finding his height an advantage: Faith was much shorter than him, and fairly slight, "who did you tell about me? After our last meeting."

"I didn't . . . I don't understand . . ." A puzzled look crossed Faith's face as she jerked her gaze up to meet his. "I didn't tell anyone."

"You didn't report it? Tell your teachers, or the guards?"

She shook her head. "No!"

Noah hated the fact he believed her. Leaning so close they were almost nose to nose, he was very aware they were both breathing heavily.

"You must have told someone."

Regaining her confidence, Faith placed her hands on his chest and pushed him away. "Look, a couple of my friends know I was in the med centre, but I didn't tell anyone about you."

He relaxed his grip on her a little, stepping back. "If you say so."

"You don't believe me?"

He sighed. "Actually, I do."

"So . . . I can go?" Faith's glance shot to the door, her expression hopeful.

Noah gathered his thoughts. "'Fraid not."

Her face fell. "Why not? I have to get back."

"Where to?"

Her face closed off again. "Never you mind."

Rolling his eyes, he motioned to the wall where she had been hiding. "Get back there, where you were." He reached for the knife in his belt, pointing it at her. "I need you to stay here, for now."

Her face darkened, but she fell silent. Noah glanced around the room. He needed to keep her here while he searched. There were a lot of drugs in this room, and he didn't have the time to keep one eye on Faith while he searched. He had no doubt she would try to escape.

An idea struck him. Placing the knife on the shelf to his left, he unfastened his belt. It was old, but strong, a good leather one, stolen from Bellator on one of Flynn's raids a few years ago. Sliding it out from around his waist, he hoped his pants would cope without it while it served another purpose.

"W-what are you doing?" Faith's voice took on a tone he hadn't heard before.

He met her gaze, puzzled. "What do you—" She wrapped her arms around her body and shrank as far away from him as she could, without melting into the wall behind her.

He narrowed his eyes, confused. "I'm going to tie you up."

Her face blanched and he could see she was trembling. Her voice was barely a whisper. "And then what?"

"And then I can—" He stopped and looked at the belt, then back at her. "Oh . . . no! I didn't mean . . ." He felt his face flaming again. "I don't want you trying to escape while I . . ." he gestured to the shelves, ". . . get what I came for. I wasn't going to—" He gestured a hand to her body and dropped it just as quickly.

"Oh." She relaxed slightly, but her arms remained firmly folded over her chest.

"Alright then." Clearing his throat, he crept towards her again. "It's just for a little while. I can't have you getting in my way, that's all. Once I'm done, I'll let you go."

She seemed to have regained some of her earlier confidence. "Do you have to?" He stared at her. "Can't you just . . . let me go, now? I mean . . . I'm not supposed to be here either. You can't leave me tied up in here . . ."

"I won't. Like I said, once I'm done, I'll let you go." He tried to lighten the situation. "I mean, I'm not leaving a good belt behind . . . I kinda need it."

His attempt at humour fell flat. "Look, I won't give you away. I swear." She clasped her hands in front of her. "I get it. We both came here for a purpose and can't leave til we've achieved it." She ploughed on, her eyes desperate. "I had a reason for coming here too, but I've got what I needed, so if you'd just let me be on my way, then I promise I . . ."

"Sorry." He felt a surge of guilt as he looped the belt around one of the shelf's metal supports. "But I can't trust you not to raise the alarm. Stay there, I'll be done soon enough."

He reached forward, taking hold of one of her wrists. She stiffened slightly but allowed him to move her a little closer to the shelf. Before he wound the belt around her arm, he paused for a moment, staring at the strange device which circled her wrist. He ran a finger over its surface, startled when it flashed brightly. Recovering himself, he eased the clip out of the way so he could fasten her wrists to the shelving without causing her pain.

"Does that hurt?" He slid a finger in between the belt and her wrist, feeling the rapid pulse beneath it.

She shook her head but refused to meet his gaze, apparently having given up fighting him for now. Sighing, he left her, moving back to the shelves to search. Working as quickly as he could, he shone the light alternately between the list and the shelf, with an occasional flash back to Faith, to check she hadn't moved. Every time, she scowled at him.

Within ten minutes, he had managed to locate four of the drugs he needed most and stashed several boxes in his pack. He knew he could have done with more, but time was against him, and he knew what he had already would suffice, for now at least. His ma would be pleased.

Stepping back, he glanced around the rest of the room, his eyes falling on a shelf at the back which was filled with dusty old books. Thinking of his ma again, he moved towards it, running a finger along the spines of each volume.

"What do *you* need with those?"

It was the first time Faith had spoken since he had secured her to the shelf. Surprised, Noah turned to look at her. "What do you mean?"

"Can you read?" Her tone was sceptical.

"'Course I can read." He felt a surge of anger. "Ah, you think we're all ignorant, right?"

She stared at him, her eyes flashing. "Well, aren't you?"

"Ma taught me to read as soon as I was old enough. I'm perfectly capable."

"Ma?"

"My mother." He grinned. "I forgot. You don't have mothers, do you?"

"We do. We just don't . . ." She thought of Sophia's mother briefly. "We don't get so attached to one person, that's all." She rolled her eyes. "Bellator's moved on since the days of the patriarchal nuclear family. We have a better, more communal style of childrearing."

Noah raised an eyebrow. "Do you now?"

"We do." She frowned, returning to her original question, clearly curious, "What would you want with these old things, though? They're not stories . . . not interesting at all."

"That's where you're wrong." Noah selected two of the books and pulled them out from the shelves. "They're *medical* books. They give information and advice. And that is *extremely* interesting."

"How so?"

Noah slid the books inside his pack alongside the meds. "When you live where I do, there *aren't* any medical centres or hospitals. But people still get sick and injured." Faith opened her mouth to speak, but Noah held up a hand to stop her. "Enough sharing. I need to get out of here."

She frowned. "Me too."

"Alright then. We agree on something."

He set his bag on the ground and moved towards her, reaching for the belt which held her in place. This time, she didn't flinch as he stepped close. As gently as he could, he pulled the strap on the belt, releasing her wrists. She rubbed them with her fingers, and he felt a stab of guilt at the discomfort he'd put her through.

"Well, it's been . . . interesting," she said awkwardly, turning away, "but—"

"Shh!" Noah held up a finger to silence her.

Clearly annoyed, she opened her mouth to protest. He leapt towards her, attempting to cover her mouth with his hand. She struggled, trying to twist away, and he found himself forced to pull her close to him, pulling her backwards into his body in a desperate attempt to silence her. For a moment, she relaxed against him, but he had the distinct suspicion she was gearing up for a second attack.

And then, in the hallway outside, a light flickered on.

CHAPTER TWENTY-TWO: FAITH

F aith strained her ears, finding herself praying for the second time that night. When Noah had entered, she'd been sure the game was up. But even as his prisoner, she felt reassured he didn't mean to hurt her. Now, there was a fresh threat.

For a moment, there was silence, but then the sound of voices drifted towards them from somewhere close by. They were no longer alone in the upper floors of the hospital.

Noah stood behind her, his arms still holding her against his chest. They were so close that she could feel his heart beating against her shoulder blades. Flustered at their closeness, and annoyed he hadn't let go of her once she'd understood the danger, she turned her head. Abruptly, he relinquished his hold on her as she turned to face him. His eyes were wide. She felt his breath on her cheek and became aware of his lips, only millimetres away. Embarrassed, she withdrew her hand and attempted to move, but the wall was at her back and there was nowhere to go.

"What should we do?" Noah's whispered question hung in the air between them.

"We?"

"Well, yeah." He glanced over his shoulder at the exit. "Neither of us should be here, so . . ."

Faith glanced around the storage room. This had never been part of the plan. How had she ended up on the same side as a boy from Eremus? But he was right. Neither of them could afford to be caught. She considered their options. Fight, or flight. But how could they fight? The only weapon they had was Noah's knife. All the hospital staff had to do was call the guards and they'd be done for.

"Hide, I guess." She kept her voice low. "Hope they don't come in here?"

He didn't look too happy but seemed to accept her suggestion. Moving slowly, he edged around the shelf Faith had hidden behind and headed for the back of the storage room, beckoning for her to follow. Unsure of his plan, she tiptoed after him, but he'd disappeared. She froze, terror coursing through her body.

"Hey!" The hissed whisper came from somewhere at the rear of the room. Here, there were several sets of shelves in a row, all containing books. The shelving units were a different style than the open ones which contained the medicines, with solid backs to them, and as Faith approached, she realised each set was back-to-back with another. She crept closer, her heart pounding.

An arm shot out from behind the final shelf. Grasping hold of her hand, Noah hauled her behind it. The last set of shelves faced the rear wall, and the gap was narrow. Clearly, whoever had stocked the storage room had prioritised medicines, because anyone wanting to look at these books would have limited space. The dust swirling in the air indicated no one had been back there for quite some time. It was a sensible hiding place. As the voices outside grew louder, Faith shifted into a more comfortable position and then kept as still as she could.

"They're heading this way." Noah's breath was hot on her neck as he leaned in to whisper in her ear. She shivered slightly.

"Let's just pray they're not up here to get meds."

His eyes met hers and she saw her own panic mirrored in them. Managing a weak smile, she turned her eyes back to the shelf, as though she might see through it and know what was coming.

As the volume of the voices increased, they heard the sound of muffled footsteps on the carpeted floor. Faith found she was still holding onto Noah's hand, squeezing it as she braced herself for potential discovery. But the voices stopped as they got closer, the conversation pausing while a door squeaked open. There was a brief pause, and Faith heard it click as it closed.

After several moments of standing frozen, Faith relaxed her grip on Noah's hand.

Noah leaned close again, keeping his voice low. "They must have gone into one of the offices."

Faith nodded. "We can't risk leaving now, though. They could come out any minute. The corridor's long and straight, and if one of us was halfway up it when they came out, well . . ."

Noah closed his eyes and groaned. "I have to go."

"You can't." She wiped a bead of sweat off her forehead with her sleeve. "They'll catch us both."

Opening his eyes, he glared at her. "I know. But he said half an hour. It's past that already. He might not wait."

"Who?" Despite the danger, Faith found she was curious. "Your brother again?"

He glanced at her, opening his mouth to speak, then seeming to change his mind. Instead, he slumped down to sit on the floor, leaning heavily against the wall. She felt a sudden pang of sympathy at his situation. She would be in trouble if they found her, but Noah? He'd be executed.

"Guess we'll just have to wait until they leave." Faith hesitated for a moment, before seating herself next to him, being very careful to make sure her arm wasn't touching his.

They sat there for a few minutes in the darkness. The voices had gone silent, perhaps muted by the office walls, but the threat was still there. They would have to listen for the door to open and close again, wait for the footsteps to recede, before it was safe to leave.

Beside her, Noah's body was taut, his breathing rapid. It struck her how sensitive he seemed, how his reaction to their situation was so like her own. He was frightened, concerned he wouldn't get back to someone who would worry for him. Again, he seemed nothing like the callous, vicious males she had been taught about. She thought about the medical books again, wondering at his interest in them.

"So," she kept her voice low, "can everyone in Eremus read?"

For a moment, she didn't think he would respond, and then he allowed his body to relax against the wall. "Most of us, to an elementary level, at least. My ma and I are better than most."

His voice didn't contain a trace of the arrogance which might have accompanied such a statement. He seemed simply to be stating facts.

"Why's that?"

There was a slight pause before he continued, as though he were choosing his words carefully. "A lot of the people where I live . . . they don't . . . value education. Reading is just . . . well, let's just say there are other things they feel are more important."

"But not your mother?"

"No."

"So, the books you took . . . she'll read them to . . .?"

"My mother tries to take care of the people in Eremus." In the shadowy light, she felt his body shift, as though he were angling towards her. "She'll find these books very helpful."

"Your mother . . ." She paused, trying to understand. ". . . she's a medic? A doctor?"

"Well, she wanted to be . . ." Noah's voice was soft, pained almost, ". . . but she didn't get to finish her training, so . . ."

Faith sat up straighter. "Training? Where would someone in Eremus go to train?"

Beside her, Noah froze. He'd said something he regretted, and she could feel him searching for words to cover what she was sure was a mistake.

"She . . . another one of our medics in Eremus helped her to . . ." he trailed off, not seeming to know what to say.

"You're a bad liar, Noah." In the darkness, she smiled at his discomfort.

He was silent for a long time. Eventually, he shifted, as though being further away from her helped him to focus. "Actually, she started to train here in Bellator, but she left the city before she could finish. She doesn't know everything she needs to know to . . . to help people the way she wants to."

"She's from *Bellator*?" Her mind racing, Faith turned to face him. In the shadows, she could just make out his profile. "How'd she end up in Eremus then? Was she kidnapped?"

Noah laughed softly. "No. She chose to leave."

"Why?" Faith shifted closer to him and was gratified when he didn't move away. "I mean, didn't she *like* living here?" Faith tried to make sense of it. "She was studying to be a *medic*, she enjoyed the work . . . it's a privileged position so she'd have a *very* nice life . . . why would she suddenly up and leave?"

There was a long silence. Noah's body had tensed again. Faith got the feeling that, if it were light enough, his eyes would be boring into her. Eventually, he spoke. "Because of me."

It took Faith a moment to realise what Noah meant, and then she felt stupid. "You mean, she was . . ." she gestured to her stomach, even though he couldn't see her, ". . . and she . . ."

"She ran away because she was pregnant with a male child." Noah said simply. "Me."

"Oh." Faith sucked in a breath. "That was . . . brave."

Noah hesitated, and when his reply came it was tinged with surprise. "It was."

They fell silent. Faith considered the courage his mother must have shown, to run away from a life of luxury and security rather than give up her baby boy. It put Faith's own rebellious efforts into perspective, and she felt a begrudging respect for the woman who had abandoned everything to give birth to the boy who sat beside her.

Noah seemed as lost in his own thoughts as Faith. After a while, he shifted closer again.

"You didn't say why you were here." His tone was lighter now, teasing almost. "I mean . . . since I've told you my secrets, I think you owe me the same."

There was a click, and suddenly Noah's flashlight illuminated the space between them. Slowly, he swung it upwards, until she blinked as it lit her face.

"Come on then. Spill."

Wiping her damp palms on her trousers, she cleared her throat softly. "Umm . . . I was looking for something."

"Yes?"

She paused, searching for the right words, wondering how much she should tell him. She was surprised to find part of her really wanted to confide in him. She pointed at the flashlight. "Could you turn that thing off?"

There was a tiny click, and they were cloaked in darkness again. She felt herself relax. Somehow, it was easier to talk when he couldn't see her. "Okay. I was looking for information . . . which would prove something . . . something I believe . . . I *suspect* to be true."

In the shadows, she could only make out his silhouette. Somehow, he seemed larger, more solid, an almost *comforting* presence. He didn't speak but waited for her to continue.

"I attend a special school . . . The Danforth Academy. It's a great honour." She twisted her hands in her lap as she spoke, wondering how he might react to what she was telling him. "The girls who go there are selected at the age of ten. We're all chosen because of our potential."

"Potential? For what?"

"Potential to do great things for Bellator, I guess." Faith hurried on, surprised she didn't have a better response. "And, when we're at the school, we get the very best of everything. Food, living quarters, clothing, education . . . honestly, it's amazing."

He shifted slightly, and she sensed his question before he asked it. "Where do you all live before that?"

"Bellator citizens are all assigned to an area of the city from birth. Usually, the one where their biological mother came from. We don't have traditional parents . . . not like the old world. Instead, we live in larger communities where the adults share the responsibility of bringing up the young. Before I was selected for the academy, I lived in the Garner Borough. Shared accommodations . . . shared responsibility . . . everyone working together." She paused, wondering what it might be like to call someone mother, or brother.

"Isn't that . . . kind of lonely?"

"No!"

"Shh!"

"No." Faith lowered her voice again as she heard the note of panic in Noah's. "We all support one another. Every woman in Bellator has equal rights . . . is surrounded by other women . . . like I said, it's our responsibility to look out for each other."

"But you said . . ." he sounded puzzled, "you said life at the academy is amazing . . . like it was better than the life you had before . . ."

Faith frowned. Put like that, it did seem less than equal. She struggled to phrase it better, to explain herself more clearly. "No. I don't mean in monetary terms . . . I mean we all start off the same, with the same rights, and the same choices . . ."

"But some people make better ones, and end up in a better situation?"

"Um . . . sure. Yeah. I guess that's right."

He pressed his point. "And some are randomly chosen for a better life at the academy?"

"It's not random. We're chosen because we show promise."

"Because you work hard? Are stronger? Fitter?"

Faith found herself floundering under his scrutiny. They were never expressly told why they were chosen. Just that they were special and deserved the opportunity.

But Noah had moved on. "Okay. So, you're chosen. How does your school operate?"

Back on more solid ground, Faith found her voice again. "We attend the academy from the ages of ten to twenty. While we're there, like I said, we get the very best of everything, but we're also contributing to Bellator."

In the shadows, she saw him cock his head to one side and imagined him frowning. "How do you do that?"

Now was the part where she was uncertain. She had always accepted their role at Danforth as a position of privilege, but her recent questioning of the system was the reason for her presence in the hospital tonight. Still, she attempted to give the standard response.

"As students at the academy, we get to trial things. Any recent inventions, any scientific or technological developments . . . we get to use them first. Give feedback on how good they are, tell the companies that created them how they might be improved . . . that sort of thing." She slumped back against the shelving. "At least, that's what we're told."

"You think they're lying to you?"

She shrugged. "I don't know. Recently . . . we've been taking some new daily supplements, supposed to improve our health."

"Let me get this straight . . . they're *testing stuff* on you?"

"Well . . . I mean, not exactly test—"

"That's what it sounds like."

"It's supposed to be stuff which helps us. Strengthens our bones, cleanses our bodies, makes us fitter, that kind of thing."

She trailed off, not knowing why she was defending the academy.

"Is it anything to do with this?" He felt for her hand in the darkness, and when he found it, ran his hand across her wristclip as he had earlier. The display came to life, flashing up the date and time as it always did. Flustered, Faith pulled her hand away.

"They might see the light." She turned off the display before continuing. "And no."

"What is it then?"

"It's a wristclip."

"A what?"

She sighed. "A helpful device, that's all. It has a flashlight, a camera, a messaging system . . . that kind of thing."

He stiffened. "Can they track you with it?"

"They can. But I turned that function off tonight." She gestured to a series of buttons on the side of the device. "Look here. This button allows me to access the regular menus. But if I do this . . ." she toggled through to the administrator screen, "and pop in a password-"

He frowned. "Password?"

"A specific series of letters and numbers." She tapped in Anderson's code to demonstrate. "It takes me to this menu, where I can turn off whichever feature I want."

"That's a relief." Beside her, she felt him relax. "The wrist thing aside though, it does kind of sound like they're using you as test subjects for anything new they invent." Noah whistled softly. "Even if it harms you."

"Well, that's why I'm here, actually." Faith bit her lip, thinking of Serene. "A girl I know . . . not a friend really, she's a little older than me, but . . . well, she died recently." Embarrassed at the tears which filled her eyes and threatened to fall, she swallowed hard. "A couple of us . . . well we think they lied to us about the reason for her death. We figure what they told us about her didn't add up."

He leaned back against the wall, satisfied with her explanation for the first time since she'd started speaking. "And you came here tonight to try and get some answers."

She nodded, then realised he might not be able to see her. "Yes."

"And did you?"

She sighed. "Yes."

He sighed. "Well, I guess things here aren't so rosy after all." He moved even closer to her, so their arms lay alongside one another. "I'm sorry you have to go through that."

Slowly, she leaned into him, grateful when he remained where he was and didn't pull away. He was tall, and solid, and she had to admit the warmth he radiated was comforting.

"What are you going to do now that you know?" As he spoke, she could feel his chest rumble slightly beneath her head. It was an odd, but not unpleasant sensation.

"I'm not sure what we *can* do." She shuddered. "I mean, it's not like we can leave . . . and if we—"

"Ssh!" Gripping her arm, he leaned forward, straining to listen. There was the sound of a door opening again, and voices outside in the hallway. They waited, their bodies tense, for the click of it closing again.

For a moment, it seemed like they were in luck. They heard the door close, and the sound of footsteps on the carpet. But instead of fading away, they grew in volume. Then there was a clicking sound which came from much closer, and they heard someone open the door to the storage room.

"Just need to get some more braxipane, before I go back down." The voice was far too close for comfort, and the footsteps which followed it came right inside.

Seconds later, there was another click, and the entire room was flooded with light. Faith found herself staring at Noah, seeing him properly for the first time. His jade-green eyes looked right back into hers. She held still, not daring to breathe.

She couldn't remember when Noah had taken her hand again, but he was clutching it as though he'd never let go. She looked away, and found herself staring at his skin, more calloused than hers, and a small scar which ran along the back of his thumb. She wondered what had caused it.

On the other side of the shelves, the medic hummed under her breath, her casual calm totally at odds with their terror. She fumbled with the boxes, dropping one on the floor and cursing under her breath as she bent to pick it up. A moment later, Faith heard a faint tapping sound which she knew was the woman operating the datadev, presumably recording the meds she was taking. And then, as quickly as she had arrived, she left, plunging them into darkness again. As the door closed behind her, Faith felt herself sagging back against the wall.

"You okay?" Noah let go of her hand. Faith found herself immediately missing its warmth.

"Think so." She closed her eyes and stretched, trying to release the tension in her shoulders. "That wasn't much fun."

When she opened them, Noah was already standing, fumbling with something at his waist. She realised, as he pulled the buckle tight, he was putting his belt back on. As her heart rate returned to normal, she reflected on how long they had been trapped together. It seemed like hours since he had secured her to the shelves.

Finished with the belt, he turned to face her. "Think we're safe to leave now?"

She pushed herself off the wall and stood up, creeping to the edge of the shelving and peering into the space beyond. Turning back, she was startled to find him standing just behind her. When she recovered her voice, she gestured to the thin line of light along the base of the door.

"Guess we need to wait til—" As she spoke, the light went out. "There. We're as safe as we'll ever be, I guess."

They moved into the open space closer to the door. Beside her, Noah snapped on the flashlight, sweeping it across the room. He moved a few paces forward and stooped to examine something on the floor.

She moved towards him. "What is it?"

"Nothing." He stood up quickly. "Thought I saw something, that's all. Didn't want us to have . . . left any trace we were here."

"Good plan."

He pointed the flashlight in her direction again, making sure he kept it at a low level so it illuminated their faces but didn't blind her. Once again, she found herself appreciating his sensitivity.

"Will you—" She found herself curious. "Do you think your brother will still be waiting?"

"I hope so." He frowned. "If not, I . . ."

She reached for his hand instinctively. "I'm sure he'll still be there."

His eyes widened at the touch, and he pulled away. "I'd better be off. Stay—" He stopped and took a less demanding tone. "I mean . . . would you mind . . . waiting here? Give me time to get out, before you . . .?"

Stung, she took a step back. "You still don't trust me?"

He hesitated. "I want to, but—"

"That's fine." She cut him off. "You go."

For a moment he looked like he was about to protest, but eventually he closed his mouth and just nodded.

"I'll give you a couple of minutes, that's all." It came out harsher than she had intended. "I have to get back too."

"Sure. Thanks, Faith." He raised the flashlight slightly, angling it so it lit her face more clearly. "Bye then."

She looked at the floor, unwilling to let her face betray her. "Goodbye, Noah."

They stood, frozen, only a couple of feet apart. For a moment, she thought he was going to step forward and take her hand again. And then she saw his boots retreating and heard the door sliding open. When she looked up again, all she could see was Noah's hand easing it back into place.

She was alone in the dark again.

CHAPTER TWENTY-THREE: NOAH

As Noah walked back down the hallway, his entire body was trembling. He and Faith had been trapped in the storage room far longer than either of them had expected, and he had no idea what he would do if Paulo had returned to Eremus without him. Creeping back down the stairs, he heaved a sigh of relief they were deserted. When he reached the door at their base and peered through it, the corridor beyond was empty.

Hurrying across it, he dodged into the hallway opposite. It was narrow and quiet. That was the main reason he and Paulo had chosen it when they had passed this way earlier. Jogging as quickly as he could without making a noise, he reached the far end and turned right, making his way back to the rear of the building, where he and Paulo had clambered through the broken window to gain entry. The hospital was huge, and his exit was still several minutes away. He wondered if there was a closer exit, which would save him precious time.

He reached another junction in the endless maze of corridors and was about to turn the corner, when he heard voices.

"Evening Suzie! Good shift?"

A woman, presumably Suzie, groaned. "Pretty dull. Hardly any admissions. The biggest excitement was a broken window in the Curie Wing. Admin's in a real flap about it."

Noah ducked into the closest doorway, feeling the sweat trickling down his spine. A locker door banged closed, as the conversation continued.

"Probably Martell and her cronies playing basketball on their break again." The original speaker chuckled. "It'd be just like them to leave the scene of the crime."

"Serve em right if someone saw it happen and reported them." Suzie sounded grumpy, and Noah wondered if she was as eager to leave the building as he was. A door clicked open, the faint sound of the wind telling Noah it led to the outside. "See y' tomorrow, Martha."

"Bye."

Noah lurked in the doorway until Martha's footsteps retreated in the opposite direction. When it was silent again, he peered around the corner. The space beyond was empty, for now, and he hurried along until he reached the external door. It would be a much faster exit than their original point of entry, and if people in the building were aware of the broken window, leaving via the same route was probably a stupid idea.

Glancing outside once more, Noah could see no sign of Suzie, nor anyone else. It was now or never. Hauling the door open, he dodged through it, not wasting time by closing it behind him. Outside, he found himself in what he thought was a parking lot and raced across it towards what had to be the main exit. The lot was too well lit for his liking, and he still needed to figure out where he was in relation to the meeting point, but his first objective had to be to escape the grounds of the hospital and conceal himself in the darkness of the streets beyond.

The street the lot was located on was thankfully quiet, and he hurried along it in what he thought was the direction of the main street which ran along one side of the hospital. When he reached the end, he was relieved to find he was right. Consulting Paulo's map, he worked out that Atwood Street was three streets over. He raced across the busier road and took a circuitous route to his destination, hoping this would prevent him coming across any unsuspecting Bellator citizens.

Within a few minutes he was turning into Atwood Street, and from there it wasn't difficult to locate Jackson Avenue. He rounded the corner, his heart pounding. The department store was there, as Paulo had promised, and he located the doorway his brother had indicated with no problem.

It was empty.

Slumping against the wall, he stared out at the street. It was quiet, as promised, and a sensible place to meet. If he'd been on time. Glancing up, he noticed the sky to the east was growing lighter, a faint pink tinge warming the horizon above the buildings. It would have been pretty, if the thought of being in Bellator in broad daylight wasn't so terrifying.

His mind raced. What to do? Should he try and make it back to Madeleine's alone? He didn't know if she'd let him in without Paulo. He wasn't even certain of the route. Unbidden, his mind went to Faith, who had surely escaped from the storage room by now. Was she also creeping through the streets, noting the rose-coloured sky, her heart thundering in her chest? He worried what would happen to her if she were caught, and then wondered why he cared.

A noise further down the street had him tensing, and he shrank back against the wall. Reaching for the knife in his belt, he held it out with shaking hands. He didn't want to attack an innocent Bellator citizen. Chances were it wouldn't be a guard, but someone simply heading for an early shift at work. Once upon a time, he had fantasised about being able to overcome one of the *evil* Bellator citizens, but after only two visits, his viewpoint of the people who lived here had altered beyond recognition.

He would attempt to subdue whoever it was, just so he could escape. Then, he would run. Attempt to find Madeleine and pray she would help him. He leaned forward slightly, readying himself to take the approaching person by surprise.

But when the figure came into view, it was familiar.

"Noah?" Paulo's voice flooded with relief. "Where on earth —?"

Dropping the hand which held his knife, Noah flung himself at his brother. Paulo returned the embrace for a second, tightening his arms around Noah's back, but just as quickly, he tensed up and stood back.

"No time." He jabbed a finger at the sky. "This way."

He set off in the direction he'd arrived, leaving Noah to follow, struggling to keep up. It took them several minutes to retrace their steps to Madeleine's home, and she let them in with a stony face.

"You found him?" She grimaced. "Cutting it close, Paulo. Too close."

"Sorry, Madeleine." His brother was penitent. "Won't happen again."

Noah didn't dare speak but lowered his head in shame as he passed the older woman. Within minutes they were hurrying along the tunnels back to Eremus, the slamming of Madeleine's hidden door ringing in their ears.

For a while, Paulo was silent. The sound of his boots stomping up the tunnel in front of Noah filled him with trepidation. Would he ever be allowed on another raid? He was surprised to find the feeling which immediately followed this was disappointment he would never see Faith again. How had she gotten under his skin so quickly?

He remembered the warmth of her arm alongside his, echoing a position he and Ruth had lain in hundreds of times. It had felt different. Of course, it had. He knew Ruth well; Faith was a complete stranger to him. He hadn't felt relaxed in her company, and his heart had been racing the entire time. But he'd been in constant danger. His elevated heartrate was not surprising. And Faith was from Bellator, his enemy. Still, he couldn't shake the fact he felt like he'd be missing something if he never saw her again. That the racing heart was an indication of excitement, as well as fear.

He glanced up at Paulo, who had been charging along in front of him, so fast he could barely keep up. Picking up the pace even more, he had almost caught up to his brother when Paulo came to a complete stop and Noah had to put a hand on his shoulder to keep from bumping into him.

"Woah! Watch it."

Paulo spun to face him. "What happened then?"

"I got them." Noah jerked a hand at the pack on his back. "The drugs."

"Wonderful." Paulo's tone was sarcastic. He turned and began walking again, maintaining a slower pace so Noah was able to keep up. "At what cost?"

"At no cost, aside from a minor heart attack when I thought I might be trapped in the city for good." Noah attempted a smile, which quickly faded. "I'm guessing you went through a similar thing."

"Hmph."

Noah sighed. "I got trapped in a medical storage room. I managed to get hold of the meds Ma wanted . . . some of them, at least, but then we heard someone coming, and . . ."

"Wait a minute," Paulo stopped again. "*We?*"

Swallowing hard, Noah cursed his mouth for the second time that evening. "Um . . . when I got into the storage room, I wasn't exactly alone." He held out a hand at the alarm on his brother's face. "Don't worry, it wasn't anyone who'd be a threat to us."

Paulo grabbed hold of Noah's t-shirt and thrust him up against the tunnel wall, so hard he could feel the rough surface of the rock jabbing into his back.

"Oww!"

"*Everyone* in Bellator is a threat," Paulo hissed. "Anyone you met . . . unless they were one of our informants . . . *anyone,* is a concern." His eyes were blazing. "Look, I risked a lot to bring you along on these raids. A *lot*. You can't just—"

"Okay. Okay." Noah held up his hands and Paulo relaxed his hold. "I get it." He straightened his clothes as Paulo backed off. "Would you listen?"

Paulo gave a sharp nod. "Let's walk though. They'll be worried enough about us as it is."

Somehow it was easier to confide in his brother when they weren't making eye contact. They settled into a pace which was slow enough for him to speak comfortably, and he began to tell Paulo about Faith, being very careful not to reveal that this wasn't their first meeting.

"See, she wasn't supposed to be there either. That's why I figured she wasn't much of a threat." He thought about it. "She was . . . nice. Not at all what I figured a Bellator citizen to be. She goes to some fancy academy . . . but it didn't sound like all that great a place to me."

"Oh yeah?" Paulo looked interested. "Why not?"

"I don't know . . . she mentioned some tests the students had to take part in . . ."

"Aren't tests a part of any school?"

"Not those kinds of tests. More like . . . medical tests?" Noah shrugged. "It sounded . . . I don't know . . . odd. I don't think she'd be a threat. She seemed to trust me." He thought about her demonstrating how to deactivate the wristclip, feeling a little guilty for memorising the password sequence she had keyed into the device. "She was . . . nice."

"*Nice?*" Paulo regarded him, an amused expression on his face. "You mean you . . . liked her?"

Noah blushed. "Um . . . yeah, I guess so." He hurried to change the subject. "So you agree she doesn't pose a threat?"

"I guess not. I mean . . . if you're right and she wasn't supposed to be in there either." Paulo nodded at the tunnel ahead. "Almost there now. I expect there'll be a party of anxious folk waiting for us."

Sure enough, when they reached Eremus, a small knot of people was pacing the tunnel. Flynn, Ruth, and several of the other raiders enveloped them at once, relief flooding their faces.

Ruth got to him first. Noah found her arms wrapping around him tightly, as though she would never let go. "Thought you were—" she muttered into his neck.

He patted her shoulder and pulled away. On the other side of the tunnel, Flynn and Paulo were holding what looked like a pretty awkward conversation. Most of the other raiders had hurried off, tired from the raid and satisfied their companions had safely returned.

Flynn slung an arm around Noah. "Had us worried for a minute there."

Paulo turned away, scowling.

"Want something to eat?" Flynn called after him. "Anna saved you some food from dinner last night."

"I'll get something later," Paulo threw over his shoulder. "Need to see Jacob."

Flynn's face fell. Clearly the rift between the two men had yet to heal, and Noah knew Flynn's easy physical contact with him hadn't helped. Pasting on a smile, the older man turned back to Noah and Ruth. "Hungry?"

Noah nodded. "Where's ma though?" He swung the backpack off his shoulder. "Got some of the meds she wanted. For Harden."

Flynn's eyes lit up. "She'll be pleased. Actually, Harden's a little more stable. Seems like his body is trying to fight the infection, but I know your ma will be thankful she has the drugs."

"I'll take them to her if you like." Ruth held out her hand. "I'm not hungry, and keeping busy . . ." she shrugged, "well . . . it helps, you know?"

Noah swung the pack off his shoulder, unzipped it, and handed the boxes of drugs to her. "Thanks. I could do with some rest."

She smiled sadly. "No problem. I'll run it over to the med cave and try to persuade your ma to come get some rest. I don't mind sitting with Harden for a while."

"Thanks, Ruth." Flynn's smile was grateful. "Appreciate it." He glanced at the tunnel where Paulo had disappeared only moments earlier. "Let's go, Noah."

Ruth hurried off up the tunnel, the boxes of meds firmly clutched in her hands. Noah turned back to Flynn. In the dim light of the tunnel, the man who, to all intents and purposes was his father, looked old. His skin was grey and the wrinkles which had appeared around his eyes and mouth lately seemed more pronounced. Striving to ease the man's suffering, he nudged Flynn with his shoulder. "Where's that food you promised me, then? I'm starving."

Flynn looked back at him, brightening at the prospect of having someone to look after. "This way, my good sir. I'd be happy to serve your dinner." He gave an exaggerated bow and then winked. "That's how they do it in Bellator, you know."

Noah chuckled. "Is that right?"

As they returned home, Noah's mind wandered to an academy where all the students were treated like royalty. *Were* their meals served in such a way? Just how much luxury did their lives encompass? And, in the end, was all the indulgence in the world worth it, if you had to pay for it with your life?

Not knowing why he felt so concerned about a girl he hardly knew, he put his hand into the pockets of his trousers, searching until he found the item he was looking for. Drawing it out, he stared at the locket in his palm. When he'd noticed Faith had dropped it, his first instinct had been to hand it back. It must have fallen off in their struggle, and he felt responsible for her having lost it. But something had made him pocket the tiny necklace, a souvenir of their meeting.

Now all he could think about was how he'd taken something which belonged to Faith, without her permission. What would happen when she couldn't explain its absence? What if, by taking the necklace, he'd put Faith in danger?

CHAPTER TWENTY-FOUR: FAITH

Faith had made it out of the hospital without issue, racing back towards the school as the light crept across the sky, chasing her the whole way. Skirting the quad, she'd almost slipped as she swung herself up into the branches of the tree beneath her window, catching herself at the last minute and making the climb to her window in record time.

Once back inside, she felt a stinging sensation in the palm of her hand. Glancing down, she could see she'd torn her skin on the trunk of the tree as she saved herself from the fall. She clutched it to her chest to stem the bleeding, grateful to find Sophia was awake.

Her friend set to work repairing the damage. "If anyone asks, we'll say you fell and cut it during the run yesterday." Sophia frowned in concentration, her fingers deftly pulling the bandage taut as she sprayed it with the holding gel and waited a couple of seconds before letting go. "There."

"Thanks." Faith flexed her hand, marvelling at the tidy job.

Sophia leaned back, her face concerned. "What happened then?"

"Hold on a minute. I just need to . . ." Faith went to the cabinet by her bedside. "I took some photographs in the hospital . . . just need to . . ." She opened the drawer and took something out.

"What's that?"

"Portable minidrive." Faith held the tiny black disc against her wristclip and tapped the display a few times. "Diane gave it to me . . . so I could copy anything I found at the hospital onto it." When the minidrive had finished emitting a series of beeps, Faith deleted the images from her wristclip and pushed the tiny disc to the back of her drawer. "There we go. All done."

"Okay. Spill." Sophia leaned closer to her best friend. "You were back so late. I thought you weren't going to make it."

Faith thought back over her evening. "I was trapped for a while." Sophia's eyes widened. "It was okay, though. Just had to wait til the coast was clear before I got out." Settling back on the bottom of Faith's bed, Sophia waited for more. "I got in okay . . . managed to get hold of a keycard—I was lucky there." Feeling guilty, she had left it on a windowsill on her way out, hoping that Tech Jackson wouldn't get into too much trouble. "Anyway, I found a medical storage room which had a datadev with hospital records on it."

Sophia's eyes were like saucers. "Did you find something?"

Faith nodded. "We were right. Some of the information was restricted, but I found out femgazipane is a new drug, only just available, and untested."

"Untested?"

"Uh-huh. It doesn't have an approval date yet." Faith mused. "I'm guessing that means its full effects aren't known."

"But," Sophia was horrified. "They're giving that drug to *us*? *Before* it's been approved?"

"Looks like it." Faith leaned closer. "I'm fairly certain that's what they gave to Serene."

Sophia's eyebrows shot up. Faith knew her friend had been convinced Danforth had their best interests at heart. To discover they perhaps didn't, had come as a shock.

"And there's more." Faith took a deep breath. "I . . . when I was in the hospital, I met someone . . ."

Sophia looked confused. "You said nobody caught you."

"It wasn't someone who worked at the hospital. No one who would have *caught* me, so to speak."

"Then who?"

"Promise me you won't freak out?"

Sophia nodded her head solemnly.

"Well, I was searching the datadev and I heard someone coming, so I hid. When the person entered the storage room, they didn't switch on the light . . . turned on a flashlight instead. So, I figured they weren't supposed to be there either. Anyway . . . they found me." She paused, seeing Sophia's face was pale. "Remember you said you'd be calm." Faith waited until Sophia nodded before continuing. "It was a male . . . a boy . . . from Eremus."

"Erem—" Sophia appeared to choke on the word.

"But he was, I don't know . . . he wasn't . . . like they tell us." Faith struggled to explain. "Like, we talked, when we were trapped together, and—"

"Wait a minute," Sophia found her voice again, "you were trapped *together*? I thought you meant . . . you said heard someone coming and it turned out to be this Eremus boy . . . so . . ."

"It was. The *first* time I heard people in the hallway, I mean. He tied me up—"

"*Tied you up*?" Sophia sat bolt upright.

Faith held out a hand in defence. "Only so I couldn't interfere with what he was doing, and . . ."

"What *was* he doing?"

"Just taking some meds."

"So, he was stealing."

"Well . . . yes, I suppose he was . . . but he needed the meds. *They* needed them." Faith struggled to explain Noah's reasoning.

"Imagine living somewhere that didn't have a healthcare system, where you couldn't just go and get painkillers for a headache or drugs if you were sick." She wasn't sure she was doing a very convincing job. "Look, he . . . he didn't hurt me."

Sophia reached out and squeezed Faith's hand. "Well, that's something, I suppose. Was he awful?"

"*No*." Faith's answer was instant. "He only secured my hands because he figured if he let me go, I'd raise the alarm. You can't really blame him for not trusting me. Apparently, someone back in Eremus really needed the meds. That was the only reason he was in the hospital." She fell silent for a moment, watching her friend process the information.

"And you said you were stuck there . . . together?"

Faith nodded. "We heard voices and hid. They didn't catch us. When we were sure the people outside had left, we made our way out. Separately."

"And that was it?"

"Yes. Don't suppose I'll see him again."

Sophia sat back against the footboard of the bed, her expression bemused. "You sound almost *sad* about it."

Faith shrugged. "I just think . . . the academy lied to us about the treatments . . . and they deny the existence of Eremus. Maybe they're lying about everything. *Maybe* . . ." she squeezed Sophia's hand, "men aren't the horrible beasts we've been told."

"Maybe." But Sophia didn't sound convinced.

Faith stretched her tired limbs and groaned. "I need a shower before breakfast. Wake myself up. I'm going to struggle to stay awake today."

"At least you got back safely, and without being caught."

"Yeah, that's something." Faith bent to squeeze her friend's hand. "Sorry if I kept you awake worrying."

Sophia shrugged. "I'll live."

As Sophia returned the squeeze, Faith's wristclip vibrated. Glancing down, she saw Diane's name appear on the screen.

"Diane wants an update." She gestured to the device. "I can't *message* her about this. I'll have to talk to her in person."

"Leave it til you've had a shower." Sophia stood up and hauled Faith to her feet. "She can wait ten minutes. You're shattered."

Faith reactivated the location function on her wristclip before removing it and placing it on the desk. Then, she allowed Sophia to hustle her into the bathroom. Soon she was standing under a torrent of gloriously hot water, rinsing off the stress and sweat of her midnight adventure. She wondered how the people of Eremus kept clean. Surely there were no hot showers for them? Yet Noah hadn't seemed dirty, and his scent had been a pleasant, if unfamiliar one, reminding her of the outdoors, of trees and the wood burning on the fire the teachers had lit on last year's camping trip.

As she towelled off, she realised her neck was bare. Panicked, she searched through the pile of discarded clothing on the bathroom floor. Nothing.

"Dammit!" She knew she'd been wearing the necklace when she had left the academy. She must have lost it at some point during the evening. She hoped it wasn't lying somewhere in the storage room. At least on the street, or in the communal areas of the hospital there could be an explanation for its presence. She would have to wait a week and declare it lost. Although there would be a penalty, they would provide her with a new one. But if it were found in the wrong place . . .

Trying not to think about it, she took some deep breaths. Dressing quickly, she emerged from the bathroom feeling calmer, until she saw the grave expression on Sophia's face.

"You got an alert. From Anderson."

Every Danforth student was given a state-of-the-art wristclip as part of their Academy Welcome pack. It was the first of many gifts which made the programme so desirable to the Bellator citizens. The alerts could be customised to let the user know who was contacting them, but some were pre-programmed and couldn't be altered. Messages which came from inside the academy had a range of different tones: there was one which informed them of changes to their schedules, one for medical appointments, and one, which was especially shrill, that indicated a personal meeting with Principal Anderson. The girls joked it was the Call of Terror.

Faith picked up the wristclip with trepidation. To get *that* type of notification this early in the morning couldn't be good. She grimaced, as she read the most recent message. "I've got a meeting with Anderson at eight a.m."

Sophia squeaked. "That's in ten minutes!"

Faith twisted her still-wet hair into a knot on the back of her head and looped her academy scarf around her neck. Hopefully, the principal wouldn't notice the missing necklace. Checking her appearance in the mirror, she figured she looked about as dutiful as she was ever going to.

She turned to Sophia. "Can you make sure you see Diane? Pass on what I've told you?"

Sophia paled slightly at the thought of independent contact with the older girl but nodded. "Of course." She hurried to Faith's side, throwing her arms around her and hugging her tightly. "I hope it goes okay. Whatever it is . . ."

"Thanks."

It took her fewer than five minutes to reach Anderson's office, where she stood outside, trying to take in slow breaths to calm herself. She knocked on the door, hearing the sound echo through the mostly-silent building. It was still early. Most of the girls wouldn't be up yet.

For a moment, there was no response. Just as Faith raised her hand to knock again, the door burst open and she almost ran into Avery Lassiter, her knocking hand almost aiming a punch at the perfect face. The older girl's smile quickly morphed into a sneer.

"Been anywhere unusual lately, Hanlon?" She arched an eyebrow, then turned and called over her shoulder. "Professor Anderson, there's a *student* waiting out here to see you."

"Send her in."

With a sweep of her hand, Avery motioned for Faith to enter the office, one eyebrow raised. "See ya later." She bent lower, whispering in Faith's ear. "*Much* later."

With that, she turned and glided up the hallway, swaying her hips as she went. Faith sighed and took a deep breath.

She entered the office, which was only dimly lit at this time of the day. It faced the opposite direction from Faith and Sophia's room, and the sun had yet to climb high enough in the sky to light it well. Peering into the shadows, Faith saw Anderson sitting at her desk, her head bent over a datadev. The faint glow from the display cast an eerie shadow across her features. She didn't even raise her head to greet her visitor.

"Sit."

Faith lowered herself into the chair and waited. She stared at the painting which hung on the wall to the left of Anderson's desk. The date scrawled on the bottom denoted it had been painted in 2078, and was titled "The Violent Truth." It depicted a horrific scene of a woman being attacked by a group of men. There were at least seven of them in the picture, all leaning over her with leering faces. Several of them carried weapons, whips, chains, and knives, and the woman had slashes all over her arms and face.

It had always made Faith shudder just looking at it. But today she studied it with a different viewpoint. Noah was a man . . . well, a boy. But he would grow to be a man. And she couldn't imagine him for a moment as one of the men in this picture. They were painted as savages, almost animalistic, with hairy faces, sharp, bared teeth, and long fingernails which were really more like claws. Noah's skin had been as smooth as her own, and his teeth were nothing like the sharpened molars in the image. Was it *all* fictitious?

"Faith Hanlon." Anderson glanced up from her datadev, her eyes sharp. "Where were you last night?"

Her heart sinking, Faith attempted to conjure a convincing lie. "At what time?"

"At the time when you should have been resting in your dorm room, as curfew instructs," Anderson snapped.

"I . . . I umm . . ." Faith found her hand on the scarf around her neck and adjusted it awkwardly, hoping she hadn't drawn unnecessary attention to it.

"Were you, in fact, out of bed when you should have been asleep, and roaming the streets somewhere *outside* of the academy?"

Faith wondered how much Professor Anderson knew. Deciding it might not be much, she kept her response vague.

"I wasn't feeling well . . . and I couldn't sleep." She hung her head, attempting to look contrite. "I went for a walk . . . to . . . to calm myself."

Anderson frowned. "Where did you go?"

"I just did a circuit of the streets surrounding the academy. I . . . I've been feeling very . . ." she went for a version of the truth, hoping it might be more convincing, ". . . upset by what happened to Serene."

"Were you close?"

"Well, not very, but I spoke to her several times, and she was such a . . . so lovely . . . and now she's . . ." Faith buried her head in her hands, hoping she might gain some sympathy and reduce her punishment.

Anderson was quiet for a long while. So long, Faith glanced up to see what was delaying her impending sentence. She watched as Anderson tapped some information into her datadev, then swiped a hand across the screen, bringing up a holo-image which slid up into the air between them. It shimmered there, a silvery barrier between herself and the principal. Another tap, and a video began to play. Faith recognised the street at the side of the academy and saw herself appear over the top of the wall. She slid to the ground, glanced right and left, and hurried out of sight.

"These cameras were installed for the safety of students at this school." Anderson's tone was hard. "In case outsiders attempt to break in. We didn't expect to find evidence of students breaking *out*."

Faith said nothing. Her heart thundering, she prayed the hospital did not check their own surveillance equipment as carefully, or at least no connection had been made between the academy and the hospital which would cause them to look closely at the films from the previous night. For her own sake, and for Noah's.

"You put yourself in danger last night. The curfew here is for your own good, to keep you safe and ensure we know where our students are at all times, so we can protect you." Anderson leaned forward. "These recordings are routinely reviewed, but there is no way we could monitor them constantly. You're lucky we have other students in the school, more obedient, more vigilant students, who care enough to keep the rest of you safe."

Faith's mind was racing. *Other* students? Was Anderson saying . . .

"This morning I had a senior student come to my office very concerned she had woken in the night, gotten up to open her window for some fresh air, and spotted a fellow Danforth girl appearing over the wall, racing across the quad, and scaling a tree to re-enter her room, when she should have been in bed."

Avery. Faith thought back to her arrival at Anderson's office. It would be just like her to use information on fellow students to get in with the faculty. And her parting comment now made a lot more sense. Yet there was no way Avery could have known where she was going. And so far, the principal had made no mention of the hospital. If Faith stuck to her story and acted contritely, maybe she would get off with a lighter punishment.

"Of course," Anderson went on, "it was you that this student saw. She felt bound to report it to ensure your safety, to make certain you understood what you were risking by sneaking out."

"Of course." Faith lowered her head, cursing the older girl's scheming. "I'm sorry. It won't happen again."

"I'm sorry to hear you've been struggling with Serene's tragic passing." Anderson didn't look in the least bit sorry. "I will of course recommend you for a course of therapy with our counsellor, if you feel you might need it. But, you understand, there must be some sanction given, to make the severity of your actions clear to you, and also to send a message to any other student who might seek to . . . *emulate* your rash behaviour."

Faith braced herself. This was it.

"You will therefore serve no less than a fortnight's detention. One hour per day, with Professor Kemp, starting tonight. She will make sure you understand the purpose of the academy rules, and know not to breach them again." Anderson leaned back in her chair, her eyes boring into Faith's. "Do you understand?"

Faith nodded. "Yes. I do."

"Then you may go."

Faith got to her feet and turned to leave, making sure she maintained her sorry expression. Inside, she was grinning, knowing it could have been so much worse.

As she reached the door, Anderson spoke once more. "Oh, and Hanlon?" Faith looked over her shoulder at the woman who sat behind the desk, her face stern. "Any more of this, and you won't get off quite so lightly, you hear me?"

"I do." Hoping against hope the situation wasn't made worse by her necklace being found in the wrong place, Faith hurried out of the office with her head down.

CHAPTER TWENTY-FIVE: NOAH

A few days later, Noah approached the medical cave, the books he had taken from the Bellator hospital clutched under his arm. He'd been waiting for the right time to pass them on. Now that Harden was on the mend, his ma had less on her mind and would be able to appreciate them.

She'd been thrilled with the meds he'd brought back, but Paulo's story about his late return to the meeting point had worried her. Noah had played the situation down as much as he could, but she was still alarmed by the close call. He was hoping the gift of the medical texts would help persuade her he would make a skilled and capable full-time raider.

He hadn't mentioned Faith, of course. So far, the only person he had confided that information to was Paulo. Since his brother hadn't been anywhere near their cave in the days since the raid, Noah knew he didn't have to worry about him giving his secret away. But he had admitted, to himself at least, his reasons for wanting to raid had changed.

He still wanted to gain respect. But part of him wanted to see Faith again, though he didn't know why. He was intrigued by the girl he had run into twice now, and he felt strangely empty at the thought of never seeing her again.

As he approached the cave, he could hear voices. ". . . sure you're feeling up to it?"

It was his ma's voice. She must be talking to Harden, her only current patient. He couldn't hear the mumbled reply, but when his mother spoke again, she was clearly responding to someone else's comment.

"Your temperature's been normal for the past two days, so I guess if you feel strong enough . . ."

Inside the cave, Noah heard movement. Hoping Harden was on his way out, he ducked in through the door.

"Hey, Ma."

His mother turned. She looked pale, but less tired than she had been when he had left for Bellator. He knew the part she'd played in Harden's recovery had helped to ease her conscience about Dawn's death. The fact the drugs Noah had brought from the city had played a part in that made him very happy.

"Noah!" Her face curved into a smile as she handed a pile of clothing to Harden, nodding to the curtain she had rigged as a privacy screen on the other side of the cave. "You can get changed over there."

Harden clutched the clothes to his chest and hurried away, not even glancing at Noah. When he had disappeared behind it, Anna came towards him, leaning close and squeezing his arm.

"To what do I owe this pleasure?"

Noah proffered the books. "I brought you something."

Anna looked surprised but accepted the gift. As her eyes scanned the title of the first book, they widened, and she moved it aside, looking at the one underneath. "Wait, where did you —?"

"The raid. I saw them and figured they might be useful." Noah shrugged, embarrassed. "I mean, you always say you wish you knew more . . . and they're pretty old . . . Bellator seems to have a more sophisticated way of storing information now . . . but I thought at least they might tell you *something* . . ." He trailed off, uncertain.

His mother glanced up from the books. "They'll tell me a *lot*."

"Oh. So . . . they're good?"

"They're amazing." She opened the first one, scanning the list of contents. "Look, there's a section on anaesthesia," she caught his puzzled look. "That means when a patient is knocked out during a procedure—stops them from feeling pain while it's happening." She turned the pages with reverence. "Lots of modern drugs do the job, but there are older ways . . . using specific plants and herbs . . . they'd be far more accessible for us here in Eremus . . ." She looked up, her eyes filling with tears. "If I'd had some when Dawn—" She swallowed hard. Shooting a look at the screen to ensure Harden hadn't yet appeared, then stepped forward and put her arms around Noah, pulling him into a brief, tight hug. "Thank you."

"S'ok." Noah felt his face growing warm. "I'm glad they're helpful."

She stepped back. "Listen, have you finished your shift for the day?"

He nodded. "I was shifting rubble, but they've almost finished carving out the new section of tunnel. There's not much to do, so they let me off early."

"Want to hang around here for a while? I still have some work to do, but you can help me with it if you like." She leaned closer. "Harden's leaving, by the way."

Noah was relieved to have this confirmed before he agreed to stay. "Sounds good."

"It's settled, then."

Behind the screen, the rustling noises had stopped. A moment later, Harden emerged, fully dressed. He cleared his throat as he approached.

Noah regarded his bully. "How are you?"

Harden stopped a few feet away. "Better."

"That's good." Noah dropped his gaze, staring at the floor.

After a pause, Harden turned to Anna, proffering the roughly-sewn gown she insisted patients wear if they stayed any length of time in the cave. "I . . . wanted to . . . I mean, thanks for . . ."

Anna accepted the gown. "No problem. It's my job." She moved towards the rear of the cave, placing it in the basket to be washed. "You will come back if you feel worse?"

"Sure." Noah's ma shot her patient a stern look and he threw up his hands. "I *will*!"

"Alright then. I've given instructions to Flynn that you're not to be put on heavy duties for at least a week. Should give you time to recover properly." She nodded briskly and hustled into the small internal cave which opened off the main one and served as a storage room. "You take care now."

Left alone, Noah and Harden stared at one another. Noah couldn't move. He cursed inwardly, willing his feet to turn his back, to walk over to the med cabinet, anything but stand here waiting for his newly-recovered enemy to attack. He braced himself for a cutting comment which never came. Instead, Harden dropped his gaze to the floor.

Thinking back to the terror which had seized him during the raid, Noah forced himself to breathe deeply. After a few seconds, he found his feet were free. Feeling a surge of triumph, he strode to the med cabinet and busied himself sorting through the boxes on the shelves. There were not many, and the job would not be convincing for long. But at least he had taken some action.

Before he ran out of boxes, he heard Harden move. Not towards the exit. Instead, the boy came closer, until Noah could feel Harden standing directly behind him.

"Hey Madden." Harden's usual antagonistic tone was absent. "Seems like you might be more suited to raiding than I thought." Noah didn't turn but raised his head to show he was listening. "Scoring the meds, I mean."

Noah remained still, waiting to see if there was any more. For a moment there was silence, and then a shifting of feet which suggested Harden had expected a reaction.

"Guess I'll see you on shift, then." Noah heard Harden's footsteps retreating. They paused at the entrance, giving Noah another chance to respond. When he didn't, Harden continued. "If you can keep up. See y'around Madden."

Noah turned, but Harden had already disappeared from the doorway. Trying to quash the tiny ray of hope at his enemy's almost pleasant treatment, he restacked the meds. Harden would never be his best buddy, but even being ignored by him would be a vast improvement to what had gone before.

He was closing the cabinet as his mother emerged from the back. "Harden gone?" she enquired, the exaggerated innocence in her tone belying the fact she had clearly left them alone on purpose. "Did you two talk?"

Noah shot her a look. His mother was often far more perceptive than he gave her credit for. "He was . . . nicer than usual, I guess." He shrugged. "Didn't exactly thank me for getting the drugs which saved his life, but . . ."

His mother laughed. "Well, at least he was pleasant."

"That's going a little far."

"Maybe he won't be so hard on you from now on."

"Maybe."

Anna's eyes turned serious. "You know, his ma only came to see him that once. I mentioned to her at breakfast he was ready to come home, but she didn't come to collect him."

"She didn't?" Noah didn't know what to make of this information.

"No. She didn't."

Feeling awkward, Noah moved to the rear of the cave. "Want me to take care of this laundry?" He gestured to the bin which held used bandages, gowns, and towels.

She nodded. "In a minute. Sit down, Noah." She gestured to one of the chairs in the cave. As he followed her instructions, she walked to the door and glanced out into the tunnel beyond, pulling the curtain over the space before returning. Taking a seat beside him, she looked him directly in the eye. "There are things I've been wanting to tell you."

He straightened, unsure what was coming. "I'm listening."

"I wanted to explain . . . properly . . . why I didn't want you raiding. I mean, now you know I came from Bellator." She dropped her gaze. "It's silly really. But when I ran away . . . I made myself a promise. I told myself I'd never let Bellator get their hands on my son. Not ever. And . . . I think when you wanted so badly to go there . . . I was terrified if they caught you, they'd know about your origins and . . ."

She fidgeted, her fingers twisting back and forth in her lap as she spoke. "I know it doesn't make any sense. How would they even know? If you were caught, you'd be treated like any Eremus citizen. They'd execute you on the spot." She looked up again, her eyes blazing. "That's why this whole situation with Paulo is so . . . so awful. I'd obviously be just as devastated if he — but you have to understand, he was *on a raid* when I met him . . . at the age of *nine*, and . . . I don't know. I didn't have a say in him becoming a raider because he kind of already *was* one."

"Ma," Noah reached for her hand, "maybe he needs you to tell him . . . what you just told me. Then he'd understand."

Her eyes shone with tears. "You think?"

"I do."

She managed a weak smile and then wiped a hand across her forehead. "There was something else I wanted you to know about that hospital you visited with Paulo. I spent part of my medical training there. In the fertility section, in their labs . . . everyone does it. Part of the training rotation. But towards the end of my time there, I heard some things which worried me. *A lot.* So when I heard you'd been stuck there, in *that* hospital of all places . . ." She shuddered.

Noah leaned forward. "What kinds of things did you hear?"

His mother sighed. "Oh, I don't know. I didn't trust some of the more senior doctors in the hospital, especially those working in the fertility clinics. There was gossip . . . whispers about money being diverted into secret research. I asked a friend of mine to do some digging into it. She wasn't in the medical sector, she was still at the university, but she was a whizz with accessing the datadevs."

Noah thought of Faith. "What did she find?"

His ma shrugged. "Nothing, to be honest. She was convinced the information was there, but it was very well protected. And then . . . well, I was selected for reproduction, which took over my life after that." She stood up and started pacing. "They assigned me to a hospital in a different part of the city, which was a huge relief."

"Because you were—"

"Because I had concerns about the doctors at Bellator General, yes. But even in a different hospital, I became more and more anxious about the pregnancy. Once I knew the implantation had been successful, I was relieved, but then I got attached to you." She shot him a wry smile. "I started worrying you might not be female. And, well, you know the rest. You were a boy, and I was instructed to go for a deletion. I couldn't bear the thought of it, so I ran away. But I never forgot about those rumours. And when I heard you'd been stuck in Bellator General, of all places, well . . . surely you can imagine the negative feelings that brought back for me?"

A shiver ran down Noah's spine. He opened his mouth to confide in his mother about Faith, the academy, the girl who'd died, but the curtain at the entrance was jerked back and Ruth appeared. Her face was creased with worry.

"Ella had a fall . . . hurt her shoulder." Ruth's eyes darkened. "Anna . . . she can't move it."

"Where is she?" As his ma hurried to the basin of water to wash her hands, she fired questions over her shoulder. "How long ago was this? Is she alone?"

Ruth answered them in turn, practical as ever. "She's in the east tunnel. Happened about ten minutes ago. Paulo's with her."

"I'm coming now." Anna jerked her head at Noah. "Grab some of the pain meds and follow us, okay?"

He barely had time to nod his agreement before she was out the door, Ruth hot on her heels. Gathering his thoughts, he grabbed the drugs his mother wanted and hurried after the other two, praying Ella's shoulder wasn't seriously hurt.

CHAPTER TWENTY-SIX: FAITH

As Faith left the dining room that evening, it was already dusk. The Herstory classroom seemed different, more intimidating without the other students to command Professor Kemp's attention. Her teacher was already there, the small, crumb-filled plate in front of her suggesting she'd had to cut dinner short. Her grumpy expression supported this theory, and Faith took a deep breath as she entered.

"Come in." Professor Kemp looked up, her grey eyes serious behind the wire-rimmed glasses. Faith had begun walking towards her usual seat when her teacher spoke again. "Sit up front, please." Reversing awkwardly, Faith slid into the seat Kemp had indicated. "I have to say I was . . . disappointed to hear you'd received these detentions, Faith." The professor's frown deepened. "Disappointed, but not surprised, sadly."

Faith stared at the floor, ashamed to engage with the teacher who, though intimidating, she had always respected.

"Look at me." The command was non-negotiable. Faith raised her eyes to meet her teacher's. "That's better. Now listen. This *has* to stop. You've always found it a little difficult to follow the rules, but this time your actions were rash and dangerous. You could have gotten yourself into serious trouble, sneaking out like that."

"I'm sorry." Faith felt her face growing warm but forced herself to go on. "I really am. I know I was breaking the rules, but I still don't see how I was putting myself in *danger*." She hurried on before she could lose her nerve. "I mean . . . Bellator's a safe city. You're always telling us how lucky we are to live here, where we're so well protected. We all know Eremus no longer exists . . ." she watched her teacher's face closely, ". . . and without that threat, *surely* there's nothing to fear."

To her credit, Kemp's eyes hardly flickered. "I know what you're saying, Faith, but there are dangers everywhere we go. We don't always see them, but . . ." she shrugged, "they're there. You can never be too careful." She shook her head and tapped a button on the datadev which sat in front of her. "Look, I have work to do. You're required to complete an assignment in each one of these detention periods. I've already sent you the one for today. You'll be free to go in an hour . . . as long as it's finished."

Kemp turned back to her datadev and Faith knew she'd been dismissed. Kemp swiped a finger over the screen until she found the right document. Once she had, she bent over the screen and began to read, an expression of intense concentration on her face. Faith mirrored her actions, logging into her own datadev. Navigating to her messages, she hit the latest one from Kemp and read the title.

"Write a five-hundred-word essay on the establishment of the Danforth Academy."

Faith groaned inwardly. She already knew a fair amount on the subject, and it wasn't exactly thrilling stuff. Begrudgingly, she opened a blank document and copied the assignment title across. Once done, she sectioned off her page into the various topics she would need to cover, filling in the information she already knew and highlighting what she needed to research. Clicking the Seek button, she brought up the school's website to begin.

As the page loaded, the email icon flashed in the corner of her screen, and she tapped on it to find a second message from the professor sitting at the front of the room. Glancing up in surprise, she could only see the top of Kemp's head. Clearly, whatever she had sent didn't require them to have a conversation. Faith looked back at the screen, tapping on the message to read it, hoping fervently it didn't contain a second assignment already.

It didn't. Instead, Kemp had sent her a link to an article written by a woman called Felicia Danner. Faith presumed it was aimed at helping her with her research, and was grateful for the support, however quietly it was offered. Opening it immediately, she began to read.

Written in 2102 and titled "Forging a Healthier Future: Danforth Academy Finally Opens Its Doors," the article focused on a delay in the opening of the school, which Faith had never heard about. Interested despite herself, she scanned the text, wondering what problem could have almost prevented Danforth from opening in the first place.

Her eyes were drawn to a paragraph around halfway down the page.

Plagued by difficulties from its earliest days, the Danforth Academy has struggled to get the go-ahead. Some citizens have questioned the cost of the academy's build and upkeep, its exclusivity, and the cutting-edge education techniques insisted on by its founder, Health Secretary Abigail Danforth. The outspoken leader has often courted controversy, most notably last year when she fired Madeleine Leigh, the distinguished biochemist. Leigh had been heading a committee advising the government on its medical practices and procedures. Her sudden dismissal provoked many questions which Danforth brushed off with her trademark nonchalance, claiming they'd simply had a "difference of opinion." All in all, the controversial new school and its creator have had more than their fair share of troubles.

Faith jumped to her research document, copying the key points across to the appropriate sections of her essay. So, Danforth had been Health Secretary before she had become Chancellor in 2104. Interesting. It made sense the school had been named after its creator, and the woman's interest in modern education techniques was no secret.

Faith read on.

Danforth has stated that the selective school will only admit the most promising young citizens. Along with receiving the best education in the province, the chosen few will have the privilege of using cutting-edge technology, unavailable to anyone else in the city. The new academy divides the Bellator population: many are excited about the prospects it might offer our younger citizens, while some are concerned about the consequences of the progressive techniques used by such an establishment.

Faith stopped again to make additional notes. It was interesting to discover there had been objections to the academy in the first place. Faith hadn't realised this, and in the light of her recent discoveries, it seemed important. She skimmed the rest of the page, her eyes settling on an entry at the bottom, which teased a different story.

Special Feature: Abigail Danforth

As Danforth Academy opens its doors, we take a closer look at the formidable woman behind the high-tech educational establishment.

Intrigued, Faith clicked the link. The article was lengthy, but fascinating.

Destined for greatness: does our beloved Health Secretary truly have the best interests of Bellator at heart?

Abigail Danforth is a bit of an enigma. Born in 2065, at a time when the disastrous effects of the Vardicus virus were still being felt, little is known about her childhood. It must have been tumultuous, though. Any female growing up in the ruins of the old world cannot have had an easy time. As a dwindling number of men struggled to retain their command over women, resorting to more and more heinous acts of violence, many young women found life a struggle.

But Danforth rose like a phoenix from the ashes of the outdated society. Showing extreme promise in school, especially in the sciences, she eventually went on to train as a bioengineer. In 2087, she accepted a job at the prestigious BellaLab Corp, where her ground-breaking innovations brought her instant success.

At the tender age of twenty, she became one of the founding members of the Women's Independent Party. It was at this time she first began her intensive involvement with the government of Bellator.

Her reaction to the great Barbarian Revolt of 2094 brought her the most renown. After the capture of several vicious male specimens who had run riot across the city for several hours, she put forward a solution which would both protect Bellator citizens and modernise its reproductive systems. Her Seed Bank concept, enabling Bellator to safely freeze sufficient male seed to procreate healthily for generations to come, was widely accepted as the perfect solution to a society without male citizens. When it was successfully implemented in 2097, Danforth became the obvious choice for Health Secretary.

Since then, there has been no stopping her. From imposing increasingly severe sanctions on the drudge population to banning certain pre-Vardicus texts, Danforth's quest to revolutionise the city's systems has often been compared to a juggernaut. And some citizens have begun to question her constant drive for change. Scientist and prominent member of the Bellator Justice Association, Madeleine Leigh, who worked alongside Danforth at BellaLab Corp for several years prior to being dismissed from her post, has her doubts about Danforth's motives. "There's no question Abigail is a driven, brilliant woman," Leigh told us, "but many of her ideas have dubious origins, and her somewhat radical plans for the future of Bellator, should she rise to the position of chancellor, are of great concern."

In a recent press conference, Danforth hinted she has her eyes on the leadership position. Many in the city would welcome her. I spoke to Joanna Anderson, recently appointed principal of Danforth Academy. "Abigail Danforth is a formidable woman who wants the best for our city," she told us. "We shouldn't be questioning her pursuit of excellence; we should be embracing it."

But is Leigh right to be worried? When I questioned her, Danforth was quick to reassure me that the women of Bellator are of the utmost importance to her. She went to great pains to stress the importance of protecting our beloved city in the future. "Bellator can't bury its head in the sand. There will always be new challenges. We must not be afraid to embrace new concepts, which might seem radical, but will ultimately empower us to anticipate and overcome any future trials."

Reassuring words from a confident leader? Or something more sinister? We'll have to wait and see. Whatever happens, Leigh assures us the BJA will be on the sidelines, watching Danforth and taking action—

A noise made Faith glance up. Standing in the doorway, her face stony, was Anderson. Behind her stood Professor Mitchell, Faith's technology teacher. At the front of the room, Kemp had also noticed the intrusion.

"Good evening, ladies. Did you need something?" She looked almost shaken. "I can assure you this young woman is hard at work on her assignment for the evening." She glared at Faith as though daring her to disagree. "She knows she has to stay until it's complete."

Anderson gave a sharp nod at Kemp. "I'm afraid I need a *word* with our detainee."

As the principal moved towards her, Faith glanced down at her screen, ready to toggle back to her research document. She had to at least look like she was making progress with her assignment. Instead of the Danforth article, her screen already displayed her notes for the essay. Surprised, she tapped at the base of her screen, searching for the article, but it had disappeared.

Anderson's sudden arrival must have caused her to inadvertently tap one of the keys on the datadev and shut it down. Shrugging internally, she turned to face the more pressing issue. Her principal was now bearing down on her with a furious look on her face. Faith attempted to look contrite.

"Good evening, Principal." She gestured to her screen, which had the beginnings of a half-decent essay at least, considering she had only arrived in detention fifteen minutes earlier. "I've made a good start on today's assignment. You're welcome to read over what I have so far."

Anderson didn't even glance at the screen. Instead, she held out her hand. "Wristclip."

Despite the fact that she'd already deleted the incriminating images, Faith's heart sank as she removed the device and placed it into Anderson's hand. The principal swept back to the front of the room and handed it to Professor Mitchell who used a slender cable to connect the device to the datadev on Kemp's desk, gesturing to the other teacher to move aside. Kemp reluctantly complied, and within seconds, a holo shimmered in the air above them, displaying a large, technicolour version of Faith's home screen.

As the professor began to study the information, a rush of heat came over Faith. Had she not followed Diane's advice, she would have really been in trouble right now. She couldn't believe how naïve she had been. Those screenshots sitting there innocently on the tiny computer had been little grenades waiting to blow up in her face.

Professor Mitchell did not waste time. Opening the settings tab, she inputted an admin password and began navigating through a series of files Faith had never seen before. A number of boxes popped up one after another, as the professor's fingers flew over the keys at lightning speed. Faith watched, her hands shaking, as various commands appeared and disappeared with alarming speed. She only managed to read a few: recall . . . restore . . . deleted . . . but it was enough to turn her body cold.

Suddenly, the wristclip let out a series of beeps and the words 'data restored' hovered in the air. Mitchell tapped the datadev once more and Faith's home screen reappeared.

"It's done." Nodding at Anderson, Mitchell vacated the chair.

Wasting no time, the principal sat down and began jabbing a finger at the various command buttons on the screen. First, Faith's email inbox hovered in the air, the list of messages separating her from the two teachers. It was difficult to read it backwards, but once she worked it out, she was puzzled to see the second email from Professor Kemp had vanished. It crossed her mind Kemp might have deleted it, worried she'd be in trouble with Anderson for giving Faith extra help. But this wasn't the time to wonder.

Finding nothing suspicious within the email folder, Anderson moved on, navigating in and out of the various applications: reminders, homework schedules, the music player, the teleapp. With every move, her finger crept closer to the image folder. Faith cringed, unable to take her eyes off the holo.

She was trying to steady her breathing when Anderson hit the right button. Immediately, the holoscreen was filled with numerous pictures. Faith's heart sank. Somehow, Mitchell had recovered them.

It didn't take long, after that. The incriminating images were among the last she had taken, and within seconds the first one was floating in the air in front of them, condemning her. Serene's name, the information from her private medical file, and the data on the femgazipane record hung in the air, taunting her.

Faith clenched her fists by her side. There would be no lenient punishment this time.

The silence which followed seemed to last for an age. Nobody moved, and Faith was unable to make out the expressions on her teachers' faces for the barrier of light which screened them from her. But she knew they were less-than-happy.

Anderson tapped a button. The holoscreen disintegrated. Faith was left staring at the principal, whose eyes were blazing with anger.

"You lied to me, Hanlon." Faith stared at the carpet. "Stand up."

At first, Faith found herself unable to move. Fear seemed to have commandeered her limbs, imprisoning them. When the command was repeated though, in a sharp, unrelenting tone, she had no option but to follow it.

"Stand. Up." Faith did as she was told. "You're coming with me." Anderson yanked the wristclip out of the datadev on the desk and pocketed it. "And you won't be needing this."

As Faith walked towards her, she glanced down at Kemp. The teacher had a strange expression on her face, one of resignation and something else. Fear, perhaps? What did the professor know that she didn't? And was she, at least partly, on Faith's side?

As their eyes met though, her teacher's face was cloaked with disappointment. Feeling abandoned, Faith turned to follow her principal into the hallway, her legs trembling.

"**W**ait up!"

Hearing Ruth's voice behind him, Noah slowed his pace. They were both heading for the canteen, where Jacob had called an urgent meeting for the raiders. He'd been most insistent that everyone be there, but no one was sure why.

As he waited for his friend to catch up to him, Noah scrutinised her closely. She had a little more colour in her cheeks, but he was sure she was thinner than she had been a few weeks ago. The strain caused by Dawn's death had not been helped by Ella's injury the previous evening, and Noah was concerned.

"Hey." Noah took her hand and squeezed it for a second. "How's she doing?"

"She'll live." Ruth extricated her hand, motioning for him to keep walking. "Anna promised she'd stay with her for now. She's trying to brew a natural painkiller . . . using some plants and herbs from the woods."

"That's good."

Noah yawned. It had been a long night, with not much in the way of sleep. When his ma had reached Ella, she'd quickly realised the damage to her shoulder was quite serious. Enlisting the help of Paulo and Flynn, she had brought Ella back to the medcave on a makeshift stretcher. Her patient had screamed the entire way.

Once there, Anna had gone to work immediately. Grasping a pair of scissors, she had cut away Ella's shirt, exposing her upper body. There was an odd bulge at the front of her shoulder, just underneath the strap of her bra. They had all looked away, either out of respect for her privacy or squeamishness, though Ella's agonised moans suggested she didn't care who was looking at her.

"It's dislocated." His ma had shaken her head, before sending Noah to fetch what painkillers they had.

Working quickly, she had persuaded a distraught Ella to swallow a pill and done her best to cool the injured area with a wet cloth. Ruth had stayed by Ella's side, stroking her hair and whispering words of comfort into her ear. Then they'd had to wait for the painkiller to start working. It took an age, but eventually Ella's groans had faded to whimpers.

Anna had nodded brusquely. "I'm afraid that's the best we can do."

Noah remembered his ma beckoning to Flynn and Paulo, leaning close to whisper instructions into their ears. He had always marvelled at his mother's ability to take charge in difficult situations, and this was no different. Between them, her assistants had held Ella still, Flynn keeping her legs in a vice-like grip, while Paulo held down her good shoulder.

"She's going to scream," Anna warned, as she took up her own position on Ella's injured side.

The room had felt unnaturally hot. Without a role in the procedure, Noah had watched his ma rotate Ella's shoulder, manipulating it in a number of different directions. She'd been right. The painkiller Ella had been given clearly didn't cut it, and she howled. The process had taken an age, and Ella's cries had become animalistic, reminding Noah of the rabbits and squirrels which got caught in their traps, often badly injured, but still alive.

Instinctively, he'd moved closer to Ruth, who had refused to let go of Ella's hand, yet looked horror-struck by her sister's pain. Paulo and Flynn had fought to keep the patient steady as his ma continued to put pressure on the joint. Finally, she was satisfied the shoulder had shifted back into place. Gently placing Ella's arm across her body, she had beckoned to Noah.

"Hold the arm in place while I get her a sling."

Noah had obeyed. Ella had fallen silent, and the group of people around her were similarly subdued. Anna had made quick work of securing Ella's arm in the sling and sent the rest of them away to rest, aside from Ruth, who had insisted on staying. Anna had a second cot in the cave for this specific purpose, and Ruth had decided to try and sleep there.

The three men had made their way outside together, exhausted by the intense experience. Noah was grateful the emergency had united them, temporarily at least. They had hesitated in the doorway of the cave, an awkwardness hanging over them.

"Thanks for your help there," Flynn had gone to slap his nephew on the shoulder, then thought better of it. His arm hung in the air between them for a second, before he let it drop to his side again.

"No problem." Paulo's expression had been guarded. "Ella needed me."

"We *all* needed you." Flynn had shifted from one foot to the other. "Couldn't have done it without you."

Paulo had shrugged. For a moment, it had seemed like he would say something else, but instead he gave a quick nod and turned to go, with a quick 'See y' tomorrow' thrown over his shoulder.

Noah and Flynn had walked back together, a little disappointed. Noah had worried he might not sleep, but as soon as his head hit the pillow, he had passed out. When Flynn had woken him this morning with the news of Jacob's meeting, he still felt tired.

Now, Ruth turned to him as they walked along. "Your ma was a marvel last night."

Noah allowed himself a smile of pride. "She's pretty good, isn't she?"

"Not sure what we'd do without her." Ruth scrutinised him. "She was telling me you brought her some books . . . from the raid?"

"Yeah." He shrugged. "I figured they might have some helpful information . . . stuff she doesn't already know, of course."

"They're good, she said." Ruth's tone was earnest. "I think she was up most of the night reading after I fell asleep. She hated that she didn't have any anaesthetic for Ella last night." She paused. "You know, the drugs they have in Bellator that knock you out before an operation?"

Noah made a face at her. "I know what anaesthetic is."

"Okay. Okay." Ruth held up her hands. "Guess you're not the medic's son for nothing. But really. She said if she could've fixed Ella's shoulder without pain, she'd've felt a whole lot better."

"I think we'd all have felt a lot better." Noah grinned despite himself, giving an exaggerated shudder as he remembered Ella's screams.

"Well, yeah," Ruth elbowed him. "But I think *Ella* had the worst of it."

"I know." Noah admitted. "But it was a pretty stressful night for all involved."

"It was." Ruth agreed. "Anyway, your ma went out to look for the plants she needed this morning. Figures she'll be able to use them to make a solution that might have a similar effect."

"Oh yeah?"

"Isn't it brilliant? I mean . . . just think of how much better off Ella would've been if Anna'd been able to put her arm back while she was *asleep*."

"Definitely," Noah agreed. "Though I'm going to try very hard *not* to fall over . . . you know, avoid needing any medical intervention at all."

"Good plan." Ruth was laughing as they approached the canteen door. "How're things with Paulo? Looked like he was acting a little more friendly last night."

"Not sure." Noah shrugged. "He was fine during the emergency. But afterwards, when Flynn tried to talk to him . . ."

"No good, huh?"

"He was a *little* nicer, maybe. But he didn't come home with us."

"I'm sorry." This time Ruth was the one reaching for his hand. She squeezed it briefly before letting go.

They entered the canteen and hurried inside, where a group of raiders had gathered in one corner. Jacob had yet to arrive, but Paulo was already there, speaking to Dan Clark, and Noah spotted Harden with his friend, Sil, and some of the other, more junior, raiders. Noah tensed, but as his eyes met Harden's, the other boy's head inclined slightly, in a movement which might have been construed as a nod. Noah stared at the bully, but he had already looked away. Still, as he and Ruth approached, there were no sly looks or cruel jibes sent his way.

They took a couple of seats on the edge of the group and settled to wait for their leader. For a while, they were silent. Noah realised how long it had been since he had properly spent any time with his friend. With the raids, the attack, the rift with Paulo, and Dawn's death, there had been too much going on. He'd missed his friend's company and quiet support.

He hadn't even told her about the last raid. Not properly, anyway. Wondering how she would react to him meeting, talking to, and actually *liking* a Bellator citizen, he was about to confide in her about Faith when she spoke again.

"What do you think the meeting's about?" Ruth glanced around at the assembled group. "Looks like he called every raider past and present."

Noah's gaze followed hers. It was definitely a big group. "Guess he wants to talk about his next move. When we were sent on the last raid, he hinted at something. Said we were there to scope things out, gather more weapons . . . ready to take action . . . s'pose this must be it."

"About time." Ruth's expression was hard. "Those Bellator bastards need teaching a lesson."

Noah recoiled at the bitterness in her voice. While he understood her hatred of the attackers who had been responsible for Dawn's death, he had never heard her speak with such loathing of the *ordinary* citizens of Bellator. How could he tell her about Faith now?

He was still struggling to find the words when Jacob arrived, striding to the front of their group and up onto the podium, where he turned to face them. He looked refreshed and determined, unlike Flynn who stood beside him, his face worn from lack of sleep. The raiders fell silent as they turned to listen to their leader.

"Morning, everyone." Jacob beamed at them, his smile a touch too wide for Noah's liking. He resembled the crocodile in one of the books his ma had used to read to him as a child. "I come bearing good news."

The raiders exchanged grins and nods of appreciation at Jacob's positive tone.

"Look, you're all aware of how angered I was by the recent attack on our people." Noah felt Ruth stiffen next to him as Jacob shot her a look of sympathy. "We lost a valuable member of our community for the first time in many years, and," he shifted his gaze to Harden, "it could have been even worse. Clearly, it has shaken our community. But things here have changed. In the old days, we would have doubled the restrictions in our community, staying inside almost permanently while we mourned our losses, making *certain* our camp was concealed from the forces Bellator sends to hunt us down."

He paused, looking around at the crowd of assembled Eremus citizens. Raising a hand, he jabbed a finger into the air in front of him as he spat his next words at them.

"No more!" Several of the raiders jumped at his sharp tone. "No more, I say. For years, I've been searching for a way we might exact some revenge on the Bellator people, to gain ground in our struggle for men to be recognised once more. They attempt to deny our existence . . . paint us as violent, vicious creatures who don't deserve to live . . . and I for one will no longer stand for it.

"For years, people have told me there's no way we can fight them, no way to even the imbalance of power and resources. That in any fight, Eremus wouldn't stand a chance against the mighty Bellator. And that may be true." Ever the showman, he looked around at his captive audience, lowering his voice so they had to strain forward to listen. "But what if we changed our plan? What if . . . we chose to attack cleverly, stealthily?"

Around Noah, the raiders began murmuring, exchanging glances with one another as they tried to work out what their leader meant. Above them, Jacob continued the performance.

"I've spent the past few years gathering weapons and storing them in one of the caves far below the surface. Few people know the extent of this cache, but little-by-little, every time I sent raiders into the city, I was collecting. Stealing ammunition, guns, grenades, explosives. Bringing them back here not for immediate use, but to keep for a time when we might need a surplus of weapons." Another dramatic pause. "And now, that day has come."

Around them, Noah could feel the excitement building. Jacob had always been a great speechmaker, and this was one of his finest. But while Paulo, Harden, and the younger raiders looked eager, Flynn's face was troubled. Noah felt a dread creep over him. What exactly did Jacob want them to do?

"While we cannot beat them in a direct, hand-to-hand battle, it has been my intention for many years now to target and destroy various major sites in the city. Sites which are *vital* to Bellator's survival." Jacob went on, building to a dramatic conclusion. "The first of these hits will take place on our next raid. That's the reason you're here today." He paused, looking around. "So I ask you: what does Bellator need most to ensure the survival of its people?"

Jacob stared around at the assembled group, his eyes flaming. For a moment, there was a confused silence, but then people started to stir, to think about the question he had posed.

"Their government buildings?" one young raider suggested.

"Schools?" This came from somewhere at the back.

"Their defence system?" Harden called.

Beside him, Ruth started forward, her hand raised. "Hospitals?"

On the podium, Jacob thrust a hand towards Ruth. "Almost." He turned to Paulo, who stood at his side. "Want to come up and tell them about your plan?"

Noah tensed. What part did Paulo play in all this? He glanced at Flynn, who looked just as confused. Smoothing his hands down the front of his jeans, Paulo stepped onto the podium beside Jacob. He cleared his throat and began to speak, his voice deep and steady.

"I've spent a long time thinking how we could achieve more from our raids. More than stealing a handful of supplies which allow us to eke out a difficult existence here, in hiding. Jacob's right. We can't just blast in there and fight. The guards would defeat us in minutes. But there is another way we can get at them." Noah's brother looked around the room, his eyes meeting every one of the other raiders standing around him. It was a move Noah had observed Jacob pull off many times. As he continued, Noah wondered if Paulo had been taking lessons from their leader.

"Bellator ensures the continuation of their female community through a strict breeding process, where healthy females are selected to be impregnated and reproduce at the optimum stage of their lives. Aside from those bred specifically to be drudges, all male foetuses are eliminated. The females are brought into the care of the Bellator authorities, allowing them to continue their virtually single-gender society. *This* is where their weakness lies."

Jacob nodded approvingly, stepping forward to deliver the final blow. "If we can destroy the building which they use to store the frozen male seed, they will *no longer be able to* procreate in this way."

"Without the seed bank, they can't reproduce." Paulo clarified. "They'll die out."

"Which will force them to turn to us for help," Jacob finished, with a satisfied nod at the whispers which rose among the raiders.

"The seed is stored at the back of the Bellator Hospital, in what they call the fertility unit." Noah had to force himself not to react as Paulo mentioned the location. "We'll go into the city at night, as we would usually. Noah and I visited the hospital on our last raid, and I was able to get a good sense of its layout. The plan is to plant a large number of explosives around the perimeter . . . blow it sky high. Then we get out. Fast."

"There'll be no more risk than on a usual raid." Jacob reassured, glancing around at the concerned faces of some of the raiders. Then his voice turned almost gleeful. "And they won't know what hit them."

"We're planning to carry out the raid in two weeks' time." Paulo took over again, warming to his theme. "Until then, we'll all attend daily training sessions. Rehearse our positions. Make sure we can all play our part. For this to be a success, it's vital we work as a team."

"Normal routine for today, but we begin our preparations tomorrow." Jacob said. "Meet us at seven a.m. sharp in the training room."

Stepping down from the podium, he motioned for Paulo to follow him. Flynn was still standing off to one side with their neighbour Dan, his face creased with concern. He clearly hadn't known about the big plan in advance. Noah wondered why.

"Coming?" Ruth elbowed him.

"Sure."

"Clever man, your brother." They began to wander out of the canteen together. "It's a bold move."

Noah nodded. "It is."

"If we can pull it off though, it'll have a massive impact." She nodded approvingly. "First time we have a plan that might actually *work*. I mean . . . to improve our position."

"Yeah," Noah agreed.

But as he walked to the tunnels to start his shift, he could only think of Faith, and the damage their explosions could do to anyone who happened to be in the hospital at the wrong time.

CHAPTER TWENTY-EIGHT: FAITH

There were no windows in the room Anderson had locked her in. Faith had a vague awareness of time passing because the light turned on and off automatically, marking what she could only assume was day and night, but that was all.

She'd been here for ten days. Once she'd realised she wasn't going to get out any time soon, she'd tried to keep count. Every time the light flicked on in the morning, she scratched a line in the wall behind her cot. After that, she tried to keep herself occupied, dreading the moment the illumination abandoned her. When she was plunged into darkness, she counted the minutes til she could escape it again.

She had little in the way of furniture: just a small cot, a desk, and a chair. One corner of the room was walled off, and in the tiny space beyond was a toilet and a small basin. She was thankful for the basic bathroom access, but wished she had a shower too.

She was hungry. Very hungry. While Anderson's punishment didn't stoop as far as to starve her, she was definitely being denied access to the food she was used to. She received only two meals a day, and they, like her accommodation, were small and basic. Soon after the light came on, a drudge would unlock the door to her room and bring in a tray, picking up the one from the previous night before leaving again.

The same process was repeated around an hour before the lights went off again, allowing her time to eat what there was of her meal before she could no longer see what was on her plate. Other than the drudges, she had seen no one. She'd tried speaking to them. Multiple times. Each time the keycard beeped to unlock the door, she readied herself to approach them. But despite trying a number of different approaches: demanding answers, cajoling, grasping their hands, and even, once, crying, none of them had responded to her.

She had been hoping one day Arden would arrive with her food, but, so far, she had only seen the same two drudges. Neither of them had any interest in speaking to her. In fact, they'd both backed away in alarm when she had stood up and moved towards them.

She couldn't blame them though. She hadn't showered since Anderson had brought her here. The few attempts she'd had at washing in the small basin had not really improved the situation. And she was very aware of the trouble the drudges would be in if they were caught speaking to her. Still, she wouldn't stop trying.

She glanced down at her bare arm. Anderson had not returned her wristclip, and she had no way of contacting Sophia or Diane, no idea what was happening in the outside world. All the time, she worried. If Anderson knew *she'd* been in the hospital, the principal might have them check the footage from the cameras there. If they followed up on her visit, they would no doubt spot Noah in the footage. The thought of getting him into trouble too, plagued her.

She'd had a lot of time to think since she'd been in here. To consider the lies the Danforth Academy told its students. In fact, the lies Bellator told its *citizens*. There were no two ways about it. Danforth students were not selected for their intelligence and promise. They weren't at the school to provide feedback on Bellator's newest inventions and technology. Instead, they were apparently chosen at random: a group of children who the city's scientists could test their newest drugs on without fear of reprisal. Because the girls selected were, for all intents and purposes, dispensable.

A sense of betrayal swept over her, searing and bitter. How was Danforth getting away with this, she wondered? And how many people knew about the school's true purpose?

If she ever got out of here, Faith vowed, she would find Noah. Hell, she'd walk all the way to Eremus, if she had to. Noah's mother had done it, hadn't she? Life there had to be a whole lot better than being a prisoner in Bellator, one of the academy's victims. But after more than a week of tiny meals, no visitors, not even a brief spell of time outside to exercise, she was beginning to doubt she'd ever feel strong enough to find a way out.

Faith had taken to pacing the room, small though it was, to try and get rid of her anxiety. Being cooped up in one place did not agree with her. She'd developed a short routine of stretches and exercises which kept her body active. And she'd tried to keep herself mentally busy: reciting her times tables, recalling key quotations from the Bellator Literature texts they had studied last year, and even singing songs, challenging herself to remember all the words. But there were still long periods of time where she had nothing to do but stare at the ceiling.

Right now, she assumed it was morning. Her breakfast had been delivered a few minutes ago. As usual, it contained a slice of unbuttered bread, an apple, a small sliver of cheese, and a glass of water. It had been the same every day since she'd been here. She tried to ration what she was given, but usually she was so hungry when it arrived that it took every scrap of willpower not to gobble it all in one go. Having polished off the bread, she had just taken a small bite of the apple when she heard the familiar sound of the keycard unlocking the door.

Startled, she sat down on the bed and swallowed hurriedly, almost choking on the fruit in the process. It wasn't time for another meal yet, she hadn't even finished this one. Who was entering her cell? When Professor Kemp poked her head around the door, Faith found it difficult to stop her heart from racing. Realising how quickly she had become accustomed to the lonely repetition of her routine, she cursed herself for allowing the simple arrival of a teacher to alarm her.

"How are you?" Her professor stepped into the room and stared around at its contents.

"I'm fine, thank you." Nothing could have been further from the truth, but Faith was in enough trouble as it was. Appearing to be argumentative would not make things go in her favour.

Professor Kemp was holding some books and papers in her hands. Moving to the desk, she put them down. "Persuaded the principal you needed something to do in here." She pointed at a notepad and pencil, as well as a couple of battered novels. "These are mine. She won't permit you to have anything digital in here, but I figured you might appreciate these, no matter how old fashioned."

Faith found herself fighting tears. The books might be outmoded, but desperate times called for desperate measures. She'd spent so many hours in here with nothing to do that she appreciated anything which offered a distraction.

"Thanks," she managed to whisper.

"It's alright." Kemp gave her a small, tight smile. "That's not the only reason I came though." She hesitated, running a finger along the spine of a book as she spoke. "I have to take you to the med centre. An appointment."

Faith's heart sped up again. What kind of appointment? She was dying to ask but knew Kemp was unlikely to answer. She managed a small nod and gestured at her half empty plate. "Will my breakfast still be here when I get back?"

Kemp looked troubled. "Of course. I'll make sure that it is."

"And c-could I . . . could I use the bathroom first? I mean . . . before we go?"

"Of course." Kemp blushed slightly. "I'll wait outside." She retreated from the room, closing the door behind her.

When Faith was ready, she tapped on the outer door. Kemp was waiting for her, along with a drudge. With a start, Faith recognised Arden, cursing. It was typical he would be assigned to care for her at a time when they were unable to speak privately. Their eyes met though, and he bowed his head ever so slightly. Faith took it as a sign he understood what Anderson was doing to her.

"Hold out your hands." Kemp gestured to Faith's wrists and turned to Arden, who handed her something. "Together."

Faith proffered her wrists and watched in growing horror as a set of clasps, attached to each other by a thin cord, were positioned loosely around them. Kemp held a device up to the cuffs and they emitted a soft beeping sound as they pulled tight. When the noise stopped, the restraints prevented her wrists from moving further than a few inches apart.

Kemp handed the device back to Arden and jerked her head outside. Faith moved after her into the hallway, subtly tugging on the cords which bound her hands. They were strong, and the more she struggled, the tighter they became. In the end, the pain of the contracting restraints was too intense to bear. Faith gave up, focusing on following Kemp through the maze of corridors.

Arden fell into step behind her, and she was grateful for his presence. He might not have any power to help her, but she knew he was on her side, and it went some way towards easing her loneliness.

She wondered how Kemp was planning to get her to the med centre. Any Bellator citizens they saw in the street would notice the cuffs binding her wrists. Surely Anderson didn't want the public suspecting Danforth students were being mistreated? But Kemp took a different route through the academy. They exited though a door which was unfamiliar to Faith, ending up on a quiet avenue which ran along one side of the building.

Kemp directed her straight into a waiting comcar, which swished away from the curb as soon as the three of them were inside. As they travelled, Faith tried to adjust to being outdoors again, alarmed at how long it took her to stop feeling disorientated. She knew why they weren't worried about anyone seeing her wearing the cuffs. It was clearly still early, and the streets were deserted. With no traffic, the comcar had them at the front entrance of the med centre within a few minutes.

It looked totally deserted. As she was hustled into the reception area, it struck Faith that she was totally alone. Her thoughts returned to Serene, and she had to force herself to breathe slowly as she walked behind Professor Kemp. What exactly was this appointment for? Why was she the only one here?

One of the usual technicians sat behind the desk and seemed to be expecting them. She looked up with a bright smile, her eyes dropping to the cuffs on Faith's wrists only briefly. "Faith Hanlon, right?"

Kemp nodded. "Yes. Can you take her straight in?"

"Of course." The technician tapped a button at the side of her datadev and, almost immediately, another tech appeared. "Natalie will take you through right away."

Natalie was tall and thin, and not nearly as smiley as the woman at the desk. As they followed her down the hall, Faith observed there was an obvious reason why she hadn't been selected to work on reception.

Turning abruptly, Natalie disappeared through the door to one of the treatment rooms. Kemp followed, motioning for Faith to come too, and indicating Arden should remain outside the door.

Inside, Faith was shaking, though it wasn't particularly cold. She took a seat in the patient's chair and waited. A thousand thoughts, each one worse than the last, chased through her head.

She could fight. But how could she overcome the technician *and* Professor Kemp? She'd barely eaten in the last week. She could ask to go to the bathroom and sneak out through the window. But Kemp would probably insist on going with her, and anyway, where would she go? Her thoughts flew once more to Noah, and she fantasised for a moment that she might run away with him to Eremus. But how would she find him? And would he even want to be found? With her around, he'd be a prime target for the Bellator guard. No Eremus citizen would want that.

Natalie was still fiddling with her equipment and Kemp appeared to be losing patience. "Can you hurry, please? It's *imperative* this is done quickly. I thought you had been made aware of that. We need to get out of here before . . ." she jerked her head at the door.

Natalie glowered at Kemp, but she gathered her equipment and crossed the room to Faith. Bending over her, she pushed up her sleeve, looking slightly taken aback at the cuffs. She recovered herself quickly though, and busied herself looping the usual tourniquet around her patient's upper arm.

Faith attempted to distract herself from the sharp pinprick in her skin, studying the drugs on the shelves as she usually did. But the lettering on the boxes seemed to dance in front of her eyes, making it impossible to read. She gave up and looked down, noticing there was a vial attached to the needle which protruded from her arm.

She looked at Natalie, surprised. "It's empty."

"Well, yes." Natalie rolled her eyes. "It has to be if we're filling it with your blood. If it was already full, there'd be no room."

Faith ignored the sarcasm, her heart fluttering wildly in her chest as she realised the appointment was simply a blood test, probably her regular one. Being locked away had definitely affected her perception of time, but now that she thought about it, the senior class was due its next one. She was so relieved that she didn't mind when Natalie filled a second vial.

A moment later, it was over. "All done." Natalie released the tourniquet and hauled Faith's sleeve down.

"Thanks," Faith managed.

Kemp tutted at the tech, before ushering Faith out into the hallway, glancing at her wristclip as she did. She muttered something under her breath as she headed back towards the lobby with a determined stride. As they reached it, she ground to such an abrupt halt that Faith almost slammed into her. When she looked up, she could see the reason why.

Filing into the med centre for their regular blood test was the entire senior class. The expression on Kemp's face told Faith they were supposed to be gone by now, avoiding being seen by the rest of Faith's peers. There was little Kemp could do about it now, though. Holding her head high, the professor marched Faith past the line of girls and hurried her towards the centre's exit.

As they emerged on to the street, the end of the line was just approaching the doors. Faith's heart leapt as she spotted Sophia, whose face lit up at the sight of her best friend, then quickly paled as she spotted the cuffs. Managing a brief smile which she hoped would go some way to reassuring her friend, Faith followed Kemp outside into the weak sunshine and allowed herself to be guided towards the comcar.

Kemp climbed in first. As she did, Faith felt Arden close behind her. Too close. For a moment, she was anxious. But as she ducked her head to follow her teacher, she felt his hand close around hers, sliding something into her palm. A folded scrap of paper. Grateful for Kemp's conversation with the comcar driver, Faith managed to tuck the note into her sleeve.

As she settled into the seat next to Kemp for their return journey, the message felt like it was branding its contents into her skin. Staring out the window at the city, Faith fought to keep her face blank, imagining what the note might say.

CHAPTER TWENTY-NINE: NOAH

As Paulo continued to fire questions at them, Noah slumped lower in his seat. The raiders had gone over the plans for the attack so many times now that his head was spinning, but his brother seemed determined to continue the assault until every single one of them knew the plan inside out.

"Where are you stationed?" Paulo jabbed a finger at Ruth, who was sitting to Noah's right.

She didn't hesitate. "Bellator Hospital entrance on Marshall Street. Left-hand side of the main doors."

The accusing finger switched aim and Noah jumped. "What's your objective?"

Startled, Noah thought quickly. "Prevent anyone from exiting the hospital."

"Good." Paulo gave a sharp nod. "The hope is the hospital will be quiet, it being the middle of the night and all, but we don't want anyone getting out and raising the alarm before we're ready to leave."

He turned to Jan, one of the older raiders. "And you?"

"Get to the central circuit breakers and cut off the hospital's power."

"Why?" He barked, but Jan went on, unintimidated.

"So when we detonate the explosives, the hospital won't be able to raise the alarm."

"Not immediately, at least." Paulo frowned. "But we'll have to act fast. Now, they'll be placing the explosives around the fertility unit. It's empty at night, aside from security, so the risk to life is as small as we can make it. There won't be any employees there."

That was the only consolation. Flynn's main concern had been the loss of innocent lives, and he had said as much to Jacob. The raiders had always been careful in the past, taking plenty of resources from Bellator, but never putting lives at risk unless they had no other option. In the years Flynn had been raiding, the only Bellator citizens who had died were guards who had put the lives of Eremus citizens in danger. This, the council could live with.

But a plan to blow up an entire building? That hadn't gone down as well, despite Jacob's persuasive delivery. The fact he had delivered it to his raiders before consulting the council had ruffled a few feathers, but he had smoothed the waters since with meetings where he had argued the benefits of the plan far outweighed its risks. He had promised to minimise the loss of life, and, in consultation with Madeleine and her resistance contacts, had done his best to ensure the only people likely to be near the fertility unit at night were a couple of guards.

The picture Jacob painted about the benefits of his long-term plan was very appealing, and most of the council had agreed that, in the long run, taking out Bellator's fertility stores would place their community in a better position. With no male seed to continue the race, it was hoped Eremus might engage in talks with Chancellor Danforth. Talks in which they could broker peace, ask for Bellator's respect and protection, and attempt to have them consider reversing the laws which banned male citizens from the city.

Flynn and Anna weren't convinced, and they'd talked about little else at home since the meeting. After years of successfully hiding away, Flynn felt going head-on with the Bellator government was asking for trouble. And Noah's ma knew more about the inner workings of the city than anyone. She was worried, and Noah was inclined to trust her judgement where Bellator was concerned.

But the attack was going ahead, with or without their approval. Noah had been glad to find he was assigned to the group running interference on the other side of the hospital from the fertility unit. Being a safe distance from the highly-volatile explosives, and not being responsible for *planting* them suited him fine.

"Paulo?" Jan looked concerned. "When I turn off the juice, what happens to the patients who're staying in the hospital? Overnight, I mean. Aren't some of them hooked up to machinery that uses the power?"

"Good question." Paulo gave her a brief nod of approval. "Madeleine's associate tells us there is a backup generator. Should kick in before any harm is inflicted. And in the event of an emergency . . . like a complete loss of power . . . it's programmed somehow . . . you know . . . focuses its efforts on the life-saving stuff. The machines which are keeping patients alive will be the first things back online. Clever, huh?"

Jan's face did not relax. "I suppose."

"The communication systems are less essential, so they won't come back online as fast. It means the loss of power shouldn't endanger anyone but will give us enough time to get everything in place before the comms are back up and they can alert the authorities." He turned to Harden. "What's the only problem?"

"The external doors."

"That's right." Paulo grimaced. "Because they're emergency exits, the backup power will be restored to them pretty fast too, so there's a chance someone might try to get out that way to raise the alarm." He nodded at the group. "That's what the rest of us are there to prevent."

Harden mock saluted. "Got it, boss."

Ignoring him, Paulo pressed on. "What time are the bombs scheduled to go off?"

This time Harden's buddy Sil, a slight girl with dark hair, responded. "Four a.m."

"And what time are we to be in place from?"

"Two a.m.," Sil continued. "Remain concealed, watch the hospital entrance, report any suspicious activities at our side of the building to you or Jacob."

"And," Harden finished, all humour absent now, "prevent anyone from leaving the building until the explosives are in place."

When he had discovered he and Harden were on the same team, Noah had not been happy. But in the days following Harden's release from the medcave, there had been no cruel remarks, no physical assaults, not even a sly elbow in the ribs as they passed in the tunnels or the canteen. And while the ex-bully hadn't spoken pleasantly to him, he was definitely more willing to tolerate Noah's existence in peace. Noah wasn't complaining, and it definitely made their current assignment less stressful.

"Alright." Paulo cleared his throat. "And when the other group is ready?"

"We wait for the signal they're in place, then retreat to Atwood Street," Noah recited, eager for the interrogation to be over. "When the rest of the team join us, they'll set off the explosives. As soon as the bombs go off, we leave."

"Via our assigned exits, of course," Ruth added quickly.

One of the teams on the previous raid had managed to get hold of some remote detonators, which meant they could trigger the bombs from a safe distance. This meant the Eremus citizens weren't being put in unnecessary danger, but had the added benefit of allowing them to beat a rapid retreat while the city dealt with the chaos of the explosion. This had put most of the raiders' minds at ease about the safety of the mission, but both Ruth and Noah were still concerned about any Bellator citizens who might be close to the fertility unit at the wrong time.

After going over a few more details, Paulo seemed happy his team knew what they were doing. "Great work tonight. You know the plan well. As long as Jacob's team does the same, we'll be in great shape on Saturday night." He glanced around at the group. "Any questions?"

Harden raised his hand. "Once the explosives destroy the seed bank, what's our next move?"

Paulo raised an eyebrow. "Nothing's confirmed yet. But if all goes well on Saturday, I think you'll find Jacob wants to set up talks with Danforth. To start negotiations."

"What kind of negotiations?" Sil enquired.

"Not sure yet." Paulo shifted his gaze to the door, as though he expected their leader to arrive at any moment. "All I know is . . . without the seed, Bellator's in a difficult position. Jacob wants to take advantage of that. Gain some power over the city."

Harden exchanged an excited glance with Sil. "Bout time those Bellator folks got theirs."

"Let's not get too cocky though," Paulo warned. "Not yet, at least." Glancing around at the group, he grinned. "We'll meet once more tomorrow to go over everything." He held up a hand at their groans. "Both groups together, this time. Now I *know* Anna and Sam wanted more volunteers in the canteen, so you can all get over there and help out for the rest of the morning."

Spurred on by Ella's injury, Noah's ma had recently begun work on a new project: creating anaesthetic from naturally occurring ingredients. After reading sections of the Bellator medical books, she had begun scouring the woods for a range of different plants, returning with an alarming number of seed pods, buds, and leaves. Their cave at home had been filled to bursting, Flynn and Noah complaining about the scent, which was sometimes so strong it made them dizzy. Armed with the right ingredients, Noah's ma had worked like a woman possessed. He had watched with fascination as she crushed various buds, boiling them with a combination of leaves in her quest to create the elusive drug.

A few days ago, she had burst into their cave, triumphant. She'd managed to create a solution whose ingredients mimicked the ones in the medical books she had been reading. The only thing left to do was to try it. She had persuaded Flynn to acquire a live squirrel from one of the hunters, and used a small amount of it, firstly to make the creature drowsy, and then to put it to sleep for a short period of time. When it woke up none-the-worse from the anaesthetic, she had set about making more.

Since then, she had tried it on Sam, Flynn, and Noah, adjusting the ingredients each time to ensure the solution did the trick without endangering anyone. When Noah had woken from a fifteen-minute doze caused by the drug his mother was calling Sleepsol, he'd been struck by an idea.

"What if we put this stuff into small spray bottles?" he'd remarked, sitting up on the bed.

"Spray bottles?" His ma had looked puzzled.

"It's fairly watery, right?" He picked up the small bottle of solution and turned it over in his hands. "I mean, it'd work as a kind of spray . . . a mist?"

"Sure. But I don't follow." She had looked up from the copious amounts of notes she was making. "It makes far more sense to just give it orally."

"Not for the purpose I'm thinking of."

His ma had cocked her head to one side, amused. "Just what are you cooking up in that brilliant head of yours?"

"Wsshhh!" Noah had aimed the bottle in her direction. "Enough of this, sprayed right into someone's face, would have an effect, wouldn't it?"

"It'd probably cause them to pass out." She had taken the bottle from him and moved over to the table. "Bit of a dangerous way to treat patients."

"But what if we weren't? Treating *patients*, I mean." Noah stood up and moved towards his mother. "What if we were . . ." he grabbed her round the neck from behind and mimed spraying the bottle into her face again, "defeating an enemy?"

She had frozen, and for a moment Noah thought she was angry. He had loosened his hold on her and allowed her to turn and face him. "That, Noah, might just be an excellent idea."

She had gone to Jacob and Flynn, explaining the concept carefully. The idea that the raiders could carry a bottle of the solution with them and use it to safely knock out the Bellator guards without actually hurting them was very appealing. Jacob had openly praised him for the idea, and even Paulo, though a little unwilling to share the limelight, had begrudgingly agreed it was a practical solution to a persistent problem.

Since then, they had trialled it in spray form, and found that, nine times out of ten it caused a person to experience dizziness, disorientation, and pass out. Seeing its value, Jacob had ordered Anna to create large quantities of it. Shifts had been altered so Eremus citizens could help with the production line. Cora and Beth had taken charge of the foraging efforts, sending groups of people out every day to gather large quantities of valerian, clove, kava, and cinchona. Since then, Anna and Sam had taught several citizens how to combine the key ingredients. Others had been assisting with bottling it, preparing a solution for every raider to carry on the raid with them.

Noah, at least, felt far safer with the solution as a weapon instead of a knife or a gun. Of course, Jacob would insist on them being armed with other weapons, but he planned not to use them unless it was absolutely necessary. He knew most of his fellow raiders preferred the protection of an old-fashioned weapon, but something non-lethal was far more his style.

Since he'd started training for the raid, he'd had several dreams which had featured Faith. Each one had placed her in progressively more dangerous situations, and every time he had woken up before he'd been able to save her. In the most alarming one, *he* had been the one standing over her, holding a knife that glittered in the moonlight. The concept of being able to spray something harmless in her face to knock her out with no long-lasting effects was definitely a welcome one.

An elbow in his ribs brought him back to the present, and he turned to see Ruth staring at him. "You ready to go?"

"Sure." He stood up and they made for the door, following the rest of the raiders out.

Ruth leaned close to Noah. "Your mum really got this stuff to work then?"

"She did." Noah beamed. "Tested it out on Flynn and me over the past week. *Several* times. It's surprisingly effective."

Beside him, Ruth chuckled. "I can't believe you dreamed this up." She squeezed his arm affectionately. "Actually, I can. It's very *you*."

He felt himself blushing. "I don't know . . . it just came to me. When Ma tested it out on me, and I felt how powerful its effects were, I . . ."

She leaned closer. "It's not a criticism. To want to save innocent people is a good thing." She punched his arm, backing away. "Good to know not everyone's as bitter and twisted about the Bellator citizens as me, huh?"

"Still think they're all bad?" Noah asked.

She shrugged, her face losing some of its humour. "I know they're not. Doesn't stop me from blaming them all for being part of the system which killed my ma."

Noah understood. Once again, he opened his mouth to confide in her about Faith and then shut it again as footsteps echoed up the tunnel from behind them. They turned as Paulo caught up to them.

"You both on your way to Anna?"

Ruth stood up. "Yes. Did you need something?"

"Umm," Paulo looked uncomfortable. "Noah, I . . . um . . . I was wondering if you could . . . stay here for a little while? Help me with something else?"

"Sure." Exchanging a surprised glance with Ruth, Noah nodded. "You go on. Speak to you at dinner?"

"Sure thing. See you later." Ruth turned and walked away, hurrying to catch some of the other raiders.

"She doing alright?" Paulo peered after her. "Jacob wanted me to check that she was okay to be on the raid. You know, he wouldn't usually let her come so soon after Dawn . . . but with the size of the mission and all . . ."

Noah turned back to his brother. "She'll be fine," he said, with more confidence than he felt. "She's partnered with me. I'll keep an eye on her." Paulo nodded, seeming satisfied. "What did you need, then?"

For a moment, Paulo looked confused. Then he turned abruptly, beckoning for Noah to follow. "Jacob wants me to check over the weapons. Thought you could help me out."

As he followed Paulo out into the tunnel and deeper into the further recesses of the cave system, Noah wondered if his brother was trying to find a way to heal the rift. While he didn't relish being in close contact with numerous lethal weapons, Noah did appreciate the chance to smooth things over with his brother. Maybe he could get them all talking again. He hurried to keep up as Paulo moved further ahead.

"How're you feeling about the mission?" Paulo threw over his shoulder.

"Good, I guess. I mean . . . nervous, but who isn't?"

"Nerves do you good. Keep you safe."

They walked on in silence for a while. Eventually, Paulo turned into the tunnel which led to the cave where Jacob was storing the mysterious boxes. Pulling aside the red curtain, he gestured for Noah to enter. They both had to stoop to avoid banging their heads on the low ceiling.

"That girl you met." Paulo's voice echoed back to him, slightly distorted by the tunnel. "You ever think about her?"

Noah was wary of answering. They hadn't spoken about Faith since the night of the raid itself. Noah wasn't sure what the appropriate response was.

"Um . . . a little, I guess?"

"Where'd you say she came from? Some special school?"

"Um yeah . . . Danforth Academy."

"And you said she believed they were being used for . . . research?" Paulo turned into an unfamiliar cave which lay on the right-hand side of the tunnel.

Trailing him inside, Noah nodded. "Yeah. They're told being selected for the school is a privilege . . . that they'll get to try out all the latest tech, give feedback to the manufacturers, that kind of thing. But Faith . . ." he blushed, "that's her name . . . believed the academy might be using them to trial potentially dangerous meds."

"Really?" Paulo stopped in the middle of the space, turning to Noah with a shocked expression. "The school is *testing* stuff on them?"

"Yeah . . . I guess so." Noah had thought about this a lot since the raid. He warmed to his topic, noting Paulo's interest. "Sounds awful, doesn't it? Can you imagine having to undergo medical treatments just so some scientist can see how they turn out?" He shuddered.

Paulo moved to the rear of the cave, reaching up to lift down the lantern that hung on the wall. "Can you imagine having the medical capabilities to be *able* to test out new drugs and procedures? Like we could ever do that here . . ." He pulled a box of matches from his pocket. "And this girl . . . Faith, you said? She was in the hospital that night to . . .?"

The question hung in the air between them, as Noah considered his answer. "To get information." Noah remembered their conversation. "She never said exactly what. But it felt like she'd figured something out . . . something important, about some treatment they were being given . . . She told me a girl at her school had died and they'd tried to cover it up. She thought it was linked to the testing . . . or the drugs maybe. She was in the hospital to work out . . . what had gone wrong."

"It does sound like they have a pretty bad deal." As the match flared, Paulo's face was illuminated. He stared at Noah, his expression intense. "So, these girls . . . the Danforth Academy students . . . they have to be pretty important to Bellator, right?"

"Important?" Noah couldn't hide his surprise. "They're hardly important if they'll let them *die*."

"But they *lie* about how they died . . . right? To the other students." Paulo replaced the lantern on the wall, where it cast eerie shadows across the contents of the cave. "Perhaps because they want to test similar drugs on them again in the future?"

"I guess so." Noah shook his head. "I just felt so bad for her, you know? I mean, even if she *found* the information she was looking for . . . what could she *do* about it? It didn't sound like she could just . . . leave."

"No." Paulo walked over to one of several chests which had been stored in the cave, beckoning Noah to follow. "Did she tell you anything else? Where the school was . . . how many girls attend it . . . who was in charge?"

Noah shook his head. "I don't think so. Not really."

A look of disappointment flashed over Paulo's face briefly, but was quickly quashed. "Poor girl. I don't envy her." He turned away, nodding at the chest. "Better get on with this, then."

He levered the top off the first chest, revealing a startling number of guns and large amounts of ammunition. Noah couldn't stop his mouth from falling open.

Paulo caught his expression. "Jacob's been building this stash for years. He *really* wants to get even with Danforth."

"Get even?" Noah was curious.

"Never mind." Paulo turned away. "It's pretty impressive, isn't it?"

Impressive was not the word Noah would have chosen. And as he began dividing up the assorted weapons with his brother, he couldn't keep Faith's face out of his mind. Haunted by thoughts of her smooth, pale skin being pierced repeatedly by vicious metal bullets or poison-filled syringes, he prayed she would be nowhere near the hospital when the Eremus bombs went off.

F aith lay on the uncomfortable cot and read the message for what seemed like the hundredth time. When she had first returned from the med centre, she'd been hopeful. The fact that she had been taken to attend her usual appointment suggested Anderson still had her on the same medical programme as the rest of the girls. She'd thought they might begin to allow her a little more freedom, at least give her a chance to explain what she had been doing at the hospital.

She'd been wrong. Delivered back to her cell, her days had resumed their previous routine: the bare minimum of meals, delivered by a silent drudge, and endless boredom.

She had the books which Kemp had left her, but it was difficult to focus on their content. The only reading matter which held her attention was the now much-crumpled note. Its message was encrypted, which told her one thing: its author was Sophia. Her friend loved ciphers of all kinds, and had clearly put her hobby to good use. It was a sensible precaution. Sending the note was a huge risk.

But while her best friend loved puzzles and codes, Faith had never been a fan. And Sophia seemed to credit her with a higher intellect than she possessed. Despite staring at the lettering for hours, she still had no idea what the message said.

She pulled out the slip of paper once more, willing the words to rearrange themselves into order.

rubbqjeh wkqht qj qsqtuco.

juqsxuhi qsjydw ijhqdwubo.

jebt oek qhu iysa.

qhtud mybb xubf.

iudt hujkhd cuiiqwu.

Sighing, she pushed herself into a sitting position. How did ciphers work? She knew they used replacement letters in place of the original ones. If she could just work out the pattern Sophia had used, she'd be able to read the message. Reversing the alphabet had given her nothing but more nonsense. Frustrated by her lack of success, she had given up. But she owed it to her friend to try harder.

Grabbing the notepad and pencil Kemp had left her, she wrote out the alphabet, keeping her letters neat and even. Racking her brain, she tried to remember Sophia showing her various ciphers. She had never paid much attention, though she did remember something about shifting letters over by a certain number. She numbered each letter normally, A – Z, 1 – 26, then wrote the alphabet out again, moving the numbers along by two letters, with no success. Trying to remain positive, she repeated the process with three letters, then four. Nothing.

She considered special numbers Sophia might have chosen. Six, the number of their current shared room. Nine, their old dorm. Twelve, Sophia's supposed favourite number. Still, the message remained indecipherable. About to give up, she tried sixteen, their shared age. It required a lot more movement, as the number was so high, but when she had worked out the first short sequence of letters, she was staring at the word Bellator.

Excited now, she worked feverishly to unscramble the puzzle in front of her. It took her a while, but fuelled by excitement, eventually she found herself reading a set of words which made sense.

bellator guard at academy.
teachers acting strangely.
told you are sick.
arden will help.
send return message.

She sat back, satisfied with her handiwork. Sophia would be proud. The message suggested her actions had led to stricter security measures in the academy, presumably to prevent anyone else being tempted to act in the same way. The fact that Anderson had lied about the reason for her absence was no surprise. The academy was definitely trying to cover up what she'd done and continue as normal. And it didn't sound like she'd be allowed out of her cell any time soon.

The only positive was Sophia had been talking to Arden, who had obviously agreed to help where he could. And the idea he might pass messages between them was comforting. She tore a page from the notepad and considered a reply. She would have to write it, then use the same cipher to disguise it. When she might pass it to Arden was anyone's guess, as he had not returned to her cell since her visit to the medical centre. Still, it was worth a try. She got to work.

After half an hour she was satisfied with her efforts. She had an encrypted return message, written on a slip of paper small enough to pass to Arden without being seen. It conveyed the bare minimum of information, vital things she felt Sophia should know. It told her friend she had been locked up, was being fed, and still seemed to be accessing the same medical treatment as the rest of the class. It also conveyed Anderson knew she had been at the hospital, and cautioned Sophia against any further investigation. Faith had included the final warning for Diane, but was confident Sophia would realise this and pass the message on.

She was just checking over her message when she heard the door's autolock release. She just had time to thrust the note into her pocket when the door burst open. She looked up, expecting Kemp, but instead, she was faced with Principal Anderson. Faith felt her heart jolt at the unexpected appearance. Behind the principal stood a tall woman in a white technician's uniform.

"Hanlon." Anderson's tone was flat. She strode in and glanced around the room suspiciously. "I assume you're not getting yourself into any further trouble."

Faith stared at her, unsure of the expected response. "Um . . . no." She fought to keep her voice from shaking, determined not to let the woman see how frightened she was. "No, I'm not."

"Good." Anderson beckoned to the tech. "Come in and get set up."

The woman came inside, pulling a trolley filled with medical equipment behind her. Sweeping Faith's books to one side of the table without ceremony, she hauled the desk close to the cot and lined the trolley up next to it.

The tech beckoned Faith over, pointing to the cot. "Here, please."

Faith obeyed, sitting down as instructed, her eyes fixed on the woman in the white coat. She opened a drawer in the front of the trolley and took out a number of items: a fresh pack of syringes, a vial of a strange, turquoise liquid, a cannula, and small datadev. She tapped on the screen, which let out a series of beeps. Then she held out the device and directed her gaze at Faith.

"Name?"

"Faith Hanlon."

The datadev beeped again, then began speaking, its tone robotic. *Faith Hanlon. Bellator Resident 21719. Student at Danforth Academy. Age sixteen. Recent bloods normal. No markers present.*

The tech seemed satisfied. Tapping the screen again, she put down the device. Unlocking the doors at the base of the trolley, she pulled them open to reveal a machine of some kind. She tapped some buttons on the control panel, which blinked brightly, and the machine began to make a low humming sound.

Taking a sanitising solution from her bag, the tech coated her hands in it before donning a pair of latex gloves. She attached a length of tubing to the machine and secured the other end to a cuff made of a dense-looking material. Reaching for Faith's arm, she slid the cuff up it and tightened it in place before flicking a lever on the front of the machine.

"What's this for?" Faith managed.

"Just a simple procedure." The tech barely looked at her. "We need to keep an eye on your vitals while it's going on."

She selected a syringe and began tearing off its packaging.

Faith glanced at her principal, fighting to keep her voice steady. "What procedure?"

Anderson shot her a look. "Nothing for you to be concerned about."

"But you need to track my vital signs? That's not—"

Anderson held up a hand. "You relinquished your right to any say in what happens to you when you decided to leave the school without permission in the middle of the night. If you're so interested in finding out what goes on in a hospital, you should be *fascinated* by this." Her voice was heavy with sarcasm.

Faith fell silent, focusing instead on the tech. The woman had opened the vial of liquid and filled the syringe with it. Her mind was racing, searching for an option, any option, which would allow her to escape the mysterious treatment. She was fairly certain they were about to administer a dose of femgazipane. But no matter how she looked at it, she couldn't stop them. Even if she fought them off and managed to escape her cell, how far would she get before they caught her?

No. She had to hope whatever they were about to inflict on her had been altered or improved since Serene's death. Anderson was giving them the treatment for a reason. Her aim wasn't to kill them. Surely, the doctors had learned from what happened and made changes to the drug's makeup? The logic didn't make her feel any better.

The tech reached for Faith's arm again, her hands ice-cold. She held the limb out straight and pressed down in the crook of Faith's elbow until she found a vein. Working swiftly, she inserted the needle, securing it with a piece of meditape. Then she picked up the vial of liquid from the table, holding it up to the light to check the label.

Faith found herself shivering uncontrollably, though the room was quite warm. She closed her eyes, trying to relax her body. Her stomach churned and for a moment she felt like she was going to throw up. She heard the technician uncap the vial and felt her attach the solution to the tube which snaked into the vein in her arm.

"Won't be long now," the tech murmured.

As the meds began to flow into her system, Faith had to force herself to breathe, dragging air in through her nose and letting it out as slowly as she could through her lips. Yoga breathing, aimed at promoting calm. It didn't stop her heart from stuttering in her chest in the most alarming way, and she wondered if she was having a panic attack.

She couldn't bear the alternative: that the drug was already taking effect.

Her head began to swim. Was this it? Had this been Serene's reaction? If so, surely the tech should be pulling the cannula out to prevent a repeat occurrence. But the woman only watched Faith quietly as the mysterious liquid invaded her body.

Faith lost track of time. It felt like the tech had been sitting there for hours, feeding the poison into her system, yet it might only have been minutes. Anderson tapped her foot impatiently. Outside, Faith thought she heard the yells of the girls on the basketball courts, the ball rebounding against the asphalt. There was a faint scent of something sweet, like honey, and her skin felt very hot, almost as though it were burning

And then there was darkness.

When she woke, the room was empty. Anderson and the tech were gone; all trace of medical equipment had been removed. Once again, the table only contained Kemp's books, piled untidily to one side. When Faith tried to sit up, she found the room was spinning and lay back down again.

For a moment, she wondered if she had dreamed the strange encounter, but the telltale pinprick of blood in the crook of her elbow suggested otherwise. Beside the bed was a cup of water, which she managed to lift to her lips. She had only taken a tiny sip when she lost control of her hand and spilled a generous amount down the front of her shirt. Managing to lower the cup to the floor with difficulty, she collapsed on the sheets and allowed the darkness to take her.

Later, she came to again. This time, she was desperate to visit the bathroom, only she knew she didn't have the strength. For a while, she lay still, trying to stop the room from spinning. Her need became more pressing. Realising her other option was ending up with a wet bed which was unlikely to be changed any time soon, she rolled her body off the cot and managed to land on the floor without hurting herself. From there, she crawled, agonizingly slowly, to the bathroom. For once, she was glad the room was so small: it meant she didn't have far to go.

Once she had emptied her bladder, she tried to stand, but the sensation of dizziness overcame her once more and she slid back to the floor. Rubbing a hand across her sweat-covered forehead, she leaned heavily on the toilet bowl, its cool surface providing a small amount of relief.

The next time she woke, she felt an intense need to empty the contents of her stomach. This time she was grateful she hadn't made it back to the cot. It was all she could do to position her head over the bowl before she threw up violently, over and over, until she was certain there could be nothing left in her system.

Feeling slightly better, she managed to kneel over the sink long enough to splash some water on her face and rinse out her mouth. Then she repeated the slow crawl back to her cot. Her remaining energy went into hauling her leaden body back onto the bed, where she sank into the sheets and sobbed.

She was alive, but for how much longer?

She must have slept for a long time. When she opened her eyes, the room was no longer spinning, and this time she found she was actually able to stand and walk to the bathroom. Washing her face and upper body the best she could, she rinsed out her mouth and felt a little better. When she staggered back to the bed, she noticed she'd been given an additional blanket. At least two meals had been left on the table, confirming the length of time she'd been unconscious. Finding she was actually hungry, she gobbled down a decent portion of the food, which was better than her usual fare: four bread rolls; a dish of stew which was still good, despite being cold; several hunks of cheese; and an apple. She ate quickly, cramming the food into her mouth in a way she knew Sophia would disapprove of.

Sophia. Faith slid her hand into the pocket of her trousers and sighed with relief. The note was still there, undiscovered. But she knew how worried her friend would be. Polishing off the apple, she stood up and tried some of her usual stretches. While she didn't feel strong enough to complete the entire workout, she felt vastly better than the previous day. Or days.

The shrill beep of the autolock made her jump. Hoping her visitor might be Arden, she held on to the note, keeping her fingers in her pocket. But though the figure who entered was familiar, she was not welcome.

Principal Anderson stopped just inside the door, wrinkling her nose in distaste. "You stink."

Faith almost laughed. "If you'd let me out to have a shower, maybe I wouldn't."

Anderson waved a hand, dismissing her. Wasting no more time, she came into the room, followed by the same med tech. Faith's heart began to race, but the woman closed the door without wheeling in a trolley. Instead, she carried a small medical bag. Crouching down beside Faith, she made short work of drawing two vials of blood.

"That should do it." The tech turned to Anderson. "I'll get it over to the lab and fast track it."

"See that you do." Anderson nodded briefly as the tech packed up her bag and left the room.

Thankful the visit had not involved a second dose of the powerful drug, Faith turned her attention to Anderson, who had placed a datadev on the table. She tapped her fingers over the screen impatiently. Seconds later, a ringtone indicated she was making a call.

"Chancellor Danforth's Office," a tinny voice sounded from the datadev's speaker.

Danforth? Faith's brain scrambled to explain why Anderson would come here and put in a call to the chancellor.

"It's Principal Anderson. She's expecting my call."

"Of course." There was a series of clicks, and then the secretary's voice again. "Putting you through."

Anderson swiped her hand over the screen until a holo appeared in the air. Chancellor Danforth's face appeared, large and unsmiling, hovering in the air over the table.

"Morning, Joanna." The voice was commanding, even over the datadev's sound system. "How is she?"

"See for yourself." Anderson motioned to the bed where Faith lay. "She's had a rough few days, but seems to be coming out of it now. She hasn't thrown up since the first day, and she's now strong enough to stand and walk around a little. No lasting after-effects that we can see."

"Then I think we're close to getting it right."

"Looks like we might be." Anderson smiled. "And we'll know soon enough. Her blood sample has just been taken over to the lab."

"Alright. I'll call them this afternoon for the results. We can go ahead with phase two as discussed if you're happy to?"

"I am. I'll get everything ready on this end."

"Good. I'll expect a report by the weekend."

The holo quivered slightly, and Danforth disappeared. Faith stared at Anderson, her eyes wide.

"What's Phase Two?"

"Never you mind." Anderson bent over the datadev, tapping and swiping until the screen went blank. "You've proved yourself useful after all, Hanlon. Just not in the way we thought you might."

Faith opened her mouth to ask another question, but Anderson was already on her way out. Stowing the datadev under her arm, she tapped the keycard against the door and pulled it open after it had beeped.

"Get some rest." She called over her shoulder as she exited. "You'll be needing it."

Chapter Thirty-One: Noah

Noah and Ruth crept through the darkened streets of Bellator side-by-side. It was just after one in the morning, and the place was deserted. Happy to be partnered with someone other than his brother for a change, Noah was also enjoying the opportunity to see more of the city. The tunnel exit they had been assigned to did not lead into a citizen's home, but instead came out in a small, wooded area somewhere on the outskirts. It meant a far longer hike to their destination than Madeleine's house would have, but Noah didn't mind.

Previously he had only seen the inner-city areas, which were all fancy high-rise buildings, glittering towers housing businesses, health centres, offices, and department stores. In contrast, when their group exited the woods, they found themselves on the edges of a residential area. The streets which he and Ruth were led through by Jan and Dane, another of the older raiders, were narrow and the buildings which flanked them were box-like and plain by comparison to the city skyscrapers.

Most of the Bellator women lived in community groups, in shared housing, his mother had told him, travelling into the city or out into its surrounding areas to work or study each day. The buildings here looked small but were fairly well-kept. A few had window boxes filled with plants and flowers, and some of the building entrances had bicycles chained outside. The streets were only dimly lit at night, and there were very few lamps on in the windows of the houses. The women of the city were mostly asleep.

It hadn't been difficult to stay in the shadows as they made their way into the city centre. Jan knew the route well, and kept to the quieter streets, avoiding the busier thoroughfares which were used by the odd comcar or transvan at night. They hadn't spoken since they had emerged from the relative shelter of the trees, having agreed in advance it was safer to remain silent. They were all dressed in dark clothing, similar to what might be worn by the Bellator women, with hoods up to shield their faces.

Entrance to the city during the raids was always carefully controlled, ensuring the larger men who stood out as starkly different from the Bellator females came in from the places closest to the centre. Being on the streets for a shorter period of time reduced their chance of being spotted. Because the raid was a large one, it required greater manpower than usual, so the groups had been forced to use a larger range of tunnel exits to access the city.

Since Dane and Noah were not particularly bulky, it was considered safe for them to travel through more of the city's streets. At a glance, their slight builds might be taken for those of female citizens, though both men made an effort to slouch as they walked. If the group was approached by any of the Bellator women, Jan and Ruth were primed to speak. Spinning a few sentences together might allow them to blend in and avoid being caught. The hope was they wouldn't meet anyone at all, but they all had a bottle of the anaesthetic spray in their pockets, just in case.

Noah knew his ma had worked through the night with her team to ensure they had a large enough supply of Sleepsol for all the raiders. They were hopeful the potion would be really useful, limiting the damage caused by their attack, which was a larger one than Eremus had ever attempted. Noah's group had set off earlier than those heading straight for the city centre, knowing they had the longer walk to contend with, but they were almost there.

Jan reached a corner and peered around it, beckoning for them to follow close behind. They turned onto a street which was better lit and dominated by a sturdy-looking wall which ran the length of the opposite side. The light-coloured stone had a dense, leafy plant creeping all over it and the buildings set well behind it were large and imposing. Noah was just wondering at the building's purpose as Jan jabbed an elbow in his ribs.

Following her gaze, he spotted the cause of her panic. At the far end of the street, there was a gap in the wall which housed an ornate gate, the heavily entwined sections of metal denying access to the buildings behind it. Two security guards had just emerged from the gate. They weren't looking in the raiders' direction but gesturing the other way and speaking to one another. They had large guns strapped to their shoulders.

"Over there." Jan's hissed whisper startled him. "*Now!*"

He started to run. Dodging across the road behind Jan and the others, he followed them onto a side street which ran behind the building. When they had reached relative safety, they paused, panting. Jan checked the street once again.

"Don't think they saw us." She wiped a hand across her brow. "They'd be after us if they had."

"That was close." Dane whistled softly.

"Too close. I've used this route for years. School's not usually guarded like that."

"It's a school?" Noah peered up at the wall, his heart pounding.

"Yep. We'll have to be extra careful. We don't want any more unwelcome surprises." Jan reached over to adjust Dane's hood, which had fallen away from his face. "Keep it *covered*."

"Yes, boss." Dane shot Noah a brief wink. He wondered at the older man's calm.

"We'll have to go this way." Jan pointed further along the street. "Runs round the side of the building. It'll take us a little longer, but we can't use that route now. Too risky. Better pick up the pace though. It's 1:15 already."

She turned and made off along the street. Noah followed, the pounding in his chest continuing. Halfway along, the wall disappeared, making way for a metal fence similar in style to the gate the guards had been protecting. Through the slender gaps in the fretwork, Noah caught glimpses of sports fields, a circular track of some kind laid into the grass, and a garden with benches and overhanging trees.

A sign on the fence caught his eye. *Private Property: Danforth Academy.*

He froze. Faith was *here*. Just the other side of the fence, *metres* away from where he stood. He glanced up at the buildings which lined the opposite side of the field. Surely, some of them must be sleeping quarters. The thought that Faith could be in any one of them had him rooted to the spot. His eyes darted back to the fence. It was certainly sturdy, keeping him from entering the academy grounds, and her from escaping.

He thought back to the armed guards, wondering how she had ever managed to get out to visit the hospital in the first place. She was brave, that was certain.

A sharp smack on the arm brought his attention back to the street and he glanced down at Ruth, who looked furious. Further down the street, Jan and Dane were also glaring at him.

"What're you *doing*?" she hissed. "There's no time for sightseeing."

He shook his head, guilt washing over him. Ruth was right. He couldn't risk the mission, put his friends lives in danger for a girl he barely knew. Shooting his friend an apologetic look, he hurried after her, promising himself he wouldn't do anything more to delay them. But as he raced alongside his friend, determined to erase her anger, his thoughts kept straying to Faith and how close he had been to her. The knowledge of her school's location was now etched into his brain.

They reached the rally point, the doorway of the department store he had previously met Paulo, just after 1:30 a.m. His brother greeted them with a glare, a walkie talkie clutched in his hand. The rest of the group was already there.

"Sorry, Paulo." Jan was quick to defend them. "There was extra security along the route. Had to make a detour."

His expression turned to one of concern. "Any problems?"

"No. We weren't seen."

"Excellent." Paulo beckoned them to gather around him. "Jacob's team is in position on the opposite side of the hospital. They've already begun planting the explosives. You know your places, right?" Numerous nods confirmed this. "Jan, Dane, you go first. Get to the circuit breakers as soon as you can. We have to take the power out before we can detonate."

"Right you are." Jan jerked her head at Dane and the two of them slipped off into the darkness.

"The rest of you get in position and wait." Paulo pointed towards the hospital. "Hopefully we won't need to take any action, but we keep those exits guarded, make sure no one gets out and sets off the alarm."

A noise from the street beyond made Noah jump, and the group instinctively shrank back into the doorway. Paulo held up a hand for their silence, and they froze as a figure appeared around the corner. With a sigh of relief, Noah saw it was Harden.

"Anything?" Paulo whispered at him.

"No." Harden ducked into the doorway beside them, slightly breathless. "I scouted the front entrance and either side of the main building. No major emergencies at the moment. The lights are on, but the staff inside look like they're staying put."

"Good. Looks like we chose a quiet night. Let's hope it stays that way." Paulo raised the walkie talkie to his lips. "Jacob, come in."

"Paulo?" The ancient device crackled, distorting their leader's voice.

"Everything's ready here. Power should be out momentarily and I'm just getting the others in place."

"Great news . . . we'll wait to hear . . . out." The walkie talkie went silent.

"Over and out." Paulo clicked the button off and stuck the device onto his belt. He jerked his head at the rest of them. "Off you go, then. I'll presume you're in position in five minutes. As soon as you're there, Jacob and his team will get busy. Your eyes stay *glued* to those exits, got it?"

They gave a collective nod and Paulo waved them away to their various positions. Noah headed for the street with Ruth, waiting a while as other raiders headed off in pairs, timing their entrance to the main street to avoid being noticed. When Harden and Sil had disappeared around the side of the hospital, Ruth jabbed her elbow into his side. They darted across the road together.

Their own position was as close to the hospital's main entrance as they could get without being spotted. There was an enclosed section of greenery to one side of the entrance. Outside it, a small sign read Memorial Garden, and Noah assumed it was a place for quiet reflection, perhaps used by those who had lost someone in the hospital. Deserted at night, it had tall trees and was surrounded by a large box hedge which would easily conceal the two of them. From there, Noah and Ruth would have an excellent view of the entrance.

The main doors to the hospital were lit but currently deserted, but Noah still shuddered at the memory of his last visit. He and Paulo had passed this way just as an ambulance had screeched up to the entrance, numerous medics rushing out to deal with the emergency. Beating a rapid retreat around the side of the building, they had only just escaped notice. Noah had felt far safer once they were away from the well-lit entrance.

"Harden was right." Ruth slipped into the garden and stood behind the hedge, peering outwards. "Looks quiet."

Noah nodded. His nerves were still on edge from the narrow miss with the guards at the academy, but even he had to admit that, so far, the hospital seemed fairly empty.

"You alright?" Ruth was staring at him. "You're acting weird."

He had to smile. Ruth was never one to mince words. Checking the coast was clear again, he gestured to the ground. "Think we could sit? We can still see the entrance, and it might be a long wait."

"Spill it." She was already lowering herself to the ground as she spoke. "I know *something's* bugging you." She looked shamefaced. "And I'm sorry . . . I know I haven't had too much time for you lately, what with . . ."

"S'alright." He reassured, settling down beside her. "I guess I'm just a bit shaken up by the guards we saw before . . ."

"That's not it." She shook her head. "When you stopped and stared into the school grounds on the way here. You held us up when you *knew* we had to go. Risked the mission." She leaned closer, staring into his eyes. "That's not like you."

He hung his head. "I know."

"So . . . what then?"

"I'm . . ." he hesitated, still nervous of how she would react to the truth. "I guess I'm worried . . ." he searched for something which might convince her, ". . . about how many people we could hurt here today. I mean . . . we've reduced the risk as far as possible, I know, but . . ."

Ruth's face fell. "It's more than that. You were like this before we even got to the hospital." She shifted away from him. "You just don't want to tell me."

Noah hated how well she knew him. She was his best friend, she knew he wasn't telling her the truth, and it hurt her.

"Okay." Relenting, he searched for the right words. "The last time I was here . . . something went a little wrong."

"I know all that." She looked frustrated. "You got trapped up there." She gestured to the hospital. "You were late to meet Paulo. He was frantic you wouldn't make it back . . . that something had happened to you."

"Okay. Well, what you don't know, is . . . when I was trapped in the hospital storage room, I . . . I wasn't alone." He watched Ruth's expression darken and hurried on. "There was a girl . . . a Bellator citizen . . . she wasn't supposed to be in there either. We . . . we talked . . . a little. She told me about her life. Ruth," he grasped his friend's hand in his, begging her to understand, "they don't all have it as easy as you'd think."

Ruth snatched her hand away. "You mean the reason you're all worked up is . . . cos you're frightened this . . . *girl* might still be here? In the hospital? That she might get caught up in all this?"

"No! Well, m-maybe." Noah found himself stuttering as he attempted to make his friend understand. "She goes to that school we passed before . . ."

"Danforth Academy?"

"Yeah. That's why I stopped." He pressed on, seeing his friend's shock "I just, I couldn't stop thinking about how she could have been lying asleep in one of those rooms . . ." he felt his face colouring in the darkness, "and *now* I can't stop imagining her in the hospital, when Jacob's setting up explosives and triggers and . . . I mean, let's be honest, we don't know how this will go down, do we? What if he blows up the entire hospital?"

Ruth stared at him. "Exactly how *likely* is it she's in there right now? I mean, she sneaked in *once* before. Did you get the impression she made a habit of it?"

"Um . . . I guess not." But Noah's mind went to his first encounter with Faith at the medical centre. "At least, I hope not."

"You saw the security outside the school. It's not likely she'd try to escape again at night if they have guards at her school." Ruth looked back at the hospital entrance. "So, unless she's having some kind of midnight treatment, I think she's safe."

"You're probably right." Noah felt foolish, but Ruth's words were comforting. "I mean . . . what are the chances of her being here?"

"Exactly." Ruth shifted her position slightly, changing the subject. "Jeez, you'd think grass would be more comfortable to sit on."

Noah waited until she was looking at him again. "You're not mad?"

Something in her eyes shifted and she let out a sigh. "That you seem to have gone a little crazy over some Bellator girl? I guess not." She raised an eyebrow. "That's not to say I *approve*, of course, but . . ." she shrugged, "I've had the time since . . . since my ma . . . well, let's just say I don't blame *every* Bellator citizen for what happened in the woods that day. I'm sure your little lady is far away from all this in her ivory tower. Privileged *princess* that she is."

"She's not—" Noah began to defend her but trailed off when he saw his friend was grinning. He slapped her lightly on the arm. "She's nice. Honestly, if you—"

But he fell silent as she held a finger to her lips. In the distance, there was a sound. As they listened, the unmistakable sound of footsteps on the pavement outside the hospital grew in volume. Not just a single pair either: *numerous* feet, all walking in this direction. Noah scooted forward to peer around the hedge, then lurched back into position with a gasp.

"People." He pointed, and Ruth took his place, staring out at the approaching group.

A dual line of girls, walking side-by-side in formation, heading straight for the hospital. Back in Eremus, they had been over what to do to prevent people leaving the hospital, to stop them from alerting the wider city to the potential attack. They'd also discussed the potential for an emergency arriving at the hospital and decided the safest thing to do in that case was to allow them to enter. Emergencies were always dealt with swiftly, and a quick call to Jacob to delay the detonations until the entrance was clear of people again would not be a problem.

But they hadn't discussed what action to take if a large number of Bellator citizens attempted to *enter* the hospital in the middle of the night. It could hardly be an emergency if there were so many of them, all arriving on foot, at the same time.

But what possible treatment could they be receiving at two a.m.?

As he crouched beside Ruth, watching the line of girls marching past in silence, his worst fears were realised. Large numbers of young girls, *totally innocent* young girls, entering the hospital at a time when they were preparing to blow part of it up. He felt a stabbing pain in his chest at the idea.

And then, he thought his heart would stop altogether. At the rear of the line, flanked by the same guards who had stood outside Danforth Academy earlier, was a familiar figure.

Faith.

Beside him, he felt Ruth turn to stare. "That's her?" He nodded and she whistled softly. "Then I guess I was wrong. Looks like she has a midnight treatment after all."

CHAPTER THIRTY-TWO: FAITH

Faith had tried to fight them off when they'd come for her. But she was weaker than usual. The drugs she'd been given were still having some negative effects, rendering her unable to put up much of a struggle against the Bellator guards who arrived with Anderson. Perhaps anticipating resistance, the principal had replaced the drudge in favour of a pair of grim-faced uniformed women who were armed to the teeth.

There was no sign of Arden, and hadn't been since the last med centre visit, so Sophia's note was still buried in her pocket. The *only* advantage to being marched off to the hospital in the middle of the night was the tiny possibility she might catch a glimpse of her best friend and be able to reassure her she was alright.

"Where are you taking me?" she had demanded of Anderson. The Principal didn't usually accompany them on visits outside the academy.

Her question had been ignored. Instead, she had found herself manhandled into the same cuffs as last time and bundled down to the academy's front entrance. Anderson didn't bother with a comcab. The cover of darkness had seemed sufficient guarantee that the wrong people wouldn't catch a glimpse of an imprisoned student.

When she had seen she was being marched to the hospital alongside the other girls from the senior class, Faith had made up her mind to cooperate. If she didn't struggle, maybe they'd let their guard down a little. Her appearance had caused a small stir among the other seniors, but a sharp look from Anderson had silenced their whispers. Faith had been placed at the rear of the line, and was surprised to find herself standing behind some girls from the junior class. The guards stationed either side of her meant there had been no opportunity to speak to her friends. Yet Anderson had joined Professor Kemp at the front of the line, so Faith felt hopeful.

She had not immediately seen Sophia, but spotted Avery. The older girl's usual veneer of perfection seemed chipped: her hair pulled into a hasty ponytail and her pale face devoid of its careful makeup job. Clearly, this visit had been sprung upon the girls. Under normal circumstances, Faith would have laughed at Avery's lack of poise, but her concern over the reason for the midnight outing had far outweighed any amusement she felt.

She had seen Diane too, a few rows ahead. When she and her protectors had joined the line, some of the girls had turned at the sound of their footsteps. Diane's eyes had widened as they met Faith's, taking in her formidable escort. Once she had recovered from her shock, Diane had shot Faith a rare look of sympathy before turning to follow the others.

The roads were as quiet as they had been the last time Faith had sneaked out. She wondered, as they approached the hospital, whether she'd choose to do it again if she was given the chance. While she was glad the adventure had proved some of her suspicions about the academy, it had led directly to her current situation, which was pretty bleak. Yet it had also led her to meet Noah, an encounter which, somehow, she couldn't regret.

The lights blazed from the hospital's entrance, but otherwise it seemed quiet. As they headed for the front doors, Faith couldn't stop her body from trembling. *Why* were they all here, in the middle of the night? A feeling of dread threatened to overwhelm her as she considered the recent treatment she'd undergone. Could the principal intend to repeat the procedure on them *all*? And if this was the case, why bring Faith along?

She had no answers. She only knew the nighttime venture could not be a positive one.

In the reception area of the hospital, they were met by a tech she had never seen before. The woman directed them down a corridor at the rear of the lobby and through a door into a large waiting area. They all took a seat, the guards guiding Faith to a chair on the other side of the space from the rest of the girls. As she sat down, she looked for Sophia, eventually spotting her friend sitting close to the door, her body tense. A look of intense relief flooded her features as she saw Faith.

Before Faith could even muster a reassuring smile, a door on the other side of the room banged open, and a familiar figure strode in. Faith's heart began to pound as she recognised the medic who had visited her at the academy and administered the drugs which had knocked her out. She beckoned to two other techs, who came forward alongside her and stood facing the girls.

"Good evening," she began, "I'm Dr. Sanders. You're here today to undergo a small procedure. Nothing major, but it will require you to stay here for a few hours so we can observe you. My colleagues," she gestured to the women either side of her, "will assist me in ensuring you all receive the best care throughout the process. We are just preparing the ward for you all," she gestured to the door behind her, "and then we'll get you checked in and settled."

The news was received with silence. The senior girls glanced at one another with concern, but none of them dared to speak. Faith's heart was pounding so loudly she was surprised the guards couldn't hear it. Whilst she hadn't died from the treatment like Serene, she had no wish to inflict the horrific sickness on the others, and had no idea what its *long-term* effects might be. Her eyes met Diane's. She could see the same fear reflected in the other girl's expression.

Anderson had moved across to talk to Dr. Sanders and beckoned one of the guards over. They bent their heads together in intense discussion, motioning to various girls around the room every now and again. Faith glanced at the guard who had been left with her. This woman was the smaller of the two, though she still had a formidable gun strapped to her belt. She was currently staring at something on the screen of her wristclip.

Faith looked across at Diane again. Nodding very slowly, she tried to communicate something of her desperation to the other girl. Diane mimicked her nod, then stretched widely, one arm extending into what Faith could see was a gesture. No one else noticed she was pointing, but when Faith followed the direction of Diane's finger, she understood. Nodding at her confidant once more, she turned to the remaining guard, adopting a pained expression.

"Excuse me?" The guard ignored her. Raising the volume of her voice a little, she tried again. "Um . . . excuse me?"

The guard glanced at her sharply. "What is it?"

"I . . ." Faith made sure to fidget in her seat convincingly, "I need to . . ." She pointed a finger towards the bathroom. "I have to go."

The guard rolled her eyes. "Now?"

Faith squirmed a little more. "Yes." She took a little gasp of air, as though her need were immediate. "Please? I'll be quick."

The guard shot a look at Anderson, who was disappearing into the ward behind Dr. Sanders. The other guard remained outside the door but looked as though she had been instructed to stay there.

"You'd better be." The guard took her arm and pulled her roughly to her feet. "Hurry up then."

Faith followed her to the bathroom door, where she was afraid the woman would insist on going inside with her. She watched as the guard gestured to her partner and disappeared inside. Faith followed her, wondering how she could make sure she ended up alone. Inside, the guard prowled along the line of stalls, glancing up to check there wasn't a window in the room.

Apparently satisfied, she turned, thrusting a finger in Faith's face. "Don't be long."

"I won't." Faith proffered her bound wrists. "Umm . . . could you remove these? Just for a minute?"

The guard sighed, then fished the control out of her pocket and released the cuffs. "No funny business, alright?"

She waited for Faith to nod before retreating, presumably to stand outside the door. Faith went into the first cubicle and waited nervously, with no idea whether or not Diane would be allowed into the bathroom at the same time as her. One thing was certain, they wouldn't have long.

But Diane didn't let her down. A moment later there was the sound of voices outside, and then the door burst open again. Faith stayed still, not wanting to give herself away until she was certain it was Diane and they were alone. A single pair of footsteps made their way into the bathroom, and Faith heard the door to the next cubicle bang shut.

"Faith?" Diane's voice.

"Diane!" Faith felt tears rushing to her eyes and was glad her friend couldn't see her. "Can't believe they let you in!"

"Had to lie, say it was an emergency trip." Diane sounded vaguely amused. "Said I'd been having stomach cramps all day and they let me right in." There was a metallic click, as though Diane had shot the bolt across the door. "So, where've you been for the past week?"

"Anderson found out about my little trip. She has me locked in a room somewhere at the back of the academy, close to the teachers' offices."

"Is she taking care of you?"

"Mostly. So far, at least." Faith made a face and then remembered Diane couldn't see her. "Food's not always been great."

"Any idea why they brought us here in the middle of the night? There was no warning."

"I think so." Faith took a breath. "They brought that medic . . . Dr. Sanders . . . to the academy a couple of days ago." She closed her eyes at the memory. "She injected me with a drug."

"A drug?"

"I think . . ." Faith hesitated to go on, "I think it might be linked to the one they gave Serene. Did Sophia . . ."

Diane cut her off. "Yeah. She told me what you found out. I get that whatever they . . ." her voice faltered for a moment. ". . . *tested* on Serene was what killed her." She paused. "But you had a dose . . . and you're still here. How come?"

"I've no idea. Maybe they adapted the drug? *Learned* from what happened with Serene?" Faith played with the note in her pocket, wondering if she could ask Diane to pass it on. "I don't know, but whatever they're doing, they seem pretty determined. And the fact they've brought us all here, in the middle of the night . . . what if they're going to give it to everyone?"

Diane grimaced. "How did it affect you?"

"I was sick. For several days, I think. Weak . . . passing out . . . throwing up . . ." Faith shuddered. "At least I'm still here, though."

"For now." Diane's abruptness sent a hot flush through Faith's body. "What if they plan to give it to us *regularly*?"

Faith's head was starting to pound. "I can't imagine."

There was a brief silence. Eventually, Faith heard Diane shift in the cubicle next to her. "We have to *do* something."

"Like what?"

"I don't know . . . stop them somehow . . ." Diane sounded desperate. "We can't let them just—"

"Perhaps we could . . . delay it at least?" Faith sighed. "It was awful, Diane. I don't want you all to have to go through it too."

"Okay, delay it then. That sounds more possible." Diane sounded a little more hopeful.

Faith cursed. "They'd only bring us back here another time though . . ."

"True." Diane said. "But what if we delayed it and, in the meantime, managed to get the word out somehow . . . tell the government? Make sure they knew what was going on at the academy."

Faith felt the desperation threaten to overwhelm her. "Danforth's in on it."

"What?"

"Danforth. She knows. Anderson spoke to her from my room." Faith sighed. "I think she's the one *behind* it all."

"Well . . . what about the media?" Diane wasn't giving up. "The people of Bellator don't know what's happening to us. If the citizens knew . . . they'd do something to stop it . . . surely? She couldn't keep just . . . *using* us for some experiment."

"I guess it's worth a try." Faith was grateful for Diane's determination. "But we have to act *now*."

"Let me think." Diane was tapping something against the door of the cubicle, a mad repeating pattern which sped up as she considered their options. "We could—"

But before she could continue, the door to the bathroom was pushed open again.

"You two about done?" the guard growled.

"Just coming now." There was the sound of water rushing as Diane flushed the toilet.

Faith did the same, before opening the door of her cubicle. She wandered out to the basins and began washing her hands as the bathroom door slid closed once again, the guard's face disappearing. Seconds later, Diane appeared at her side.

"Sophia's been worried sick you know," she hissed out the side of her mouth.

"I know. Tell her I'm okay. And I miss her."

"You can tell her yourself." Diane's eyes roamed the room before returning to Faith's, glittering dangerously. "I know what to do."

Faith followed the other girl's gaze to the wall at the far side of the bathrooms. Protected by a glass panel was a small button. Above it, the words 'Fire: Emergency Use Only.' Her eyes widened as she glanced back at Diane.

"That's brilliant."

Diane winked. "Well, *I'm* brilliant."

Drying her hands, Faith walked towards the emergency panel. A hand on her shoulder stopped her.

"Nope." Diane pulled her backwards gently and pointed to the exit. "You're in enough trouble already. Out you go."

"No!" Faith turned. "I'll stay with you."

Diane just shook her head. "No, you won't. Get back out there, so they don't think you're involved." She stepped forward and thrust her arms around Faith, enveloping her in a brief, almost painful embrace. When she let go, she pushed Faith abruptly in the direction of the door. "Now go."

Her hands shaking, Faith exited the bathrooms. Only when she was outside again did she remember the note in her pocket. Too late now.

She began to count under her breath. "One-two-three—"

The guard bore down on her, cuffs in hand. But before she had a chance to re-secure Faith's hands, a shriek ten times louder than an ambulance siren tore through the air.

N oah and Ruth stared at one another in horror. Panic flared in both sets of eyes as the alarm's shrill scream circled them. Blinding terror jolted through Noah's body: someone had discovered Jacob and his team! He searched his brain for the backup plan, but something in his head seemed to have stalled.

Ruth recovered first, creeping forward to peer round the hedge. She gestured for him to join her. Since the girls had entered the hospital, the entrance had been quiet, but the alarm had changed things. They had a clear view now: the main doors had been flung open and, as they watched, various techs hurried out, ushering patients into the warm night air. Once outside, they were directed to various muster points, where medics with clipboards began taking stock.

"They're evacuating," Ruth hissed.

"Makes sense." Noah swallowed. "If they know about the explosives."

"If that were the case," his friend gestured to the positions of the different groups, "why would they stay so close to the building?"

Noah looked again. Ruth was right. If they were aware of the bombs, the techs would be moving the patients as far away from the hospital as possible. He glanced back at the doors. A stream of medics continued to exit, now bringing out patients in wheelchairs and on trolleys. But all of them followed the same pattern, assembling in specific places on the hospital forecourt.

"I don't get it." Ruth frowned.

"What?"

"It's too organised. There's no panic." Ruth glanced at him, her expression dark. "We can't stay here. Let's get back to the rally point. Work out what Paulo wants us to do."

"Abandon the mission, surely."

Ruth raised her eyebrows. "Don't count on it."

"Are you kidding? If we stay—"

"All I know is, Jacob was pretty set on this mission. He won't be happy if we have to go home and all those explosives go to waste."

Noah groaned. "Great." He pointed at the far side of the garden, focusing on their escape. "Best way to get out without being spotted?"

"Yeah. Faces the right direction, at least." Ruth set off, edging around the garden until she reached a place where the hedge was a little thinner. She began pushing her way through. Noah followed, emerging on the main street which ran along the side of the hospital. He brushed a few stray leaves from his shoulder and glanced up and down the street. Seeing no one, he nodded at Ruth and together they darted across the road.

The doorway on Atwood Street wasn't empty. Paulo was already there, his face thunderous. He looked up as they approached.

"Is everything—?" Ruth stopped, waiting for his reply.

"Not sure." Paulo curled his fingers into his palms. "Can't get hold of Jacob at the moment. But I had a status report fifteen minutes ago. He said they'd set up just under half of the explosives without any issue."

"You think they've been caught since then?" Noah's voice shook. "Flynn's with him, right?"

Paulo ignored his question. "What did you two see?"

"An alarm went off." Noah gestured back in the direction they had come from. "People started to flood out of the hospital but —"

"But it was weird, Paulo," Ruth interrupted.

Noah's brother turned to her. "Weird? How?"

"They were all . . . lining up. Like, in specific groups. It was really *organised*." She frowned. "But if they'd heard someone was setting off bombs, wouldn't they have been . . . I don't know . . . *running*? As far away from the hospital as possible?"

"You'd think so. Sounds more like an evacuation. They have drills for them, like, if there's a fire or something. Wouldn't be a drill in the middle of the night, though." Paulo raised the walkie talkie to his lips again. "Jacob. Come in, Jacob." The small black device remained stubbornly silent, and Paulo dropped his hand in frustration. "You see anything else interesting?"

"A large group of girls were taken in. Before the alarm went off." Noah thought of Faith, being marched to the hospital in the middle of the night. "Not sure what procedure they'd be having in the middle of the night . . ."

". . . but they didn't look like they were ill or injured," Ruth finished for him.

Paulo looked thoughtful. "How long ago?"

"Around twenty minutes?" Ruth glanced at Noah for confirmation.

"Yeah." Noah frowned. "We didn't see them come out again. At least, not before we left."

"If it *is* an evacuation, there'll be meeting points all around the building." Paulo pulled out the plan he had sketched for the purposes of the mission. "There are lots of different exits," he jabbed a finger at each side of the building, "and they'll be brought out by whichever is nearest."

"You mean they could evacuate close to Jacob's group?" Ruth's eyes were wide.

Paulo traced his finger to where the fertility unit was. It ran along the rear of the hospital. "Shouldn't think so. They won't have taken patients in there at night. At least . . ." he looked concerned, ". . . I don't think so." He looked up from the map.

"Paulo," Noah took a deep breath, "these girls . . . they were from Danforth Academy."

"Really?" Paulo looked up from the map. "That girl you met . . . Was she with them?" Noah nodded and Paulo's eyes widened. "Interesting."

"Why *interesting*?" Noah felt a sense of dread creep over him. "You think they might have been headed for the fertility unit?"

"I'm sure they weren't." Paulo frowned. "But you said they were . . . testing stuff on these girls . . . secretly . . ."

"*Testing* things?" Ruth interrupted. "You didn't tell me that part."

Paulo ignored her. "Their arrival here . . . in the middle of the night . . . it has to be linked to the tests, surely?"

"I'm not sure." Noah shoved his hands deep in his pockets, trying to stop them shaking.

Ruth shifted her feet impatiently. "What do we do, then?"

"I don't know. I need to speak to Jacob, or—" Paulo froze, motioning them back into the shadows at the back of the doorway.

From the street came the sound of footsteps, pounding on the pavement. When Harden and Sil raced into view, Noah felt like his heart might explode. They were followed by several other members of Paulo's group, and hustled into the doorway one after another.

"We saw . . ." Harden was panting.

"They were . . ." Sil seemed in a similar way. "At the side of the hospital. They're bringing everybody out."

"Same thing at the front." Ruth confirmed. "Like you said, Paulo, they must have different exits for different patients."

"Which definitely means the entire hospital is in the midst of being evacuated." Paulo brought the walkie-talkie to his mouth again. "Jacob. Come *in*."

Noah shot Harden a look. "Did you see any girls?"

Harden turned to him, a smirk on his face. "Looking to bag yourself a pretty little Bellator babe, Madden?"

Ruth scowled. "No, you idiot. We saw them all marched in through the front. They didn't come back out again."

"There *was* a whole bunch of girls, brought out together." Sil chimed in, a puzzled expression on her face. "But they weren't in hospital gowns like the other patients we saw. Looked like they'd just come in off the street, almost."

A look of concern crossed Paulo's face as he stared at the silent walkie talkie. Gesturing to them to stay where they were, he checked the street was clear and wandered a few metres away from them, attempting to reach Jacob again. As he left, another four raiders from their team appeared round the corner. Jan and Dane were the only two members of Paulo's team left to return now.

"We'll be heading back, right?" Sil leaned closer to Noah and Ruth, her face creased with concern. "I mean . . . once the rest of the group gets here. We can't stay if the entire city's on alert."

Ruth shrugged and gestured to Paulo. Finally, the walkie talkie crackled to life, and his face flooded with relief. "At least they're alive."

"For now." Harden glanced up and down the street, his eyes wild. "Don't you think we should just be getting the hell out of here?"

"Not until the whole team's back."

"But once they're all here, we'll go. Right?" Harden persisted.

Ruth's gaze remained fixed on Paulo. "Does he look like he's ready to abandon the mission?"

Paulo continued to speak into the device, gesturing wildly in the direction of the hospital.

"They're not seriously considering going *through* with it, are they?"

"Not sure." Noah watched his brother closely. "Before the alarm went off, Jacob confirmed they had some of the explosives in place. If the alarm is nothing to do with us, then . . ."

"He can't expect us to go back there . . . can he?" Sil's voice cracked slightly. "Not with all those people around."

"Jacob won't want to throw away those explosives. Took him too long to gather them." Ruth warned. "Plus, if we abandon the ones which are already rigged, and they're found tomorrow, we'll have put Eremus in danger without doing any damage here."

"If he can, Jacob will set them off. At least the ones he has ready." Noah had heard Jacob's tone when he spoke about the weapons. He was proud, determined. "He won't give up. Not now."

"Noah's right." Ruth nodded. "If he detonates the ones they have in place, at least there'll be *some* impact. He's been planning this raid for years."

"Are you kidding?" Sil had gone pale. "Our role was to keep people *inside* the building so they couldn't raise the alarm . . . so we could manage a quick getaway. They're *all* outside now. The chances of us being caught are way more—"

She stopped abruptly as Paulo returned. "Jacob's team is okay. No one's spotted them yet, but with all the emergency services rushing to the hospital, the situation's much more dangerous."

"At last, some sense." Harden jerked a hand over his shoulder. "We're heading out then?"

"Not quite." Paulo shook his head. "New plan. We're going to skirt the outside of the building. Head to the east side of the hospital."

"But that's where we just came from." Harden complained. "There are *people* there."

"*Lots* of people," Sil echoed.

Paulo didn't seem to hear them. "Jacob wants to have an impact on Bellator. He's still going to blow the explosives, but they haven't had time to set them all up. The seed bank will be damaged, but not destroyed." The group was silent now, waiting for Paulo to go on. "We need to go further, do more."

Noah's heart sank. "So, what's the plan?"

"Hostages."

"Hostages?" Sil was alarmed.

"Yep." Paulo glanced out to the street, checking it was still empty. "Look, Jacob's going to blow the explosives in the next ten minutes. When he does, it'll cause more chaos. Provide a distraction we can take advantage of."

"To kidnap some of the hospital's patients?" Noah hissed.

"Yes. Specifically, the girls from the Danforth Academy." Noah's heart sank as his brother continued. "It's perfect, don't you see? They're *important* to the authorities. They *matter*."

Noah stared at his brother, horrified. Ruth reached out, clutching his hand as Paulo ploughed on, not even glancing at the rest of them. The group around them shifted, exchanging worried glances.

"It'll send a strong message to the Chancellor." Paulo's voice was charged with desperate emotion. "You said these girls are important to Bellator. If we take them, Danforth *has* to take notice."

"But . . ." Noah pulled his hand away from Ruth's, stepping towards his brother, "they're innocent. They shouldn't be *used* . . . I mean . . . I *told* you about Faith . . . I *trusted* you . . ."

Paulo shot him a look. "Sorry. But when it comes down to it, what's more important? Protecting some spoiled rich girl from the city that denies our very existence? Or protecting your family?"

"I know what you're saying," Noah knew he sounded desperate, "but we can't kidnap them . . . they . . . she'll never . . ."

"This isn't a discussion, Noah." Paulo's face hardened. "We're taking them. That's it."

"And Jacob said—"

"Never mind what Jacob said. We have to move, or we'll be too late."

"What about Jan and Dane?" Ruth reminded Paulo.

"They have a walkie talkie. I'll message them to go directly back to the tunnels." As Ruth's face fell, Paulo turned away. "They're experienced raiders. They'll be fine."

Noah wished Jan and Dane were back. He was sure they wouldn't be on board with the new mission, and Paulo would be more likely to listen to them. But there was no stopping his brother. Paulo checked the street once more, before darting out into it. The rest of the group followed, their concerned glances and slower pace evidence of their uncertainty.

Noah hurried to catch his brother, grabbing onto his arm. "Paulo, please . . ."

"We won't hurt them, if that helps." Paulo shot him a look. "We'll knock them out with the Sleepsol, then carry them back with us."

"And they'll wake up terrified in a darkened cave."

"Pretty much what we've been stuck with all our lives, isn't it?" Paulo hissed, yanking his arm free of Noah. "Let's see how they like it."

Noah gave up, dropping back into the rest of the group. Kidnapping Faith? In all the daydreams he'd had about seeing her again, not one of them had involved him forcing her to return to Eremus with him. She'd think he'd betrayed her. And she'd be right.

But what could he do about it? If he refused to follow orders, he'd look like he was betraying his people. And Paulo was right. He *should* feel more loyalty to Eremus than he did to a girl he barely knew. But it didn't feel right.

They hugged the shadows until they reached the main road, which was filled with emergency vehicles arriving to attend the alarm. Jabbing a finger in the opposite direction, Paulo diverted onto another side street and they hurried along it, heading for their new rally point via a circuitous, but safer, route.

Eventually, they found themselves in a narrow alley with a tall, chain-link fence blocking their exit. Paulo pointed upwards and began to scale the barrier. One by one, the others followed. When it was his turn, Noah felt the cold metal of the fence cutting into his fingers. Closing his eyes, he forced himself to keep climbing. At least, he reasoned, if he was with the team who were taking the girls hostage, he could attempt to protect Faith.

He was the last to jump down from the fence on the other side. The second his feet hit the pavement, Paulo was off, racing ahead to a bend in the alleyway. Peering around the corner, he gestured back to them. All clear. Noah hurried to catch up with the rest of his group who were huddled together at the end of the street, all eyes focused in the same direction.

Noah followed their gaze. Standing, lined up in silent rows outside the east entrance to the hospital were the Danforth girls. Their expressions, those Noah could see from this distance, ranged from confused to terrified. He couldn't immediately spot Faith, and for a moment he hoped she was still inside the building.

Edging close to the street, Paulo nodded grimly. "I'm just waiting for Jacob's little *distraction*." He nodded toward several guards who stood, shielding the academy girls. "Should get rid of them. Then we go in."

"Go in . . ." Sil's voice faltered, ". . . how?"

"I know this wasn't part of the plan, but we have to think on our feet." Paulo circulated the group, instructing them. "I promise you, we won't hurt them." He took out his can of Sleepsol. "Here's what we're going to do. Work in pairs. Threes if you have to. When the guards are gone, approach the girls, use the solution to knock one of them out, then get her back to the tunnels."

Noah couldn't help but wonder what they would do with the girls when they reached Eremus. A horrific thought struck him.

"Paulo!" he hissed.

"Look, Noah, I know you're not—" His brother began to argue but stopped at the look on Noah's face.

"There's something else. If we're *really* going to do this." Noah pointed at his wrist. "They all wear a device fastened to their wrist. It has a tracking system of some kind."

"Good call, brother." Paulo's eyes travelled to the girls on the other side of the road. "We take them off and dump them, then. No good them being able to trace us back to camp."

"Could we maybe . . . just turn them off?" This came from Ruth. "I mean . . . couldn't the information on them be . . . *useful* if we can access it at some later date?"

This time, Paulo's eyes gleamed. "Another great idea." He turned to Noah. "You know how?"

Hating himself, Noah dropped his gaze. "Yeah. They have a menu accessed by a password, a series of letters and numbers." He reeled off the sequence three times, hating himself for remembering it. "Once you key it in, you should get access to a menu." Noting the confusion on some of the surrounding faces, he searched his mind for a better explanation. "It's a list of choices. Select the one which says *location* and turn it off. Got it?"

Paulo nodded. "Alright. So, remove the devices from their wrists and pass them to myself or Noah here." He jerked a hand at his brother. "We'll deactivate this location function and keep 'em safe til we get back to Eremus. Once you get rid of them, head straight for the tunnels. Okay." He jerked his head towards the hospital. "Get ready."

The group shifted, shooting nervous glances at one another, but obeyed the order. A moment later, they had divided themselves up and were crouching, out of sight but ready, spray cans in their hands.

Satisfied, Paulo nodded. "As soon as you hear the explosion, and the guards leave, get straight in. Don't hesitate. Take advantage of the chaos."

"What if the guards don't leave?" Harden asked.

Paulo shrugged. "There aren't many. I'm betting at least some of them will go to investigate. If some stay behind, I'll deal with them."

As his brother finished speaking, Noah spotted Faith. She was standing off to one side, separated from the others, a guard standing right next to her. Noah wondered what she'd done to deserve the armed escort. She didn't look frightened or bewildered, like the majority of her fellow students. If anything, she was smiling. He couldn't imagine why.

His eyes were still fixed on her slight figure as a deafening blast echoed through the air. The ground beneath them shook, as though a thousand frightened deer were galloping past.

Paulo straightened up. "Time to go."

CHAPTER THIRTY-FOUR: FAITH

F aith's ears were ringing. Her eyes were squeezed shut, and when she managed to open them, she realised she was lying on the ground. All around her, the other Danforth girls were in similar positions, the orderly lines from a few seconds ago shattered by the earsplitting boom. Faith ran her hands over her body, checking for injuries. Although she felt like she'd been assaulted, there appeared to be no physical damage.

She wondered if the explosion was anything to do with Diane. Pulling the fire alarm was one thing, but actually setting off some sort of bomb? Faith dismissed the idea quickly, deciding an attack like this had to have been planned by someone with access to explosives. She was pretty sure that counted out a mere schoolgirl.

She glanced around, searching for the guards who had been glued to her shoulder all night. They were nowhere to be found. Glancing at the building, she was confused. The door they had exited through was intact, the building still standing. She pushed her hands into the ground and stood up. The sky on one side of the building was clear, a star shining here and there in the carpet of darkness. But when she twisted her head in the opposite direction, the billowing clouds of smoke told a very different story.

Whatever had happened, it had come from *behind* the building. But the explosion had been a powerful one, damaging at least part of the hospital. She looked for Sophia, panicking when she couldn't see her. In the distance, the fire alarm was still ringing. Or maybe not in the distance. Perhaps her ears had been damaged by the noise.

She took a few cautious steps, aiming to try and find Sophia. Her legs held her up, just about. She'd only gone a few paces when she came across a fellow Danforth girl, curled up in a ball on the ground. Bending down, she placed a gentle hand on her shoulder. It was Avery's friend, Farrah. Her face was pale and her lips a thin, taut line.

"You okay?" Faith bent close, not knowing why she was whispering. "I think it's over, whatever it was."

Farrah uncurled her body slightly. She looked around, her eyes darting like a frightened rabbit's. "You sure?" Faith nodded and Farrah relaxed slightly. "W-where's Anderson? And Kemp?"

Although Faith had looked for her guards, she hadn't sought out their teachers. She glanced around, not immediately spotting either of them. It struck her perhaps they were unguarded for once. She figured the guards had gone to investigate the disturbance and wondered if Kemp and Anderson had done the same.

Might this be a chance to escape?

Perhaps, she decided. But not before she'd found Sophia. She couldn't just abandon her without a word, especially after what her friend had gone through since Faith's recent disappearance. She turned back to Farrah, about to offer more words of comfort, when a figure emerged from the gloom to one side of her.

"Farrah!" It was Avery, dazed and confused, stumbling towards them. "My head!" She pressed a hand to her temple. "What happened?"

Faith took an automatic step back from the older girl. She glanced down at Farrah, who seemed unable to speak.

"I figure it was a kind of . . . explosion?" Faith shrugged. "Maybe an accident . . ."

"Accident?" Avery's voice, in sharp contrast to Faith's, was shrill and panicked. "Bellator doesn't have accidents like this . . . we're under *attack*!" Her eyes were wild, flicking back and forth between the hospital doors and the street.

"I think it's over though." Faith stepped a little closer, trying to calm Avery. "I mean, the explosions seem to have stopped."

"But where are the teachers? Those guards who were with you? Hospital security?" Avery's tone was reaching a pitch which threatened to burst eardrums. "We have to take shelter . . . get somewhere safe!"

Despite the words indicating a desire to flee, Avery remained rooted to the spot. Faith raised a hand to the other girl's forehead, which her own hand still covered. "Are you hurt?"

Avery flinched at her touch. In doing so, she flung her hands out wide, and Faith could see her head was uninjured. Certain that Avery was panicking and not physically hurt, Faith's concern for Sophia returned. She eased Avery into a seated position next to her friend. Surely, the two girls could look after one another while Faith continued her search.

"Stay here. I'm sure help will be here soon."

She straightened up, her gaze skimming the figures in front of the hospital exit, indistinct in the dusky gloom. She had only taken a single step away from Avery and Farrah when she had the strange sensation she was being watched. She spun round, expecting to see Sophia or Diane, but found herself staring into a familiar pair of green eyes.

"Noah!"

Without thinking, Faith flung her arms around his neck, pressing her body against his. The warmth he radiated was wonderful, and she didn't want to let go. For a second, he responded in kind, tightening his arms around her. Then, abruptly, he stepped back. Pulling away, she peered into his face. He looked unhappy, almost pained.

"Why are you—?"

And then she realised there was someone else standing next to him. In fact, there were several others, all moving inwards, honing in on the scattered group of Danforth girls.

She looked back at Avery and Farrah in horror, as several shadowy figures approached them. Faith was certain they were both male. They had to be from Eremus. There was no time to shout a warning before they pounced. Farrah's eyes flashed with fear at the sudden appearance, and Avery struggled to her feet, letting out her signature high-pitched scream. When one of them raised his arm and aimed something at her face, Faith cried out. But instead of a gun, the object he held emitted a fine mist.

Avery's screech ensured she took in the full force of whatever was in the bottle, and the sound died away. She blinked rapidly, staggered a few paces to the left, then reached out a hand as she fell sideways. One of the men caught her easily. His partner stepped close, bending over Avery. Terrified the older girl was being murdered, Faith opened her mouth to call out. But before she could find her voice, the man backed away, following his partner as he strode away into the darkness with Avery in his arms. Another pair repeated the process with Farrah, who was silent, but terrified. The spray had a similar effect, causing a rapid collapse which allowed the two figures to scoop her up between them and carry her off in the same direction.

Before Faith could even call out to try and stop them, she realised the same thing was happening all around her. An alarming number of the stricken Danforth students were approached by similar figures. Taken by surprise, most of them offered little resistance. An arm was held out, a burst of spray directed into the girl's face. The effect was fairly instantaneous, causing the victims to seem dizzy and disorientated, stumble and lose control of their limbs, before collapsing into the arms of one or more of the assailants.

On the far side of the courtyard, Faith finally saw Anderson and Kemp. They, too, were being assaulted by the mysterious spray, but instead of being taken anywhere, the men left them lying on the ground. A yell to Faith's left caught her attention, and she turned to see Diane struggling against the two figures who were attempting to take her. Kicking out and squirming, she appeared to repel at least one of her attackers, sending them flying. Faith was surprised to discover the cry emitted by the injured party sounded female.

In the end, it took three of the assailants to pin Diane down and spray the substance into her face. Faith could see her friend was trying to hold her breath, but eventually she had no option but to inhale. Moments later, she was dragged away like the others.

Faith turned back to Noah, beginning to comprehend his sudden appearance. He was standing slightly further away from her, his hand clutching the same aerosol spray as the others. His hand was at his waist though, and he appeared to be struggling with the idea of using it.

"What—?" Faith stumbled over the words, shaking her head uncomprehendingly. She motioned to the girls all around her. "Where are you—?"

But she never finished the sentence. The figure beside Noah stepped forward, seeming to suffer none of the same reluctance when it came to assaulting her with the spray bottle. As the hand was raised, Faith tried to run, but her attacker stepped forward, grasping hold of her wrist. Unable to escape, Faith sucked in a brief breath which she attempted to hold as the figure in front of her thrust the spray even closer to her face. The struggle caused the person's hood to fall back, and as the mist enveloped her, Faith realised her attacker was female, and not much older than she was.

"Noah!" the girl hissed.

Taking advantage of the momentary lapse in her concentration, Faith took a step back, attempting to twist out of the girl's hold. Spots danced in front of her face as she stubbornly refused to allow her body to take another breath. As she fought, Noah came to life, moving towards her and grasping hold of her around the waist. The force made her collapse sideways, and they tumbled to the ground together, Noah landing painfully on top of her.

For the second time in as many minutes, Faith found her body pressed close to his, but this time it was against her will. Memories of the images from Herstory lessons played in her head in a dizzying pantomime. Noah pressed her body to the ground and turned his own face away as his partner thrust the spray towards her again. She felt its damp liquid envelop her.

Fearful of passing out, Faith let go of her breath and sucked in a new one as fast as she could. An intense, earthy taste made her gag, and she knew she'd ingested at least some of the substance. As she gave up the fight, her limbs felt heavy. The world swam in front of her as she stared up into the smoky sky. Noah's fingers slipped to her wrist. Finding it bare, he moved to check the other, encircling it gently. She realised what was happening: the Eremus citizens were removing and deactivating the devices which could help Bellator track them. Something Faith was certain they'd learned about from the boy who was now using the information against her. For a moment, she met his gaze, which was filled with a mixture of confusion, fear and what might have been guilt.

Her last thoughts were of Sophia, and whether or not she had escaped the attack. Was she, too, being carried off to Eremus? As Faith lost consciousness, she thought about where she was headed, unable to believe it was the very place she had once considered a potential sanctuary.

N oah watched Faith's eyes flutter shut, struggling against the effects of the Sleepsol. He'd known his ma's solution was powerful. But when he'd imagined using it, he had pictured them knocking out armed Bellator guards in an effort to escape, not incapacitating innocent schoolgirls and carrying them off like cavemen.

She'd fought hard. Had more warning than the others. He'd found himself incapable of hurting her. He'd stood, useless, giving her plenty of time to take stock of what was happening around her. Hardly the surprise attack it should have been.

In the aftermath of the explosion, which had been more powerful than Noah could ever have imagined, it had been easy to swoop in and take advantage of the chaos. It was almost like this had been their original strategy. The second the bombs had exploded, the guards accompanying the Danforth students had raced off to find the attackers, leaving the girls mostly unsupervised.

Noah's head was still reeling from the rapid change of plan. Paulo was decisive, he had to give him that. It stung, though, that information Noah had confided in his brother had been used *against* the Danforth girls so callously. They were just as much victims of the city's cruelty as his own community and had played no part in Bellator's violent attacks on Eremus. Paulo knew that. Yet it had made no difference.

His brother and Harden had been the first ones in, taking out the only people left protecting the girls: their teachers. After using the Sleepsol on the two women, they had left them lying unhurt on the ground before moving on to collect and disable the dangerous devices on the girls' wrists. It was a wise move, and meant the rest of the group could focus their efforts on knocking out the students and carrying them away. Noah's hands had been shaking so badly, he'd been relieved the only device he'd had to deactivate himself was Faith's.

A few minutes after the bombs had gone off, new sirens ripped through the night, indicating more emergency services were on the way. Driven by fear, Paulo's group had acted fast, taking as many of the girls as they could without putting themselves in more danger. As Noah and Ruth had hoisted Faith into their arms, he'd heard Paulo shouting at the remaining raiders to retreat. They had their hostages, the fertility unit was seriously damaged, and his brother didn't want to risk any more Eremus lives.

As they struggled along with their awkward burden, Noah knew Ruth was furious with him. For his hesitation, which had put them both in danger. For his inability to use the spray to anaesthetise Faith, which had meant she'd had to step in and take the lead. Stumbling through the back streets of the city, half-dragging, half-carrying Faith between them, his partner was silent and seething. But now was not the time to discuss the matter. Their priority was to get out of the city, and fast.

They had lost sight of the other raiders in the general confusion. Once Faith had passed out, Ruth had taken charge. They'd managed to lift their captive and hold her in a position they could maintain and then headed for one of the tunnel entrances which was closer to the city centre. Ruth had used it previously; it branched off an alleyway which ran behind one of the city's factories and would provide the rapid exit they needed.

It only took them ten minutes to reach it, and they encountered no one. All the time, the sirens wailed in the distance behind them. The image of those vehicles changing direction, moving away from the hospital and racing towards the escaping raiders played in Noah's head over and over, causing his throat to close up until he could barely breathe. He wondered whether he had inhaled some of the Sleepsol.

Terrified he might pass out, he fought to overcome the dizziness threatening to envelop him. He was already responsible for abducting Faith. He didn't want to be responsible for hurting her physically as well. He drew in deliberate deep breaths as they hurried along and was relieved when he began to feel less faint.

"This is it." Ruth directed them into a tiny alleyway. It was the first time she had spoken since they'd left the hospital grounds. "The tunnel entrance is just ahead."

They struggled the final distance, stopping close to a drainage cover set into the road.

"You got her?" Ruth hissed.

Noah nodded, and she relinquished her hold on their prisoner, moving towards the rusted disc of metal.

Glad his head was clearer now, Noah encircled Faith with both arms, making sure her head was supported by his shoulder. Now he thought about it, Faith didn't seem heavy at all. He wondered how much she'd had to eat recently. Her face was pale, the shadows underneath the closed eyelids were purplish and bruise-like. A sense of guilt settled over him like a heavy blanket. She was here because of him. The victim of a sudden and shocking abduction.

He thought back to their first meeting, of the beliefs she held about men. What had she said? She'd been afraid he might hurt her; surprised when he didn't. The women of Bellator believed all men were vicious. Weren't the Eremus citizens living up to this image by terrifying the girls in this way?

At that moment, he hated himself.

Ruth was still struggling with the cover, which remained stubbornly closed. At the end of the alleyway, two figures appeared. For a moment, Noah tensed, but as the people came closer, he realised it was Jan and Dane.

"Noah?" The older woman's voice was low and gentle. "Everything alright?"

Dane's eyes were fixed on the girl in Noah's arms. A look of horror overcame his features. "Is she dead?"

Noah shook his head. "Unconscious."

"Then why are you—?"

"New plan." He shrugged. "Jacob's orders."

The pair exchanged glances but grasped the danger of the situation. As they hurried to help Ruth, Noah felt Faith stirring in his arms. He glanced down at her, alarmed.

"Noah?" She stared at him, sounding confused. "What are you . . .? I didn't . . ." Her eyes focused suddenly, and her face darkened. "What are you *doing*?"

"I didn't mean . . . I can't . . ." Noah stumbled over the words. "Please, let me . . ."

But her eyelids fluttered closed again. Noah cursed inwardly, knowing he deserved her accusing stare, but unable to find the words to defend himself. A harsh, grating sound startled him, but when he glanced down, he saw the others had finally managed to pry the cover open. Beneath it, the black, yawning mouth of the tunnel gaped, threatening to swallow them whole.

Jan and Dane slid through first, waiting below to support the unconscious girl. Ruth motioned to him impatiently, and together they lowered Faith into the darkness. As Noah descended into the tunnel depths behind her, he felt the blanket of guilt threaten to suffocate him once more.

The journey back to Eremus was a difficult one. Along the way, Noah's group came across other members of their group, most of whom carried a similar burden. The further they walked, the heavier the girls became. The rocky floor of the tunnels was uneven and had always been tricky to navigate, but with the additional weight and near-darkness, it became a minefield. Paulo instructed them to pass the girls between them at intervals, sharing the load, but by the time they reached the outskirts of their own community, they were exhausted.

"Let's head for the canteen for now," Paulo gestured. "It's big enough to hold us all, and we can work out what to do from there."

Once more, Noah and Ruth secured Faith's arms around their aching necks and set off. As the raiders brought the girls into the canteen, a small number of anxious citizens hurried across to see what was happening. Noah and Ruth chose a table close to the door, placing Faith down as gently as they could. Harden and Sil lowered the girl they carried onto the next table along. Noah turned to face his ma, who was at the forefront of the waiting group, her face taut and pale. She could never sleep when any of them were on a raid, and this one had been riskier than most.

"What have you—?" She paused, staring around at the Danforth girls, taking in their identical clothing.

Noah avoided her gaze. Behind his ma, another figure pushed to the front of the group. It was Sarah Porter.

"Where did these girls come from?" she demanded.

Paulo strode forward. "There was a change of plan."

"A change of—?" Anna's eyes narrowed.

"Yes." Paulo stiffened. "Things happened which we didn't . . . anticipate. We had to adapt."

"That's it?" Sarah glared at them. Behind him, Noah could feel Harden stiffen. "No further explanation?"

"Sarah's right. Why are these girls . . . these *Bellator* girls . . . here in Eremus? Our home?" Anna walked forward to the closest girl, bending to listen to her breathing. "And what did you do to them?"

"We only knocked them out." Paulo's tone was defensive. "Your Sleepsol worked well."

Noah felt his mood darken further as his mother's face blanched. "You mean . . . you used my solution . . . to knock out these . . . these young women? And brought them back here . . . for what?"

Paulo looked slightly cowed at Anna's tone, but he ploughed on. "An alarm went off before we were ready to detonate the explosives. We had to act fast. These girls are valuable assets to Bellator."

"Assets?" For the first time since they had arrived, Noah spotted Ella standing with Cora, who had a protective arm around her. Her arm was still supported by a sling. She stepped forward, her eyes blazing. "They're just *girls*. A similar age to us, by the looks of things." Beside him, he felt Ruth stiffen. Ella took a few steps towards the tables where the Danforth students lay, her eyes filled with concern. "Poor things. They'll be so frightened when they wake up."

"Maybe so," Paulo continued. "But that can't be helped. These girls . . . these *citizens* are worth a lot to the Bellator government. Their absence will be noticed."

Anna took a step towards Paulo. "That's exactly what I'm worried about."

"Where's Jacob?" Sarah glanced at the entrance to the canteen and back again, her eyes blazing. "Did he *instruct* you to do this?"

"Well, no . . . I mean, not exactly . . ." there were audible gasps from the raiders surrounding Paulo, "but we know he wants to have an impact on Bellator . . . to make a difference . . ."

"Wait a minute." Jan spoke up, her tone incredulous. "You mean these *weren't* Jacob's instructions?"

Faced by the hostility of his fellow citizens, Paulo drew himself up to his full height. He opened his mouth to continue, but footsteps in the tunnel beyond stopped him. As one, the Eremus citizens turned to see the other raiding group burst into the canteen.

"Paulo! Noah!" Flynn hurried forward. "Thank God!"

Jacob wasn't far behind him. "So glad you—?" He stopped, staring around the canteen at the Danforth girls as the remaining raiders hurried into the cave behind him. "What's all this?"

Paulo flushed, but stood his ground. "When we spoke . . . I know you said to get everyone back here straight away, to avoid the explosion, but . . ."

He stopped speaking, as Flynn broke away from the group and hurried to Faith's side, bending over her. "Are they alive?"

"Yes!" Paulo took a step towards his uncle. "All of them. We took good care not to . . ."

"Explain yourself," Jacob interrupted, his gaze zeroing in on Paulo. "What happened after our last conversation?"

Paulo kept his gaze on the ground, shifting from one foot to the other. "I knew you weren't sure if the explosives you'd managed to set up would completely destroy the fertility unit, so . . ." his eyes blazing, he raised his gaze to Jacob's, "I figured when the bombs went off it would be a perfect distraction . . . I wanted to do something else to get at Bellator, so . . ."

"So, you figured you'd kidnap some of its citizens?" Jacob's look was stern, but he looked intrigued despite himself.

"They're not just ordinary citizens." Paulo hurried on, determined to explain himself. "They're from a fancy academy in Bellator . . .. you have to be specially selected to go there. I'm not sure why, Noah didn't find that out, but . . ."

Noah felt his face grow warm as all the eyes in the room turned to him. "I . . . it was when I . . . got trapped in the hospital," he managed. "I met one of the students from the academy. She didn't tell me much, but . . ."

"You're saying these girls are important?" Jacob demanded.

Noah nodded. "I'm not sure why. But I think . . . the government . . . have them at the school for a specific purpose."

"Just think, Jacob. These girls are part of a government project." Paulo stepped closer to Jacob, his confidence growing. "Maybe something *Danforth herself* set up."

Jacob's face hardened at the mention of the Bellator leader. "Okay. So, you figured if you took them, Danforth would have to sit up and take notice."

"She'll take notice alright," Anna's tone was shrill, and Noah could see his ma was frightened. "When she comes *looking* for these girls . . . what happens to Eremus?" She jabbed an accusing finger at Paulo, who blanched. "What have you *done*?"

"You weren't there. There wasn't time to think properly," Paulo protested. "Seemed like this was . . ." He paused, his face hardening. "No. This *is* a good idea . . . one which will have the impact Jacob wants."

"But don't you see?" Flecks of saliva flew out of his ma's mouth as she spoke. "You've brought the wrath of Bellator on us all, you *stupid—*"

Jacob stepped forward and held up a hand. For a moment, Noah thought he was going to join the attack on Paulo, but instead, he focused his gaze on Anna. "Let's all calm down. Paulo's right. Our explosives went off, but we hadn't had time to set them all up. We don't yet know how much damage they caused. Paulo was aware of this and made the decision to take these girls hostage as a way to get at the Bellator authorities. We could spend all day arguing about whether or not it was a good idea. But they're here now. There's nothing we can do about it. And who knows? Maybe having a bargaining chip to use with Bellator in the future will be a good thing."

"A *bargaining chip*?" Anna gestured to the girls. "They're barely more than children!"

"A fact I am well aware of." Jacob straightened, glancing around the room. "They won't be hurt."

"Jacob's right." Suddenly, Sarah was by his side. "We'll treat them well. And they could prove to be a real asset."

"What about the Bellator authorities?" The question came from Dan, who stood with the other raiders in the cave entrance. Noah heard the fear in his neighbour's tone. Around him, there were similar murmurs of concern.

Jacob turned to face him. "What about them?"

"You don't think they'll retaliate?" Exasperated, Flynn raked a hand through his hair.

"And risk the lives of their precious citizens?" Sarah waved a hand at the girls. "Not likely."

Jacob nodded. "Danforth will have to listen. And she can't just send the guards in this time. Not while we have these girls here with us."

Noah looked down at Faith. She lay still now, her eyes closed as though she simply rested. Her face was calm, but he couldn't banish the memory of her horrified expression. He didn't think she'd ever forgive him for what he'd done. No matter how well they were treated here.

The moment when she had first recognised him had been both thrilling and terrible. She had hurled her arms around him and for a moment he'd felt heroic, but the sense of shame which quickly followed had been difficult to ignore. Knowing she had turned to him for support when he was the one who had betrayed her trust was agony. He took a small step towards her, but stopped as a shrill scream pierced the air, echoing painfully around the cave walls.

Every eye in the room flew to an older girl, who was sitting bolt upright. Her shriek had woken some of the others, who also began to stir, staring around them in various states of confusion and terror. One girl pushed herself to her feet and began to stagger drunkenly across the cave, zigzagging this way and that as she fled from the group of strangers. As she passed Ella and Cora, the pair stepped back in alarm. But before she could even get close to the exit, Harden stepped in her way, thrusting an arm out to prevent her from escaping. He thrust her down onto a bench with a force that made Noah wince. Giving up, the girl cowered away from him and began to cry.

On the opposite side of the canteen, another girl had darted away from her captors and raced towards the food preparation area. She was fast, and before anyone could reach her, she had grasped hold of a knife from the counter and thrust it out in front of her.

"What do you want with us?" Her voice was calmer than he had anticipated.

Jacob took a couple of steps towards her, his hands outstretched. "We're not going to harm you."

"That doesn't answer my question."

"Hand over the knife." Jacob stopped moving and waited. "And no one will get hurt."

"Why should we trust you?" The girl's eyes were wide. She backed up a little further at Jacob's approach. "You *kidnapped* us."

Flynn joined Jacob. "I know how it looks. But we . . ." He continued walking forward until he was only a couple of feet away from her. ". . . *genuinely*, we aren't going to hurt you."

"Stay back!" The girl brandished the knife and didn't back away. "I'll use this if I have to."

Flynn stopped walking and raised his hands in surrender. "You don't have to do that."

The girl stared at him, her eyes fierce. The hand which held the knife shook slightly, but she continued to hold it high, in front of her body.

"Let. Us. Go." The words were spoken quietly, but the tone was one of determination.

"I'm afraid we can't do that." Jacob stepped alongside Flynn.

The girl's gaze flicked between the two men, as though weighing her chances. Every eye in the cave was focused on them, the other girls seeming to hold their breath. Noah guessed they were all assessing what would happen when one of them challenged the might of their captors.

He glanced at Faith, noticing she was also sitting upright, her eyes fixed on the girl with the knife. But instead of a wary fascination, she looked terrified. Clearly, the rebel was someone she cared about. He wondered how far the girl would go. She looked determined enough, but she was totally outnumbered, with no weapon other than the knife.

"What are you hoping to achieve here?" Jacob's tone was almost mocking, and Noah noticed Flynn shooting a frustrated look at him. "You have a kitchen knife. It's probably fairly blunt." Noah, who had spent plenty of time in the canteen sharpening the carving equipment, knew this was a lie. But he had to admire Jacob's quick-thinking. "We," Jacob pulled a gun from its holster on his belt, "have weapons capable of causing *far* more—"

"We've already said we won't hurt you, though," Flynn cut across him, and now it was Jacob's turn to look annoyed. "And we won't. But you have to put the knife down."

Taking a risk, he stepped towards the girl, holding his hand out for the weapon. At the same time, Jacob thrust the gun forward, taking aim. The girl took a small step back, seemed to make a decision, and then charged forward, brandishing the knife in front of her.

But she'd hesitated a second too long. Anticipating her move, Flynn managed to sidestep it, twisting around behind her and out of harm's way. Jacob was slower, and the girl's knife caught the sleeve of his jacket, slashing through it.

He swore loudly, lowering the gun as his free hand clutched his arm. Flynn grasped hold of the girl's wrist from behind, twisting it until she cried out and the knife clattered to the floor.

The danger over, Flynn kept hold of her, but this time his grip did not look so harsh.

"What's the damage?" Flynn nodded at Jacob.

"No damage." Their leader brought his hand away from the torn sleeve. It was clean. "Ruined a good jacket though." He glared at the girl, whose eyes still flashed with fury.

Recovering himself, Jacob motioned to the rest of the raiders. "We need to put them somewhere they can't cause any more trouble."

Sarah stepped forward. "We can take them down to the training rooms for now."

Noah watched as his ma stepped forward. "I'd like to check them over. Make sure they're not suffering any ill effects from the Sleepsol. *If*, as you say, we intend to take care of them."

"Tomorrow." Jacob shot her a look. "You can look them over tomorrow."

For a moment, his mother looked like she was going to argue. But as Sarah took charge, directing the raiders to escort the girls out of the canteen, she closed her mouth again, changing her mind. But Noah knew his mother. If she had something to say, she wouldn't stay silent for long.

CHAPTER THIRTY-SIX: FAITH

When Faith woke, she was disorientated. The darkness surrounding her was almost complete, diluted only by a faint glow on the opposite side of the room. It took her a few moments to work out she wasn't in a room, but a cave. How it was possible to tell night from day down here was anyone's guess. The dim light filtered into the space from the tunnel outside, where whoever was guarding them had a small lantern.

Faith's entire body ached. She had never had to sleep on the ground before and felt like she'd been beaten by the punishing rocks beneath her. The thin covers their captors had provided did not offer much protection from the chilly air which circulated in the caves, and they smelled odd. At first, many of the Danforth girls had rejected the scant protection, disgusted by their poor condition. But the next few hours spent shivering had changed their minds, and now they had all overcome their revulsion and had the blankets wrapped firmly around them.

Beside her, Sophia stirred. When Faith had woken up in the large cave which acted as a dining area for the Eremus citizens, the first thing she'd done was search for her friend. When her eyes had lighted on the small, pale figure, crouching on a bench close by with terror in her eyes, Faith had felt twin surges of relief and dismay.

Reaching out for her friend's hand, Faith squeezed it gently. Sophia's eyes flickered open and she stared around, confused. Faith watched her try to work out where she was, going through the same thought process she had herself a few minutes ago. A look of stunned realisation crept over Sophia's face as the events of the previous night came back to her.

"Hey." Faith tried to smile.

"Hey yourself." Sophia rolled on to her back and stared at the darkened roof of the cave. "You alright?"

"As alright as I can be, I guess. You?"

"Not really."

They fell into a silence for a moment, processing the situation. She could almost hear Sophia's brain working, sorting through the evidence they had in front of them and trying to come to a sensible conclusion. Eventually, her friend rolled to face her again.

"You think they planned this?"

"Planned it?"

"You know . . . knew what they were doing ahead of time." Sophia shifted slightly in the darkness. "I mean . . . if they'd intended to keep prisoners . . . well, it doesn't seem like they were exactly . . . prepared."

"I was thinking the same thing," Faith admitted.

"We are in Eremus, right?"

"Looks like it."

"I mean . . ." Sophia dropped her voice to a hushed whisper as someone close by rolled over in their sleep, "up until a few weeks ago I didn't think Eremus even existed . . . but to find it's here . . . wherever *here* is . . . and much bigger than Bellator might've imagined, well . . ."

"Well, what?"

"Well, it's pretty incredible, that's all." Sophia shrugged. "That they've lived here, all this time, hidden away. Bellator thinks they're all dead."

"Wait a minute." Faith propped herself up on one elbow. "Let me get this straight. You *approve* of the people who kidnapped us in the middle of the night and dragged us back here?"

"No." Sophia shook her head. "That's not what I mean. Let's just say I admire their cunning." She shifted closer to Faith, dropping the volume of her voice even lower. "But I'm still not sure our kidnap was part of the plan." Faith could feel Sophia's hot breath on her cheek now. "Listen, that boy . . . the one you met in the hospital . . . did you see him yet?"

Faith felt her face flushing in the darkness. "Yeah." She cleared her throat. "He's the one who carried me back here . . . well, him and some girl."

"The tall, skinny guy?" Sophia sounded like she was frowning. "He didn't seem like one of the . . . um . . . more aggressive ones."

"Maybe not, but . . ." Faith took a deep breath and voiced her biggest fear. "I've been thinking maybe that's his purpose. He's non-threatening. Maybe . . . maybe *he's* the reason they took us. Maybe it was *me* . . . I mean . . . his conversations with me which—"

"Wait a minute . . . conversations. As in, there were more than one?"

"No . . ." Sophia's tone was so disapproving, Faith couldn't stand to tell her the truth. "I mean the different conversations we had whilst we were stuck in the hospital together." Sophia was silent, and Faith wasn't sure her friend had believed her. "But what if . . . what if they *sent* him? To talk to me. Or at least . . . someone *like* me. To seek out someone who the Bellator authorities would miss."

Sophia pushed herself into a sitting position. "If that were the case, if their aim were to kidnap, then like I said, they'd be better prepared." She gestured at the cave they were housed in. "They'd have somewhere secure rigged up to hold us captive. This is just an ordinary cave . . . the entrance is wide open . . .

they have to constantly guard us. I don't think he was a plant. More likely he was doing undercover research on the hospital. And in the wrong place at the wrong time in terms of bumping into you."

"I guess so." Faith saw the reason in her friend's words but wasn't sure it made her feel any better.

Sophia seemed to sense this and reached a hand out for Faith's. "Hey, there was the explosion as well. I mean . . . that had to have something to do with them, right?"

"I suppose."

"I'd be willing to bet on it." Sophia squeezed Faith's hand. "I'm sure it came from somewhere on the other side of the hospital. And it sounded like it did an awful lot of damage."

Faith shuddered, hoping the buildings the bomb had damaged had been empty. "What do you think they're going to do with us?"

"Well, if they know we're of value to Bellator, they shouldn't hurt us. At least, I hope not." She paused for a moment. "I mean . . . if we do as we're told, try not to aggravate them . . . we should be okay. We won't be worth much as hostages if they don't keep us safe."

"I hope you're right." Faith gripped her friend's hand tightly. "How long do you think they'll keep us here for?"

"Who knows." Sophia returned the squeeze and extricated her hand gently. "How about we try to get a little more rest? I don't know about you, but I feel like we might need our strength for whatever's coming."

Sophia lay back down, shifting around until she was comfortable. Faith attempted to follow her lead, knowing her friend was right. But even when Sophia's breathing deepened and she began to snore softly, Faith couldn't stop her mind from racing. Flashes of the previous night's events scrolled through her head, Noah's face appearing more often than she would have liked. Within a few minutes, her hands were curled into fists, the nails cutting into her palms.

No matter what happened next, she was glad to have escaped from the academy. Sophia's theory, that the explosion had been the main aim of the Eremus people and the kidnap an afterthought, rang true. She might find herself better off here. Certainly, her situation back in Bellator had been dire.

But if they were being held as hostages, that meant they would be used as leverage for Eremus to broker a deal with Danforth's government. And that meant, at some point in the future, they would be *sent back*. Faith went cold at the idea, remembering the barren cell, the loneliness, the meagre food supply.

She wondered for a crazy moment if Eremus might allow her to stay, but rejected the idea quickly, feeling stupid. They were hostages. Useless to the community, unless they were eventually returned to Bellator in some kind of an exchange.

Giving up on sleep, Faith stood, creeping to the door. If you could call a gap in the rock a *door*. A dirty, ragged strip of material covered the space, offering a small amount of privacy, but the lantern's glow was proof a guard was posted right outside. Eremus wasn't taking any chances. After her episode with the knife, Diane had refused to go quietly, and once they'd been brought down here, she had attempted no fewer than three different escapes.

Every time Diane had run, she had been brought back by one or more guards. The first time, she'd managed to blast right past the woman seated outside their cave, but the guard had given chase and, with the assistance of a couple of others, dumped a kicking and screaming Diane right back in the cave. Her second two attempts were less successful, as the Eremus citizens, who had learned from previous experience, were ready for her. In the end, she had given up, storming off to sleep on the far side of the cave, away from the others, who had huddled together for warmth and comfort.

Diane had guts, that was for sure. But Faith wasn't sure escape was the best plan, at least not right away. She wanted to wait, figure their situation out before she made any rash decisions.

From what she'd seen as they had been marched down here, the cave system was huge. An endless series of caverns and tunnels which networked their way underground, covering what must be a huge area. Attempting to sneak out of here was pointless. Anyone crazy enough to try it would either get lost or fall and injure themselves. No. Faith was willing to wait and see how the Eremus community treated them before doing anything rash.

Peering through the curtain, she could see a pair of booted feet, and the legs which belonged to them, stretched across the tunnel. She wondered if the guard himself was asleep. Listening carefully, she strained to hear his breathing over the sounds of the sleeping girls.

She sighed, thinking of Noah again. No matter which way she looked at it, he had told his community about her. About the school, Serene's death, the drug testing, and the wristclips. And he had recognised her outside the hospital, she was sure of it. For all she knew, he had told his leader to target the Danforth girls.

She couldn't believe the previous day she had been wishing— yes, *wishing*—to escape to Eremus. Actively considering finding Noah. What a fool. To imagine he would help her, a spoiled little rich girl from the city, rather than seeing the opportunity she and her fellow students provided for his community. He was a good actor, that was all. And when she saw him again, that's what she'd have to be. She couldn't show him how much his betrayal had hurt.

A noise outside in the tunnel startled her and she recoiled into the darkness of the cave. The guard's foot shifted as another pair of boots approached.

"Takin' over?" The current guard sounded like he was stretching. "Bout time. I'm shattered."

Faith couldn't hear what the new arrival said in return. But she was aware of the sound of shuffling feet outside, indicating the first guard's departure. She stayed still, waiting for his replacement to settle into place, but instead, she heard footsteps approaching. She froze, unable to move without alerting the new guard to the fact she was listening just behind the curtain.

A second later, a hand grasped hold of it, pulling it open. Noah peered into the cave, shining a lantern over the sleeping group. Finding himself face to face with Faith, he leapt backwards, and for a moment, the fabric fell back into place. Faith took a step away as he recovered, so when the curtain was pushed aside again, she was not standing quite as close.

"Faith." His voice was soft, low. "Are you alright?"

She stared back at him, willing herself to stay calm.

He took a step towards her, stretching out his hand. "Are you hurt?" She tensed, and he dropped the hand to his side. "Look, I'm sorry."

She straightened up, glaring at him. "What for?"

He hesitated. In the dim light from the lantern, his expression was kind, earnest. Faith found herself wanting to step closer, to feel his arms around her the way they had been outside the hospital. She clenched her fists, cursing the impulse. He noticed and took a step back so he was standing in the doorway again.

"I'm sorry . . . for everything, I guess." He hung his head. "You have to understand, I didn't mean for this to . . ." He gestured at the girls inside the cave. "This . . . well, it wasn't supposed to happen."

Faith stared at him, furious with herself as her eyes pricked with tears. She wanted so badly to believe him. But she'd believed him once before, and look where that had got her.

"I trusted you." She fought to keep her voice steady.

His face fell. "I know."

"Did you betray me?"

He raised his eyes to meet hers. "No!"

"You didn't tell *anyone* about me? About the academy . . . the tests . . . my friend's *death*?"

His silence was all the evidence she needed.

Taking a deep breath, Faith stepped towards him. He regarded her hopefully, as though he expected her to forgive him. When she was within an arm's reach, she stopped.

"Like I said, I trusted you." Faith made sure her gaze was fixed on him as she spoke the final words. "I won't do it again."

Without another word, she turned and withdrew into the darkness. As she settled down beside Sophia with her back to the door, she knew he was still there. She refused to turn and look, even though the light from his lantern illuminated the cave for a long time.

Eventually, when she thought he might stand there all night, she heard him step back into the tunnel, letting the curtain drop behind him. As he moved back to the guard post, she buried her head in the blanket. It was a long time before her body stopped trembling.

Later, Faith wondered what would happen in the days ahead. Sure, she had escaped the horrors of her Bellator prison. She was back with Sophia, and there would be no more blood tests, no more drug trials. But she was still trapped. She had simply replaced one cell with another. Only time would tell whether the new captors treated her any better than the old.

But the new Faith *would* be different. No rebellious behaviour, no more rash decisions which only led to trouble. Lying there, Faith vowed to be clever. To behave, to listen, and to learn about her new surroundings.

When the time came to make a move, one way or another, she would be ready.

H e didn't know what he'd expected. But as he sat, slumped against the wall outside the training-room-turned-prison, Faith's expression was etched in Noah's mind. Gone was the look of trust, the smile of relief she'd given him when he'd appeared outside the hospital. Even the hurt which had emblazoned her features when she'd realised he was kidnapping her would have been preferable.

But when she'd faced him at the door of her cell, her face had been cold. She hated him. And he didn't know how to change that.

With little else to do, he thought back over the events of the past few days. Questioned everything he'd done. How had things come to this? His ma was furious with him, Paulo had betrayed his trust and, from what he'd said so far, Jacob seemed hell-bent on using the Danforth girls in his vendetta against the Bellator authorities. He was already talking tactics, discussing ways they might use the girls to get Danforth's attention, to make demands, to force her to cooperate.

And maybe he was right. Perhaps violence was the only way to get Bellator to listen, to take notice. Noah wanted a better life as much as anyone in Eremus, but he didn't want innocent people to be hurt in the process.

And the girls from the academy were definitely innocent. Noah couldn't get past the fact he was the one responsible for landing Faith and her friends in this situation. He'd begged Mick to switch guard postings with him tonight, knowing he wouldn't be able to sleep until he'd had the chance to attempt to apologise to Faith.

Her rejection had hurt. But it had also strengthened his resolve. He *wouldn't* let anyone hurt her. Even if it meant buddying up to Jacob and Paulo, taking on raids which were even riskier, going against his ma and Flynn.

She was his responsibility now. And, whatever happened, he wouldn't let her down.

Want more?

Want to continue Faith and Noah's story?

Dependence is the second book in The Bellator Chronicles.

A bitter betrayal. An unwilling hostage. An impossible choice.

Kidnapped in the aftermath of the explosion which rocked Bellator, Faith is a prisoner in the rebel community of Eremus. As she plots her next move, she struggles to come to terms with Noah's betrayal. He proved what she was always taught – men can't be trusted.

But in this harsh environment, Noah may be her only ally. Bitterly regretting his actions, he does everything he can to regain Faith's trust. And when he defends her from the ruthless rebel leader, she finds herself falling for him.

Then Faith learns that Bellator wants her back - for all the wrong reasons. Caught in the middle, she doesn't know who to turn to. As the reckless actions of the leaders on both sides endanger someone she loves, Faith realises she has become a pawn in a much bigger game.

Can she save her best friend without playing into the enemy's hands? And, if she succeeds, will it mean leaving Noah behind?

The second book in the Bellator Chronicles, Dependence is filled with intense drama, gripping action, and a pair of star-crossed lovers you'll be rooting for long after lights out. Perfect for fans of The Selection, Noughts and Crosses, and The Handmaid's Tale.

OTHER BOOKS BY CLARE LITTLEMORE

The Flow Series

Flow
Break
Drift
Quell

A drowned planet. A terrible secret. A girl desperate for answers.

In a world where sea levels have risen to unimaginable levels, an isolated society exists. Life in The Beck is tough. Floodwaters constantly threaten existence, and rules must be followed to ensure the survival of the entire society.

Sixteen-year-old Quin knows the Governor is hiding something. When she receives a sudden promotion to the Patrol Sector, she hopes the extra freedom will help her expose his lies.

Life in Patrol is not what she expected, though. The new recruits train hard, and failure is not tolerated. When she attracts the attention of the handsome, mysterious Cam, he warns her that asking questions could get her killed.

But Quin can't resist. She digs deeper and discovers that there's more to Cam than meets the eye. With her heart and her life on the line, Quin has to decide how far she is willing to go to protect the people she loves.

If you love The Hunger Games, Divergent and The Giver, this gripping dystopian series by Clare Littlemore will keep you up all night.

Author's Note

Thank you for reading Compliance. I hope that you lost yourself in the dual worlds of Eremus and Bellator, just as I did when I wrote the book. I love building relationships with my readers. If you enjoyed Compliance and would like to receive updates when I'm releasing a new book, sign up for my readers' club:

https://clarelittlemore.com/newsletter?signup=compliance

If you sign up, you'll receive a regular newsletter with giveaways, book recommendations, special offers, the occasional free short story, and (of course) details of all my new releases. I promise there will be no spam. I hate spam.

AND WHILE YOU'RE HERE...

You can make a big difference.

Being an indie author, it can be difficult to get my books noticed. And reviews are really powerful. If you liked reading Compliance, please consider spending a couple of minutes leaving an honest review (it can be as brief as you like) on the book's Amazon page, on Goodreads, or similar. It genuinely doesn't have to be long - often just a single sentence is enough to convince someone to give a new author or series a try. I'd be eternally grateful.

Thank you very much.

About the Author

Clare Littlemore is a young adult dystopian and sci-fi author who thrives on fictionally destroying the world with a cup of tea by her side. The tea will often be cold, because her characters have a way of grabbing hold of her and not letting go until the final page of their story is finished. They regularly have the same effect on her readers. Clare lives in the North West of England with her husband and two children.

Come and say hello!
Facebook: https://www.facebook.com/clarelittlemoreauthor
Instagram: https://www.instagram.com/clarelittlemore/
The Last Book Cafe on Earth Facebook group:
https://www.facebook.com/groups/lastbookcafeonearth/
Twitter: https://twitter.com/Clarelittlemore

ACKNOWLEDGEMENTS

This book would not exist without the support of so many people. In the past, I have attempted to list them all, and, inevitably, I always forget someone.

This time, I will simply say thank you to my wonderful editor Beth Dorward for all her patience, and to my amazingly talented cover designer, Jessica Bell, for coming up with an exciting concept for my new series, which both fits with and is different from the covers of The Flow Series. I also need to mention the fabulous Lyn Blair for her unwavering support with so many aspects of this series.

After that, there are too many people to name. So if you listened while I hammered out a complicated plotline, beta read an early edition of Compliance or bolstered me when I was concerned I'd never get to the end of the manuscript, thank you. If you brought me endless cups of tea while I tapped away at the keyboard, commented on early ideas for cover designs, or helped my to edit my blurb, thank you. If you proofread the book (sometimes more than once), considered my suggestions for possible titles, or waited patiently until I'd finished the chapter before I helped you with your homework, thank you. If you bought copies of my previous books and waited for this one without complaint, thank you.

A lot of work goes into writing and publishing a book. And many hands make light work. To anyone who helped me, even just a little, to get this book finished, thank you. You know who you are.

And, finally, to my readers. Thanks for your patience in waiting for this book. I know it's been a long time coming. I hope it was worth the wait.